Finney, Ernest J

California Time

CALIFORNIA TIME

western literature series

OTHER BOOKS BY THE AUTHOR

Birds Landing

Winterchill

Lady with the Alligator Purse

Words of My Roaring

Flights in the Heavenlies

California Time

ERNEST J. FINNEY

UNIVERSITY OF NEVADA PRESS / RENO, LAS VEGAS

Western Literature Series

University of Nevada Press, Reno, Nevada, 89557 USA

Manufactured in the United States of America

Design by Carrie Nelson House

Library of Congress Cataloging-in-Publication Data

Finney, Ernest J.

California time / Ernest J. Finney.

p. cm. — (Western literature series)

ISBN 0-87417-311-6 (alk. paper)

I. Title. II. Series.

PS3556.I499C35 1998 97-36561

813'.54—dc21 CIP

The paper used in this book meets the requirements of American National Standard for Information Services—Permanence of Paper for Printed Library Materials, ANSI Z39.48-1984. Binding materials were selected for strength and durability.

A portion of chapter 5 was published as "Sequoia Hunters" in *Other Voices* 9, no. 24 (Spring/Summer 1996).

California Time is a work of fiction. While readers may recognize several Great Central Valley locales, all names, characters, and incidents are products of the author's imagination and are used fictitiously. Any resemblance to actual persons, living or dead, or to events in the lives of actual persons is entirely coincidental.

07 06 05 04 03 02 01 00 99 98 5 4 3 2

for Nan, again

CONTENTS

ACKNOWLEDGMENTS

Over the years, a number of people have contributed enormously to my understanding of Central Valley life. I'm grateful for their insights and their answers to my many questions. My thanks to:

Harry and Yoshino Watanabe
Dick Brown
Ellen Brown
Lyman Gorrell
King Raygoza
Bill Leoni
Michi Tokumoto
Junior De Soto
Charlie Rodriguez
Peter and Judy Hopper
John and Karen Webster
Dan and Vera Azevedo
Yoshino Hasegawa
Jay Johnson
Larry Ritchie
Dean Levitan
Jeff Ritchie
Rick Carlstrom
Leon Holcomb
Frances Sanchez
Joyce Cox
Jim LaRue
Bud Erickson
Stan and Marcia Milham
Linda and Don Yamakawa
Clyde and Vernetta Smith
Nick and Toya Parenti
Matilda Vartikian

PATRICK HART—1928

chapter 1

The Valley had no calendar. Time in California wasn't measured out in months; it was by crops. Spring meant strawberries, then the apricots, cherries, peaches, and it was summer, hot as fire; tomatoes, squash, plums, Thompson seedless, figs. Fall, still blazing hot, was cotton, persimmons, pomegranates, walnuts, almonds. Winter was oranges, tangerines, and lemons. Then the dead time arrived, tule fog like a thick spread of moonwash hiding the sun, and you couldn't be sure you were awake or alive, everyone laying low, waiting for the first almond blossoms in February, when time started up again. Clocks were just ornaments here.

He'd been managing the hotel since '23, five years now, but it was only Saturday afternoons that registered, when everyone came into town, some in their Sunday clothes, some in washed-out cotton dresses and overalls. Parked cars angled down Main Street from one end to the other, stores all open, crowds of people walking the length of the commercial blocks, then back again, visiting, stopping to talk and sit a while on the benches in front of the stores. Watching the passersby from his favorite spot in the lobby, he'd now and then catch a glimpse of himself in his new double-breasted suit in the lobby mirror. He didn't look like his father anymore. The way the barber slicked back his receding hair made his forehead look higher than it should be. Little blue eyes, red Irish skin, pug nose, chinless mouth; you would have to call the sum total ugly, there was no question about it. But the suit looked good. He tipped his hat to the folks going by the hotel, and they called back, "Hello, Mr. Hart." "Afternoon, Patrick." "Pat, has the Doghouse got a new shipment of hooch? I'm still carrying a headache from last week's."

"You're going to like this new batch. Made it this morning in the Californian's cleanest bathtub, up on the fourth floor. Aged to perfection." That got a general laugh.

He held the door open for three women who went into the coffee shop for some refreshment. He knew a lot of the people now. The townspeople were easy; he saw them every day, on the street or in the fraternal organizations he belonged to, the Order of Moose and the American Legion. Chamber of Commerce. But he was getting to know by sight and name some of the farmers that lived out in the country. They might come into the hotel's dining room for dinner on a special occasion: a good crop, a wedding or a funeral. He recognized them from his rides with Ray Hamada, who'd been here since the '90s, when there was nothing but tall grass and oak trees, and because of Elton McInteer: as the superintendent of the Land Company, Elton knew everyone, for business reasons.

He'd first come to town in the month of August. He hadn't known what to expect. Whenever anyone at the Land Company office in San Francisco had mentioned the valley they'd laughed, as if a big surprise was awaiting him. "Patrick, wait until you get there. You'll see." It hadn't taken him long to see that the valley was bad enough, but the town was the worst of the bargain. Five blocks of downtown, alleys behind every store, railroad tracks running across the middle like a badly stitched scar. Because it was the county seat, there were a couple of extra buildings: a courthouse with two cannons, French 75s from the Great War, in front, and a jail. A few blocks of big homes with sloping lawns shaded by trees that made the streets into tunnels. Middle-sized houses with screened-in sleeping porches hung with wisteria that got hosed down at night to cool off the breezes. Then lots of modest homes on small lots, interspersed here and there with an old farmhouse, tank house and barn next to it, on a couple of acres, overtaken when the town spread into the open fields of the countryside.

To end up here in this burg was hard to swallow. He'd gone everywhere a ship could float from the time he was twelve. He'd seen the capitals of Europe. He'd put into every port in South America, was on one of the first ships through the Panama Canal, had sailed around Australia and New Zealand. California was barely civilized. The Great Central Valley was a blank space on the map of the country. It was like being buried alive.

"You'll see, Patrick," they'd said. See what? He hadn't understood that it might be a joke. He'd met with Mr. Reid, the American Land Company director, in Sacramento as scheduled. The meeting went well. Reid asked after mutual acquaintances in Boston and then they got down to business. He was offered the job. Reid shook his hand and didn't seem to notice the porcelain prosthesis. "Your references are the best I've seen in a long time. You're more than qualified for the position. The hotel, the Californian, is our southernmost endeavor in the state; you'll be on our frontier, so to speak. We have other investments in that area: several cattle ranches, some acreage in grain, some groves, a sawmill, some oil leases, a winery—I'm not sure what all. We're not Southern Pacific railroad, God forbid, but we're prospering."

The next morning he got the 4:20 A.M. train down the Great Central Valley. It didn't take long for him to decide that the joke was there was nothing to see: the valley was empty of people, vacant. Every hour or so the train stopped at a station that looked exactly like the one before it. Only the names on the signs nailed to the roofs changed. Lodi and Stockton. Manteca, Modesto, Merced, Madera. Looking out past the station, he could always spot the hotel; it was always the tallest building, sticking up like the center pole for a circus tent before the canvas was put up, amid the surrounding business buildings. Then houses and shacks. Then there was nothing again, nothing but the yellow grass smoothed out flat, moving in the direction the wind blew, the wild game that ran from the sound of the train, antelope or deer, and the rounded hills in the distance. He could see what he thought were mountains to the east, but it was hard to say: the sun turned everything into a glaze or sheen of light. They crossed a trestle over a river with a strip of green on either side, a line of trees, small houses, several times. But the rest remained barren, yellow and unending. Sometimes the yellow weeds became uniform and he guessed it was a crop, but wasn't sure what kind. Sometimes there were big green squares of trees, the limbs sagging with fruit. Cattle once in a while, long strings of cows following each other as if they were going somewhere. You could go for miles before you spotted a road, much less a house or barn. Central California was uninhabited.

Though all the windows were open in the club car, it was stifling by two in the afternoon. The speed of the train didn't make any difference; the hot wind blowing into his face felt like it was bruising his skin. He ordered glass after glass of lemonade and held the iced surface against his face. The ice didn't last long enough to help. The other passengers were scattered around the seats far apart from each other, as if to keep a distance in case someone should melt.

He counted 172 telegraph poles before he saw another house, water tower next to it, topped by a windmill. A tank house, someone had corrected him, the water supply for the house. Civilization. Big limp trees in rows, the leaves bigger than a maple's, with kids on their hands and knees underneath, picking up fruit off the ground and putting it in buckets. Figs, someone said. It was all mysterious. He couldn't stop looking back, trying to figure out what he was seeing. It wasn't like passing through a foreign country; it was like a journey in a dream, where you had to make up the names for what you were seeing.

His stop was next. There were no porters, and his trunks were dumped from the baggage car onto the depot platform. No one else got off; he was there alone in the hot sun when the train pulled out for Bakersfield. He walked around the station looking for a taxi, but there didn't seem to be any. The depot was downtown, and he had just decided to walk to the hotel and come back for his trunks when someone hailed him from the shade of the loading dock. "If you don't have any more sense than to stand there in the sun and wait for something that's never going to come, you're not going to last very long around here." He could make out a straw boater in the shadows. "Come on, my Model A is over there; we can load your gear and I'll take you to the hotel."

"How do you know that's where I'm going?"

"You're either a salesman or the new manager at the Californian; either way that's where you'd go. Or you can stay out here until one of the stationmaster's relatives arrives and charges whatever he thinks you have in your pocket to take you there. By the way, my name is Ray Smith. I'm a longtime acquaintance of Elton McInteer." He was standing at the other end of the big steamer trunk now, some kind of Chinaman, Oriental, but a little taller than most, with thick shoulders and eyes so slanted you couldn't see the whites. He acted like he owned the place, the very heat.

They loaded the trunks into the Ford truck. He had taken off his porcelain hand on the train and put on his hook. The gun case was last. Without asking, the Chinaman unstrapped the end flap and pulled out the 25/35 lever-action Winchester he'd been talked into buying in Chicago by a passenger who needed fifteen dollars. "You might need this out west," the man had said, as if the place was still wild. The Chinaman was aiming down the barrel, and when the stationmaster came out the door he swung the rifle around toward the man and and cocked it with his thumb.

"Go ahead, Ray, shoot me. It'd be worth it, to know they finally hanged you," the stationmaster said. Ray pulled the trigger. The stationmaster jumped back inside. Ray was laughing so hard he couldn't stop. "I, along with most other people, dislike the thieving railroad," he said when he could talk. "Come on, I'll take the long way and show you the city." People knew the Chinaman, waved, and he honked back. He did a running commentary as he drove. "Don't go in that place; even before Prohibition it had the worst rotgut in the world. Alma's, cleanest girls in town. Full measure in that grocery store, even if they are Jews. You can depend on the Bank of Italy; they'll treat you right there. And how did you lose your hand?"

He usually told some cock-and-bull war story, but this time he told the truth. "A female acquaintance cut it off with a cleaver because she thought I was stepping out on her."

Ray looked over at him, jammed in the front seat with the gun case and valises. "You may fit in around here after all," he said.

"Let me ask you one. How did an Oriental get the name Ray Smith?"

"You Occidentals are all the same, always looking at differences instead of similarities. Because my last name is very common where I come from, which is Japan—as common, in fact, as Smith—I renamed myself Smith when I came to the United States. But the newspapers call me the Yellow Peril, which I like a lot better. If I hadn't already established Smith, I'd use that."

He couldn't tell if Ray was crazy or not. He didn't try to pay him; that would have been a mistake. "Come on in. I've got a bottle of Canadian Club."

"Some other time. My son Mats was supposed to have been on that train. I haven't seen him in years, but he's probably as slow-witted as everyone else in my wife's family. I know he got on the boat in Yokohama, and it takes fourteen days. I had the train tickets waiting for him at the offices on the docks in San Francisco. His mother is sending him just to get even with me for never going back to Japan."

That had been his first day in the valley.

In his first year, in '23, he'd lived in the manager's suite on the first floor behind the front desk. For some reason he couldn't sleep in the hotel. It took him forever to conk out, and then he'd be awakened by the slightest noise. He moved his room upstairs to the second floor. It was a little better. There was no street noise, but the roomers were always coming and going and he'd count their steps on the wooden hallways. He'd never had this trouble before. Sometimes, waiting for sleep, he'd think how much the hotel was like a ship. Maybe that's what he missed, the rocking of the boat. The rooms were like cabins, the dining room like the ship's saloon. There was a barbershop too, a coffee shop. He'd been a purser. A purser on a ship and a manager at a hotel, they were really almost the same. Constantly checking that the passengers were happy, the ship's services running smoothly.

Not that the hotel looked like a ship. It was a square six stories of yellow glazed brick that took up almost a whole block, counting the garages and storage sheds across the alley. It was the tallest building in town, seventy-one rooms, each with its own toilet, sink, outside window, transom, and double bed; if you wanted a bath, it was down the hall. And it was the hub: the Chamber of Commerce met there on Wednesdays and the Moose on first Mondays; wedding receptions were held in the banquet room and juries were sent to eat in the coffee shop. When people said, "I'll meet you in front of the hotel," everyone knew they meant the Californian.

The window-lined lobby and front desk faced Main Street. Four big fans hung down like fronds on a palm tree from the embossed-tin ceiling, keeping the room cool. Wall mirrors by the elevator reflected the glow of the ceiling lights on the polished wood of the front desk and the seventy-one brass keys hanging in front of their cubbyholes. All the sofas and chairs were tufted oxblood leather with claw feet; he'd insisted on that. The two potted plants by the front door, his nod to tradition, seemed out of place in the lobby, almost sad and lonely. Doors led from the lobby to the barbershop and coffee shop and bar, closed since 1919. The Californian was a first-class establishment, except for the speakeasy across the alley.

No one took Prohibition seriously here. You could always get Dago red from the Italians or homemade German brew, which was pretty good. And Canadian whiskey from Vancouver was abundant on the West Coast. The hotel sold wine with dinner and beer on the sly. The hotel bar was officially closed, but the storeroom across the alley, which everyone called the Doghouse, did a brisk business in drinks. The bourbon was forbidden, but the city police were understanding as long as there was no trouble. It was the pigeons that were the trouble.

The goddamn pigeons had got into the vent system and were nesting there. He did what everyone advised: poisoned corn, toy snakes from the five-and-dime, silhouettes of owls, even wire mesh over all the openings. But he could hear them cooing all night long now. He still wasn't sleeping well. It wasn't until the end of his second year at the hotel that he thought about moving up to the roof. There was a glassed-in enclosure where the hotel linen had been hung to dry before the new steam-heated drying unit was put in. He would go up to the roof, look around, and imagine sleeping up there. You couldn't hear the street or hotel sounds, and the pigeons never landed there. He moved a cot up to the enclosure to give it a try, and he slept like a baby. It was like being on the bridge of a liner. He could see across the valley to the coast range of mountains on the west side and to the Sierras on the east. He was the captain of the ship. And the pigeons trailing the wake, wheeling across the sky, were like seagulls.

Ray had come into the hotel a few times during his first couple of months, but most often to pass through to the alley and then into the Doghouse to get himself a quick drink. Ray was a busy man. But one Saturday he came into the lobby wearing a new suit, a thick gold chain looped between two pockets of his vest, carrying a walking stick with a silver knob in the shape of a monkey. Slant eyes, slicked-down black hair under the gray derby, straight-backed. "Mr. Smith," Patrick couldn't help saying. He had found out that Ray was one of the largest landowners out by the river and that his real name was Hamada.

"Mr. Hart, you're looking well."

"And you look prosperous, Mr. Smith." They were still formal in that mocking way.

"When I deal with investors, which I did this morning, I like to be on an equal footing, at least in the sartorial department."

It wasn't noon yet, but he said, "Ray, how about a drink?" He had one of the waitresses go into his office and get a bottle of bourbon and some ice and soda. They sat in a corner of the lobby where they could look out onto Main Street, hidden from passersby.

He'd always wondered, so he asked after the first drink, "How did you learn English so well?" Ray didn't have a trace of an accent. It was his looks that always made you notice his perfect English.

"Why's it so surprising that a person can speak his adopted country's language? You speak English."

"But I was born here, and the Irish spoke English before they came over."

"Well, I spoke English before I came here, too. My father was an importer. Our chief clerk was Occidental, born in Baltimore, Maryland. It was our business to know English."

They sipped, talking, watching the Saturday crowd pass in front of the hotel. Swarms of kids with small white bags of hard candy, their Saturday treat. Women looking hurried and worn, the men standing in groups on the corner talking like they had all the time in the world. "Look at these people," Ray said. "Peasants. Coolies. They came here to escape the landowners, and they're doing here what they did where they came from, drowning in their own sweat."

"Except that they can buy land here. Be their own boss."

"I've been here since '91 and I've never seen one that would take a chance beyond twenty acres and two full meals a day in his belly. Sure, some of them might own land, but they're still slaves to the packers and the banks. They're still working for wages. Their imaginations have been bred out of them. I don't know why they bothered making the voyage."

"I'll tell you why. My grandmother told me her father's brother back in Ireland was harnessed like a horse to a plow with five other men. The owner had them flogged when they stepped out of line. The animals were treated better than they were."

"That's all good exercise," Ray said.

"Not if you're Irish," he said, indignant.

"What does that have to do with anything, what nationality anybody was or is? This valley is for the taking. It's what you claim, not what you happen to be. What you own, the crop you bring in. When I first came, it was grain and cattle. A ten-thousand-acre place was about the right size. When grain went bust after the war, the serfs came in and planted twenty, thirty acres in vines or fruit, whatever their family could work. They made a living. It won't last. All they're really selling is their backs, their labor. When the cheap land runs out, their kids will start arguing over who gets the property. In three generations most of the valley will belong to a handful of landlords, just like it was back where these people came from, and they'll be working for the owners again."

They went into the dining room and had lunch and talked about the stock market, making money and losing money, commodities. He must have told Ray about the pigeons. When they came back and sat down in the lobby again, he noticed a well-dressed Oriental standing out in front on the sidewalk, waiting for someone, he thought. There were a lot of Chinese in town; there was a restaurant and a grocery store, a laundry. He was enjoying himself talking to Ray, who had a wealth of information. He sent for another bottle. When a clerk came over to show him some freight invoices, he excused himself and said he'd be right back.

When he did come back, Ray wasn't there. Then he heard the first blast. A pigeon came down hard against the cement curb. People were stopping on the street, looking up at the hotel roof. There were more shots, and three birds sailed down like old hats. He was headed across the lobby for the stairs when he saw a policeman come running down the sidewalk, yelling up toward the roof, "There's an ordinance against shooting in the city limits."

Then Ray's voice called, "I've been retained to rid the premises of these vermin-infested fowl. The health of the city and the sanitation of this hotel must supersede any ordinance."

"I just wanted you to be aware of the law, Mr. Hamada."

"I appreciate that, Sergeant."

The cop watched for a while as Ray blasted away, then walked on down the sidewalk. He got the bellboy to go out and start picking up the dead birds.

When Ray came down it was because he was out of ammunition and the glass of rye he'd taken up with him was empty. "It's thirsty work," Ray said. "I didn't get them all, but I will." He lay down on the lobby sofa and closed his eyes. "I'm going to rest a minute," he said.

He was just thinking he should call the clerk over to help him take Ray up to a room when the Oriental who had been standing outside came into the lobby, walked right up to him, and shook his hand. "I am a Christian," he announced in stiff English. "I will take him home." He pulled Ray up by the arm. Ray didn't resist. They walked Ray out the side door to where his Ford was parked and laid him in the back. Patrick put his shotgun in next to him and waved to the young man as he drove away. Could that have been Ray's son, he wondered? Probably not; he wasn't like Ray at all. He found Ray's derby in the lobby when he came back in, and he put it on the shelf in his office. He thought he'd better take a little rest himself.

It wasn't long after that that Ray took him up to the hunting camp for the first time. They had been talking about going hunting for the last four months, but he never thought they'd go; it was just talk. It had started to cool off a little, not much, but enough that you weren't sweating all day long. He wasn't sure if he could even shoot a rifle with one hand, but he took the lever-action Winchester anyhow. He had never hunted anything before, but he was out back in the alley waiting when Ray drove up.

Ray had a young woman sitting in front with him, someone he didn't recognize, not one of Alma's girls. Stretched out in the back of the truck on a tarp was the young man who'd said, "I'm a Christian," still in a suit and tie, asleep. "Who's that in back?" he asked, getting in beside the woman.

"It's my goddamn boy, Mats," Ray said, shifting gears. As soon as they left town the road turned to dirt. The mountains didn't seem to get any closer; after an hour they looked just as far away as they did from his glass room on top of the hotel. The woman didn't say anything, kept her eyes closed, rocked against his shoulder as they finally started going up the switchbacks into the hills. It was still dry up here, yellow grass, sagging brush. Looking back, you couldn't see the buildings in town anymore, just the flatness of the valley separated into squares of cultivated land. They got higher and the valley disappeared behind the ridges and the trees. When they stopped by a creek to put water in the radiator, he noticed the quiet. Not a sound, not even the creek made a noise. They passed a pack station, a couple of buildings, corrals filled with mules and horses. Ray honked but didn't stop, kept going up, raising dust that filtered up the shafts of sunlight piercing through the tops of the trees. The trees seemed to get bigger the higher they went—not just at the trunks but taller too: you couldn't even see the tops sometimes. It was all new to him. It was almost dark when they got to the camp. He could make out the outlines of tables and outbuildings. They had eaten sandwiches on the way as Ray drove. No one said much: it was too hot, too uncomfortable. Ray never stopped unless he had to. He'd cursed the road, the car, and his boy in the back, who kept getting sick.

Tired out from the drive, he grabbed his bedroll. As soon as he lay down he was out. When he woke up it was cold, still dark. Ray was standing over an open fire. The woman was cooking. It went fast after that; he couldn't keep up with what he was seeing or doing. It was the place, the mountains, the forest; it was too big, too much to understand. Sometimes he was struck dumb with what he was seeing: trees tall enough to reach into the clouds. They were camped at the upper edge of the timberline, and they could look down on the forest. There were still patches of snow further up on the rock ridge.

The girl's name was Mabel and she did the cooking but went out with Ray and him in the morning to hunt. Mats, Ray's boy, stayed in camp. They left early that first morning, the sun just coming up, Mabel carrying the pack, following Ray on a path he could barely see. They chanced on a buck with four or five does out in a meadow and Ray dropped him and one of the does. Mabel dressed them out and put the hearts and livers in a canvas bucket. They went on, and when Ray pointed at another buck eating berries off some brush, he fired his rifle and dropped the buck, just like he'd been hunting all his life. By noon Ray had killed two more bucks. "We're in luck," he said. "I can get the Ford up here." They ate lunch in a meadow, red onion sandwiches and hot tea, Mabel cooking the livers and hearts over the coals. Nothing had ever tasted better in his whole life. He fell asleep on the green grass, just stretched out and closed his eyes and that was all he remembered.

He woke up at the sound of whooping and yelling but couldn't see anyone and closed his eyes again. Pretty soon Ray was kicking at the soles of his boots. "That was good," he said. "You go help yourself; we all came up here to have some fun." He must have hesitated. "Go on, she won't mind. Mabel's a good kid." Ray handed him a half-full pint of rye. He went.

This place was like paradise. Nowhere he'd ever visited with the ship, no other country, came even close to it. He didn't want to go back, after the ten days of hunting. It was like being a stranger in the most perfect place you could imagine. Make-believe. He'd just wander around sometimes, looking at places he knew no one had ever seen before, not even animals, probably, up here. He found a tree with its center burned out, the charred space bigger than a room. For the first time in his life he picked a bouquet of flowers and gave them to Mabel. She was touched, he thought, and passed him extra gravy at dinner. She seemed to be enjoying herself. She was a well-spoken girl, "Good mornings" and "Good evenings." She read to Ray while he shaved, usually from the business section of the newspaper they'd brought up, commenting as she read. "Navels look good this year. Walnuts, too. Apples are going to be a branch breaker, they say." She drank like a man and could raise hell like one when she got a snoot full.

But the more Mats tried to get along, the worse Ray treated him. "Don't try to build a fire; you'll end up burning yourself. And I don't need my rifle cleaned; you lost the goddamn front sight the last time you tried. Just sit there, Mats." He gathered wood and read. Mabel ignored him too. Ray sent Mats off to fish the last day before they went back to town, but he didn't catch anything.

After they came back down to the valley he found himself staring up toward the mountains sometimes, as if he'd left or lost something up there. Elton said that people from the valley had been going up there to hunt for years, sometimes in a big group, sometimes just a couple of fellows. It depended on how the crops turned out, if anybody made any money. He told that to Ray. "Him and his money. I go up there anyway, even if I go broke. The cheapskate, he works for another man for wages and he still worries." The interesting thing about having Ray for a friend was you got to watch someone else do all the things you'd only think about doing yourself because you didn't want to suffer the consequences. Probably that was why Elton hated old Ray most of the time.

They never made a formal appointment for these rides. Elton would see him in the hotel or bar and say, "Patrick, I've got to go out and see one of my farmers Wednesday. I'll pick you up at ten." He usually did. Standing by the two big front doors, looking out to see if Elton was going to show up, he watched as people started drifting into the dining room, the ones that had money. 1928 wasn't a good year, everyone was saying. But then it was always either feast or famine in the shovel-and-dirt business, as Ray called it. Everything he knew about this place was from either Elton or Ray. He had never met a happy farmer: they had either just succumbed to disaster or just averted one. There was no middle ground. And from what he'd seen in the couple of years he'd been here, they enjoyed the situation. They expected fire, flood, or pestilence, so they were never disappointed. It had been like coming to a different world, coming from Boston and then the port cities to the Great Central Valley, as they called everything down the middle from Redding to Bakersfield. The best piece of ground in the U. S. of A.—Elton said that.

He'd never learned how to drive. It hadn't been necessary, working on a liner, living aboard ship. Then he'd lost his right hand in 1918. He was too old now, he told himself. So he waited to be driven to see the countryside. He never let on to Elton how much he enjoyed himself on these outings. If Elton knew, he'd stop asking him.

Elton McInteer ran this end of the American Land Company business: tenant farms, the grain elevators, stockyards and a milling operation, packing sheds and wineries and the rest. He didn't have anything to do with the hotel but was always stopping in and inspecting the place as if he did. It was two years before they started calling each other by their first names. "Well, what do you think, Pat?" They took drives—making his rounds, Elton called it—down dusty roads. Ray didn't even need a road; he'd go cross-country, driving right through someone's land. Ray was always in a hurry.

Elton was a bunghole at times, condescending, impatient with anyone who didn't know as much as he did, always dressed in a businessman's suit and vest and tie, looking at least ten years older than he was, which was almost forty-five. Elton cultivated his resemblance to Calvin Coolidge.

They went east from town, one of his favorite routes. A mile out, the blacktop turned to gravel, then dirt. Elton tested him as they drove. "What's that grove over there, down that side of the road?"

"Olive trees."

"What about this one?"

"Nectarines."

"Peaches." Elton was pleased when he corrected him. He'd missed that one, but he kept getting better, asking Ray questions, looking things up in books. He read all the agriculture news in the papers. Did Elton report on him to Sacramento? Probably: he was always going up there to see Mr. Reid. They had made the game harder a few years ago; he was also supposed to guess what country the people who worked the property had come from. He liked the game, but he didn't always like Elton.

"Who owns those vines over there?" That meant Elton bought the

Thompson seedless for the raisin packing shed. Elton was steering the big touring car with one hand, slowing down, the dust catching up to them. "What do you say?" They were getting closer to the house now, board and batten, tank house, storage shed filled with stacks of raisin trays, chicken run and vegetable garden. A big oak tree for shade.

"Italian," he said.

"You were lucky," Elton said, stopping the car in the road.

He wasn't lucky; he could tell by the plum tomatoes in the garden and the geraniums and carnations in old olive oil cans on the porch, and by his new theory, too. A smell of something delicious cooking reached all the way to the road. "There were no weeds in the grapes," he said aloud to throw Elton off.

The owner came out, short and thick, wearing washed-out overalls, a cotton work shirt, flat cap. There was no way to know whether he could speak very much English or not after he said good afternoon, because Elton did all the talking about crops and prices and the Italian did the nodding, his foot resting on the running board. "And give my best to Mrs. Palestini," Elton said before driving off. He'd given the farmer a nickel cigar, always a sign the man was in his good graces.

Elton had said it before, but he said it again now: "Italians will work themselves to death for you, probably pound for pound the best all-around laborers the Good Lord ever developed. They're like horses. Portuguese are next, but you have to tell them twice. Mexicans same way. Filipinos, you demonstrate and then point at them so they know it's them that have to do the work, not you. Who owns that place over there?"

"Figs. Armenian."

"They're like mules; they think they're smarter than you. But they'll work. They'll speculate, too; take a chance on what's going to be the next big cash crop. How could you tell?"

"I could read the name on that lug box over there in that shed—Vartanian." Elton had been in California for over forty years, about the same amount of time that Ray had been here, but it was like they'd never seen the same things. They knew each other well enough: Elton called Ray a son of a bitch, and Ray never mentioned Elton's name if he could help it. When they met, they were cordial. Elton was most interested in acquisition, yields, and cash. Ray was a speculator, an innovator. Ray invented ways to make money.

"What about this place?"

Small dairy, a dozen cows standing out in an enclosure up to their hocks in manure because there were no drains or high spots. A bunch of kids with red hair playing on baled hay. It wasn't English they were yelling. He was going to say Danish but instead shook his head. Scandinavians, Germans, same as Dutch, all thickheaded and tightfisted, hanging on to four cents of the first nickel they ever made. "Portuguese. The manure, when it's that high and should have been hauled away a month ago, it can only be Portuguese."

"This is the Brazil place. Portuguese, but from the Azores, not the mainland."

"I just hope they clean those cows off before they milk them."

"I don't drink milk anyway," Elton said.

Just like there were Irish and Italian and Polack neighborhoods in cities, there were places in the valley where various nationalities had congregated. The Volga Germans spoke Russian and grew tree fruit up by Sanger. The Swedes named their own town Kingsburg. There was a town of Negroes, Allensworth, named after the colonel who started the colony, where they grew cotton. But even if the nationalities didn't congregate in one area, you could tell who they were by what they grew; that was his new theory, anyhow. The big strapping Yugoslavians grew Malagas for raisins. The Dutch and Portuguese always had dairies. Danish too. Armenians grew citrus and figs. Mexicans were cattlemen. Basques had sheep. The Italians grew vines, but they could make any crop grow. He'd told Ray his theory once.

"Bullshit, Patrick. These pitiful dupes try to raise whatever they grew back where they came from, and when that fails they try whatever can make them a dollar. Your peon whites from Iowa, say. If they grew corn back home, they won't last long around here, so they adapt into chicken farmers or pecan growers. And what do the Irish grow?" He started laughing, slapping his leg. "Kids, twenty to a bed, shanty Irish. The Chinese grow little grocery stores. Rich white farmers who own wineries and canneries and packing sheds and mills and most of the good land grow crops of greenbacks.

"Your theory doesn't hold water in the valley, Patrick. This place breaks all the rules because it's so new. Untried. No one is sure what will work here or where, so they have to experiment. The past doesn't count here. You can lose your nationality in this place. You have to be able to follow your wildest dreams, steer with your imagination, not settle for being a slant eye or a wop. The people who can do that are the ones who'll last in this hellhole. Come on, let's go over to Alma's and see what the whores have to say about your theory."

He saw Ray's son, Mats, once in a while: he'd stop in the hotel to say hello. They had breakfast together a couple of times. If Ray was there and saw Mats coming, he'd step out the back door. Mats brought in his new wife and introduced her, nice-looking woman, Harriet. Taller than Mats was, and could speak English well enough. He'd heard that Ray had sent to Japan for a bride for Mats. He had heard from someone else that Mats was farming now, had some acreage out north of town. Mats was proud of his new wife. Patrick took them to lunch in the dining room and tried to entertain them, teased Harriet. She giggled at everything, but there was no real hilarity. They were both so controlled, so serious about responding correctly. Mats said they'd been married in the Presbyterian church. They'd picked the right outfit, he thought.

And he saw Ray more often, now that they had the contest going. It was to see if they could screw their way through all the whores in the county and end up at Alma's by Valentine's Day. At a rough estimate there were about seventy professionals at harvest time, and half that in between. One of the problems with the contest was new whores kept appearing and old ones disappearing. They were always phoning back and forth to report the count. It was a lot of fun. After Veronica cut off his hand he'd learned a valuable lesson about entanglements. It was like Ray said, women were supposed to be fun. He'd pay for his pleasure; it was cheaper in the long run.

He was godfather for Mats and Harriet's daughter, Reiko, and went to the ceremony with Ray, who behaved himself, even with a snoot full. Reiko Ann Hamada. He had that inscribed on a silver baby cup. Ray was whispering to him through a whiskey breath, "Get married, Patrick, and have the next one," his whole body shaking with stifled mirth. He didn't see what was so funny, himself. He had no plans of getting married, but he wasn't ruling out the possibility. The Irish always married late anyway; he was only thirty-six years old. "It's you I'm worried about," he whispered back to Ray. "You already have a dozen kids; isn't that enough?" Ray laughed out loud. It sounded like a bark, and the minister jumped. The rumor was that Ray had kids all over the countryside. There were other people in the church, farmers, neighbors of Mats, Portuguese and Italian, looking around the building as if the devil might appear any moment in a Protestant church. A handful of Japanese Christian bachelors, all in their best suits. They seemed subdued, half the size of Ray.

Three years later they did it all again with Mats and Harriet's second child, a boy, Grayson. Ray was sober that time and muttering. "What kind of a name is that? I asked the silly girl and she said it was an American name. I know where she got it, from those goddamn novels she reads."

After the ceremony Ray wanted to take everyone over to the hotel for lunch, but Mats said he had to get back to his place; he was right in the middle of harvesting. Reiko, the little devil, took his hand and said, "We go, Uncle Pat," and started up the sidewalk. Everyone else followed.

It was a good lunch until the baby started crying. "Feed the goddamn kid, Harriet," Ray said. Harriet tried to rock the baby quiet, but he started screaming. "Don't you think we've ever seen a tit before?" Ray yelled at her. She got up, her face red, and took the baby into the women's lounge. Mats just put his eyes on his empty plate. Ray was finishing his fourth glass of wine. "I hope you have more sense than your mother, Reiko," he muttered.

Ray would bring the grandkids into the hotel sometimes. They were both hellions. Reiko never shut up once she started talking. And if she didn't like whatever she was eating, she'd turn her plate or glassful of milk upside down on the table. Ray would just laugh and order something else for her. Grayson, when he wasn't shrieking, was crawling under the tables, bothering people. He'd grab a lady's purse and spread the contents on the floor and take the things he wanted to play with. The worst was, both were smart kids. Grayson could read before he went to school. Just take a newspaper and go from page to page. You couldn't shut him up. Ray thought it was funny. Reiko would insist she had to help the desk clerk; she'd stand on a chair and check in the guests. People seemed to think it was cute. She was always wanting to help the cooks in the kitchen or the waitresses in the dining room. When Ray came in with his grandkids, the staff hid.

HORTENSE

chapter 2

I was awake, waiting, listening, hearing my sisters' breathing, the windmill catching a night breeze from across the pasture, the five-hundred-gallon water tank filling. I could see my mother through the doorway, placing the kindling crisscross on the newspapers in the firebox before striking the kitchen match against the top of the cast-iron stove. It was like watching myself in the mirror; I was so much like my mother. My sisters and two brothers all looked like in-betweens: some were tall like my father with blue eyes like my mother; some were short like her with brown hair, brown eyes, like Dad's. I had everything like my mother—hair the color of carrots, blue eyes, big rear end—and all in the sixth grade.

I always felt happy when I woke for another day, as if I were alive for the first time. Every day was a surprise: to smell wood smoke while I was still under the warm covers and hear the mooing of the cows seemed brand-new and interesting. It was 4:30, and the cows knew that better than the clock on the kitchen table. They were shifting their feet by the barn door, waiting to get inside out of the cold so they could stand in a stall with clean hay to eat and get rid of that big sack of milk. Susie's was so swollen sometimes that it dragged on the ground like a pillow between her legs. It had to be uncomfortable.

Last year in school I heard a boy call a girl a cow. It surprised me. A skunk, I could see that, a polecat, a bitch dog, maybe. But a cow? I liked cows. If I could be an animal, it would be a cow. Holstein. I wouldn't want to be anything else. A chicken? I liked chicken. I asked Reiko about it. Because both girls and cows had teats, she said. I knew that mine were already big, in the sixth grade. I wouldn't mind being Susie, who gave four gallons a milking. I took care of Susie, washing her, every inch, while the water was still warm, rinsing the rag again and again, using my fingernails to scrape the muck off her legs. Then I'd scratch her forehead, feel her nose to see if it was nice and wet.

When I was younger I'd kiss Susie, let her lick my face. Susie would moo when I held out the framed pictured of the Virgin Mary, and she'd give it a nuzzle before going into the stall to be milked. She didn't need a rope; Susie always moved along with just my hand on her neck. Cows cry: I'd seen that a lot of times. When they got branded or sick, big tears came down their cheeks from their eyes. Susie cried when another cow died. I tried to take my time, milking, when I came to Susie, give her time to eat and rest, but it wasn't always possible. Susie didn't kick, but I still fastened her head to the feed trough like the others. Then I milked, my head resting on Susie's flank. When no one was looking I took milk from another cow and poured it into Susie's bucket.

Pretty soon it would be rush rush, everyone up, my father and brothers milking a lot faster than I was, and my mother and sisters running, filling the twelve-gallon milk cans from the buckets on the loading dock before we heard the truck. I thought of the cows like they were trees like back east, trees that gave maple syrup. Cows gave sweet milk. I'd seen the picture in a book about trees. But you couldn't pet a tree or kiss a tree.

I told Reiko. "Are you crazy?" she said. "Cows are animals. The trees are just trees."

"You water cows like peach trees."

"Do peach trees shit manure?"

"They lose their leaves."

Reiko wouldn't answer after that.

The alarm went off and I jumped out of bed, making the springs bounce like I'd practiced, waking up my sisters. Dressed, old wool trousers of my brothers, three sweaters, and then rubber knee boots.

My mother had the kindling going good, and I put more wood in the firebox.

I was the second outside after my father, who had the electric light on in the barn. I hurried, humming, so the cows knew I was coming. I could hear my mother hitting the celling with the broom handle to wake up my brothers upstairs. I wondered how long the electric bulb in the barn would last. It was two years old, from when they brought the wires out to the dairy. The one in the kitchen had already burned out twice. We didn't have to go to bed early now, or use coal oil lamps like before. When it was new, I got up one midnight and turned on the light, just left it on, watching it, to see if they still sent electricity through the wires all night, when no one needed it.

When the cows were milked I led them out to the pasture so they could make more for the evening milking. Milk factories. I had to hurry, eat breakfast and not miss the school bus. My brothers had already eaten and were going across the field to work for Mr. McInteer in the packing shed.

I washed in the cement laundry trays on the back porch, soaping my face and then down to my belly button. I held my teats together for the mirror; they grew more than anything else. I rinsed and put on my bra and underpants I'd washed last night. Reiko and I had bought bras in town at Woolworth's last summer. I needed one. Reiko didn't. Size of walnuts. Mine were like oranges. I dressed fast, put on my school dress, ate breakfast while I made my lunch, already hearing the bus but knowing it hadn't come yet. Dipped some homemade bread in the bacon grease and put last night's meat between the two slices. Grabbed a cluster of Malaga grapes from the pantry and poured Log Cabin syrup on another heel of bread and wrapped that in waxed paper too. And I heard the school bus for real and ran, brushing my hair, passing my sisters going into town to high school the other way on their bikes.

Reiko and Grayson were the first ones to be picked up. I was the second on our road. Reiko moved over so I could sit next to her. Grayson was right there, hanging over the edge of the seat. He was a pain in the ass. I was going to be glad to be in high school someday, because he wouldn't get there for another three years.

By ten o'clock I was getting sleepy in the warm classroom. I could feel my head roll on my shoulders and couldn't stop my eyes from fluttering closed, then open. I thought how the cows look as they sleep: they rock their weight from their hams to their legs. Sweetly bovine. I wanted to put my head down on my chest and sleep and sleep.

The bell made me jump, and we were out for noon recess. I used the inside toilet, warm and clean, no checking for black widows that might have decided to spin a web on the wooden seat. No flies. Just a flush and begone. The new school was like a castle. Lights and toilets and heat. Coming here was like getting a rest from the dairy. A moo moo here, and a moo moo there.

I missed the cows when I was in school. I pretended the kids were cows, lowing like they do back and forth as they chew their cud in the pasture. We looked like animals, sitting at our desk stalls, whispering back and forth. We were held there too, not able to get out of our seats without asking, except to use the dictionary.

Reiko sat across from me, and we'd go to the back of the room to look up words. Reiko could spell anything. We looked up *glamorous* and *exotic* and *penis* and *vagina.* When it was my turn I usually looked up *cow.* There was a drawing, and I'd study the names I didn't know: *pastern, dewclaw, hock, brisket, withers.* Then Reiko would grab the big dictionary and look up words that she thought would make me hate cows. *Bovine, sluggish, stolid, bucolic.* Some were good and some were bad. I didn't care. *Pastorale.*

We waited for the bus after school, and that town boy came over our way and started in. "Cow, fat cow. Hortense the whore." I pretended I was chewing my cud. I didn't listen. But Reiko heard this time, and she got ready for him when he came closer. She had her books held together with an old harness strap, and when she swung that geography and history and math book right into his big mouth, he went down with a thump. He made more noise than the pigs did at butchering time when their throats were cut and we were trying to catch the blood in pans to make sausage. He ran off squealing and we hopped on the bus.

The next morning they called us into the office. Reiko said it was an accident. The boy's mother was mad and said it wasn't, and he was going to have a scar. I looked as bovine as I could, head down, arms crossed, tail still. Reiko glared right back at the woman. They couldn't do anything: her grandfather had given the land for the school, just handed over the deed for three acres, after the school consolidated and we got buses to ride in. That's why I didn't have to go to the one-room school my brothers and sisters had gone to. The woman said something under her breath, and Reiko put her thumb to her nose and waggled her fingers at the woman's backside when we got out of the office.

I never minded the long ride home. The bus was high up and you could see across the country, better than you could from our tank house. It was like the yellow bus was a big number two pencil and we were drawing the lines separating the properties.

We passed the Italians' place. The father had chased the priest off his front porch with a broom once. My sisters knew the boy's sisters. We could see him pruning the vines. Julian. He used to come to school, but he didn't anymore. It was cold and he had on an old horse blanket coat and stocking hat. He moved down the grapes, clipping, not even turning when the bus passed, like the vines had him by the throat and he couldn't get away.

The bus divided the vineyard from the big squares of peach orchard. We cut through grain fields, went around a big oak, then alfalfa fields, and then finally came to our dairy. I said good-bye to Reiko and ran up our road as fast as I could. The cows knew I was home and would be waiting at the end of the road, and I'd be yelling, "I'm back, Susie, I'm back."

Hortense

Saturday was better than any day of the year. Maybe not better than Christmas or Thanksgiving, but those two were only once a year. Saturday came every week. On Saturday we went into town, Reiko and I, most often on Mr. Hamada's flatbed, but sometimes in Reiko's grandfather's Ford. My father didn't have a machine yet; we got what we needed from the delivery man. If we were lucky the grandfather would drive, and then the fun would begin. He'd say, "Come on," when we got to the hotel, and we'd go into the coffee shop and he'd say, "Order anything you want" when we sat down at the counter. We'd have hamburgers and root beer. Mr. Hamada would go into the Doghouse, and we'd sit there in the coffee shop, all happy. Even Grayson behaved himself. Then we'd go to the matinee or see our friends from school and visit all the stores, one after another, Sears, Penney's, and the rest, or just walk back and forth on the cement sidewalk, up and down Main Street, eating hard candy from Woolworth's out of white paper bags. You couldn't ask for more than that. They knew I had to be back for milking, and we always left at four o'clock.

When it rained heavy and the ground soaked through and the sun tried to come out, it brought the fog. You couldn't tell heaven from earth. When I went to get the cows I couldn't see my hand in front of my face. I couldn't tell if I was walking on the ground or on a roof, the fog was so thick, wet and white like milk. Susie would find me and then call the others, and they'd follow us back to the barn.

I washed the others first and then Susie, took her inside to milk. Put my forehead against her side and started. The long spurts made the bucket sing, and I could hear the voices from her stomachs talking to me in my head, in a soft language. Once my cousin Del tried to get a cow into a stall and got kicked; then when he started milking she put her foot in the bucket and when he got it out she shit all over his shoulder and arm. He got so mad he grabbed her tail and broke the bone, made it stay up like a U. I closed my eyes and put my hands over my ears that time, not to hear the bawling.

Both my father and my brothers were gentle with the cows, but some dairymen, if they were really mean, would hobble the cows so they couldn't kick, tie a front leg back so the cow kept busy trying to stand on three legs and couldn't do anything bad. And then the cow would get mean back, and in the end the butcher would be called. Our cows were happy cows. Susie allowed Grayson to sit on her back when he came to visit with Reiko. My father would kid Grayson and say that you had to crank the tail of the cow to get the milk out. Grayson would pretend he didn't know better and try, and we'd all laugh.

The lazy cat came in. I always waited until she got close enough and then I'd give her a long squirt in her open mouth until the milk bubbles came out her nose. When no one was looking, I got the book and wrote down the amount of milk Susie gave with the pencil. Instead of a two, I put four gallons. Susie was six years old and still gave enough milk for us to keep her. I mentioned that as often as I could. She was never going to be sold to the meat man.

We didn't usually go to church unless something good had happened: my sister graduated from high school and got a job with the telephone company; a lot of the cows had twin calves in the spring; there was early rain and we got an extra crop of alfalfa. Then we'd go on Sunday. It couldn't hurt, my father said. He spoke in English to us when he remembered, so we'd do better in school, but I liked to hear him talk in Portuguese to my mother. The church was called Saint Rose of Lima and wasn't far away, at a place where there used to be a ferry before the bridge was built across the river, which happened the year my dad came here from the Azores. We could walk across the fields to church, or just start down the road, and someone going that way would pick us up in their car. We never went to confession: my father said we were exempt because we had a dairy; there was no time to do anything bad. And we ate meat on Friday because it was good for you. We invited the priest for dinner once a year—more, if he was Portuguese and was funny.

The day before Christmas we cleaned the barn, swept it out good, scraped the floor, knocked the cobwebs down, then hosed the place before putting down clean straw. I cleaned the cows extra good before bringing them in to get milked. They all behaved themselves; they knew what was coming. My mother would fill pans with oats and pour molasses over the top, to thank the cows for the milk and for letting us live good. Each cow got her own banquet; they liked that.

Later we got our stockings full of fruit and nuts and candy, and sweaters my mother made us. My father would tell us stories about the Azore Islands, where he grew up, and how poor they were, so they could only afford to have a goat, no cows. I knew cows were at the manger when Jesus was born, and he'd tell about that when I asked, how cows were blessed for having witnessed the birth of Jesus. In some countries, he said, they were sacred and couldn't be killed even if you were starving to death.

What was even better than Christmas was the Holy Ghost festival, when the Holy Spirit descended like a dove at Pentecost. There was always a procession from the Grange Hall to the church, with a band, and girls who were old enough got to dress up in long dresses like Queen Isabella did when she gave food to the people after her marriage. And that's what we did, after Mass and the procession back to the Grange Hall, fed sopas to everyone that came, not just the Portuguese but anyone who wanted to come and eat with us. I had watched my sisters march in the procession and I was old enough, now that I was eleven.

Our procession was in April, the first in the valley. The other parishes would follow, one after another, every Sunday for months. I was going to be in the queen's court. A high school girl was going to be Queen Isabella. Reiko was going to wear a nun's habit and pass out pieces of sweet bread as we walked. She was allowed to be in the procession because her grandfather bought new uniforms for the marching band.

It was exciting getting ready, borrowing gowns from the older girls, long white satin dresses and velvet capes that dragged on the ground, and diamond tiaras that you wore on your head. I had watched my mother change the gowns to fit my sisters, but it was my turn now to stand on a chair while she pinned up the hem. She had to let out the waist for me and shorten the skirt. My father and brothers would be working in the Grange Hall kitchen all night before the procession, helping to make the sopas. One year almost a thousand people had come to eat. All the Portuguese families in the church donated something for the sopas: meat, cabbage, or bread. My mother baked for days. She had never bought a loaf of store bread in her whole life.

My heart was thumping as we started the procession from the hall to the church. The band was playing a hymn, and we were all singing, and so were all the people lined along the streets, watching us. We had to walk very slowly so we wouldn't trip over the capes of the girls in front of us, slowly up the church steps and down the center aisle, with all the candles burning on the altar. All of us in the procession sat in the front rows. I was sitting next to Reiko, and she was shaking, she was so excited. Mr. and Mrs. Hamada were there with Grayson. Reiko said her father thought that Catholics weren't Christians and she might get in trouble if the Presbyterians found out. I saw our neighbors, the Palestinis, there too. They were Italians, and came for the free feed. My father said the Italians weren't Christians, even if the pope was in Rome.

After Mass, we marched back, the people lining the streets again. The sun was out, shining down into our eyes, and I thought we might be blinded and get lost and end up in heaven. I was right behind the queen, and behind me was the big statue of Our Lady on a platform on poles carried by four men. In front of us were the Knights of Columbus, wearing their Christopher Columbus hats with their swords out resting on their shoulders, and then the band in their new uniforms, and then the kids dressed as nuns and brothers, passing out bread. My mother would never let me dress as a nun when I was younger. She said it was bad luck. Reiko was acting like a nun, crossing herself and bowing to the people. I had showed her how to do it. I had been to her church once. It was like sitting in the school gym. There was no smoky incense or candles, no statues or stained glass windows. It wasn't like a church at all.

All of us in the procession got to sit at special tables in the hall where everyone could see us. They passed around the tin grape pans full of sopas, four to a table, six persons to a pan, but I was too excited to eat. I chewed on some pickled fava beans someone put on the table, and drank a Coke. Grayson came and sat with Reiko and me and was helping himself to the food, piling up the chunks of boiled meat, avoiding the cabbage, and then ladling the broth on top. I had no appetite. It was hot in the hall. The band was playing, and you couldn't hear yourself think, they were so loud. I saw my mother and went over and hugged her and my sisters. An uncle bought me another Coke, and I went back and shared it with Reiko and Grayson.

There was a dance later, but we had to get back home to milk. My mother promised me we would go to at least three more festas and I could be in those processions too, following the queen through the other towns across the valley. I didn't mind taking off the gown and putting on my work clothes when she said that. I could wear it again this year, and next year I would be chosen again, for second or third princess, probably.

I ran to get the cows. They knew it was Sunday because I had put them in the pasture where the sweet grass grows. The only trouble was, the fence wasn't good by the river, and they could get out. No matter how fine the grass was where you put a cow, it would try and get out and go somewhere else, just like people. I had to call for Susie, and when she didn't come I walked out until I saw the herd and saw where the fence was broken again. I got the cows moving toward the barn and hurried them up so I could go look for Susie.

Everything went topsy-turvy when this happened. It would take time to find her; Susie liked to roam. It was only the smartest cows that got out. I got a halter and her cowbell, so I could ring for her to know I was coming, then went into the kitchen. "Susie got out. I'm going down to the ditch to find her; tell Dad for me." My mother's back was to me and she was trying to get the lard in the big skillet to melt even by sliding it back and forth and then banging it on the top of the stove. She turned around and put her hand on my cheek. "You're not going to find Susie anymore," she said.

I was still out of breath from running, but I could feel the warmth of the kitchen. "She can't have gone far."

"We butchered Susie for the Holy Ghost festival." She stroked my cheek and neck.

"No, Mama. She was still giving four gallons; it's in the book. No, Mama."

"Hortense, she was too old, she was barren. It was the best way, to celebrate Pentecost instead of selling her to some stranger to butcher."

My brother started yelling, "Hortense, come on, I have to milk. Come on." I went out and started washing off the cows. I couldn't help it; I started crying. I had raised Susie from a calf. I put her cowbell around my neck. It rang softly as I cleaned, then hugged each cow around the neck, to make them all feel better.

GRAYSON

chapter 3

Granddad took me into town on Saturday and we left Mother and Father and Reiko home. We went to the feed store, the post office, the bank, and then to the barbershop, and each of us got a haircut and I got a sucker. Then we went into the restaurant and I had American food, a hot beef sandwich and a glass of milk. I ate it all because Granddad said to.

Then we went into the Doghouse behind the alley and I had a ginger ale and listened to Mr. Hart and Granddad while they talked and laughed. "You going to be a farmer like your grandfather?" Mr. Hart asked me. I nodded. Granddad said Irishmen were great talkers but that's all they could do.

We took rides sometimes, after Granddad would make a bet with Mr. Hart or someone at the bar. We went up to Sanger once, where the end of a sixty-mile-long wooden flume came down from the mountains. They'd run water through it, Granddad said, and they'd float lumber down to be stacked and dried and sold at the big yard there in town. We drove up there, four or five cars, to see, once. The flume was like a big ditch, but up in the air, up on stilts like the legs of a railroad trestle, made out of wood, as deep as our water tank. Standing underneath it, you could feel drips of water from the leaks and you could hear the boards hitting the wooden sides as they rode on the water and followed the curves of the flume down out of the mountains. We drove further into the hills until we came to a house built right up against the wooden flume. We all got out and Granddad talked to a man who lived in the house. There were some men up there on the edge of the flume, and Granddad put me on his shoulder and we went up the ladder. They all knew Granddad, and he gave them a drink out of his bottle. I could look down and see the water run by, and I started counting the big planks, as big around as a field lug box, but long, as they passed. One of the men stopped a plank when Granddad said, "That one," and Mr. Hart tried to grab me off his shoulders. "Leave the boy, Ray," he said, but Granddad yelled, "Make sure those welshers don't run off," and he whooped and jumped on the plank and we were off. We went fast. Granddad had his arms out for balance. I could feel the spray on my face, and Granddad was singing in Japanese. "Faster," I yelled for him. "Faster!" It was like walking on the top rail of a fence, but the fence was moving. When we came to the end I was yelling, "Let's do it again," but Mr. Hart grabbed me. "The hell you say!" He gave Granddad a double eagle gold piece, and so did the other men.

We didn't always do something good. Sometimes we drove a long way just for a look at something Granddad wanted Mr. Hart to see. North, one time, to see some German farmers that came to the valley from Russia. We had lunch with a family Granddad knew. They put out a good spread, but it was like eating with a row of tree stumps; they were big people and didn't talk much. My grandfather liked these people because they worked hard but had no luck. The soil was so-so, and they didn't get the yields to make a go of the place. Granddad bought a lot of different seed from them and listened to them about growing citrus, which he was thinking about going into himself.

Another time Granddad took me south with him and Mr. Hart, past Earlimart and then west to Allensworth. I read the signs. We were going to talk to some farmers who were growing cotton and knew what they were doing. Experts, Granddad said. We stopped at a house where a man named Reverend George lived.

He and some other people took us around to the fields and showed us their crops. They talked about their problems with some water company that was taking their share. But there was plenty of fruit, they called it bolls, on the cotton plants. One of the kids showed me how to open the green bolls and eat the stuff inside. It tasted like spearmint.

These kids were the color of prune plums, except that the bottoms of their feet and the palms of their hands were pink. They showed me. At lunch I asked the reverend why that was, and Granddad started laughing, but the man explained, "Everyone in the world was black once, but the Good Lord decided that he'd turn all the people pink for a change. He made a pond filled with magic water, and if you washed yourself in there you'd become pink. And all the folks ran to do the Lord's bidding and jumped into the pond. By the time we got there, there wasn't very much water left, only enough to put our feet in and the palms of our hands." I was going to ask about their insides, because I could see their tongues were pink, but Granddad told me to eat my soup so I did.

After lunch I took a nap with the other kids in the family and we pretended to close our eyes and sleep while Granddad asked questions about cotton. We played patty-cake without talking or squeaking the springs of the bed, and one of the girls let me look in her mouth to see how far back it was pink. She had lost her milk teeth. And I let her pull my eyelid up to find the rest of my eyeball. She whispered in my ear, "How did you get eyes like that?" and I said back, "From Japan." I asked her where she came from and she said, "The middle of the sun." I asked, "Is that why you're so burnt up?" and her older brother giggled. "Mississippi," he said, and I knew that was a state, and he told me enough times until I could spell the word, and then I fell asleep.

The big girls read to us later, when we walked over to their library. All the people in the town were the same blackness, and the big girls weren't mean like Reiko and didn't hit me. When we were ready to go, the reverend gave me a small book with Jesus pictures and stories and Granddad said, "You want him to be a Bible-thumper like you, George?" The reverend thought that was funny too.

On the way home Granddad was telling Mr. Hart they'd settled on Africans for growing cotton in the South because they were more used to the heat, being closer to the equator. "Labor has always been a problem in this country, because it's too big, so people can move on. It's a trick to know how to keep labor poor, so they don't get ideas. They would have tried Irishmen down there too, but they're too dumb to know when to come indoors when it's raining."

When Mr. Hart got excited his face got red and he waved his hook in the air like he was looking for the pull string to a lightbulb. "They should have tried you Japanese," he said. "They might have taught you some manners with a whip." Granddad always laughed when he got Mr. Hart's goat. I knew Granddad was Japanese and a farmer and a Californian and American. But I decided that I would just be Californian. That's what Mr. Hart said he was.

Mr. Hart looked like one of the pigeons that lived around the hotel, with his big belly and his smooth silk vest and his hair slicked back. Before we ate dinner with Mr. Hart, he took us into his office and showed us his new rifle. It had a big hoop where the lever used to be. "It was the blacksmith's idea. I think he's got it right this time," Mr. Hart said. "I can fit my hook around the rim and be able to jack in and eject the shells easier." They let me hold the rifle and work the action. "You want to go hunting with us?" he asked me. I nodded again, but I knew my father would say no. He did every time, and Granddad would slam the front door. He asked every year, and I would shout "I want to go" and scream and cry, but my father always said no. My grandfather yelled once, "Mats, you want him to turn out like you?"

My grandfather had his deer horns nailed onto the side of his shed and they were turning white in the sun like bones. Over three hundred points, I counted one time. Mr. Hart showed me his trophy. It was the buck's whole head with fur down to his neck hanging on the wall. My grandfather held me up so I could touch the big brown glass eyes and scratch the nose. There was a moose head too, hanging over the doorway between the lobby and the dining room. It belonged to the club that had meetings at the hotel.

I sat on Granddad's lap going home so I could steer better. The Model A went off the road a couple of times, and I almost got a night bird on the road but he flew off. Granddad was talking to me in Japanese, but I could understand some from the hour each day my mother taught me and Reiko the language. We lived too far out to go to the regular Japanese class.

I made the turn into our place and Granddad woke up good when we hit the wheelbarrow and pushed it into the chicken shed and knocked the hens into the air. My father came out then and Granddad was yelling at him for putting the wheelbarrow in our way, and my mother took me inside. I had a good time, I told her, the best I ever had in my life. When my father came in he said I was never going to go with Granddad again. I didn't carry on because he'd said that before a lot of times, and I always went anyway when my grandfather came for me.

I went to school with my sister. The bus stopped for fat Hortense standing by the road handing spring grass to the dirty cows through the fence. My grandfather always wondered why the dairy people couldn't figure out they needed a drain where they kept the cows so the piss and rainwater didn't puddle. He said things like that when we drove around with Mr. Hart, who didn't know anything about farming.

The bus stopped at the Italians', but no one ever came out . "I'm not the truant officer," the driver said, and we went on. My grandfather stopped there once when the family was making wine. They had a press in the cellar and the big boy turned the handle on top of it, forcing the cover down against the grapes. The juice came out the bottom. The cellar was filled with wooden barrels and Granddad kept testing the barrels with a tin cup. He'd take a sip and hand it to Mr. Hart. There were fruit flies everywhere, like sand blowing in your face from a wind. I didn't like it. Granddad kept asking the Italians if he could stomp on the grapes with his feet. They all laughed a lot.

I had to do good in school because my parents told me to, and not bring shame on my family by breaking the rules. Do my best. So I did. Most of the time. School was easy if you did the homework. But I had trouble with clocks. Even with Reiko there to remind me, I'd forget. Pitching pennies with the other boys in the second grade, I would forget and miss the bus. I would tell myself after the last bell, stop, the big yellow bus will leave you behind, but I'd keep lagging the pennies against the backstop, like I wanted to miss the bus. When I did, I'd walk home by myself the long way through town, stopping to spend my pennies at the grocery for bubble gum and licorice sticks, walking slow when I came to the Californian to see if Granddad was there, or Mr. Hart. He saw me once, walking by slow, and came out, took me to the restaurant, and bought me a piece of lemon pie à la mode. Told me I was almost ready to go hunting with him and Granddad.

No one came out this time either, and I got to the end of town and started the long walk home. My father said if I missed the bus I had to walk; he wouldn't come in for me. So I walked, but I liked to walk; he didn't know that.

I stopped at the Italians'; they had a little pond by the pasture with ducks swimming around. I put my books down, picked up some good rocks, and took aim. The ducks knew enough to swim to the other side. They were good throwing rocks, and when the ducks got hit they honked and the feathers flew.

The big boy came out of the house, yelling at me, but I couldn't understand him at first. His face was as red as a strawberry, and his big hands were the size of sugar beets. He yelled in English finally, "My papa says you stop throwing stones at the water chickens or I kick your ass." I started running. He didn't chase me very far.

When I got home my mother was sad. And I was almost sad because she was sad. I explained I missed the bus while she gave me my dinner. My father came in and put his hat on the nail and watched me do my homework. He was sad too. I told him I was the only one in class who knew all their six tables. He was still sad. Later Reiko grabbed me by the arm and twisted it above my head, and pulled my hair until my eyes got wet. "Shame on you," she whispered. "Shame, shame, shame. You're a bad boy," and she twisted my arm more until I thought it was going to come out of the socket. "You better not miss that bus again," she said.

The bus stopped for the Italian boy again, but this time Reiko got off after the driver said something to her, and went right up those stairs. The mother came out then and Reiko talked to her. Then the father came across from the shop, and Reiko talked to him too. The driver started honking the horn. The Italian boy came down the walk tucking in his shirttails and got on the bus. I got down behind my seat, in case he remembered me, and watched. He sat there like he didn't know where the school bus was going to end up.

Whenever I saw Reiko that day, there was that big Italian boy, right behind her. He was there in line waiting for the bus too. When the driver stopped at his place, she had to tell him to get off. And she yelled out the window, "Be on time tomorrow, Julian."

"I've seen smarter fence posts," Hortense said, and I laughed too, and Reiko glared at both of us.

Julian was like Reiko's shadow: you saw her, you saw him. Even in the library. He'd sit there and read a book, his big nose almost touching the page, like he was counting the words with the tip of it. I'd watch to see if he'd turn the page, and he did every time Reiko did. It always surprised me when I spotted Julian; it was like seeing a farm animal inside the school. He already had hair sprouting up under the collar of his shirt and thick on his arms, in the seventh grade, and he shaved too; I knew because I could see where he cut himself in the same place every morning.

He started coming over to our place on Sunday after he finished his chores. He'd stand there by our back porch until Reiko came out. She would let him help with the chickens, cleaning off the eggs for market. And he was there when we came back from church the next Sunday too, sitting on our back porch like he didn't have anything else to do.

At first no one knew what to do with him or what to say. My mother didn't like to speak English in front of strangers, and my father was busy. After church he got ready for work on Monday. Our new acre of strawberries always needed something: besides the regular work getting the ground ready, planting the sets, weeding, irrigating, and picking, you had to have the crates made to put the berries in. The truck had to be able to run to take them to market. Something was always breaking, the pump to our well or the universal joint on the truck, or it was time to put up the scarecrows to keep the birds away.

But sometime before the end of March my father would take time out to start the chrysanthemums. It was his pleasure, he said. He had learned how when he was a boy in Japan. He told us once it was a mum on the Japanese flag, not the rising sun. Granddad said bullshit when I told him that. "That's for sissies," he said.

My father had an old table with tin flour bins that he used only for his flowers, starting the slips from last year's plants in pint clay pots, labeling them in Japanese for color and kind. When they got bigger they went in quart-size pots and then in gallon pots. If they were going to be cascade mums they went in five-gallon wooden tubs that fit onto the waist-high stands he'd made. Julian started helping my father. He started out just helping to mix together the dirt, humus, and sand that the mums grew in, and packing it in the pots.

After Reiko looked over Julian's regular homework we played school sometimes, and she was the teacher. I didn't like that much. If Reiko said you had to stand in the corner and wear a dunce cap, you had to do that right away. We played school in the old chicken coop. Sometimes Hortense would come over; then she was the teacher and Reiko was the principal. Julian didn't mind. He would do whatever he was told, as long as it was Reiko who told him. "Recite your twelve tables," Reiko would tell him. He knew them. "He just looks stupid, but he's not," Hortense whispered to me.

After a while my father said Julian knew more about growing mums than he did. A natural farmer. My grandfather would have said that. Always sticking his big finger in the dirt to see how much water was in the soil. I saw him take a taste of some soil once, just a pinch between his forefinger and thumb, like it was salt. He couldn't be around the mums without making some adjustment, turning a pot more toward the sun, checking both sides of the leaves for black spot or white fly eggs, pinching the buds off here and there so the blooms on the plant would be big as saucers. I'd pretend to help, but it was no fun. Reiko would stay just to order Julian around. She'd write with a grease pencil, translating the Japanese into English for him on the pots. Pink spider. White curve. They had at least a hundred pots on the table and more scattered all over the yard. They had built ten new stands out of four-by-fours to hold the five-gallon tubs for cascades. When the cascades bloomed, they looked like waterfalls of flowers, pink or white or yellow or red or lavender, all the way to the ground. Mums bloomed too late for the county fair, but there were flower shows in November put on by garden clubs. My father and Julian were always going to take them to the shows, but they never did. They stayed in our yard. Julian took some home for his mother and his aunt. Reiko took some to her teacher and made me take some to mine too. Then the frost would kill them, and they'd start all over again next spring.

My grandfather showed up one Sunday. He only stopped when he had a snoot full, on his way back to his place. I was too big, but he picked me up and put me on his shoulders. Walked around then, looking over the place. "You might as well have stayed in Japan, Mats, if you're just going to farm a few acres. You got the whole valley to grow crops in." Every time my father listened to my grandfather he went broke. Once in cotton, once in poultry, and once in walnuts, all before I was born, except for the walnuts. That's what my mother said. She never came out of the house after she bowed to Granddad from the doorway. She helloed over to him, offered food, and said good-bye.

Granddad watched Julian. He was forming a hoop of baling wire for the cascades to grow down, and Reiko was helping, fastening the wire crosspieces with the pliers. Grandfather liked Italians: he said they were the best workers in the valley; that's why he liked them for tenants. He always called Julian "Macaroni." He said something to my father in Japanese, but my father wouldn't answer. *Keto,* I knew what the word meant, hairy white, and that they were talking about Julian, and my sister too, but Reiko didn't hear. They were watching them, Reiko on her knees by Julian, holding the wire for him to bend, his big hairy arm on her shoulder. "Julian, go get some potash in the shed," my father said. "It's time, if we want any buds."

After that, Reiko had to help my mother in the house when Julian came over. We were too old to play school anymore, anyway. But Reiko still let Julian sit by her on the bus while she read his school papers, using her big gum eraser to make changes. I would go out and talk to him, but no one else did. My father stopped doing the mums. Pretty soon Julian stopped coming over on Sunday and grew his own mums at his place.

When I found out Julian got to go hunting, I decided I was going too, even though my father said no. I was going anyway. I started for Granddad's place but Reiko caught me on the road and slapped the spit out of me and chased me all the way home, hitting my legs with a switch.

Hortense was allowed to come into the house. She came over all the time. She and Reiko would lie on the double bed in Reiko's room and read *Silver Screen,* turning the pages slow, talking about the movie stars in the photos, giggling, snapping their gum. From the place where I liked to sit in the hallway, I could watch them and I could see my mother alone in the kitchen too. She could hear them from there too, and sometimes when they laughed, she would too.

PATRICK HART—1932

chapter 4

If a person wanted to listen in a little town like this, he could hear anything he liked about anything or anyone at all. There'd be a lot of rumors about himself, he knew, if he bothered to listen. But the main topic of conversation was farming, which included the weather, the Land Company, and Ray Hamada. The hotel was considered neutral ground, as if the money that was spent in the Doghouse didn't go straight up to the Land Company's main office in Sacramento.

Elton wasn't just disliked anymore, he was hated by a lot of people around the valley. He was known as a sharp operator, someone you had to be wary of in a business deal. He'd brag, "I just acquired an orchard of Elberta peaches for a song" or "I had to foreclose on this forty acres of oats today, broke my heart," and he'd laugh. Hard times made it easier for bad characters like Elton. This business depression brought out the worst in people. There were still a few valley families and corporations bigger than the Land Company, but Elton was keeping score: "We're gaining, Patrick. In another ten years we'll own more than anyone else in the valley. We'll run this part of the state someday. We'll show the Southern Pacific Railroad how it's done."

He tried to stay out of discussions about the Land Company with Elton or anyone else, for that matter. But the company was a farming topic opener, and you could no more get away from it than you could from the valley heat. Every business in town was affected by what happened out in the fields. A bad year—no rain, poor crop, prices falling—was not good for business. No one built barns or bought new farm equipment or even new shoes for their kids if it was a poor year. It was like everyone was standing on someone else's shoulders in a big pyramid, and if one started to weaken, the whole group had to start leaning and waving their arms to find a new balance.

The only one indifferent to it all was Ray; he watched everything like a spectator, like one of those big condors that circled over the valley, floating impervious, not caring if every crop in the valley was ruined. He never even seemed to care that he'd lost or made money. "I've done all that," he said once. As for rumors, or what people thought of him, he'd laugh. "What do they know?" he'd say.

And there were a lot of rumors; too many to believe; no one person could have possibly done everything Ray was credited with. He'd had disputes with the railroad; he'd been accused of derailing several grain cars and destroying two trestles—this was before the state government finally took some action against Southern Pacific—and Wells Fargo Bank was supposed to have had Pinkertons on him regarding a missing ore shipment in Mariposa County. That was not to mention his problems with the government or some of the big farming families that dominated on the west side of the valley, or the amount of money he was supposed to have lost. Ray gave good advice on the commodities market, but they both always lost as much as they gained.

If Ray wasn't hated like Elton, there were a lot of people who were afraid of him all the same. He did pretty much what he wanted: driving up on the sidewalk or shooting out the streetlights when he had a snoot full, or trying to take half a dozen whores into the Methodist church to have them baptized, or driving a herd of wild cows down Main Street during the Armistice Day parade. To most of the local businessmen, he was Ray, that son of a bitch, you know what he did now? To the big state newspaper families—McClatchy, Hearst, Chandler—he was one more example of the Yellow Peril to be denounced in their crusade for stiffer exclusionary laws barring Orientals from California. The newspapers could indulge themselves in race baiting, trying to get the politicians to do their bidding, but no one in town in his right mind would ever confront Ray over what color he happened to be. When he came into people's view they saw a man, a rich man, a wealthy farmer, someone who'd got here before them and knew how to survive, someone they'd do well to copy if they had any plans of staying in the valley.

There wasn't anywhere Ray'd stop that the people didn't invite him in for supper. And there wasn't a kid in the household who didn't get a buffalo nickel, and the woman a box of three linen handkerchiefs with flowers embroidered in one corner. He had boxes of cookies and cans of hard candy bought by the gross that he passed out over the holidays, with a bottle of his favorite rye for the men. The backseat of his Model A was always loaded with things to give away.

Ray could make money on those visits too, like the one down to Allensworth where the Negroes had their town and were bringing in bumper crops of cotton. He found out how they were doing it, made two or three visits until he'd learned enough. It was a losing proposition for those people, because some irrigation outfit was stealing their water.

Ray was too far ahead of his time was the trouble. He talked him into investing in one of the first cotton gins and they lost their shirts. He set Mats up in the egg and poultry business, twenty-five thousand chickens, which was one of the biggest ranches around. But then everyone and his brother got into the business with fifty or sixty thousand chickens and the price fell. Mats didn't like the risk and got out after taking a loss. Ray couldn't talk him into getting more leghorns and enlarging the operation. He came in blazing mad for a drink after his last try at it. "I should have let Mats become a priest. That's what the idiot wanted to be, a Buddhist priest. I wrote over and told him, you go to an agriculture college so you can be some help to me over here. A lot of good that did me. He won't take risks, the dummy. He thinks farming is doing the same thing over and over again. You find a crop and stay with it. Like working in a factory on the assembly line, putting together a Ford. You don't buy more land, you don't experiment with new crops, and you don't take chances. Strawberries. He's got five acres of berries and the other thirty-five he rents out until he can afford to plant something else. He's not farming, he's sleepwalking. Wasting his time. I should have let him become a priest."

He could sit up in his glass house on top of the Californian for hours, just looking across the city to the farms further out. Now that he'd had ten years to get used to the place, he didn't miss the sea. The valley was as flat as an ironing board. Water-less. Someone must be disking somewhere because there was dirt rising up like clouds in the west. Some of the new tractors were huge machines with treads like a tank. But it was electricity that made the big difference in farming, Ray always claimed. You could work at night, and the packing sheds and rail cars got refrigeration, so fruit and vegetables could be shipped now farther than ice could last.

He opened the bureau drawer where he kept his prosthesis. He couldn't always decide which one he was going to put on. The porcelain one weighed too much. He had one made of wood by some carver Elton knew, all the fingers moved and it was painted a flesh color close to a real hand's, but he hadn't got used to it yet. The whores liked the hook; they wouldn't tell him why. He had sent for an ivory prosthesis but didn't have real high hopes it would be any better. He had got used to having just the one hand. Everything just took more time.

He examined his left hand and then held out the other arm that ended at his wrist. Was it fate that he lost the hand, or bad luck? He would still be at sea instead of in the middle of the valley if he had two hands. Everyone thought he'd lost his hand in a naval battle. He let them think that. He had come home from the war a hero, but his mother had asked, "You won't lose your place without your hand, Patrick?" Always practical, the Irish—and Irish Protestants didn't have all that Catholic mumbo jumbo to protect them. Always a plus and a minus. It was a plus to be non-Catholic in Belfast because the English were in control, but when they got to Catholic Boston it was a minus. It was another minus to have a half-drunk bartender for a father whose only claim to fame was he'd had his nose broken eleven times in the line of duty, and another minus that his mother and father had nine other children. It was a plus to have a cousin who knew someone who could get him a berth as a cabin boy on a luxury liner when he was twelve years old.

It had been like seeing a spectacle or an extravaganza, watching the rich people on the liner. The middle of the sea was where they could display their jewelry and flashy clothes, drink and gamble, fornicate. Money gave them license to do whatever they wanted. They were no different really from the working people that went into his father's saloon; he told himself that, but he kept looking at them anyhow, hoping to find something, some secret answer. He went back and forth to Europe watching them, imitating them. He didn't sound like an Irishman after a while. Back and forth. He read the books they left behind and wore the clothes they'd forgotten to pack. There was one thing he couldn't master. They knew how to look back at him as if he wasn't there. He couldn't do that for the life of him.

When he got older and became a steward he had his shore clothes made by a tailor from the best cloth he could afford. His father called him a dandy when he came back from trips, because of his fine clothes. Next door to Dunagan's was an arcade, cheap food and games to test your skill. While ashore between trips he was supposed to be helping behind the bar at Dunagan's. Instead he was firing the old pellet guns at the shooting gallery or playing pool. His father, half soused, didn't notice. Were the Irish big drinkers because everyone expected it of them, or was it that the Irish were drunks by nature? He kept his drinking to a minimum, which was a plus.

When the United States entered the war in '17, he'd had no choice: all the luxury ships were either drydocked or turned over to the War Department for use as transports. He was made an ensign in the Coast Guard, the rank equivalent to purser, since pursers were considered officers in the Merchant Marine. He couldn't believe his Irish luck. He had become a assistant purser by chance: a passenger had exclaimed, after he'd helped her fill out a declaration form, "Look at the hand this boy has!" to one of the officers. "It's beautiful." He'd never given it any thought; he liked writing, the flourishes, the sound the nib made, moving across the paper. They'd let him work at the information desk then, and after a time they promoted him to assistant purser. Then the war came, so he'd never had a chance to mingle with the passengers as an officer was required to do, or to ask the wallflowers to dance.

It was easy duty, keeping the doughboys from falling over the side into the sea, hoping along with them that the Kaiser's submarines would pass them by. It was a lark to be eating at the captain's table during the war, pretending he was a Vanderbilt or a Rockefeller. On the last crossing, just before the war ended—it was in late October, he remembered—he went ashore in Le Havre. There was every kind of camp follower; you could take your pick. He chose an Englishwoman who worked as a telephone operator at a Dutch shipping firm. She wasn't even pretty, not that you'd notice, but she could speak with an upper-class accent. He spent his days supervising the unloading of the cargo and his nights with Veronica. At first her very outrageousness attracted him. Take off her coat in a dance hall and she'd be wearing a bathing costume. She'd unbutton his trousers in a taxicab and shake hands with his hard cock. She commandeered a car one night and talked several French soldiers out of their rifles: she was going to drive them to the front. He encouraged her. "Let's go," he said, loading one of the rifles. "Let's shoot a Hun."

He got tired of her. He thought she was forcing her act, that it was studied. She wasn't a madcap, she was a working girl putting on airs with her accent. She wasn't a whore and she wouldn't take the money he tried to give her to ease his conscience. He wasn't used to all the intimacy. He got tired of being with the same woman over and over, and he didn't know where to look anymore when she jumped up on a table in a restaurant and started raising her skirts to do the cancan.

He was supposed to meet her at a dance hall but instead went to Paris for a day with some other officers. The Armistice was signed, and they stayed there to celebrate. It went on for a week. Back in Le Havre, he was sitting in a bar with another woman, his arm across the table—as if it was on a chopping block, he thought later—hand fondling the woman's elbow, when there was a flash of motion and Veronica brought the cleaver down against his wrist.

He was in the hospital for two months before they sent him home. He learned to write with his left hand, eat, caress a woman. You really didn't need two hands. He didn't want to know what happened to Veronica, but she wrote, begged him to forgive her. She was sent back to London; the French let her go because it was a crime of passion and she was a foreigner.

The minus came when he went back after the war to his position on the ocean liner. He was constantly dealing with the passengers, which had always been a pleasure for him, never servile or obsequious, always straightening out their ticket problems, cabins, dining arrangements with a dignified, friendly, reassuring air. No one ever complained that he knew of, but he felt the passengers seemed to stiffen now, as if it were unpleasant to be around a cripple, someone deformed. He would drop things, take longer than was necessary to fill out papers. He could barely read his own writing now when he hurried. The chief purser stared sometimes at his government prosthesis. He bought a good ceramic one and kept it thrust in his pocket or behind his back. The more he hid his hand, the more they noticed.

He was between trips when an uncle who knew the clerk for the executive board of the Land Company mentioned the position in

California. Manager of a hotel: it didn't call for two hands. He didn't hesitate. After the *Titanic* went down in 1912, the rules had changed: they wanted everyone on board luxury liners now to be an ablebodied seaman in a pinch. To launch a boat or to row you needed two hands. They were going to get rid of him; he knew it. It was only a matter of time. He came west.

Once every two years Mr. Reid called a conference of Land Company managers, all expenses paid, in San Francisco. He took the train up to avoid driving with Elton. Mr. Reid remembered him and made a point of introducing him to the other managers. The hotel had made money for the company. He was given a bonus, a percent of the net profit, and a full five-year contract to sign.

San Francisco was a good-time city. He picked up a streetwalker and took her to dinner, not back to the Palace Hotel, just to some good oyster bar and steak house. She was more young and fresh than pretty, and a little nervous, but after a few drinks she relaxed and stopped acting as if everyone was watching her. He didn't take her to bed, just arranged to see her the next night. He didn't even know why. She was cheap and overdressed and spoke like an illiterate. He had given her enough money, as much as if he had taken her back to her room.

The next morning he started down to the Embarcadero on the chance that one of his old liners might be in port He thought he'd see if he knew anyone, say hello. Halfway there he pulled the cord and got off the streetcar. He was done with the sea. The funny thing was that while he was strolling around the city the hustle and bustle and noise and traffic reminded him of Boston so much that he kept looking at the saloon signs for Dunagan's. But he missed the valley. He wanted to see the mountains in the distance. One of those big oak trees in the middle of nothing but miles of yellow grass. The goddamn farmers coming into town on Saturday afternoon. Main Street full of people.

Roselyn was waiting for him in Union Square. She wasn't twenty yet, he guessed, but it would be hard to surprise her. She'd been in the trade for a while. He didn't ask her where she was from or anything about herself. He took her into a department store and bought her a dress, less flashy than the one she was wearing. He watched as she tried things on. It didn't seem to surprise her that he was buying her clothes. He took her to dinner at the hotel where he knew Elton and his wife were dining, nodding at them as they were seated across the room. He'd made sure she knew that he had only one hand; he'd worn his hook the first night. Later he walked her back to her room, and left her again without touching her. Made a date for the next night. It gave him such satisfaction not to do anything. It was almost as good as going to bed. He wasn't going to be able to tell Ray about this; he wouldn't understand. He wasn't sure he understood himself. Ray was always stopping by, or phoning: "Patrick, get over to Alma's; there's a new girl. Jesus, you won't believe it. Get over there." The next night Roselyn got a little uneasy and put her hand on his knee in the taxi. He ignored it. After he let her off, he went to a whorehouse the driver knew. He took Roselyn out every night he was in San Francisco. Never touched her. It gave him such pleasure. When he took her address and said, "I'll see you again the next time I come up," she tried not to look puzzled. "You're the best," he told her.

Usually when Ray drove they went to a different place each time, but lately he'd been going due west, out past Lemoore, where the yellow grass went for miles and miles. He'd drive the old rutted roads as if he were looking for something. Then he'd stop, set the brake, and climb up on the bumper of the Model A to take a look around, God only knew at what.

You couldn't see anything but the desert unless Ray had gone so far they could see the water of Tulare Lake, and that sometimes disappeared in the summer. There wasn't anything. Ray would start going over the property marks. "Over by that outcropping, that belongs to some oil company. From here to the coast range is Southern Pacific, who got it for nothing." Some corporation owned twenty thousand acres from the road back to a fence line you couldn't see. A family he could never keep straight owned thirty thousand acres over there. He knew Ray had thousands of acres himself and was considered a big-time farmer. It was like Ray was keeping track of who owned what out here, where there was no water and no hope of ever having any.

They'd come out here at least ten times, past Huron, Coalinga, Mendota, or Corcoran, to stand out there in the wind looking into the distance. "The promoters used to tell the suckers coming west from the plains that rain follows the plow," Ray had said the last time. "There's something to that. But they might as well have said the water comes from the plow. A farmer hears what he wants to hear and he can make-believe better than anyone. But there's no water even to pump from the aquifer. There's no water down below you could drill to, except the Yangtze River and that's a little too far.

"I remember when I first came here there were farmers whose families had emigrated from Europe generations back, came late and got poor land in New Hampshire or somewhere, and kept moving west, Ohio or Minnesota, Nebraska maybe, Kansas or Montana. Went bust maybe, but kept dreaming the farmer's dream of good cheap land that would grow three crops and water enough to take a bath twice a week if they wanted to. They kept coming west until they got here, the last place, right up against the Pacific Ocean. A natural desert, but they didn't let that stop them. They got a couple of good crops at first because there was twice as much rain as normal. Then nothing. Dry farming one crop, if they were lucky. Grazing and grain.

"But there wasn't anywhere else to go; their backs were against the ocean. Then the centrifugal water pump came in and they were able to irrigate. I can remember places where you'd plow and water would fill up a furrow before you could turn the horses around at the end of the row. But they kept pumping and the water table kept dropping and now they have to drill their wells deeper and deeper. They say the U.S. government is going to build a dam up on the San Joaquin in Madera County for storing water. But there's never going to be enough. Never."

"But Ray, that's on the east side, that dam: why do we keep coming out here to the westlands where nothing can grow? This is the west side of the valley."

"Because it's the last place. There has to be some way to get water over here. Someone will figure it out someday, and make a lot of money for a little while. But farming is like going shares with the devil. You may get your way for a time, but you can't win. You're going to end up plowing in hell no matter what happens."

JULIAN

chapter 5

The summer I turned fourteen, Mr. McInteer said I was big enough to go up in the mountains to hunt and to do the chores at the camp. I knew he was going to ask me because he had talked to my father before. He had been talking about me going for years, as long as he'd been buying our raisins for the Land Company's packing shed. One time he dropped off a hindquarter of venison after he came back. My mother made sausage out of most of the meat. I had never been in the mountains before. I could see them in the fall from our place, but I'd never got any closer. When I was pruning the vines I watched the white snow up there like in a Christmas card, but I could never imagine how it would be to touch it. I could hardly wait the two weeks until we left. I didn't have a rifle, but I knew Mr. McInteer would take care of that. I daydreamed about it every morning in geography while the teacher talked.

I had been back in school for three years now, and it was easy. I understood everything. Before, there were all those words I'd never heard of and those workbooks they wanted me to do. But now I was better in freshman Latin than Reiko because it was so much like Italian. And better than Hortense in algebra because the Portuguese had to take off their shoes to count past ten. Hortense didn't think that was funny and called me a name.

I rode in the rumble seat of the Pontiac with the gear. Mr. McInteer and two other men I never saw before rode in front. I could get out of the wind by ducking down, but it was worth it to lean back and look at the places we passed. It was all rock, like the dirt had washed off the steep sides and ended up as topsoil in the valley. That Pontiac could climb those roads like a billy goat, back and forth like the roads were steps going up the side of the mountains.

We passed some houses and then there was just brush on either side of the road, with a few trees. All of a sudden a deer stepped out of the brush. Mr. McInteer leaned out his window with a pistol and shot its face off, and then slammed on the brakes. It was the size of a five- or six-month-old calf, and I slit the throat to stop it from moving. "Camp meat," Mr. McInteer said. I gutted it and dressed it down and hefted it onto the front fender of the car, and we went on.

I didn't think we'd ever get to the top of the mountain, but when we did there was another, higher, and more after that. We saw more deer, some quail, and a big bird, but smaller than a turkey. Mr. McInteer yelled back, "Grouse," after he took a shot at it and missed. It was all new to me. I'd never seen a deer before either. I couldn't believe my eyes when we came to some snow left from last year, a big patch in the rocks and shade of a mountaintop. I would have liked to walk up there and see what it felt like, put some in my mouth and see what it tasted like.

We passed some cabins made out of logs and then corrals with horses and mules. People waved. We stopped at a place that had LODGE spelled with branches up over the door, and they went in and had a drink. Mr. McInteer brought me out a bottle of Dr Pepper. I got some water from a tap and washed the blood out of the deer to keep the flies away. It didn't do much good.

Another car came up the grade and I saw Reiko's grandfather get out, and Mr. Hart from the Californian. They went in and had a drink. I could hear them inside talking loud and laughing and the clink of glasses. I just sat in the shade of the straightest trees I'd ever seen and watched the jays fight and squawk with each other. It was pleasant to just be there and sit still and not have to do anything. These trees were nothing like the big oaks we had in the valley. The one by our house was taller, I'd say. My mother had her summer kitchen out under the big limb that shaded the house, and that limb was bigger around than these trees at the base.

Another two cars came up, and one after that. Three women that I'd never seen before got out of the sedan, all dressed up, and there was a lot of yelling when they went inside the lodge. My mother had made me a lunch, two big calzoni, and I washed them down with cold water. Some green pine needles came down while I was eating and got in the crust and I ate them too before I saw them. They had a nice taste.

It was almost dark when we got started again. Everyone was yelling and Mr. Hamada shot his rifle up in the air. We went in a big line of cars up another mountain. The moon was full, like a big lamp, and the men were firing at everything, the road signs, trees, the stars and shadows.

Other men were already at the camp when we got there. It was in a clearing: a big open fire, outbuildings, a couple of tents, and a long table with benches made out of rough lumber. Mr. McInteer showed me where to hang the deer. I was to help the cook, Mabel, and sleep in the kitchen. I recognized her. She had been in my sister Mary's class. She told me to put my blankets in the storage tent. I carried two big pots of the beans she'd cooked over to the table where the fire was. Everyone started eating the beans and drinking more of the whiskey. The cook had a bottle too, and I took a sip when she wasn't looking. It was bitter and didn't taste like the wine I drank with my dinner at home. We never acted silly, either, like they were doing. Even the brandy or anisette my father and mother drank sometimes after dinner didn't make them crazy. I watched the women drink it down too, so they could yell and hoot like the men did.

Then we washed all the tin plates and ate our dinner of beans, which weren't so bad for not being like home if you put lots of salt and pepper over the top. The men were still drinking and playing cards, and someone had brought out a harmonica. The women were inside the tent; I could see their shadows from the kerosene lamps.

The cook told me to go to bed then, and I rolled up in my blankets, smelling the food in the storage tent and hearing the yelling of the men. I woke up early and gathered dried limbs for the fire without being told. Lit the kindling in the woodstove before the cook got up. She had a split lip this morning. She started frying eggs and big cuts of ham. I kept dragging in more limbs for the stove and slicing bread for the cook. Men came over with their tin plates for the food and hot coffee. We had the lamps lit on the tables because it was still too dark to see. There were no women yet. I heard the dogs before I saw them, maybe fifty hounds and three or four men on horses, with another dozen packhorses. Men were getting their rifles and filling their canteens with coffee.

The cook was still frying. She had me put a slice of ham and two eggs between pieces of bread with a slice of white onion and wrap it all in waxed paper. The hunters came by for the sandwiches. Mr. McInteer didn't say anything to me. Reiko's grandfather and Mr. Hart took two each. I wondered how Mr. Hart was going to shoot with one hand and a hook. He had a rifle slung over his shoulder. The dogs were gone, and then the men. It got quiet, and we took a break and ate.

It was getting light now, and I could see the clearing for the first time, with trees all around it like the ones down by the lodge. The cook told me to call her Mabel and to follow her with an old wooden wheelbarrow with an iron spoked wheel. After we'd walked a ways, the trees started thinning out a little, and you could see hillside through the brush, and big black things that looked like burned boulders. I wasn't looking, I was pulling the barrow behind me, head down, and so I didn't notice until we got right up to it the biggest tree in the world, standing alone by itself on a point. The closer we got the smaller I became. You couldn't see anything else. It was bigger at the base than our house, and the bark was like fur. Mabel went around to the other side and there was a big cut about ten feet up, a wedge cut out of the tree, so big you could stand up in it. There were steps cut into the bark going up to the cut. I followed her up. An old rusty double-edged axe was stuck in the wood, and she picked it up and started hacking away at the face, cutting loose chunks of purple wood. "Don't worry, the tree won't fall," she said. "This wood is good for baking; it makes the best pies in the world. I'm going to need about five loads; it burns fast." She handed me the axe. "Just chunks, please. It won't come down; it's been here too long. They couldn't fall this tree or they'd lose it down the cliff. Get busy now; I have to go back."

I didn't look up. I whacked that tree and the pieces piled up. It was after I kicked the wood down to the wheelbarrow and loaded up that I saw the tree was cut through maybe a quarter of the way. The tree was so tall I couldn't see the top, just a few branches, and the crown was stuck in the clouds. I made the first load and then the second.

Coming back, I took a breather by one of the black bumps and noticed it had bark too. It was a stump, so big it didn't seem like it could ever have been a living tree.

I took another load, and coming back this time I climbed up onto one of the stumps and stretched out. It took seven lengths of me to go across. From up there I could see more stumps; they were all over the hillside, hundreds of them, almost covered by the brush and scrub trees. I couldn't imagine them all standing up, a forest of these monsters. Each time I came back with the barrow I looked for the tree like it wasn't going to be there, like I had only imagined it, a tree that big. I finished up the loads and made a broom out of dried brush to sweep out the cut. I wanted to leave everything as neat as I could, like a secret.

After I unloaded the wood we cleaned up the camp. She got me a broom and I walked along one bench and swept the table off. I was peeling potatoes when the women started getting up, coming over to the kitchen tent in their robes, pouring coffee, not saying anything to the cook, who was opening big cans of apricots. By noon the women were playing cards at the table and me and the cook were digging into the first pan of apricot cobbler and some peanut butter sandwiches with lettuce and butter spread over the bread first, the way Mabel liked them. One of the women came over and wanted lunch, and Mabel pointed to the eggs and ham left from the morning, covered with hard grease now. The woman said something under her breath as she went back to the table.

"Four-bit whore," Mabel said.

I had been hearing the noise but I couldn't put a name to it. Shots? I'd stop and listen, trying to work it out. Mabel went into the storage tent and came back with a pair of binoculars in a case. "Take these out to that tree at the point, and you can see the drive from there."

I went. Twenty feet from the clearing, I couldn't see it anymore and I was wondering if I was going to get lost, but I kept going. I came out at the big rocks and I started climbing. From on top of them, looking way off, I could make out the valley and maybe what was the town. Looking back for the clearing, I couldn't find it until I saw the tree at the point. It stuck up high over the tops of the other trees.

I put my eyes to the foggy glass of the binoculars a long time before I saw anything I was looking for. Finally, way down the canyon, I saw the men on horseback riding through the brush, the dogs like ants running every which way, appearing and disappearing. There were plenty of shots. Then more. I followed the smoke and saw the deer. They were everywhere, plunging through the brush, as big as rabbits in the glasses. Every time they thought they had got away, there was another hunter waiting, and the dogs right behind them. More shots, and the deer still running. I watched until I thought I better get back to help. I followed the tree back.

The cook was glad to see me. "I thought they might have shot you for game," she told me. She was pretty when she laughed. "Cut up that venison," she said. I went over to the yearling Mr. McInteer had shot coming up and skinned the deer and chopped it down the backbone with a hatchet where it hung. She didn't have to tell me; I did it like we did at home. Then I loosened the hams and she started cutting up the meat for buck stew.

I'd never in my life seen such a big pot for cooking. I could have got inside, almost, and been out of sight. She browned the meat first, while I finished boning the yearling and cut up the potatoes. The hunters started coming back then, carrying their rifles like fishing poles. Some of the packhorses were carrying four or five deer. The dogs came in with a few riders and more hunters. Someone put a case of whiskey on the table. The women became more lively, getting up to greet the men by name, helping them take off their packs, getting them drinks of spring water from the milk can on the table.

When we heard the shouting and shooting, even the cook went to see. Next to the clearing there was a steep hillside that went straight down to the river. When I looked over I could see Mr. Hamada holding on to the tail of a horse that was leading the way, and Mr. Hart behind him had ahold of his belt and they were coming up the side of that bank like it was nothing. The horse was carrying a big buck. Mr. Hart was yelling giddyup giddyup, and Mr. Hamada was shooting his old lever-action rifle in the air with his free hand.

Everyone was laughing, pounding the two men on the back when they got to the rim, passing around a quart of whiskey. Mr. Hart was dusty and had a big rip in the back of his jacket and he had lost his hat, but he was in high spirits. Mr. Hamada kept yelling, "Count 'em, just count the points on that buck." Mr. McInteer had the tablet and went over to the buck. "Twenty points," he shouted, and there was some more yelling and Mr. Hamada fired another shot up into the trees.

Three long poles had been set up between the forks of some trees in the clearing, and maybe fifty deer hung there, looking as if they were watching us, hanging there by their hind legs, gunnysacks wrapped around the cavities where their guts used to be to keep the flies out. The dogs that weren't lying around like they'd died were over under the deer, licking up the dripping blood from the pine needles.

More hunters came in with more dogs. Somebody started the bonfire and sparks went up like stars. When everyone came back and all the antlers had been checked, the men started going over to where Mr. Hamada was sitting and handing him greenbacks for the first-day deer with the most points. Mabel had been cooking the hearts and livers as the hunters brought them over. She'd breaded the livers and sliced the hearts and baked them with sausage. They were tasty. I started carrying them over to the table, hot in black pans, with loaves of bread, and everyone dug in, swilling the whiskey and talking loud about the hunt like they were still a long distance from each other. I was almost running to keep up.

Mr. McInteer came over to the kitchen for something and the cook said, "Get those fat-assed whores to help us." Two of them started ladling out the stew and taking it over to the tables in tin bowls. It smelled good. Some of the men had four or five helpings. I kept slicing the bread. The apricot cobbler was popular; they ate it all up.

Everyone was feeling good by the time the sun went down behind the highest mountain. They were playing cards, sitting as near to the fire as they could because it was getting cold. Mabel and I ate by the stove. The stew didn't taste as good as it smelled. She had saved some of the cobbler back. "You have to watch out for yourself," she said.

The men around the fire were talking about the hunt, arguing who had the best stand and where they were going tomorrow. Then about last year's hunt. We could hear the stories from where we were sitting, and see them in the flames of campfire. Then about the women. Then about the war. Some of them had been in the war against the Germans.

My father's cousin stayed with us when he first came over from Italy. He had fought the Austrians in that war, in the Alps on the frontier. He told us he joined up when the army came into his part of town one night when he was sixteen and rounded up all the men. They picked out the best men and gave them rifles and marched them toward the front. They were in the trenches two days later, not knowing what was going to happen next, when the Austrians opened fire with their cannon and killed nearly all the men from his town. Later he was sent on patrol and when the patrol got to the enemy lines they saw an Austrian sentry. He was singing a song about his mother in a beautiful voice, how he missed her. My father's cousin started crying, thinking of his own mother. His officer told him to shoot the sentry. He took aim and shot the man in the back. And from then on, every day of his life, he heard that sentry singing that song about his mother. Everyone around the table was crying when he told us that.

The cook was taking sips out of her tin cup, sitting on a wooden box, and I was rinsing off the spoons and forks with boiling hot water like she showed me. It was quiet now except for the voices from the fire; it was like there was not going to be a morning. I'd never seen the stars so close or so big.

One of the hunters started talking about years before, when he had been in the logging business up in these mountains, cutting down the big trees. Sequoias, they were called. He figured his company cut down around eight thousand of those giants in the Converse Basin. When they fell to the ground, it was like the strongest earthquake he'd ever felt. "It was like we were bringing down a piece of the night sky, the way the sun began to show as the crown started to topple. Took three or four men ten days to cut one down," he said. "We used broadaxes to make the undercut, and then we used a twenty-eight-foot crosscut saw to cut through. We had to drive steel wedges in the kerf behind the saw to keep the weight of the tree from closing the path. Had to hand dig a cradle in the dirt, sometimes fifteen feet deep, and fill it with brush for a cushion so the trunk wouldn't bust to hell like a bottle when it hit the ground. We lost half the trees we felled that way.

"Sometimes a tree just wouldn't fall: the hell with gravity; forget the base was cut through. No matter what we'd try, the tree stood fast. We'd leave the area then, work somewhere else where it was safe. We lost a lot of men up there. Then we'd get a windy night or an early storm before we quit for the winter and then that tree would decide to come down. It sounded like the end of the world. I hated those trees.

"The hard part started after we got them down. Some were just too big to handle, to cut up, and we left them there where they lay. The others, we had to limb them and peel them to get to the wood. That goddamn bark wouldn't want to come off; we'd have to use iron bars to pry it up while someone would hack away with an axe. It was like the tree didn't want to die and be useful. You had to pry that fur off them inch by inch, then cut up the tree in sections small enough that the oxen could drag them to the sawmill. A lot of the time we had to drill them with an eight-foot auger, fill the holes with black powder, and blow the log in half to be able to even think of moving the section. Jesus, it was a lot of work. But they could build a good-sized town with one of those trees. There'd be enough boards and some left over."

"So that's how you got rich, Harry?"

"We didn't make a thin dime. We went broke. Bankrupt. Every company that tried to make any money on those trees failed. They were cursed."

The cook nudged my toe. "My grandfather," she said, "the first time he saw a white man cutting down one of those valley oaks, he thought it couldn't be done. He couldn't believe his eyes. He'd never seen one cut down before. He watched all day while they sawed it down. My mother told me that. My grandfather wouldn't move from that spot. They were on their way up in the foothills to get away from the heat, gather acorns; the Yokuts still did that then. But they stayed there until the big oak fell."

After she said that, I watched Mabel when she wasn't looking. She didn't look Indian. We'd read about Indians in history, but I didn't know there were any left in the valley.

After five days Mr. Hart asked me if I wanted to hunt, and I said yes sir. He showed me how to shoot the rifle until I could hit the can every time. The next morning he took me a long way from camp out on a point and told me to get behind a fallen tree clear of the manzanita bushes that went for miles, where the deer would be driven out. "Never leave your rifle; always carry it, even when you pee. Keep your eyes peeled," he said.

The cook had made me two big ham sandwiches and a canteen of lemonade. I kept thinking about them, even though I'd just eaten breakfast, until I ended up eating everything she put in the pack by ten o'clock. I could hear shooting sometimes, and the dogs, but I didn't see any deer.

The cook had loaned me her binoculars too, and I spent a lot of time finding the tree every five minutes so I'd know the way back. You could tell, not only because it was higher than the other kinds, but because it was shaped so different that it didn't seem like it belonged here anymore, that long straight shank with no branches at all until the crown at the top, like it had outgrown the lower limbs. I started moving around, getting different views, until I saw a patch of snow on the side of the mountain like the one I'd seen coming up. I didn't know what got into me, because I left my rifle and started climbing those rocks. It didn't take me long. That snow was like ice, and I ate so much it froze the inside of my head. I tried to fill my canteen, then took off my jacket and filled that. I buried an arm under the snow to see if it would turn blue. I didn't want to leave that snow, it was so wonderful.

Finally I came down and was almost back to where I was supposed to be when three does came out of the brush, and then right behind them, a buck. I froze but they saw me. They kept walking like they were in no hurry. The buck had more points than I could count. I rushed to get my rifle, but it was too late, they were past. I never told anyone.

Some of the hunters had started going back down to the valley. Some new ones came up, but a lot left, and all of the whores. The cook didn't have to work so hard; we took it easy. She sipped whiskey all day now, but could still cook. Mr. McInteer had left. He said I could get a ride down with Mr. Hamada and Mr. Hart.

I got two buckets and hiked back up to where I found the snow and brought some back for Mabel to make ice cream. She poured canned milk and chocolate syrup over the snow, then mixed with a spoon. It was awfully good, and she gave me all I wanted.

I went out another time to help Mr. Hamada pack in some meat. We cut up the buck and carried it out on packboards. He handed me his rifle when a forked horn jumped out of the brush and then stopped about a hundred yards away and looked back at us. I hesitated and he shouted, "Shoot the son of a bitch, Macaroni," and I pulled the trigger and the buck dropped. I went running and cut its throat. Ray cut out the tongue, eyeballs, and asshole and said I had to eat them for my dinner because it was my first deer, but Mabel said bullshit and threw them to the dogs.

The men who worked the dogs left, and we took the storage tent down. Mabel said there'd be twenty feet of snow on top of it by January if we didn't. I couldn't imagine snow that deep, the tree with snow piled up past the undercut. I'd heard one of the men say it was impossible to kill those trees unless they were cut all the way through. He said some had big hollows in them, burnt out by forest fires, some big enough to drive a car through, and they were still growing. I didn't believe that story.

When there weren't more than a dozen men left, Mr. Hamada said we were going bear hunting now, the hunt that was the most dangerous of all. We all went out with him next morning, me trundling the wheelbarrow full of five-gallon jars, like the ones pigs' feet come in. "Don't you dare break them," Mr. Hart said. We walked about a mile from camp, near the point where the big tree was. The cook came too and we walked together. She picked manzanita berries off the brush and put a sprig of them in my mouth to chew. I noticed no one was carrying a rifle.

When we got to the point we stopped. I was looking at the tree, wondering if it would be possible to climb up higher than the cut: What a view you'd have. You could see the ocean, probably. I heard the crash of glass breaking, but it wasn't until I got a whiff of the smell that I knew what was happening. Ray was breaking the jars on the rocks about two hundred feet away. The smell was so bad we had to move back. It was worse than any outhouse I ever smelled in my life. "Old fish heads," Mabel said, holding her nose and running in front of me.

I didn't want to ask Mabel because she could get in a bad mood easy, but back at the camp she said, "That was bait. The bears will come now. That's their nature." I wasn't sure what she meant. "They have to," she said. "They smell that fish, no matter if they've never seen one before in their life, they'll be there tonight." I didn't know whether to believe her or not.

Everyone started drinking and playing cards. The cook played and was winning. I dragged more dead limbs for the fire and sharpened all her cutting knives for her. Just as the sun started going down good everyone got their rifles and some got shotguns and pistols too, and we started back toward the tree.

We went slow, no one in a hurry to get there, passing bottles back and forth. It was too dark now to notice anything. The sun had dropped behind a peak and there was nothing to see. Everyone stopped near the big tree. The outline of the undercut looked like a big mouth ready to snap closed on us, and I stepped back and onto the cook's foot. She gave me a push off. I didn't see anything. Then I did. It was the sound they were making that made me see the shapes rooting up the ground, grunting like hogs. There were all sizes, small to as big as a Ford coupe. They didn't even notice us as we kept getting closer and closer, or hear the shells being levered into chambers and the hammers clicked back.

At a word everyone opened up at once, and with the light from the muzzle flashes I could see the bears. They didn't run. I could hear the bullets whacking against their hides, but they kept trying to feed.

I wanted to yell run, run, go hide, move, as the flashes like squirts of blood pounded the bears. Mr. Hamada was laughing; the cook was yelling something. Then it stopped and it was dark again and I was holding on to the cook's sweater. The others started back to camp.

"That's all?" I asked the cook.

She said, "We'll look at them tomorrow." Ray heard and asked, "You want to get us some bear meat tonight?" and tried to hand me a butcher knife. "Leave him alone," the cook said.

Later that night when I rolled up in my blankets I couldn't sleep. I kept seeing the bears getting shot. But maybe they didn't die. Maybe they wouldn't be there, and it would be all right. The bucks ran; you could miss. I heard someone come up to the tent. "Mabel, let's take a walk. Mabel, you hear me?" He was drunk and could barely stand and kept bumping against the pots stacked on the floor.

"Go visit your whores."

"Come on, Mabel, don't be that way." The cook got up and they went off together. I could hear Ray saying, "You sweetheart, you. Do you think I would forget my Mabel?"

The next morning I got up first and got the fire going, then the water on the boil for the coffee. The cook wasn't saying much. She got the big stovetop grill hot for the pancakes. Flapjacks, she called them. They were the best American food I'd had so far. We had them stacked a foot high before anyone else got up. She fixed me some special with strips of bacon cooked right in the batter. I put a sunny-side-up egg and a big dab of jam between each of my five pancakes, then poured on the syrup until the cakes were soaked. I tried to cut up just the top flapjack each time, not to break the eggs on the other layers so I wouldn't lose the yolk all over the plate. Mabel watched me, trying not to laugh. I liked her too.

She told me to get the wheelbarrow and I followed everybody back to the point where the tree was. It wasn't so bad in the daytime, but it was bad enough, seeing those mounds of fur from a distance. They looked like the stumps of trees. Not as big, of course, but black and dead. One raccoon wouldn't stop eating until Mr. Hart kicked him off. I stopped counting bears after twenty-five. They were in all sizes. Close up, their skins were full of sores and bloated ticks. Some of the hunters were just cutting out the hams, leaving the rest, not bothering to even gut or skin them. The cook was knocking out the big front teeth of one with a hammer, and I started helping her pick them up. Everyone went to work.

One bear had been gutshot and somehow had dug himself into a big hole in the soft ground. You could just see his tail sticking up above ground. The cubs and yearlings looked like they were asleep, if you didn't noticed the wounds. They all smelled bad, whether from eating the bait or just naturally I couldn't say. There were puddles of blood all over the ground; big shiny black horseflies looked like they were swimming on the surface. One of the men wanted to skin one out and take the fur home for a rug. He picked a bear that wasn't so shot up, and Mr. Hamada pulled the loose part back while he cut the fur away from the marbled fat with his skinning knife. We put the rug in the wheelbarrow with the hams.

The skinned-out bear reminded me of something. It was like seeing a person. Like me. My body, thick and barrel-chested, with short legs and arms. I'd read where a gorilla is close to us humans. The bear looked like some of my relatives. The cook was cutting the paws off the bigger bears now, and I loaded them on the barrow too.

I took a load back to camp with the cook. She dropped off the paws on a big red anthill on the way. "That will clean them up," she said. When I returned with my second load she was drilling holes in the bear teeth with a small hand drill. "You have to do it when they're green," she said. For lunch I helped her cut up the meat into steaks. The meat didn't smell good cooking, and when she cut me a taste, I couldn't swallow it. She pounded our two steaks with the edge of a plate for a long time. We had potatoes, too, with gravy and breakfast pancakes.

I had to ask her why those bears hadn't run for it last night. They must have known we were coming. "It's their nature," she said again. I didn't understand. "That's what the bait's for. Those fish heads make them forget everything they know. It's like what whiskey does. They can't help themselves; they have to try and get as much as they can. Wait until you get yourself a wife; then you'll understand."

I couldn't eat that meat. I tried. I chewed and chewed, but it was no use. "What's wrong with you?" she said, after I spit it out. She took a sip of whiskey. "You don't like my goddamned cooking, get the hell out of here. I mean it; get out of my kitchen." I heard the men laughing from the table. "Ingrate," she said.

Mr. Hart tried to get me to eat the bear stew that night but I couldn't. The men still went out hunting every day, and I followed along and helped pack the deer, if any. Without the dogs it was slow work. I had taken my blankets out of the kitchen tent and was sleeping under the table. The cook wouldn't talk to me or let me help her anymore.

It was getting colder and it rained one night. Snow coming, I heard one of the men say. I wished I could be here to see that. Holding my nose, I went back to the point, careful not to look at what was happening to the bears. I guessed where twenty feet of snow would come to on the tree. About as high as the top of the cut. I had this notion I would like to live in the tree, make a house in the cut. Hortense's brothers slept up in their tank house. Someone said one of these trees had been hollowed out and used for a store. I dug up several burls with my knife. The cook had said when she was talking to me that they'd grow into trees in time. If I could grow vines and chrysanthemums, I could grow sequoias.

We started breaking camp. Most of the deer had been taken down to the cooler at the lodge as they were killed, and the hunters took them home from there. We loaded the flatbed with everything. I sat in the back with the gear. The cook sat in front between Mr. Hart and Mr. Hamada. When they stopped at the lodge, they got out but I stayed where I was until they came out late in the afternoon.

When we got to the valley it was like seeing it new after being away for years, not just a little over two weeks. We let the cook off first, in the side yard of a nice house near to town. You could smell the new paint, white with green trim at the windows. I helped her with her boxes and the big trunk she had. There was a light on in the house, but no one came out. "Here," she said, and she handed me the old sock where she kept her winnings from playing cards. I don't know why, but I hugged her like I did my mother sometimes and ran back to the truck.

Later, after I was let off in front of our place and I showed everyone the horns from the buck I shot, and they showed me all the venison sausage they'd made from the deer that Mr. McInteer had dropped off, I counted the money in the sock. I hadn't thought I'd get paid too for the couple of weeks' work. I'd got to see the mountains. Snow. And a tree bigger than all the valley orchards and vineyards put together. And those bears. I could still hear the thud of the bullets as the bears rooted for the bait. Mabel had said they couldn't help themselves. Later she'd said you couldn't expect those men to, either; it was just the way things were, now. I was going to have to think about that, work out what she meant, to be ready for next fall.

GRAYSON

chapter 6

Sometimes if I was lucky and woke up before anyone else I could be at the Brazil dairy early enough to help out in the milking parlor or give Hortense a hand. The cows liked me; they didn't mind me being around. The Brazils milked thirty head, a good-sized herd for around here, so they appreciated the help when they got any.

Then when the last cow was milked and the cans were all by the door to be picked up, and the whole world was awake and the sun was up, Mr. Brazil would say in English, "It's breakfast time." He talked to the cows in Portuguese and they understood. "Come on, Grayson," he'd say. We'd take off our rubber boots and wash up. Sometimes I'd almost get dizzy enough to keel over at the first delicious smell when he'd open the door to their kitchen. Mrs. Brazil would be at the stove frying linguica, filling a big plate on the warming rack as we sat down. Then she'd start breaking eggs into the grease from the sausage and you could hear the pop as she basted the eggs with the side of the spatula. She never had to turn the eggs over and there was never a broken yolk, never. The yolks would turn from yellow to white and little bits of burnt sausage would stick to them and she'd sprinkle pepper and salt on top from big glass shakers.

Hortense would put the warm plates full of food down in front of us, and no one would speak; we'd all just eat. Mrs. Brazil would stay at the stove frying, making toast. I'd eat so much I couldn't breathe right. Mr. Brazil would say, "Eat something, Grayson, or you won't grow." Sometimes I was so full I couldn't walk. I'd sit on the porch and pant. When I did get home, I'd be so tired from eating that I'd fall asleep.

We went to the Presbyterian church in town on Sunday and I liked it all right. There were a lot of Issei like my parents and second-generation Nisei like me and Reiko. In the afternoon we went over our lesson for Japanese school in the church cellar. Reiko and I were always ahead. My mother was a good teacher. Then we'd practice writing, which was hard, too hard. Then my father would teach judo to the boys, and the girls would learn sewing. My father was a good instructor, everyone said, and once a year we would put on demonstrations with other groups. He said I didn't have any patience and wasn't concentrating enough, but I could beat anyone my size. But judo was too slow.

My grandfather came to watch once at the Buddhist church in Fowler. I won the ten-year-old class without trying very hard. We had a big feed later, and Granddad told me there was something better than judo and he would show me. But I kept practicing. I wanted to make my father proud of me, and I tried to do everything he said.

Granddad picked me up after school one day and told Reiko to tell our mother he'd bring me back that night. We drove up north to Japan Town and had sushi in his favorite place, where he knew the owner, who had been an apprentice sushi maker for seven years in Tokyo. Then we went to a gymnasium and we watched boys wearing armor like football players wore under their jerseys fight each other with sticks. It was noisy. There were four or five battles going on at the same time. They'd hit each other with the sticks, which were the size of grape stakes, until one gave up. "This is kendo. You want to try?" Granddad asked.

The teacher showed me how to do kendo. He let me hold the bamboo rod and told me where I could hit. Downward cut on the top of the head was all right, sides of the body and also the wrists, and a thrust to the throat. I practiced in front of the mirror for an hour.

Granddad sat in a chair and watched. He explained that *ken* in kendo meant sword, and this is what the samurai did when they practiced.

I wanted to try. Granddad and the teacher helped me put on the armor and face mask. I had watched the other boys hitting each other in the mirror, and I could hardly wait. The teacher was saying, "I am the teacher and you are the student, master to disciple; you must do what I say and follow my instructions. Bow now to your opponent." My grandfather was winking at me, his bullshit wink.

The first time the other boy hit me so hard he almost broke my helmet and made me dizzy but I gave it back to him harder. It was fast: you just hit and hit again and never stopped the whole time. It was like driving a nail into the floor. I did it with another boy and then another. I could barely stand up when Granddad said enough. "You want to come back?" he asked me. I nodded. I liked kendo ten times better than judo.

On the way home he told me stories about his grandfather who was a samurai and was one mean bastard. He had told me before. He used to just ride around on his horse looking for troublemakers; it didn't matter who or how many. He'd have his sword nice and sharp, ready for trouble. Once he had a fight with three brothers. He killed two and the other ran away and climbed a tree. His family begged him, "Spare his life." The samurai chopped down the tree, then cut off the last son's head.

When my grandfather brought me home it was dinnertime, and my mother asked him if he'd like to join us. "Don't mind if I do," he said, and he told me to go out to the car and bring in the food. He always bought boxes of ready-made sushi and teriyaki and udon for himself when he went up to Fresno. We sat down to dinner and ate the food Granddad had brought. The food my mother had prepared stayed on the stove. Not even Reiko said anything this time.

Once she asked our mother, "Didn't you cook when you were my age?" My father never complained, but my mother couldn't even cook rice. It was either too dry, like soap flakes, or too soggy, like paste.

"We had servants that worked in the kitchen," she told Reiko. The few times Granddad had dinner with us, he didn't eat very much. He told her, "You better learn to cook American; you'll never cook Japanese." When Reiko got bigger she tried to cook American. She was almost worse. I'd go into the kitchen to watch sometimes. My father leveled the stove because everything they fried was raw on one end and burnt on the other because the grease would run down to the low side of the pan. With the stove leveled, they cooked everything too much or too little because it was different now. When I pointed out what was wrong with the fish once, and it was her fault, Reiko threw a potholder at me and yelled, "You better get out of here, Grayson."

"You get what you pay for," my grandfather would say to me and Reiko when the three of us were driving somewhere. He liked to tell the story about our mother and father, in the days when the picture brides came from Japan; that was when Japanese men in California exchanged photos with ladies in Japan so they could choose a wife.

"There weren't any Japanese women here?" Reiko would ask.

"Very few. And there was no chance your father would ever get one of those. And I just didn't pick anyone. I wrote a friend I knew in Osaka, who made inquiries, lined up four or five I liked. I wanted someone who could do a day's work, speak some English, and make a man out of Mats. Taller than ordinary, too."

"How about cooking—did you ask that?"

"No, I forgot that too. Somehow the bastard got me a pretty girl, healthy, yes, and she could play the samisen, sing, too, but she'd been raised as a lady. And she was five and a half feet tall. That's why you kids are going to be tall. You can thank me for that. I had a country woman in mind, not a lady. Japanese ladies are delicate and simper like your mother does." Reiko had to look that word up later. "I am never going to simper," she told me.

"I knew it was a gamble, but I didn't understand the odds. I was lucky that she stayed after seeing Mats. There was one picture bride up in Reedley that took one look at her groom and caught the next train back to San Francisco and was on the return ship to Japan."

I would look at my mother sometimes and I'd think of the photo. I wanted to ask something, but I didn't know what. Reiko asked, "Did your parents like you? Why did they let you go so far away from Japan? And why did you come to California?"

"I loved my parents," she answered. "And I wanted an adventure."

When Granddad came to dinner and he brought the food, we ate like there was no tomorrow. He didn't always bring Japanese food. Sometimes it'd be a big pot of tripe stew, roast beef in a big pan with potatoes, sacks of boiled shrimp and crabs. "I spent all day in the kitchen cooking," he'd say, and he'd laugh. I'd been with him when he stopped at his friend Mabel's house and picked up a a big pan of pork chops. Cream pies were his best favorite. He loved them.

When my mother and Reiko tried to make a pie, it was always

awful. Once they used salt instead of sugar because they'd put both in the same kind of coffee can from the five-pound sacks we bought. Usually it all stuck to the bottom of the pan so they had to scrape it out with a spoon. Once they made a pumpkin pie for Thanksgiving, and when they tried to slice us pieces, the filling ran out like soup all over the plates. I didn't think Granddad would ever stop laughing. Pop just grinned. Mother too. Reiko yelled, "No one's asking you to eat it," and that got him going more.

All the farmers wanted it to rain, but only when they needed the water, not when the blooms were on the strawberries or when we were picking, and not enough to flood the fields. "Why expect rain in a desert?" Granddad would say, but he'd curse the sky if the black clouds started forming in October and the barometer started falling and his crop of cotton wasn't in yet.

The farmers drying raisins in August hated early rain the most. I'd wake up at night during raisin season, listening for the thunder in the mountain. When I heard it close, and saw lightning behind the window shades, I started dressing, listening for the first raindrops. I was out the door running for the Palestinis' with Reiko passing me up before we reached the road. Hortense was already there, stacking the wooden trays of drying raisins in the shed as they were brought to her. We ran as fast as we could between the rows of vines, grabbing up the trays of raisins from the ground. I could only carry four at a time. The drying grapes bounced around, all wrinkled and brown, as I ran, and I didn't want to lose them. It felt like it was going to pour down any second. Even the Italians weren't yelling; they were running too fast. Julian's father was hauling stacks of trays on a cart. The trays were the size of a spread-out newspaper, light, because they were made out of redwood, and the ends had a lip so you could stack them and the raisins wouldn't get crushed. We all ran like crazy people up and down those rows of vines because if the raisins got wet in the rain they'd mildew and you'd lose the crop. Most of the time, just when we'd got all of the raisins safe inside the shed, the damned sun would come up, shining so warm I'd have to take off my shirt. We'd wait to make sure, the stacks of trays by the thousands in the shed, and it would turn hot then and the clouds would leave, the sky as blue as it was in July, and then we'd have to put all the raisins back, unstack the trays and carry them out to the rows of vines. It took a lot longer, putting the trays back. I never minded, never groaned. In fact, I was so happy it was hard to look sad, because I knew we'd get invited for Sunday dinner.

Mr. Palestini could only speak Italian, but he'd take me by the shoulder and say, "Vieni qui, mangia," putting his fingers to his mouth, and we knew it was time to eat. Food was always good at the Palestinis', but Sunday dinner was the best, because a lot of the family members would show up from other farms or from town, Julian's older sisters and their husbands and kids, uncles and aunts.

There was a long table with everyone around it talking loud in Italian and English. Big loaves of bread came first and everyone would break off pieces to chew while Julian's mother and sisters went around the table ladling soup in our bowls, pouring each ladle slow, making sure everyone got enough. Sometimes it was soup and sometimes it was pasta, but it all tasted wonderful. The kids sat down at one end of the table with the really old people who sometimes didn't have any teeth. The talking got louder and louder, and with anyone else you'd think the men were going to start punching each other silly, but I knew that wouldn't happen. I'd asked Julian if they were arguing once and he said no, they were just discussing which grapes were best for raisins, Malagas or Thompsons.

Two cousins sat across the table from each other, banging it with their fists to make a point. Julian's oldest sister, Mary, started singing at the stove. A kid in a high chair started howling. Everyone was talking. The Zia, Mrs. Palestini's sister, who I always tried to sit next to, poured me an inch of red wine and filled the rest of the glass with water. I tried to be her friend, even if we couldn't understand each other. I called her Zia too, even though she was Julian's aunt, not mine. I would sharpen her pruners when we cut and tied the vines and bring her the water jug first when we picked. She was old, but that woman could work. She always wore an old black dress and a bandana over her head, and she'd stay out there all day. When I got my soup I tried to do what Mr. Palestini did, tear up my bread into a heap in the middle of the soup until it sank, soaked through, and then spoon it all up hot into my mouth. Some of the men undid their belt buckles and the first button of their trousers, thinking ahead, and I did too.

They started bringing the platters of food then, chicken, eggplant in tomato sauce, roasted meat, artichokes. The food just kept coming, and the Zia just kept putting it on my plate; she never let anything get by us without getting some. I used to worry sometimes that I wouldn't get a helping in the general confusion. The talk was easier now, like the food was slowing them up some. I ate faster than the Zia because she only had a few front teeth. When I cleaned my plate she put more on. Julian's middle sister had twin babies, and she nursed them one at a time while she was eating.

Reiko didn't eat that much. Hortense ate as much as Julian, who was trying to be a gentleman and polite and keep his elbows off the table and chew with his mouth closed. One of Julian's sisters had married a Swede from Kingsburg, and he was like them already, yelling short bursts of Italian, red in the face as anyone. I didn't want dinner to end.

After a while, though, the sisters and Reiko and Hortense got up to help clear, and someone put coffee cups on the table and bottles of liquor and another kind of wine. Julian gave me a taste of the Sambuca. It was too sweet. There was cake, but most everyone was too full. There were apples and late peaches; Mr. Palestini peeled the skin in long, thin spirals. There was steady talking again. There was a wheel of cheese. A cousin started playing the mandolin. The Zia speared me a slice of cheese and dripped olive oil on it. I'd already had two pieces of cake.

Some of the kids went outside. I stayed right where I was, the Zia talking to me sometimes, although I couldn't understand most of it. I got up to fill her coffee cup from the pot on the stove. Got her a straw from the broom to pick her teeth with. The Zia kept talking to me, and Julian's older sister leaned over and said, "She's telling you in Italian, 'Around the table we never grow old.' That's a proverb; what they say in Le Marche." I hugged the old Zia and she was pleased. I had no intention of ever leaving that table and getting old.

I told Granddad about the Sunday meal at the Italians'. "Those Wops know how to live," he said. "Eating is important. So is singing. So is having babies and so is working. The only drawback is the talking; they talk all the time. They've got brains too. But those men would never make a samurai. They like life too much. They like flowers, they like clothes, they like the way they look in a mirror. I don't know what it is. On the other hand, I saw two fight with knives once. One gutted the other. Fought to the death. As soon as the one fell dead, the other son of a bitch instead of running for it burst into tears, started to wailing like he was the one stuck. Naturally the police hauled him away. I've never understood them."

I used to dream about rain when the raisins were drying. I could show up anytime to help tie or prune, and I'd still get the feed, but it wasn't the same. Not like when the thunder and lightning came, and I was racing the Zia down the rows for the grape trays, knowing that later I'd be eating with her, shoulder to shoulder, all of us together around the table at Sunday dinner.

PATRICK HART—1937

chapter 7

It took the Depression a couple of years to hit the valley full force, but once it arrived it felt like it was never going to leave. Business at the hotel dropped 35 percent and then by '37 another 25 percent. It was going down and didn't look like it would stop. Repeal in '32 was the only good thing to occur, but few could afford the dime for a shot of whiskey anymore. The big companies stopped sending their salesmen out. They weren't making anything to sell, and there was no one with money to buy. The profit on grain and cotton went down so low that people stopped planting; they couldn't afford to buy the seed. Elton was worried: the Eastern investors were nonexistent and the Land Company was suffering. Mr. Reid had sent out word again that there would be no meeting in San Francisco this year, and no bonus. Banks were going under, farms were abandoned, land lying fallow. Ray was hurt bad financially. After a couple of drinks one night, he'd handed Ray his own stash from the hotel safe, knowing Ray had got as close as he ever could to asking for help. They still went hunting up in the mountains, but only half the hunters came now, and they didn't stay as long.

And to make it worse, the state was getting the poor from everywhere else—Oklahoma, Arkansas, Texas. He'd heard there were more people from Oklahoma in California now than there were back in their home state. For the politicians and the people with a steady income, *out of work* was just a term, but for these people it was total destruction. They were everywhere. You couldn't walk down the street without bumping into men looking for work.

Ray said it was like the big migration of Polacks and Dagos at the turn of the century, but within our own country. These people weren't foreigners, they were Americans, and they were starving and there wasn't anything anyone could do.

The pigeons were the only things that seemed to prosper, more birds every day, shitting white down the front of the hotel. He never mentioned pigeons to Ray again after that first time. Ray was complaining that you couldn't make a buck in farming anymore; they'd just sat down in the lobby after their lunch. "You can always go back to Japan, Ray." They both laughed. Ray was always saying. "Patrick, you could go back to Ireland," when he complained about the valley.

"Farmers are supposed to complain; it's a way of feeling better about the risks involved in the business, and it might keep bad luck away." Ray leaned back and lit up one of his dollar cigars. "But now, no matter what you say, every day it gets worse. Before, if you complained that probably the rain would come and knock off the blossoms, then maybe it wouldn't freeze and kill the tree. Now you can't afford to irrigate and the trees are already dead."

Ray went on talking, and he listened, looking out the window. There weren't many people on Main Street for a Saturday afternoon. There was Julian, you could spot him a block away, big square wedge of muscle. Little Grayson walked in front like he owned the sidewalk, just like his grandfather. Ray had brought Reiko and her friend, the youngest Brazil girl, in for breakfast a couple of times that month. He was a gentleman then, telling them funny stories; he had manners when he wanted to use them. He had the two girls laughing as he ordered more food than they could possibly eat, introducing them to everyone as his two granddaughters. Reiko was holding Julian's hand and Hortense's too, he noticed, as they passed the hotel on the other side of the street on the way to the Fox for the matinee.

After Ray left he went back to his office. As soon as he sat down, the phone rang. The manager of the furniture store behind the hotel told him a window in his garage attic was open and making a racket and it was going to blow off in the wind if he didn't close it. He had to do everything himself. There was no handyman on Saturday; they couldn't afford one. Christ, he thought, if he didn't shut the goddamn window the pigeons would be in there too.

He got up and went out the back way, crossed the alley and unlocked the sliding door. He hadn't been inside over there for years. The cars were all covered with dust. Once the hotel had offered day trips up to Yosemite in these twelve-seat touring cars. Now there were few clients and they didn't have any money for sight-seeing. He found the light switch for over the stairs and flicked that on. What a mess this place was, filthy. Dirt and papers had blown in under the door and there were rat droppings all over. He had one foot on the first step when a boy came out from under the stairs and ran past him. He was so startled he didn't even shout. He stepped back and turned on all the lights, then opened the doors wider to let in the March sun. The windows were down on the first touring car, and the dust had been wiped off the broken seats. He opened the car door and saw the old blanket and the half-gallon jug of water. Someone had been sleeping there. He was backing out, thinking he should call the police, when another boy came running around the car doubled over, head down, and ran smack square into the open car door with the top of his head.

He just lay there on the floor in his filthy clothes like he had a broken neck. He didn't have any socks on and his ankles were coated with dirt. His shirt had been white once. Boots were worn out. He was moving toward the door to phone when the boy got up on all fours, moving his head back and forth to clear it. The boy saw him. "We didn't steal anything," he said. It came out "anythang," slow and twangy. "We slept here was all."

He was going to answer, You can tell that to the police, when he heard the first pigeon land on the tin roof and start hopping across toward the window. "Go upstairs and close that goddamn window," he said.

The boy jumped and went up the stairs two at a time. He came down light-footed, but it might have been because he was so thin. He was tall, lanky, like those people from the Southwest. "You wouldn't have any work for a person, sir?"

He was going to say, No, not this time, but instead he said, "You sweep up in here, get all those cobwebs, you'll find a broom back there, and I'll give you dinner. Who was that other boy that ran off?"

"He's my brother."

"Get to work. I'll be back in a couple of hours, see what you've done."

He forgot about the boy once he got back into the hotel. One of the cooks was arguing with a waitress. Even in hard times, cooks acted crazy. He got the waitress out of the kitchen, and when he went back, the cook was wrapping his knives in a towel. "Floyd, it was a mistake; she just wanted to know if you were going to have the roast beef ready by dinnertime so she could put it on the menu. She wasn't trying to rush you." Last month the night clerk and the cleaning maid quit after an argument. Both had worked there over ten years, but they both left in a huff, vowing they'd never work with the other an hour longer. There were no jobs, he kept telling them, but it didn't make any difference. He cajoled the cook into staying. It was the dining room and coffee shop and the Doghouse that kept the hotel going. There were few roomers nowadays.

He remembered the kid at three-thirty and went back outside, smoking a cigar. All the garage doors were open and the floor was spotless, swept and hosed off. Two of the big cars had been pushed out into the alley and washed. The boy was inside the third car wiping off the leather upholstery, wringing the rag in a bucket of water. "What's your name again?"

"Fred Leeds, sir."

"Well, Fred, you did a good job. How much do I owe you?"

"Whatever you think it's worth."

He heard cooing and looked up and two pigeons were moving along the rafters inside the garage. "You've let the pigeons in," he yelled.

The boy hopped. "I'll get them." He noticed the boy had cleaned himself up. He was barefooted and his ankles and feet were clean. He'd washed his face and neck and he was wearing his shirt wet; he must have tried to wash it.

"You damn well better," he called after the kid. He went back into the kitchen and asked the dishwasher to fix a plate of food for the boy in the garage. He got busy at the front desk and didn't get back out for another couple of hours. The boy was working on the last car, cleaning up the chrome. He could see movement in the gunnysack on the floor, and a pigeon inside started cooing.

"How did you get them?" he asked.

"I just went after them until I could grab them."

"I'll pay you a nickel for every pigeon you can catch. They're in the attic and in the top floor. They're in the rooms again."

"I'll take care of it," the boy said, "soon as I finish here. I thank you for the dinner," he added.

He heard loud voices and looked toward the side door of the Doghouse. Ray had Mabel with him again. She didn't have to take his guff. They'd been to a few other places before they got here; he could tell by Ray's voice. "You people sit on your fat asses," he was saying, "waiting for crumbs from the Occidentals, when you were here first. You lost the whole valley."

Mabel wasn't feeling sorry for herself like she did sometimes; she yelled back, "You don't own anything, goddamn it. It never belonged to us. It can't belong to anyone."

"Bullshit," Ray yelled back. "Tell that to the farmers who got deeds and made money off the land. It's our land now, theirs and mine. I've worked mine and almost broke my back on it for fifty years now."

"You don't own anything."

Ray wasn't listening to her anymore. "You can own the air if you want, but I own my land," he said.

The two gunnysacks were bulging, moving, cooing. "What are you going to do with them now?" he asked Fred.

"I'll take them out to the camp at the edge of town and sell them to the folks."

"I don't want them to come back."

"They won't, Mr. Hart, I promise."

Cooked for dinner, that's why, he thought, smiling. The boy looked so serious. Life must have always been serious for him; he'd never seen him laugh. Fred had been there four days now, and the place looked better for it. Leon gave him a haircut for polishing the brass on the door to the barbershop, and then the kid went around the whole building polishing the brass. It hadn't been done in years, not since he'd had to get rid of the bellhops. Fred was sleeping in the big utility room where the extra help used to stay when there were banquets. There was a cot, and he used the lavatory in the lobby. The top three floors of the hotel had been closed down, and the second-floor rooms were let out by the month to pensioners.

When Fred wasn't after the pigeons, he worked in the kitchen, taking the old stove apart and steel-brushing the caked grease away. The cook always had something for him to do. And that kid could work; you had to tell him to take five and get a sandwich. But the jobs were going to run out, just the way the pigeons were running out, the way he was catching them. Then he'd have to tell him to move on. He couldn't even keep him just for his feed. There hadn't been any profit in the hotel in the last five years.

Ray stopped one morning and asked if he wanted to take a ride. They drove out to the edge of town where the Okies were camped, spread over five acres, maybe. Old Chevys and Fords, white canvas tents, and kids running all over. Everyone looked like they were waiting for something. Stood up when Ray turned down the dusty road. "Don't feel sorry for them," Ray said. "A person can starve for a while, but that won't kill you. These people are white folks; the rest of you aren't going to let them die." He stopped in front of a tent and got out. About a hundred men appeared out of nowhere. "I need six men at five A.M. tomorrow for piecework. I'll take you four, and you two over there." He told them where his place was and then backed the Model A down the road. The camp was depressing: it was like an old people's home, folks who had given up hope, just waiting, but these men and women were young.

After that they headed toward Mabel's for lunch. Ray had paid back some of the money he owed him. Things had picked up a little; he'd heard Ray'd sold some land. It didn't matter if he had money or not: whenever he walked into the Doghouse he'd yell, "Drinks on me," and every barfly in the vicinity would come running. In fact, when they'd see Ray's car coming down the street they'd hang around just to see if Ray ended up at the hotel. He'd whisper to the bartender so Ray couldn't hear, "Make it just beer and bar whiskey for these people." The barflies would order the best scotch or gin if anyone else was paying.

The lunch was good; he didn't know what he expected. He'd never been to Mabel's house before. She had made corned beef and cabbage—he realized as she sliced the meat that it was March seventeenth; she must have known he was coming. There was an old woman sitting on the porch reading the paper, gray hair back in a bun, darker than Mabel. She wore two pairs of glasses, one resting in front of the other on her nose, as she read the paper. She wasn't introduced. The place was clean and tidy. Someone must have just painted the kitchen, because you could smell paint.

Mabel and Ray didn't have to be drinking to argue. They took up their argument where they'd left it the last time they were together at the Doghouse. "Don't tell me you came across from Asia on an iceberg or some such thing. You Indians don't have any Asian blood in you, you can't have, because you're all so stupid. You don't see the Chinks and the Japanese moping around for three hundred years working for the Caucasians. Slant eyes and little nose doesn't mean anything; cats have those things and they're not Oriental."

"This is the best corned beef and cabbage I've tasted since I left Boston," he said, interrupting the argument. "Where did you get the corned beef, Mabel?" He noticed she was wearing a fashionable dress. She was an attractive woman. She wasn't going to be fat, like some her age. She must have been way under twenty when they took her up hunting that first time. He had never touched her since that one time at the camp.

"Where do you think she got it, Patrick? At the butcher shop. Now what's this crap about a tree?"

Mabel jumped up and snapped the window shade all the way up. They were eating in the nook next to the kitchen. "See that tree out there? That goddamn sequoia was brought over here from Asia the same time that we came. They only grow in China and California. We must have stopped in Japan first and seen what a sinkhole it was, so we came over here. That's the only other place they ever found these trees, in China. That Italian boy Julian grew this for me. Look, you dumb Jap. That's evidence. Indians are from Asia, and they're as smart as any Jap any day of the week."

As they were leaving, Ray handed the old woman, still reading the paper, a twenty-dollar gold piece. She took the coin without comment. Then Ray started up again. "If the thickheaded Irishmen have Saint Patrick's Day and the Chinese have their New Year's and the Italians have Columbus Day and the Americans have the Fourth of July and we have Boys' Day, what do the goddamn Indians have?"

"We don't need any holiday, because we were smart enough to get here first. We belong here. The rest of you won't last as long as we have."

He saw Ray in front of the hardware store across the street and he went over. Middle of April, and it was already hot enough for shirtsleeves. He hadn't seen Ray in a couple of weeks, not since they had lunch with Mabel. Four or five men were with him, sitting on the bench in front of the store on a Saturday afternoon.

"You can have this man Roosevelt," Ray was saying. "It's worse now than it ever was. What's he ever done for the farmer?" Halfway across the street, he realized Ray was an old man. He had stood up and was fanning himself with his hat. His shoulders were rounded and his hair had turned white; he was stooped. He was always a dandy, the way he dressed, but now his clothes seemed too big for him. Ray saw him and pointed back to the hotel and called out, "Patrick, look up there."

Up outside the fourth floor on a twelve-inch-wide ledge was Fred, going heel to toe on the ledge, reaching up over a cornice to grab a pigeon sitting on a nest. He plucked her off and dropped her in the sack tied to his waist. Went to the next nest, and then the next, putting an arm out to balance himself when he wobbled a little. The next nest just had eggs in it, and Fred tipped it down to the alley. He realized he wasn't the only one that was holding his breath when he heard Ray say, "Those Okies will do anything for money."

He hurried back across the street, took the elevator up, and tried not to run down the hall to the open window, tried not to sound excited as he called out to Fred, "Why don't you come in now? You've got enough." The sack on his belt was hanging over the ledge and looked like it would pull the boy down. "That's pretty dangerous," he said after the boy was in the room.

"I don't look down. I got most of the pigeons on this side, Mr. Hart."

"That's enough; just leave the rest."

"I could clear off the nests."

"They're okay, Fred; the wind will take care of that."

The last job anyone could think of for Fred was in the coffee shop. The night waitress had him scrape the old chewing gum out from under the counter and the booths. He went at it like it was the most important thing he was ever going to do, like he was going to be paid for how fast he could go and how well he could do it.

One of the waitresses had given Fred a pair of her husband's black and white shoes. People always forgot and left clothes in the hotel, and he let Fred go through the old leather trunks. Fred dressed up the day he left, in an old gray pin-striped suit that fit him well enough, a blue silk tie, and the two-tone shoes. He was probably going to leave the valley and try L.A., he told them. The cook had packed him a lunch, and they had collected some money. "Thank you, Mr. Hart," he said, shaking hands. The night waitress got teary and sniffed. "He was a worker," Floyd the cook said.

HORTENSE

chapter 8

I didn't see him come into civics class, but he was sitting in the back when the bell rang. Okie boy. Bib overalls. This one at least had shoes on. Some didn't. I looked down the row at him because Reiko did. We sat in front. Julian too, of course, wherever Reiko went. The teacher went back and asked his name and issued him a civics book, but he wasn't to take it from the room. They all stole. They never lasted long, the Okies. Here today, gone tomorrow. Looking for work. A handout. They didn't have anything at all.

At lunchtime he was washing pots in the cafeteria. They allowed that, so they could work for their food. I saw Reiko looking. "Okie," I said. "It'll do him good to get his hands clean."

"They're not all from Oklahoma," Julian said. "They're from Nebraska and Colorado, everywhere." You could barely understand Julian when he talked with his mouth full. When he got excited he spoke Italian. His folks couldn't speak English.

At home my parents would never speak Portuguese, just so we'd learn English. They didn't speak very well, but they tried. My older sister, when she started school and brought her books home, my folks learned along with her. They had been citizens for twenty years now. My father never stopped studying about the government once he started. He read my books and ones he'd buy secondhand, and he read the day-old newspaper the milk truck driver left each day.

When we got on the bus after school I saw the Okie boy again. He was walking barefoot down the dirt road behind the school, his two-tone shoes knotted over his shoulder. He didn't see them yet, but some of the town boys were waiting for him. I could see four or five behind the school bus shed.

We were all sitting in the back of the bus, Reiko, Julian, Grayson, and me. The bus started pulling away. It was like watching a movie out the back window of the bus, except that you were moving away from the screen and the actors were getting smaller and smaller. He got knocked down right away. Then they tried to get his shoes away from him. He was fighting them off and then he was running the other way and they were chasing him. And he kept running, faster, it looked like.

The next morning he was back, black eye and split lip, sitting in the back of the room, the teacher trying to figure out where he was in the book. Loaning him a pencil and helping him to start. They started picking on him at lunchtime, telling him what they were going to do to him after school. I'd seen this happen so many times. It was always the boys who did this: girls wouldn't be bullies. Holsteins wouldn't.

They did this to Julian too, our first year in high school. Right before school started I saw him weigh himself on a hay scale and he was a hundred eighty pounds even. When we graduated from eighth grade he didn't have a white shirt for the ceremony, but my father had one and loaned it to him. The collar was for an eighteen-inch neck, and they still had to move the button over for Julian, he was so big then. They wanted Julian to go out for the football team, but he couldn't because he was the only one left at the place. His sisters were all gone now, and his father and mother were older than my grandparents. They just had the old Zia with them, and she was almost as old as they were. He didn't mind. We never went to the sports they played in high school because we took the bus and had to get right home to help.

When Julian's mums were in bloom everyone knew, because he'd bring everyone flowers: my mother, Reiko's mother. One morning he got on the bus with a big bouquet of those flowers he'd raised. He sat in front of us next to Grayson, behind the driver. The kids made fun of him getting on.

We knew who the flowers were for, the librarian at the high school, Mrs. James, who had helped Julian look up things. She had been an English teacher once and knew how to write essays, and she helped all of us. He liked to go in there because it was quiet, and he'd help her move books when she asked. I knew what was going to happen. I had noticed the high school was like a chicken run: any bird that was a little bit different, a little stupider or smarter than the rest, got pecked to death. Well, that's what was going to happen to Julian, I knew it.

He got off the bus and the town boys were jeering him. They took the flowers and stamped on them. He looked like a cow that had put her hind foot in the milk bucket, looking back as if to say, Now how did that happen? Reiko yelled at them and made Julian come with us. The next day he had the flowers again. Even Reiko gave up on the third day. "Let's get out of here," she said when we got off the bus. The whole school was there to see. Grayson had got off the bus in front of us, instead of staying on for his stop at the junior high. He had a grape stake over his shoulder like a rifle. When a senior boy tried to take the flowers again, Julian handed the mums to Grayson and picked the boy up over his head like a bale of hay and threw him up in a hedge. That boy just froze up there like he wasn't sure how to get down. Julian took the flowers in to Mrs. James.

He was left alone after that. And he kept growing, not taller but wider. And he had that mean Italian look on his face all the time, like the co-op bull when they brought him in to the cows—crazy, so you didn't really know what he was going to do next, and no one was willing to find out. Everyone knew if they did anything to any of us, Julian wouldn't like it. When Grayson got to high school he should have got his ass whipped ten times over, but no one thought of it. Not with Julian having to go through the doors at school sideways because he was so broad.

I couldn't believe my own eyes. Reiko started talking to the Okie. Went right up to him before class. She came back to her desk next to mine, whispering that his name was Fred. I couldn't believe what she did after school, either. Instead of getting on the bus we followed the Okie down the road a ways. The town boys never came after him that day. We missed the bus and had to walk home. Julian didn't say anything; he'd do whatever Reiko said. A couple of days later we went all the way to where he was camped, about two miles from the school. He had an Okie hotel up, a white canvas tent, under one of the big oaks for shade.

He asked if we wanted a cup of water, and we sat there on upside-down buckets, drinking creek water out of tin cups. There was something about that boy. His sandy hair was always combed, the part perfectly straight. He kept himself clean too, from the creek, probably. He looked slightly to one side when he was speaking to you, like he was still thinking about what he was going to say. He was polite all right. He had introduced himself, Fred Leeds, shook all our hands. "You wouldn't know of anyone that needs work done?" he asked.

"We're going to start picking strawberries Saturday," Reiko said.

"I'd be obliged for any kind of work," he said.

We all hired each other. Julian came over when we baled our alfalfa, and we helped them picking grapes. And everyone on the road was over at the Hamadas' for the strawberries. You couldn't fool around with them; they had to be picked when they were ready for market. You got paid for what you did, not how long you were there, same as for bucking hay or picking grapes. You weren't some wage slave; you could make as much money as you wanted. That was a joke when it came to strawberries. I'd like to be working inside some store at hourly wages when it came to them. Strawberry was a fruit that was made in hell. We never saw any money, really, because it was canceled out when they helped us.

You had to start early because when it got hot, it was hot, and you started cooking out in the sun. Strawberries are peculiar; you have to pick them ripe or they have no taste, and they only last a day or two off the vine before they go rotten. You had to go fast. You picked what you could sell.

The Hamadas treated a row of strawberry plants like they were as important as a Holstein giving five gallons a milking. Beds two feet apart, and one foot between plants. They used a tape measure to make sure it was exact. Mr. Hamada patrolled the rows at night with a flashlight, my father said, pulling weeds and picking runners off and stepping on the bugs. Mrs. Hamada sang to the plants. The first crop came at the end of April and picking lasted until the first hot weather.

They kept ledgers like we did on the cows: when they irrigated after a pick, and when the next crop was due. They grew Monarch of the West berries; Reiko said they were the tastiest and had the best color. You couldn't prove it by me; they all looked the same. Julian had read about another type of berry and Mats sent away mail order for twelve sets. They were supposed to get as big as tangerines, but the soil was wrong or something. He was always on the lookout for a new variety. At the end of the season they'd let a couple of special rows go so the runners could grow out, and by December they'd be sets ready for planting. Plants could last two or three years sometimes. There wasn't anything they didn't know about berries. One time I was chasing Grayson for dumping a handful of soft berries down my shirt back and then squashing them with a slap. We ran across the rows jumping back and forth, and you'd have thought we were jumping across rows of babies, the way Mats yelled at us. I'd never ever heard Mats yell at anyone before that.

The Japanese were good pickers because they had short spines and could stoop over all day. Julian, as strong as he was, couldn't last more than six or seven hours. I couldn't go that long. Reiko never stopped. Neither did her folks. Grayson was lazy; he'd start throwing the berries at us or eating them, ask if anybody else wanted some water, anything but pick. Julian could get him to work by telling him about the mountains and hunting. He'd point over to the Sierras and say, "See that peak? No, that one, that's where we hunt. I got a buck there last year." But when the sun got serious, there was no talk; the heat dried up the spit in your mouth.

Fred was there at sunup, standing by the shack where the wooden slats for the crates were stored. We got assigned our rows by Mr. Hamada and we started picking. You had to pay attention, get just the ripe strawberries, but after a while your hands were doing the work and your brain just told you your back hurt.

We started at six. At eleven, Mrs. Hamada rang the bell. I couldn't stand up straight. We went over to where the food was spread out on a table by the shed with the scale. I wished I'd remembered to bring a sandwich. Mrs. Hamada's cooking made me lose my appetite. But I took the ladleful of green stew over my rice and put out my plate for more.

The Okie boy didn't come in for lunch. He stayed out there picking. "He said he didn't eat lunch," Julian said. "He came to work." I noticed then how far along he was. He'd picked twice as many rows as I had. More than Reiko, even. The empty crates at the end of each row were all used up, full of red strawberries for Mr. Hamada to load on the flatbed to take into market this afternoon.

"He's a picking machine," Julian said. We watched while we ate. Bent over, he straddled the row with his long legs, a boot in each furrow, moving down toward us. His hands feeling among the runners for the berries, he searched both sides of the plant, fast, faster than I could on my knees on one side of the row, having to reach over. He was picking the plants clean, too, but his back was going to break. Mr. Hamada sent Grayson out with a jar of lemonade for him, and we all went back to work. I left at two to go do my chores at home, and Julian walked with me. His family was spraying for leaf hopper.

By the time I got there the next morning the Okie was already halfway down his first row. Grayson told me they had to run him off last night because it was too dark. It went that way the whole ten days of picking the first crop. He was there before school and tried to stay during the day too, but Mr. Hamada made him get on the bus. And he was there after school, and then on the next weekend. My back hurt bad just when I breathed. I wondered what Fred's felt like. Julian couldn't stand up straight. I was too big-boned; my body just didn't bend low like that naturally.

We finished up picking on Saturday afternoon, and Julian, showing off for Reiko, jumped into the canal to cool off. Grayson did everything Julian did. Then Fred. Then Reiko. We were wearing old cotton dresses so the breeze would go up our legs, and Reiko had on a sunbonnet so she wouldn't get dark in the sun. Reiko yanked off that sunbonnet and pulled her dress right over her head and jumped in the canal in her slip. I couldn't believe my eyes. My mother would slap me silly if I did that. I splashed my feet in, but that was all. I just hoped Reiko's mother didn't see.

She swam over and dunked Fred, held him under until he came up gasping. When he tried to get out of the water she got a bear hug on him and dragged him back down the bank. That Okie boy wasn't resisting, either. I'd never seen Reiko acting this way in my life, screeching, wrestling with that boy. Neither had Julian, who was looking with his big mouth open. The supper bell rang and we ran to eat.

Mr. Hamada had him back to work around the place. So did we at the dairy. Julian's father hired him for picking. You only had to show Fred once and then stand back, whatever it was: nailing crates together or tying vines or baling hay or packing oranges. Sometimes that summer I would see him loading boxcars at the cannery or going by in a truckload of field workers. Picking fruit, chopping cotton, anything that earned money. Word got around with the farmers, and the labor contractors or farmers themselves would go out and pick him up now. He didn't go to town on Saturday to rest up one afternoon out of the week like most did. He just kept working.

But one Saturday Reiko and Grayson and I ran into Fred coming out of the hardware store with a keg of nails on his shoulders. He put it in an old Plymouth. Then his brother came out and he introduced us. Charlie was nothing like Fred. He had buck teeth and a big nose and spit when he talked. He was a backslapper if there ever was one, five or six years older than we were. He was working out past Coalinga in the Lost Hills as a roughneck for Standard Oil two days a week. Fred just stood there doing the looking while his brother did the talking. Charlie had one of those high-pitched Okie voices like he was speaking out of his snout instead of his mouth. "I'm going to be running one of those oil fields one of these days. You're looking at a future president of Standard Oil." Fred must have heard this before because he didn't laugh with the rest of us.

"And the Leeds brothers are starting right here in this county to build our future. We bought our first piece of land last week. We're going to be building a pretty big house out there before long. Maybe three bedrooms, indoor toilet, the works." He went on like that. "Haven't decided what to plant out there yet." I knew that Fred had bought a fifty by a hundred-foot lot out at the far end of our road, that he had paid the back taxes to get that lot that nobody else wanted. The soil around there was so poor you couldn't grow rocks, my father said. And to get the money for the back taxes he'd cut down the big oak that was there on the lot: they'd had to pull it down with a chain hooked to their car, after they'd cut it through, when it wouldn't fall on its own. Then they sold the wood, and then they used that money to buy the lot. Everybody knew that. Charlie was a blowhard. But we were standing there listening anyway when Reiko's grandfather came out of the hotel and saw us and waved us over.

We went running, the three of us, Grayson leading. I could already taste the Coke he'd buy us. "You want to go on a picnic out on the lake?" he said. We were already in the back of the pickup before he could change his mind.

Instead of heading out of town we drove back behind Main Street to a street with big shade trees and stopped in front of a house. I had seen the woman in the front seat with Reiko's grandfather before. I knew that her name was Mabel and that her mother was a seamstress and made the velvet capes for the Portuguese parades. But I didn't know Julian knew the woman. He was in her backyard with a shovel, digging a hole. Reiko's grandfather and Mabel went inside the house. We could hear them talking. "Well, I'm not going if you don't take that boy." She came out with a big hamper of food and we helped carry the jugs of lemonade. Julian got in the back with us.

All of us had been out by Corcoran at one time or another to fish in Tulare Lake. It was supposed to be the biggest lake west of the Mississippi, thirty or forty miles wide but shallow. There were farms all around it, but you could get to the water by following the roads on the levee. I'd heard a story that there used to be ferryboats that came down by river from San Francisco and brought tourists to fish. When it rained heavy, a lot of the farms on land that had been reclaimed from the lake went under water again.

I'd never been on a picnic before, but I'd seen how it was done in the movies. Mabel had it all: the blanket, the picnic basket, and the plates of food. We sat there and ate the fried chicken and potato salad till we were stuffed. She had even baked a flat cake with chocolate frosting. "What can that woman have for us next?" Ray kept saying. We were so full we just lay out on the ground, drowsy and happy. Mabel was talking to Julian in a quiet voice, and I listened. "We used to come out here when I was a little girl, spend the first part of the summer before it got too hot." she was saying. "We used those tules to make boats to go out in the water. My uncle showed me how. The lake used to be ten times bigger than this, miles of marsh. We could live here like royalty, between the fish and fowl. Then we'd go up in the mountains to get cool in August and September."

Grayson was awake and listening too. "How did you make a boat with tules?"

She handed him a kitchen knife. "Go cut some, down low to the roots, and don't get wet." Grayson started bringing back armfuls. And as she talked, she started making them into tight bundles six feet long and as big around as a milking bucket, tying them at each end with another tule. Grayson kept on bringing them, and we started setting the bundles out in the shape of a boat. It took her twenty minutes.

Then she put them together, using more reeds, but the greener ones. Grayson was on the boat out in the water poling himself around when his grandfather woke up. We all took turns.

"I didn't know Mexicans knew how to do this," Reiko said.

"Mabel's a Yokut Indian," Julian corrected her.

We were doing better at the dairy now; we'd signed a contract with the creamery to take our milk. Then my dad's cousin wrote from up north that there was some milking equipment for sale at a very good price because a dairy up there had gone bankrupt. My father asked if Julian could follow us with the old two-and-a-half-ton truck that the Palestinis used for hauling in the vineyard. My brothers would stay and do the milking and my father and mother would drive our truck. I got Reiko to come too, like a vacation, I explained to Mrs. Hamada, although I never knew anyone who had gone on one before. I never mentioned Julian was driving.

We went straight up the valley. I'd never been north of Fresno. My mother had packed us all a big lunch and supper. My parents drove ahead of us in the pickup, and Julian and Reiko and I followed them in the flatbed. We'd agreed that we'd all stop for lunch just north of Sacramento and for supper at Redding. We were going to camp out, sleep under the trucks if it rained. It was all farmland, just like our part of the valley was. The roads weren't bad; you could see where the WPA had made new culverts and filled the potholes. Driving through Sacramento, we could see the dome of the capitol building. We'd been driving for six hours on Highway 99, and except for the state capital, the valley still looked the same. An hour or so north of Sacramento, they had more water than we expected. Rice, we figured out when we saw the crop in the water. But we had the same miles of orchard, packing sheds, houses with tank houses behind them, barns, outbuildings. The rivers were bigger, wider; that was a change. We stopped seeing so many Okies on the road; maybe it got too cold for them up here. No one mentioned Fred, but it had been hard work to talk Reiko into coming. You could nap and wake up and you were still in the same place. Those towns were like home, Yuba City, Marysville, Chico.

We spent the night at Redding, and in the morning we cut across the top of the state to Eureka, California, where our almost-new milking machines were waiting. This part of the road went through forests and mountains and along clear-water rivers. Julian was a good mountain driver, my father said when we stopped for lunch. He was driving behind us now. Julian could go down the side of a mountain without his brake light flashing once. He ought to be good, I thought: when that group went hunting up in the Sierras, he had to do all the driving because everyone else was too drunk. I'd heard stories about what happened up there.

We picked up the machinery at a warehouse, and that took almost half a day. We had to take most of it apart to put it up on the bed of the truck. I didn't mind. These gadgets would be doing a lot of the work at the dairy now. We didn't spend any time in the city because it was too damp. Moss was growing everywhere, there was so much rain. It was raining that day, in fact. In August.

Julian tried to talk my father into going back along the coast instead of going back the way we'd come. We'd be traveling a big wedge, like a piece of pie, down to San Francisco. He showed him on the map how it was shorter, and how we could cross the Golden Gate Bridge that was just built. My father wasn't one to change his mind easily; we always went back the way we came. But my mother wanted to see the bridge, so my father finally agreed.

On that road along the coast, Julian turned into a sightseer. He stopped all the time to look at things—the ocean from a cliff, the ocean from the sand. Trees. He'd stop at stumps, even. Julian, what are you doing now, I'd yell. He told us straight-faced, "I read in this book that this highway up here is called the Redwood Highway, and I thought it might be made of that wood instead of cement." We laughed at him and he laughed at himself. We stopped at a store that had a big round cut out of a redwood tree, like a slice of salami, out in front, taller than the building. There were tags on the rings that showed how big the tree was when Jesus and Columbus and all those people were here. Then Julian started to count the rings on the thing. "Right here is when you were born, Hortense." My father's waiting for us in Ukiah, Julian, I told him. He bought a book on trees at the store, and instead of eating his lunch when we got to Ukiah, he read it. There were a lot of logging trucks on the road, and we'd hold our breath when we met one on a curve. And Julian, who was supposed to be paying attention to what he was doing, would be telling us that the sequoias in our mountains were older than these redwoods here along the road or the ones the trucks were carrying away. "It's the oldest tree in the whole country, or anywhere else on the earth."

"That oak out by your place is bigger," I said, just to kid him.

"Hortense, that oak is a midget compared to one of those giant sequoias. They say in this book that these redwoods are supposed to be taller than sequoias."

"How could anyone tell?" I asked.

We crossed the Golden Gate Bridge at night and we didn't see anything but the lights from Alcatraz and Treasure Island and the city of San Francisco. It was a relief to wake up with the dawn and see the farmland again around San Jose and then Gilroy. By Los Banos I started feeling like we were in familiar territory again. Our part of the valley.

After Labor Day we went back to school for our senior year. Reiko and I had our birthdays in October with seventeen candles. I still didn't catch on, until one time in her room she showed me a picture of Fred, just a snapshot that he didn't know was being taken. His face was turned away. The bib on his overalls was hanging down and he had his hands on his hips and you could see as plain as day he was thinking what he was going to do next. The field was the Hamadas' two acres of melons they'd tried last spring. That boy could make a shovel sing a tune, my father said. "He's so handsome," Reiko said. She kissed the picture, unbuttoned her blouse, pushed up her bra, and pressed the photo against her nipple. "Don't you understand, Hortense? I love him."

Reiko stayed over one night to help with the cooking next day for the baling crew. I had to get up in the night and I turned on the light. She had a spring clothespin on the bridge of her nose. She spent a lot of time looking in the mirror, pressing her eyelids up with her fingers to make her eyes look round.

I tried to understand more by watching what was happening. Was I going to act like that? Had my sisters? They'd crawled out the window to meet their boyfriends one night. Reiko was Japanese like I was Portuguese, but she wasn't dark, like some, or sunburned pink, like I was. More like porcelain in the sink. Thick straight black hair. Pretty. Taller than I was.

And where Fred was, Reiko was right there. Then Julian. I thought Julian might kill him, because she was his favorite, but he never said a word. And Fred never made fun of him like some of the others did, not to his face, but behind his back.

They had an Agriculture Day at the school and there were talks on the importance of farming. The government put it on. I guess they were afraid everyone was going to leave farming because of the Depression. There was a greased-pig contest in the afternoon. The person who caught the pig got to keep it or twenty-five dollars. It was a sow that must have weighed over a hundred pounds. I heard some of the boys make stratagems: they were going to wear gloves, wrap their hands with burlap strips. You couldn't use a rope; you had to catch it with your hands. They smeared a quart can of axle grease all over the pig before they let it go. And when it took off, it ran, a whole mob chasing after it, trying to grab it, but there were no handles on that pig and it kept going. Fred tried to tackle it, and he might have slowed it down some. He got covered up with grease. It was Julian who got down low like another animal, and when it came by he knocked it off its feet with his shoulder, then wrestled it till he could grab hold of its four legs. He slung that pig over his neck like you'd sling a sweater and then stood up, and all the pig could do was squeal. Reiko said he should give some of the money to Fred. Julian laughed. "Let him catch his own," he said.

I watched Reiko and I kept an eye on Fred too. He wasn't handsome like the movie stars, but there was something about the way he looked. You wouldn't expect to find his face in a movie magazine, but maybe in a church: a person who'd suffered, like John the Baptist, who in the end had his head cut off. You had to watch people's reactions to Fred to understand. Mrs. Linstrom would act silly when he came in the room for math, touching him on the arm while she talked to him. The principal's secretary would turn red when he walked into the office with one of his phony excuses that Reiko wrote for him. My own mother would keep asking him how he was, flustered, offering him food like he was a starving orphan. Mr. Hamada gave him an old wristwatch one day, when he didn't know the time. And Reiko. Even Charlie acted like Fred was different. Fred was the only one that didn't expect anything; he always seemed surprised that you remembered his name. I noticed the other girls in our classes were looking at Fred. He'd filled out over the summer, like he was eating more regular. They loaned him pencils and erasers, passed him notes and sticks of gum. He didn't seem to notice, but Reiko did. Julian understood, he wasn't stupid. But Fred didn't. The lummox.

One of the senior girls gave Fred a ride home in her father's car. He went. "See you later," he told us. It was all the same to him. He was no prize in my estimation. I could hear Reiko sniff and see tears on her eyelids. It got me mad, and I told her when we got off the bus,

"It's just puppy love, Reiko. You've got a crush on him is all; people don't die over that." I didn't say it, but Japanese married Japanese, as far as I knew.

Fred got Reiko a Woolworth's bottle of perfume for Christmas. You'd have thought it was the elixir of life, the way she talked. But it wasn't Reiko who invited Fred over for Christmas dinner; it was her father, Mr. Hamada. He could go on about Fred for twenty minutes, what a good worker he was. He didn't have to hire anyone else when Fred was around. I never went over there right after a holiday. Once Mrs. Hamada cooked the turkey with all the guts inside, and I was always afraid she might offer me some.

A week after we went back to school from Christmas vacation, I got a telephone call from Mr. Hamada. He wanted to know if Reiko was at my house. I thought fast, and I said she was over at another friend's house doing homework but the girl didn't have a phone. I said I'd go over. It was after nine o'clock. I got out my sister's old Schwinn and started pedaling. It was drizzling a little. I took the fast way along the canal banks.

Fred and Charlie had built part of a shack. There was a roof and floor but no siding or wall boards, just canvas nailed onto the studs. But there was a front door and steps, and that's where Fred was sitting, getting wet. I stepped past Fred and went inside. In the light from the kerosene lantern on the floor, I could see Reiko lying on his cot, naked. There was enough light to see her face was flour white with pancake makeup and I could smell the Christmas perfume. I got her clothes and made her dress herself while I told her what I'd been thinking in a whisper: "You're acting like a heifer in season, Reiko. You better contain yourself." And I went and told Fred too. "Shame on you, Fred."

"I never touched her, Hortense. I swear I didn't; she came out here on her own. I wouldn't do that to Mr. Hamada." I believed him, that was the trouble.

I got Reiko on the handlebars and started pedaling back. She hadn't said a word the whole time. The rain started in earnest then, and I had to pedal hard. My forehead rested between Reiko's shoulder blades, and I could feel the jolts her body made as she sobbed, and I forced the front wheel forward across the mud.

JULIAN

chapter 9

Reiko. My sister Mary kidded me when she came down on Sundays, called Reiko my girlfriend, my China doll. She's Japanese, Mary, I'd answer back. She's our neighbor. Mary knew that Mr. Hamada was our friend; he'd written letters in English to the immigration people in San Francisco for our parents. When you thought about it, you couldn't always tell between them in the valley. Until you heard the language, you couldn't always tell by looking who was Japanese, Mexican, Portuguese, or Italian. Una faccia, una razza, my mother said. Same face, same people. It was my mother who was the exception; she had blue eyes, and I'd got them too. But I looked like my father, big head, thick black wire hair, built square.

If it weren't for Reiko I'd never have gone back to school. She's the one who explained to my mother I needed glasses to read with, after the school said so. I only needed them when I read. I'd thought my arms weren't long enough. But I liked the glasses. Foureyes, they called me. Hortense was the worst; for some reason she thought the glasses were funny. She grabbed them off my nose once and put them on a cow.

Reiko was the one who showed me, helped me with my homework. I wasn't going to forget that because of Fred. She had drawn a heart in the palm of her hand, R.H. + F.L. The Okies were taking over the county; they were everywhere now. There was nothing I could do. But one time when I caught Reiko watching Fred with that look on her face, I knew what I wanted to do: choke the life out of Fred, put both my hands around his throat and squeeze, pinch his head off. She'd never even glanced at me that way. Never.

I went out back under the big oak where I'd set the flowerpots on stands. I was trying something new. I'd nailed two-by-four uprights into the trunk of the oak and built shelves across them. I had sixty-one mum sets in pots lined up on the shelves now. The top row was all with mums that were going to cascade. They needed to hang down, six or seven feet, sometimes. Spider mums on the next shelf, no buds to pinch yet. Yellow, white, pink, and lavender. Incurve mums looked okay. The button mums had black spot on the leaves. My plants had never had that before. I'd have to try looking it up in one of the books at school. I couldn't ask Mr. Hamada. He'd stopped growing the flowers; I didn't know why. Every year I'd take big bouquets to Mrs. Hamada and leave them on the steps in coffee cans because no one came out anymore when I came to visit. The Hamadas were still polite when we ran across each other, and they always wanted me to pick, but it wasn't the same. I'd stopped going over to visit.

I got started with the mums one fall when I was over at the Hamadas' and all the flowers were in bloom, the whole yard. I looked them over, thought I saw how it was done. Some of those spider blossoms were twelve inches across. The stems had to be propped up. I can do this, I said to Grayson and Reiko. I thought I could grow anything. Everybody knew Italians were good farmers. Mr. Hamada must have overheard me, because the next spring he waved me over and showed me how to separate the mums into sets. We worked together over at their place, that spring and the next one and the one after that. I liked being there with Mr. Hamada. I'd watch his hands, because he hardly ever spoke, and do exactly what he did. I liked the quietness of it.

I don't know why Mr. Hamada stopped growing the mums. Two years ago when I went over for sets, he gave me everything. Tubs, pots, and he had dug up every mum in the yard. No one came out of the house, just him. I didn't know what to say. "You don't want to keep any of this, Mr. Hamada?" He shook his head and picked up the handles of the wheelbarrow and started out of the yard toward the strawberry patch, shovels and hoes rattling against each other. I had driven over, and I started loading all of it on the truck. I couldn't think of anything else to do. There wasn't a sound coming out of the house, but still I called out, "Reiko, Grayson," knocked on the door. I didn't want to do the mums alone. We always had done the flowers together, over here. "Reiko, Reiko."

I thought I might have insulted the Hamadas, somehow. I'd heard Ray call Mr. Hamada stupid in town, and Mats hadn't blinked, his whole face was a big smile, but the other men that were standing around didn't speak, and the smile started to fade, and Mats looked sick, like he was just hit in the stomach. You couldn't tell; the Hamadas were always agreeable. I told them last year I was able to tell exactly how big the flower was going to be, even before the plant budded. They all grinned like they did when I said something hilarious. "Reiko," I yelled. I didn't tell them I could grow Reiko in one of those pots. The flowers were Reiko. If you could get a bale of cotton out of a plant, cotton that was made into clothes the shape of people, then you could grow a person in a flower. Not a real person, but how they moved, how they looked.

Once we went to a Halloween party, after I started going back to grammar school. The party was in someone's barn, and they were dunking for apples in a big washtub. They tied my hands behind my back. I couldn't get the apple to stop bobbing so I could sink my teeth in. I drove my head under the water trying to hold the apple against the bottom, but I couldn't hold my breath long enough. I was getting all wet and everyone was laughing. Reiko got down, hands tied too. "Together," she said, moving the apple toward me with her chin. With my nose I could feel the softness of her cheeks and the bone in her forehead, and she whispered, "Now," and we both bit into the apple and lifted it up out of the water at the same time.

I had never put my arm around her waist, or held her hand. Nothing. She patted my arm once when we were sophomores and I got a B+ on an essay. And now Fred. I watched the way she looked at him. I wanted to quit school. Take an axe and go over to that Okie's shack and hack it to pieces. That day that Mr. Hamada tore out all his mums, I started banging on the back door with my fist. "Reiko, I know you're in there."

"Go away, Julian. I can't come out."

* * *

I grabbed the hoe and put the file in my back pocket, slipped on the rubber boots and started toward the north section. Mr. McInteer had talked my father into planting cotton on a fifteen-acre lease, had supplied the seed. I hadn't got used to the plants yet. They were so foreign, so different from the vines or anything else, vegetables, wheat, we'd ever tried before. And you needed water, a lot, if you wanted a crop. We were using our well water too, along with water from the ditch. With the vines you used a tractor with a Fresno plow to get the weeds between the rows. With cotton you used a short-handled hoe so you could put your back into the goddamn Johnson grass that had roots longer than your leg. It was worse than picking stoop crops. If you didn't chop them down, the weeds would steal all the water and you'd end up growing the devil heads; that's what my father called Johnson grass.

I started chopping, moving down the row, raising the hoe so the corner of the blade came down under the root to get as much as I could. They'd come back anyway. I kept my head down, working toward the Hamada place until I came to their pump, about a hundred yards from their house; it was on the line that separated the cotton acreage from their place. I sharpened the hoe there, going slow, not to feather the edges, then started down the next rows. No one came out.

I knew how to keep going. I didn't mind getting so tired I couldn't think. That's what I wanted: to stop my mind from thinking all the time, let it blur into my body. I wasn't going to get any help anyhow. Sometimes the Zia was so crippled up with arthritis she could barely walk, and my mother and father had twenty-gallon tanks on their backs, spraying the vines for mildew.

It was hot even for August in the valley, twenty-three days straight of over a hundred degrees. When it got like this, it never cooled off at night. The heat just kept adding up like the sun was out all the time, night and day. People slept out on their screened porches, hoping for a night breeze; got up early and then got under cover, if they weren't farmers, until the sun started going down. Each day was worse than the day before. Mabel's family used to move up in the mountains when it got like this. I heard some kids in school say they moved over to the coast where it was cool, into their beach house for the summer, and the father came over on weekends. But you couldn't do that if you had crops. You had to live with them like you were part of the vines, a leaf, say, that kept the grapes from burning up. After I got done chopping, I had to irrigate.

The only things that were benefiting from the heat wave were the cotton and the Union Ice Company, that was the joke. You could see the cotton grow before your eyes when you started irrigating. The plants leaned toward the rush of water when I dragged the irrigation pipe to another row. You had to keep the water steady in the channels that circled the fields or they'd break and you'd lose your water going down the rows. I had to run sometimes to the end of one row to open the water flow going to the next ones. I was covered with sweat and dust, and by noon I was using the shovel to hold myself up. I'd already stripped off my shirt and kicked off my boots—too heavy, covered with mud. I stopped to eat my sandwich, took long drinks out of the gallon water jug. It was so hot I felt like my pants were cooking my legs inside a pair of stovepipes. I unbuttoned them and took them off. I wasn't wearing undershorts, I saved them for school days, but I wasn't naked because of my hair. It grew as much on my back as it did on my chest. Once, baling hay at the Brazils, Hortense said I had more hair than the Holsteins. She had brought out drinks for the crew. I spit water back at her when she said that. No one could see me out here in the cotton except the old man who grew ten acres of figs over across the road. He yelled at me when he went by in his truck, "Julian, put on your clothes; you're going to sunburn your pecker." I waved back. I was up to my balls in mud, trying to repair a ditch bank. The mud felt cool on my hot skin.

I didn't wear my glasses when I worked. I didn't need to; I could understand the plants; they weren't like people. Having the glasses was like waking up in the night and being able to see. Reiko had tried to explain to my mother about the glasses. She'd finally come back with a page out of the newspaper with a picture of a pair of glasses advertising an optometrist's office in town. My father had been sharpening his hoe on the treadle grinder and he stopped to listen. "Glasses. The school says he can't see," Reiko kept saying.

My folks could understand some English; it was just that they were never sure when they were speaking it back if anybody else was understanding them. They shouted back as loud as they could sometimes, as if that might help. But they wouldn't shout at Reiko. My mother nodded, took the paper. My sister made a special trip from Dinuba to take me to the eye doctor. My mother and father waited in the car, which was just as well, because they both embarrassed me. My old mother, fat, with a little mustache. One of my sisters had talked her into shaving it, and it had come back twice as thick now. My father would squat in the field to shit and wipe himself with cornshucks he carried around in his back pocket like a handkerchief. My mother kept the outhouse door open because of the flies, and the Zia would sit next to her on the other hole, reading the Italian paper that came every month, commenting, their drawers pulled down around their ankles.

With the glasses, after I got used to wearing them, I could see what a little fruit fly looked like on the vines, and read the words in the books better, all the fine print, when it got smaller and smaller at the bottom of the pages. And Reiko. I could see her smooth skin and the brown mole on the side of her mouth, and her beautiful teeth that made up her smile when she was happy. All of her body was tall, long neck and legs and arms. Of all the things good to look at, women were made the best of all. A big buck was nice to look at, and a sequoia was better, but Reiko was best of all. Mabel too, I could see that when she was younger she must have been beautiful.

And the glasses made me see how old my parents were. My mother's hair was all gray. My father had lost most of his, and the rest stuck out stiff over his bald round head. Neither had many teeth. My mother had been almost fifty when I was born. One of my sisters told me that. Now I was sixteen, and she was an old woman. She couldn't work out in the fields like she used to, or my father either, who was older, and neither could the Zia.

And they were in debt to the Land Company because of the cotton lease. My father had gone for the chance to make some money on a cash crop. We didn't have any money to hire anyone; it was me or no one that was going to do the work. My father hadn't known when he'd signed the paper to lease the acreage from the Land Company that under the surface dirt there was a layer of hardpan like a foot-thick cement floor that had to be blasted before we could grow anything. That land was a curse. When Mr. McInteer came around now, if my folks weren't out in the open they'd stay where they were, and I'd have to go out there and talk, stand with my arms behind my back because they laughed at Italians who talked with their hands, listening to McInteer say, "You better tell your father to get off his ass; that cotton looks like hell. You're not irrigating enough. You won't get a bale an acre, the rate you're going." Yes sir, I'd say, trying not to run for a shovel and start to work. All because we took a chance on cotton. Zia thought English was a bastard language, because the pope didn't speak it. My father always yelled, "That's why we left Italy; that son of a bitch pope owned all the land; who cares if he knows English." And now we could lose the vineyard because of these rows of cotton. Because of a plant.

Never once did my parents complain; they just kept working harder. They were going to work themselves to death, keep going until they dropped dead like some bird you found between the vines, fallen from the sky. When my three sisters came to visit they were always saying, "You can come and live with me, Mamma, Babbo, take it easy. Sell this place. Julian can work out." That was stupid; there were no jobs. I wasn't going to be a farm laborer for someone else. The freight trains passing through the valley were covered with ragged men too tired and worn out even to wave back. If the valley was bad, the rest of California was worse. They were all coming here. The Okies were everywhere, like lice. You couldn't get rid of them. What must it be like where they came from?

The only place I'd like to go if I had to leave the vineyard was up in those mountains where we went hunting in the fall. I could live up there like Tarzan. Tarzan of the Apes, I'd read all those books. The librarian told me I'd like them. I filled my lungs with air and with one hand holding the shovel over my head like a spear I gave the call, thumping my chest with the side of my fist. I did it again, a long call toward the Hamadas'. Reiko could live with me up there in the mountains.

I couldn't even go over there anymore. They all went inside. It was Reiko who'd told my mother, "Mrs. Palestini, the law in California says that everyone has to go to school." That was enough for my mother; I went back. I'd gone before, off and on, but I'd started staying home when I got scarlet fever that time. I just stayed home when I got better, and helped around the place. But Reiko said I had to go, and she gave me a handle on things, and I got up every morning and got on that bus. And Reiko made sure I did, too, or she'd come up the front stairs.

I liked school from the beginning, especially after the bus started picking us up and taking us to the new building. Hortense and I would kid each other, "Did you wash your feet in that white porcelain basin and get them clean by just flushing?" It was still a joke, even now, because some Okie woman was supposed to have said, "These California wash tubs are too small: you can't scrub a bedsheet clean in one of them." That happened at one of those camps the government built for them. But even the school in the country had been interesting—unusual, that was the word. The other kids reading about Mother, Father, and Dick and Jane. It was wonderful; you could rest up, listen to the stories; you didn't have to do anything. But then I had got sick, and I just didn't go back until Reiko came for me and said it was the law. And last week at school she said to me in English class, "Why are you always following me? Go sit somewhere else, Julian."

I had to walk by the Hamadas' place. There was no avoiding that on the way to the Brazils'. It wasn't dark yet, but the sun had gone down behind the big oak in back of their house. When I got close I saw the two heads in the metal tub as big as a watering trough that Mr. Hamada soaked in after working. Hortense said all of them used it, Reiko and her mother too. Sat out there naked steaming themselves. Cut lemons in half and squirted them on their heads and let them float on the top of the water. Then they scraped themselves instead of using a towel. I took a bath myself every Saturday night. If I needed one or not, that was the joke.

Getting closer, I saw there were three heads in the tub, and one had light hair. Fred was in there with Grayson and Mr. Hamada. There was a minute before Grayson saw me and yelled, "Where you headed, Julian?" when I thought no one was going to speak to me. I stood there feeling how heavy my hands were at the end of my arms, not quite in the yard. I hadn't caught them out in the open in over a year.

"I'm just passing by, going over the Brazils' place. I understand that they have a two-headed calf born that's still alive."

"I'd like to take a look at that," Fred said, and he stood up, streaming water.

"You're not going to eat with us?" Reiko said. He hadn't seen her standing behind the screen door, I guess.

"I'm still full from dinner, thank you." Without drying himself, he was pulling on his clothes, fast. Reiko disappeared. "I'll be here in the morning, Mr. Hamada; we'll finish up tomorrow."

We cut across the fields after we left the yard. I didn't hate Fred, or anyone.

"That's a planter's moon," I commented for something to say.

"A fella I worked for in Traver once wanted to wait to plant till the moon was right. 'We're not planting on the moon,' his daddy said. 'We're planting in Tulare County.'"

"Maybe it's a hunter's moon, then." I couldn't help liking Fred. "You going again this fall? Mr. Hart said it's going to be a good year. Deer are everywhere up there, thick as jackrabbits."

"We might go, if Charlie can get off. I like those mountains; you couldn't get a money crop to come in up there, but they're nice to look at. We're staying in this locale, now that we've got a piece of land. No one is ever going to take that away from me. I'm going to be able to look at those mountains for free for the rest of my life."

I thought about how long Fred had been here now, almost three years. He must have come in '37, though it seemed like he'd always been here. I remembered what Fred said when he saw the sequoia cut with the notch: "Holy shit, that's a tree?" He kept kicking it like he was seeing if it was real. "If you could get this thing to bear fruit, what a crop: you'd only need one."

Fred could talk when it came to it. "Mr. Hart introduced me to a clerk that's been working at the bank, Richard Cortez, and he said the banks are going to start making loans to buy land again. It's not always going to go for thirty-five dollars an acre. I never thought we'd hit the jackpot here, me and Charlie. We were riding the rods and we got off at Goshen and just started walking. We had no idea where we'd end up. But I always had hope, I never gave up thinking this might be the place."

He never stopped talking all the way to the Brazils' dairy. But the calf had died that morning. Hortense came out to show us. Her father had cut off the heads below where they were joined at the neck and put them in a crock of alcohol. She grabbed the pairs of ears floating on the top and lifted the heads. "It's a wonder," Fred said. "Now if there had been two bodies and one head, Hortense, it would have doubled your profit and been an Okie miracle besides."

PATRICK HART—1939

chapter 10

Things were still hard. No jobs, but there weren't so many men just sitting around waiting. The WPA and CCC that everyone made fun of did put a lot of the younger men to work building cement culverts and bridges around the county, fixing the roads. Hotel occupancy had picked up 14 percent in the last two months, he was able to write in his third-quarter report. They still hadn't resumed the biannual company meetings in San Francisco. What profit was there to celebrate, Elton would point out. The last had been in 1932. Elton McInteer was a genuine son of a bitch.

Ray was sick and wouldn't go to the hospital. He got out there a couple of times a week to visit, but Ray wouldn't listen to anyone, just lay there in his narrow iron bed, the four metal legs set in old tin cans filled with kerosene so no bedbugs would get at him in the night, too sick even to build a fire in the old cookstove, barely able to talk. Last time he visited he'd said, "Almost time to go hunting," and it took a long time for Ray to reply, "I'll be ready." Looking at Ray then, shrunken under the blankets, breathing hard like each breath was going to be his last, he got angry and yelled, "I'm going to get Mats if you don't let me take you into town."

"You bring that simpleton in here and I'll shoot him through the head. If I want to die like a goddamn dog, that's my business."

"You acted like a dog most of your life anyway."

Ray started laughing then. "I did, didn't I?"

This time before he left he built a fire in the stove and filled all Ray's gallon water jugs from the pump at the sink. Fed the chickens. Took the chamber pot outside to dump. Yellow pee was in the top half but the bottom was the color of blood. "I'm going," he said, but Ray was asleep and didn't hear.

Mabel was home when he knocked at the front door. He could see her through the glass, but she didn't get up from her chair. He knocked again, then yelled, "Mabel, goddamn it, I can see you in there."

"Go away." She finally got up, took her sweet time, turning off the light where she sat and turning on the one over the door. He knew Mabel had gone to some college after she graduated from high school, the Methodist one in Stockton it was, and Ray had paid her way, but how she'd ended up back here he'd never heard. She was a lot younger than he was, still in her thirties. Never married, as far as he knew. Never went with anyone else but Ray up in the mountains either, except for that one time with him. This was a good piece of property, a big lot, and the house was well built. It must have been out in the country at one time, still had its tank house, but the neighborhood was built up now, five or six new houses on the street. Her old mother had died last year, somebody said.

She didn't open the door. Just looked through the diamond-shaped glass.

"Ray's sick, Mabel; he was asking for you."

Before she spoke, he knew she'd been drinking. "You're full of bullshit, Patrick. He never asked for anyone in his life." And she turned out the light.

One of the interesting things about hard times was that they not only changed the people around you, they also brought you people looking for change. Not just the Okies, who all seemed to be pretty much the same until you met one and got to know him, like Fred, but new folks in new situations. A young man he didn't recognize had come into his office last week and started a conversation. "Mr. Hart, you probably don't remember me, but my name is Richard Cortez and I work at the bank." He went on to say he'd like to join the Order of the Moose. Personable, well-spoken, dressed like a businessman, someone who would be an asset in any organization. They hadn't had a new member in the Moose for eight years. This was a good sign. Maybe people like Richard meant better times were coming. After they saw Richard, not one member said a word about him being Mexican. It was true: clothes made the man.

Saturday was still Saturday. People still came into town, Main Street was lined with cars, but the buying was slow. When someone purchased a new car from the Ford agency it was an occasion; everyone heard about it. The few people with money weren't buying much; they were waiting it out to see what was going to happen next. People without money didn't have any choice.

He had been watching at the window and stepped out onto the sidewalk for a breath of fresh air. He noticed Grayson coming around the corner, full of piss and vinegar. Getting big now at twelve, or was it thirteen? He was almost taller than Mats. It was American food, Ray claimed.

"Mr. Hart," Grayson called out, crossing the street, shaking his hand. "Have you seen my grandfather this morning?"

"I think he's out of town." Ray had told him to say that if anyone asked about him.

"Well, if you do, tell him I've definitely almost talked my father into letting me go up hunting in the mountains this fall. But I might still need his help. Would you tell him that for me?"

"I will," he said.

He went back inside, did some work in his office. "Uncle Pat." He looked up when Reiko said his name. "Did my grandfather come in? We're in the coffee shop having a Coke, if he does."

"How have you been, Reiko, and when are you going to stop growing?"

"I'm a senior this year, and I'll stop now, I hope, because I'm five feet six inches and that's tall enough." She was so full of herself she looked like she'd burst. Confident as if she had the world by the tail. It wasn't just being seventeen. The other side of the coin was Julian, who had come in beside himself three Saturdays ago and said he was going to kill Elton.

He finished what he was doing and went over to the window again. The rug underneath it was worn from his standing at that place for the last eighteen years. Every parking place on the street was taken and it was only one-thirty. That had to be a good sign.

He went into the coffee shop. He'd forgotten about Reiko: there she was, sitting next to Fred, whom he hadn't seen in five or six months. Fred had filled out too since that time a couple of years back when he'd found him sleeping in the garage. Hortense—with that red hair you could spot her a mile away—was next to Julian. They were all having a good time. Maybe that was a sign too.

Fred spotted him. "Mr. Hart." The boy was climbing over everyone to get out of the booth to shake his hand. Julian too. "How's the pigeon population?"

"Growing, but not enough yet to worry about."

"When are we going hunting this year?" Julian wanted to know. "The oak leaves already are turning."

"I'll let you know as soon as I hear." He noticed Richard Cortez was sitting at the counter finishing up his lunch. He called him over and introduced him to Reiko and Hortense and then to the boys. It immediately made the situation awkward; everyone fell silent. But Richard spoke up.

"Well, with a new war in Europe starting up all over again, I guess it's going to be up to you farmers to feed all those people over there like the last time." That was met with silence too, but Fred asked Richard to sit down and join them, and he went back to his office.

That afternoon he got a ride out to see Ray. He fully expected him to be dead. He had described Ray's symptoms to a lodge brother who was a doctor. "I know who you're talking about. It's prostate cancer, and he could have had an operation last year but he refused. You know why? Because it would make him impotent. When I asked him, at his age was that such a important consideration if his life was in danger, he said, 'You're goddamn right it is.' Patrick, the man is seventy-four years old, for Pete's sake."

Ray was sitting up in bed reading the newspaper. Mabel was at the stove putting wood in the firebox. "There's going to be another war," Ray said. "The last one, I made a potful when I had grain and the cattle. If I knew what I know now, I'd be a millionaire a hundred times over."

Mabel never said a word, stayed in a chair by the stove. Ray kept talking; he didn't need anyone to answer. After a while he went slower, talking about something from a long time ago in Japan, a smaller island above Honshu where there was a people that were hairy, had big beards. No one knew where they'd come from, but they were up there on Hokkaido, some kind of native Japanese people. His father took him up there. Those people worshiped bears. "It's the truth," Ray said. "It's the truth. Japanese aren't religious like people around here; we can be Shinto or Buddhist, but those people knelt to big brown bears. I always thought that was so much better than the Christian hocus-pocus about virgin births and resurrection and the rest of that bullshit. I like to think that when I die I'm going to be with the bears. I killed my share. Now they can have me. That's the only thing the Indians had right; they thought it was the animals who started this whole rigmarole." He stopped talking and started breathing loud, almost snoring.

"He knows he's going to die," Mabel said. "It's just a matter of time. He's hemorrhaging. I've changed the wad of towels under him twice since this morning. His mattress is soaked through to the floor."

"Should I go get Mats?"

"He doesn't want to see him. It would just make it worse for his boy. Mats knows he's sick. Ray told me he went over there when he could still get around and gave them some things for Reiko and Grayson. Some goddamn sword and a kimono of his mother's with gold thread woven into the silk. His gold watch, his rifles, and a lot of papers. They know they're not going to see him again. He wants his ashes taken up in the mountains to the camp. Dump them up there, he told me. No funeral, just haul him into town to be cremated."

"What about the grandchildren?"

"He didn't say why, but he doesn't want anyone around."

The two bottles of rye he'd brought the last time were still on the sideboard. He put the two he'd brought this time next to them. "How will you get word to me from out here?" he asked.

"He won't last the night. Most of his blood is gone."

He tried to match her casualness. "I'll stick around, then. What's going to happen now when he dies, his place and the rest of it?"

"He doesn't have that much left. Just the home place here. Two hundred acres of walnuts, because he thought they were less trouble than most crops. Four or five sections of poor ground. All that land up in the forest. The lodge up there. He was land poor, that was the secret. Where everyone else in the valley fights over forty acres of peaches, he had forty thousand, once. He wasn't making any money. He was letting everything sit. Leasing some of the grazing rights, some of the water rights."

He didn't remember who got the cards out, but they started playing, cribbage first, then gin rummy. They could hear Ray breathing in the next room, steady as a clock. About three A.M. he opened one of the bottles of rye and poured each of them a drink in their coffee cups. She started talking again. "Some of that property he put in my name. It was after they said Japanese couldn't own land. He could have got around it, but he didn't want to bother. He said I could have it. I told him I didn't want it. I found out he put all that grazing land in the forest in my name too. I couldn't do anything about it. He was a mean old bastard his whole life."

She was mostly talking to herself. "When I was a little girl he went around with my mother; that's how I got to know him. He thought he was different than the rest of us because he was smarter, but the difference was the way he regarded everyone, and the way everyone treated him back: he could get away with anything, because he'd taken so much, land and everything else, all by himself. The only thing he cared about was the ground, the next crop, something he could grow and make a profit on. It was a contest for him. Not people. Not me, not his boy." She stopped talking and put her head down on her arm to rest. Woke up after a while, and they started playing cards again.

It was dawn. He had fallen asleep. The sky out the window was turning gray. Someone was putting on a pair of boots, slamming each one against the floor so the foot would slide all the way in. It was Ray, wearing his long johns and boots, laces hanging, an old jacket. "It's time to flood the walnuts." He went right out the kitchen door and took a shovel that was leaning against the shed wall. They both got up and followed him out. He was heading for the orchard across the yard. When he got to the first tree he drove the shovel into the ground. "This is a lot like work," he said, and fell over backwards, dead.

Mats was outside sharpening a hoe at a sit-down grindstone, moving the treadle up and down with his right foot, keeping an eye on what he was doing. He waited until Mats had finished with the hoe before saying, "Mats, your father died this morning." Mats just looked at him, testing the edge of the hoe with his thumb.

"Ray died this morning, Mats."

"You don't say," Mats said. His wife came out then and he said something in Japanese. She smiled at them. You could never tell what they were feeling, much less what they were thinking. "My father never liked me," Mats said. His wife had gone back into the house.

He had helped put Ray, wrapped in a blanket, in the backseat of Mabel's old car so she could take him into town to be cremated. That afternoon she stopped at the hotel to show him a blue and white porcelain vase she'd bought. "This is where I'm going to put Ray's ashes until we get up to the camp," she told him. She hesitated before going on. "I'm not going to miss him. But I could never say no to Ray."

For the next couple of days he kept thinking over what he and Mabel had talked about. He was forty-six years old now. For the last eighteen years he and Ray had pretty much done what they wanted around the valley in the way of good times. But what did he have to show for those years? It was a strange feeling, looking back, to realize all he could remember was a few laughs, cavorting with the whores, hunting. He'd never planted a tree, much less a son or daughter. Maybe he'd avoided becoming his father, but what had he turned himself into? Nothing. Somehow he'd avoided living his own life too. Maybe it wasn't too late.

When he saw Elton at the bar wearing dark glasses, he went into the Doghouse too. They'd taken the bandages off Elton's face, he saw. "Well, if it isn't the friend of the working girl," Elton said.

"Too bright for you in the bar, Elton? That's why you need the sunglasses? I hear you got made to look like a prize fool by those Italians. Comptroller up in Sacramento says it's the talk of the office up there. You sure put your foot in it that time. But what no one can understand is why you'd even bother. What did the Palestinis do to you?"

"They didn't have to do anything. It's my job. They had a good piece of land right in the middle of something like four sections that we own. So if I could get a bite out of it, I thought I should try. I mean, my God, they're Italians. Farm animals in overalls."

"You stopped them from ginning? Refused them at the company's place?"

"The goddamn cotton was poor grade. But they took it over to Corcoran, had a gin there do it. I never heard about it until later, or I would have stopped it."

"That's chickenshit, Elton."

"Well, that's the business I'm in. That boy of theirs is going to get himself in some trouble. I went out there to show there was no hard feelings when they paid the money up. No one came into the yard and I stayed in the car; I never trusted them. The boy comes up behind the coupe and picks the goddamn car up by the rear bumper and turns me around the other way and almost tips the thing over. I banged my head on the windshield, or I would have got out and showed him a thing or two. Then he starts hitting the car with the shovel blade, breaks the windshield, gouges holes in the hood and the roof. It was like being inside of a drum. I got out of there, but it's not over. I'll have that place. The company doesn't want me to press charges, or I would have. I'll have their deed instead."

"I thought the Land Company was trying to get along with everybody. We're not Standard Oil or Southern Pacific; we're not trying to run the state or even the valley. We need these farmers. We need their crops. You have stockholders; they don't want you to steal from these farmers. Making a buck is one thing . . ."

"Whose side are you on, Patrick? Goddamn it, farming is a goddamn business. We're not making any profits now. Those stockholders aren't getting any dividends. You do what you have to do." He had kept his voice down low, like he didn't want anyone to hear, but there was no one else in the bar. Elton got up, put some bills on the bar, and left.

He saw Julian the next week, on the street over in front of the drugstore. "Mr. Hart, am I going to get to go up to the mountains this year?" he blurted out.

"I don't know why not."

Julian went on like he hadn't heard. "Mabel isn't going if I can't."

He had to laugh. "Julian, you can go, don't worry about it. In fact, I wrote the boys up at the lodge. We're going on the twelfth. You too."

Julian started smiling. "I like that place," he said. "I always mean to get up there other times of the year too. In the spring, after the snow melts. Mabel's always talking about going. Thank you, Mr. Hart."

When they went hunting that fall they took Grayson. Julian had talked to Mats. Since Ray had died it was different. Fred came, and they invited Richard too. They needed some young blood. Everyone was getting too old. A lot of the hunters weren't even leaving the camp to hunt anymore. They sat around and played cards and told stories. Went down to the lodge's cabins to sleep in a bed at night. Alma sent up four of her best, she claimed. None of them were anything to write home about.

It rained on the second night and all the next day and snowed a little the third night. Then it drizzled. This had never happened before; the weather had always held. It was miserable. Some of the hunters left, said the hell with it, which made it bad because the more there were, the less the expenses for each person. The dog man wanted an arm and a leg to run the deer with his hounds. Pack animals. The girls didn't come cheap either. Ray had always paid for almost everything out of his own pocket. He had ways of getting it back, though. He collected from some of the cattlemen for grazing rights and water rights in the foothills. The quarry made money. And he owned the lodge and cabins. He assessed fees to the firms who brought their clients up to the camp on hunting trips, the Land Company, for one. Elton was always complaining when he got that letter. Any profit now was up to Mabel: she owned it, though the national forest thought they had a claim too. The whole thing was in the national forest now. Ray had been there before there was a national forest or a Forest Service. He'd thought that was the most pathetic misguided organization the government had ever thought up.

During the storm everyone crowded into the kitchen and storage tents waiting for the rain to stop. It poured. Mabel was trying to cook and Julian and Grayson were helping. He watched Mabel. When she wasn't drinking, she was the nicest person in the world. She still looked young. He had never approached her after that first time. She had been lying there on the hillside with her dress pulled up. "Ray said I should come over here," he'd told her. She didn't answer. He sat down and picked up one of her hands. He had a half pint and took a snort, then handed the bottle to her and she took one. "Are we going to have some fun or not?" She looked at him then. "If that's what he said, I don't care," she said.

Grayson was a humdinger of a hunter. He took to it like he'd been doing it all his life. He got a forked horn the day after the heavy rain stopped, and the day after that he walked up on a big buck who was bedded down with about twenty does and yearlings. He blasted the four point and three yearlings for camp meat. It was the first venison they'd had for the camp. The storm got the deer moving after that, and the dogs did the rest.

It was like old times, once the sun came back. The whores decided to take a bath in the big pool by the point where they'd baited the bears that time. Nearly everyone ended up in the water trying to wash their backs, cavorting in water that must have been as cold as a witch's tit. He noticed Julian didn't go in after them, went and helped in the kitchen. It was never dirty with the women; no one screwed them where anyone else could see. They each had a tent to themselves, or you could take them into your bedroll. Grayson did what Julian did. Fred and Richard were in the middle of it all.

Elton didn't show up. That wasn't unusual; people didn't make it every year. But he was glad, too, because Julian was standing up for himself. One of the old-timers called him Dago or Wop or something when Julian was dishing the food into the hunter's plate. "Don't call me that," he said. It was like one of those big stumps suddenly yelled at you, and the man jumped back.

He played cards with Mabel. She was good. He wanted to talk to her about the camp, the mountain property up here, see what she was going to do. He kept thinking about Ray and Mabel's mother, Mabel and Ray. She brought it up. "How much longer do you think we're going to come up here?"

"As long as we want, I guess. That's pretty much up to you."

"I never wanted him to leave me this place. And now I'm not sure what I should do. If I'm not careful, the county will take it for taxes. And the Forest Service keeps writing me letters."

"You can lease it to us."

She started laughing. "I don't give a damn," she said.

He thought she was laughing at him. "I'm no Elton McInteer." She laughed some more. To change the subject, he asked, "Did you bring Ray's ashes up?"

"You bet I did. That's what he wanted."

"We can have some kind of ceremony, maybe. Get everyone to fall silent for a minute in remembrance. Ray loved this place."

"Ray didn't love anything. Not the camp or even his grandkids. He didn't have any love for anyone. It was all pretend. It wasn't in his nature to have feelings, not even for himself."

The next to last morning, Grayson and Julian took six of the best dogs for a drive up a canyon full of thick brush, dead trees, and big boulders. They couldn't take the horses because of the rocks, so they ran with the dogs, keeping up pretty well, their rifles slung over their backs. Everyone could see from the point. The dogs were going crazy, crashing through the brush tracking a good scent. It's a bear, someone said; they're running a bear. It had got hot and both of the boys had their jackets and shirts off and you could see the rivers of sweat pouring off of them.

Suddenly the chase stopped and it looked like the dogs were trying to climb two of the trees. "They got puma," Mabel said. "Look how big that male is. I didn't know any were left. I thought the cattlemen had killed them all off." The boys were trying to catch their breath, sitting on a couple of rocks. Finally Grayson got up and went over and started pulling the dogs away from the tree, grabbing them by their collars and the loose skin on their backs. They couldn't hear, of course, but he could imagine the big cat spitting and growling, laid flat against the limb of the tree, raising up on his legs to spring. Grayson walked right up under the limb and pointed his rifle with one arm over his head. Then the crack, and the male fell off the limb, stiff, and bounced off the rocks, dead. They all kept watch, but nothing else happened. The female was still up in the other tree when the boys tied the feet of the mountain lion and ran a pole through its legs and started up the canyon wall.

Later he heard Richard ask Grayson and Julian why they hadn't shot the second cougar. "There's a bounty on those animals. You could have made some money."

Grayson didn't answer but Julian did. "Because I didn't want to."

He thought the last evening would be a good time to put Ray's ashes to rest. He'd told Grayson about his grandfather's request that morning, and after dinner he walked over to the cook tent to ask Mabel. She had been acting funny before dinner, not talking much or even drinking anything. But now she was roaring drunk. Julian was sitting on a box in a corner, looking away. She could barely stay on the chair she was sitting in, holding on to the arms with both hands. "Everyone's going back down tomorrow. If we're going to spread Ray's ashes we better do it tonight."

She started laughing until tears came down her cheeks. Julian was looking into space. When she could speak, she got out, "I've already done it. I've taken care of Ray's ashes."

"You put them over the point, like we talked about?"

Between cackles she said, "No. I threw them down the shitter. That's where Ray's remains belong, with the turds."

When Grayson asked the next morning about the ashes he told him, "That's already been taken care of." He didn't know how to read the look on Grayson's face.

chapter 11

The high school cafeteria closed down. Hardly anyone had any money to pay for a lunch. The kids that lived close went home. A few kids with money went downtown for a sandwich. The rest of us brought our lunch.

Most of the time I ate with Reiko and Hortense. We had always done it that way, gone off by ourselves, since grammar school. Before, we used to envy Reiko with her sliced bread and pimento loaf sandwiches. "It's because Mrs. Hamada doesn't know how to cook," Hortense said. But that didn't change things. Hortense had big hunks of homemade bread and the cheese they molded themselves and chunks of that Port sausage. She'd take a big bite out of each, just like in the field at lunchtime. But at school she didn't want anyone to see her eat it. I'd tell my ma too, you have to cut the bread and put the things inside. She'd slice the bread longways and fill it with last night's pasta and meatballs or peppers or frittata. My brown paper bag always had big round grease stains by noon. I noticed Hortense always tried to eat her food without unwrapping much of it, so no one would see. I did the same thing, and ended up eating the paper too sometimes when I forgot to be careful.

Reiko never paid any attention to the way we tried to hide our lunches, but we knew what each other was doing, envying the other kids with their Wonder Bread. I thought we were the only ones, but Kenny Rodriguez in my journalism class said he took a walk around the neighborhood at lunchtime so no one would see him eat the tortillas his mother made for him. I told him about my lunch, and we laughed and laughed. I told Hortense what Kenny said, but she didn't think it was as funny as I did. She'd heard that the Okie kids ate out by the maintenance shed because they didn't want anyone to see they had biscuits or saltine crackers for bread and drank water out of the hose to fill themselves up. Neither of us thought that was funny, because we knew one Okie who probably wasn't eating anything at lunchtime now that the cafeteria was closed. If we caught Fred at noon and tried to share any of our food, he wouldn't take even a cluster of grapes or a handful of raisins, much less any bread and salami.

When Grayson got to high school he wanted to trade lunches all the time. I had my chance at pimento loaf on white bread if I wanted. But by that time Reiko wouldn't even sit in the classroom with me, and I had stopped worrying about what the other kids thought. School was getting interesting, and I knew I'd be a high school graduate.

I took journalism because Reiko wasn't in it and I couldn't get into the agricultural welding class I wanted. The who, what, where, when, and why, Miss Bock called it. You had to write an article for every class, so I did. The high school paper was printed by the same printer as the *Valley Herald* and put inside the sports section of the town paper on Fridays. Miss Bock picked the best articles to put in, and she started using mine sometimes. I wrote an article about a man over in Reedley who invented a box-making machine that replaced sixteen men; it only took one person to run the machine. I went over and saw the thing in a peach packing shed. It would take all the pieces of wood and *bim bam bang,* you had a wooden box. It even glued a label on each end, San Joaquin Gold. After the women packed the peaches, there was another machine, the lidder, that nailed the top on. It took seconds. The fruit had just been out on the trees that morning. Then they loaded the peaches onto refrigeration cars, and in three days someone in New York City would be biting into a valley peach.

I got interested in what I was doing, but I didn't have as much time to write the articles as I needed, with just one period of journalism a day and the half hour for lunch. I couldn't stay after school for very long because I had to work at home. Miss Bock got them to let me skip physical education and use that time for journalism. I heard her talking on the phone to the dean, saying wasn't it enough that we had all been working a couple of hours before school and would do three or four hours more after school, and how much exercise did a young person need to stay healthy, anyway? After that, all of us on the school newspaper staff who wanted to got excused from physical education.

"You have a good eye for human-interest stories," Miss Bock told me. "Feature stories." Usually I couldn't concentrate anymore once anyone paid any attention to what I was doing, I was too self-conscious, but I always made myself do my homework, so I looked for feature stories. I didn't let it slide. Mr. Hamada took me to see a friend of his that grew melons over by Huron. I just took the afternoon off. There were mostly Japanese farming in that area. Mats and I were friends again. He still wouldn't grow the mums, but we talked about things. The land out there was the worst in the state, but they made those melons grow. I never knew there were so many farmers that had come from Japan, mostly growing stoop crops, vegetables and berries. And some, like Mats, had never farmed before coming to California. They couldn't even own the land in this state because of some law. Grayson's name was on his father's property. Mats told me he had studied to be a Buddhist priest before he was converted to Christianity. He'd studied at an agricultural college in Japan too, but he'd never got his hands dirty before he came to California. He stuck out his palms, and we both laughed. His hands looked like mine. Because the Japanese turned out to be good farmers, people got jealous of them. They had the worst land, hardpan on every inch of it, and made it pay and grew more crops than everyone else together, but it was chancy to get noticed for that. I knew what he meant, after the Land Company tried to take our place from us.

I did a story on an Armenian from Fowler who went broke nine times in thirty years trying to grow figs. Had to start over each time, working for someone else to save the money, bought land, and something would happen. Flood, hail one time, frost twice, drought. His wife died. He said nine times, but he couldn't even remember why for some of them.

People enjoyed the features. They wrote in to the town paper and said so. I won an award in a state high school contest in feature writing. I won another award given by the family that published the *Valley Herald.* I read one of my articles at a dinner at the banquet room at the Californian. I never had so much fun in my life.

It was nice to see my name in the paper every week. Everyone said I should become a journalist, but I wasn't so sure. You had to please too many people. When I wrote a long article on the way a lot of the Okie pickers weren't treated right, the way they were being cheated by the contractors and the big farmers, the newspaper publisher wouldn't put that in the paper. Miss Bock told me she got a phone call from the president of the school board. The publisher said it wasn't true and he couldn't print lies and misinform the public. But it was true, I'd seen it with my own eyes dozens of times, and it had happened to me too. It wasn't just the Okies that got cheated; it could happen to anyone. You were at everyone's mercy: the bank's, of course; all the governments, county, state, and federal, and practically anyone you'd sell to. When we took our raisins into the packing plant before they were stemmed, we could lose up to a ton on shrinkage. You'd think you were supposed to have four bales of cotton an acre, and you might get paid for three. Your count didn't matter; it was their count they paid you by, when it came to field boxes or bins. And if the small farmer could be cheated, a single picker didn't have a chance. There were just too many farm laborers to begin with. You couldn't keep wages up when you'd work for twenty-five cents an hour and the next man for twenty because he needed a job to feed his family. Same in the cutting sheds, two cents a tray, but they kept count. I picked cherries in Delano once, and they told me I had bruised most of the fruit in the lug boxes and I might owe them money if I wasn't careful. And when you were thirsty working out in the field, they'd charge you for the water; ten cents for a ride out to the job and two bits coming back. It was the foremen that kept your time, chopping cotton, and you'd wonder when they paid you by the hour if they'd wound their watch that morning. Probably the worst wholesale robbery was committed when they got a picking crew together. The contractor took you out to a place and you started in, worked until the trees were clean, a couple of days or weeks later. Ask for your money, and the manager would say the contractor has your cash, but no one would ever find the man again. That happened to me a couple of times and to Fred a lot of times. No wonder those Okies were up against it all the time. There were a lot of farmers who treated them fair, but there were a lot that didn't. The small farmers like us and the Brazils and the Hamadas traded labor back and forth between us; we couldn't make any profit if we had to hire someone, except for Fred. Every one of us found some way to hire and pay Fred. The way he worked, you got twice as much out of him as you would anyone else.

I couldn't rewrite that article like the publisher wanted; there'd been nothing left to say. Miss Bock said there wasn't much she could do. The people who paid for the advertising didn't want to hear any criticism: it was all economics, supply and demand. They supplied the cash and demanded the right stories in the paper. And I was trying to be fair, too. I never wrote one word about what the Land Company tried to do to us.

It got so the *Fresno Bee* and the *Bakersfield Californian,* when they needed someone to cover something in between the two places, they'd call Miss Bock and she'd assign me. The county fair, a Grange meeting, the school board. I stayed up on election night to phone in the count. Kenny Rodriguez too; we covered together sometimes, lectures that could put you to sleep in thirty seconds. Once we were supposed to cover a talk, but the speaker turned out to be a union organizer and in the middle of his speech some men came running into the hall with axe handles and started beating up the people at the front table. No one had to say "Meeting adjourned" that night. When the circus people came to town they sent over some press tickets and Kenny took his two little brothers and I took Grayson and Zia Maria. The two newspapers each paid a nickel an inch, and I could spread those words farther than an Okie could white gravy.

Mr. Hart sold me an old Underwood from the hotel. My mother used to stand behind me, watching like I was making magic, writing a new language on the kitchen table. I couldn't stop, sometimes. One article would lead to another. A farmer who was trying to grow oranges with paper-thin peel. Another who made a hair tonic out of grapes and put some in my hair to show me. The new alcala cotton that was supposed to be the best in the world. A woman who had to dress up like a man to buy some of that new cotton seed to grow on her place because they only sold to men.

I did it easy. It wasn't hard to write about the place. I'd lived my whole life here and had been listening to the stories and talking crops as long as I could remember. You had to be careful with people, though, because they might think you were making fun of them, or the way they talked. I could understand a Portuguese or a Mexican speaking Spanish better a lot of the time than I could an Okie. I hurt an Okie's feelings once, an old man's. We were talking and an old rattletrap car went by full of kids and family. The back end of the sedan had been cut off and made into a truck bed. "Will you look at that?" I said. "There goes a rich Okie; he's got two mattresses." He didn't change his expression or say anything, but later I found out that was his granddaughter's and son's families. I had been talking to him because he was digging out the stump of one of the big old oaks with a shovel. He would dig down until he couldn't go any further and use an old hatchet to hack at the roots. "That tree goes all the way down to China," he told me. I had never met anyone that would even think of trying to get one of those oak stumps out by those roots. I'd never even heard of anyone trying blast one with dynamite or burn one out. The farmer was going to pay him twelve dollars and fifty cents if he could get it all out. He'd already been working for a week. I had passed by a dozen times wondering what he was doing before I stopped to interview him. Words can hurt as much as a punch in the mouth. I stopped with a water jug after that, and some raisins that he accepted after I explained about the iron in them and the extra energy it gave you. I learned the old man's name, Marvin Monroe Milton. He had owned property once, eighty acres in Oklahoma. It made you wonder what anyone would end up doing.

I took a girl in my history class out to a movie and then out to an abandoned farmhouse I knew next to the river, just to see if it was going to be any different than with the women at Alma's. But the girl didn't want to do anything but kiss and let me play with her tits, so I took her home. It was probably a good thing, because you start that with someone and you knock them up and the next thing you know you're a husband and a father. I heard a lot of comments about that up at the hunting camp. "I never ruined a good girl," one man said. "Never in my life. If I wanted a screw, I went to the whorehouse. I'd take out the best-looking girls in town but never lay a hand on them."

Richard Cortez was too smart for his own good. He had everything worked out beforehand. His father was a doctor, he had uncles that were doctors, and he would have gone to college too except for the hard times. His father had lost his money on the stock market and Richard had to find work like everyone else. He let you know he thought he was different. But he always outplanned himself. He was so afraid of disease he would use three or four rubbers on top of each other at Alma's, and the whores would laugh and then get pissed off because the rubbers would start coming off when Richard was fornicating. He called it that.

Hortense used to tease me about Reiko, but she chased after Richard worse than anyone I ever saw. I kidded her some and she yelled at me, "You shut your big Italian mouth." Laugh, I almost choked. Richard would take her hand in the movies and then Hortense wouldn't let go the rest of the day. Poor Richard.

Fred. Once I appreciated that he didn't care for anything but work, not even the money he got for breaking his back, then I could understand him. Then I liked him more. It was just the next job that mattered for him. I don't think it was the money he made or even the place he was building that kept him going like that. He didn't even like to take the time to eat. I dragged him into the kitchen to eat with us when he worked in the vineyard, but he never enjoyed it, just picked at the food, wanting to get back outside.

The first time we all went up to the camp the whores wouldn't keep their hands off him. It was a sight. "Women who should know better are acting foolish over that kid," I heard one of the old hunters say. Fred never noticed anything. He heard what people said, but when it was about him, he disregarded it all. It was like he never thought he was a real person that other people might comment on or see except when he was working. His folks had died of typhoid along with two sisters, and he and Charlie were put in a school for boys. When they got big enough they ran away—Charlie had told me this one time; Fred was twelve and Charlie was four years older. They rode the rods and hitchhiked to California.

Mabel kidded Fred at camp, said he was trouble where women were concerned. Some of the whores said he was better-looking than a movie star. The whores started quarreling over him then, and Mr. Hart had to tell him to pick one, goddamn it, and stick with her, and he finally did. He never noticed the fuss they were making over him.

Mabel was nice to everyone if she wasn't drinking. I'd go into town sometimes just to visit with her, sit in the parlor and talk, or I would help her with something around the house, bring some fruit. She read my articles in the paper, and she'd tell me good stories she'd heard, or people to go and see. I helped to paint her house one summer. I knew she had a job, but I never understood what she did until she showed me one day. In the back room she had an office with a big table and all kinds of paper and a little machine and books. She made braille books for the blind. She got orders from people that wanted a certain book, and she'd copy the regular print book into braille. She'd taken a course in college to learn how to do it. Her mother had been a seamstress. She never mentioned her father, or Ray, for that matter. Her last name was Hastings. I knew she was a Yokut, but one time when we were kidding around she said she was a Swede, like over in Kingsburg. She wasn't as dark as my father, and sometimes you could see red in her hair and her eyes were more green than brown. She used to let me sit with her while she worked at her desk. I'd read or just watch her. I'd put my hand near hers like I was just resting it there and pretend it was touching hers.

Reiko must have heard what Fred had been up to at the camp, probably Richard told Hortense, who could never keep a secret, because Reiko stopped being crazy after Fred. Hortense had told me what Reiko did, going to his shack that time. I lost all my respect for Reiko after that.

We all went to the Portuguese festival when they made Hortense the queen. It really didn't have anything to do with God. The Brazils believed in the Virgin Mary and the three children from Fatima; Hortense told me that; the rest is horseshit, she said. My family thought the Catholic Church was just something else that you had to get around, like the government or the immigration people. They thought that even now in California they weren't free from the pope, that if they were ever sent back to Urbino they'd have to pay up. When a priest came around for something they'd hide in the house. The Zia went to church sometimes, but the rest of the family only did when there was music, like with the Queen Isabella procession.

The Hamadas were the strictest religious people I'd ever seen. I'd get confused when they said that Catholics weren't even Christian, but whatever made up a good person, Mats was it. They never missed church, tithed, and tried to live by the Golden Rule. I never heard Mats say a bad word about anyone, and he had plenty of opportunities, the way he was treated sometimes. I never asked Grayson about what he thought. He went into town every Sunday morning wearing his best clothes, and Reiko too. Never missed.

Richard didn't want to talk about religion. He belonged to the Moose Lodge and was a Mason. He was a couple of years older than we were, and had a lot more answers. Fred said once that somewhere on the road to California he kissed a snake at a revival. We all started laughing so hard he never got to finish. We were drinking beer out of quart bottles at his place. What did it feel like, Richard wanted to know, and we'd start up roaring again. I don't think he ever said.

After the procession we were all standing around waiting for Hortense and for the food to be ready. Everyone was there from our road. They were still playing the music and then Hortense came toward us in her white dress with the diamonds and the ermine cape and her attendants. People were clapping and I went up meaning just to say something funny, congratulations, your highness, but I put my arms around her and I ended up kissing her on the mouth. I had watched her for ten years marching in these parades, and now she was the queen. I went on kissing her. Everyone clapped louder. I could feel my face turning red. "What do you think you're doing?" she said. "I just wanted to congratulate you," I told her.

Finally the sopas was ready—it was something you wouldn't want to eat every day, ten pounds of boiled beef with broth and cabbage—and I was sitting between Mrs. Hamada and Grayson at a long table, digging into a hunk of pretty stringy braised dairy cow with my fork. We were all having a good time. There was wine to drink if you paid for it, but I wasn't having any. The Hamadas never drank. Mats said he'd never tasted spirits. I was finishing my fourth helping when some kid came up and whispered that someone wanted to see me outside. I got up and so did Grayson and Fred. We went out back. The sun was going down. Six or seven boys stepped out from behind the shed with Richard. "I'm going to whip your ass," Richard told me.

Most people just want to fight with words, which is a lot better than busting your knuckles on someone's hard head. That's what I thought was going on here. "You keep your hands off of Hortense," Richard said. I didn't know what to answer. I looked over at Fred. I'd seen him run, but he wasn't scared: he just didn't like to mix it up, get red-faced and out of breath for nothing. He could fight. They had him cornered under the bleachers at school one time and he came up with a Okie knuckle-duster, the handle of a number ten washtub, and he started laying into those boys. They didn't like that much. Grayson looked like he was going to get another dessert for supper.

Richard's friends were town boys mostly. I knew a couple by sight. "I never meant to offend anyone," I said. "I've known Hortense my whole life." Richard took a swing at me. I stepped back. He was always bragging about when he wrestled on his high school team in the hundred-seventy-five-pound class.

"You yellow-belly coward," he said, and he swung again.

"I'm not going to fight you," I said. I don't know why I said that, but it just fed the flames. Someone else came up and pushed Fred. Grayson flipped him into the air and he landed on his back. And everyone was swinging then. There was yelling and the constable came running and we started running too.

It was dark and I didn't know who was panting next to me, hiding on our hands and knees in the nectarine orchard across the road. It was Richard. He started laughing. "I would have cleaned your clock," he said, and he laughed again. It was over for him, and he thought it was funny now. But for me it was just starting. I was feeling sick and I wanted to smash Richard's face. I was going to grab his head and stab my thumbs in his eye sockets, but Grayson came up then, and Fred, and I got up and started walking to get away, then running, until I got to our place. I took a long time to get over that feeling of wanting to hurt Richard.

Once Fred started he would never stop; you had to take the hoe away from him before he'd come in, and then he'd argue, "Goddamn it, I was just getting going here." But occasionally I'd see Fred cut loose, relax some. Richard stopped by the place, said he was on his way to Fred's and did I want to come along to a Saturday night wingding. Fred had already mentioned that Charlie might be back this weekend. I got in Richard's old Buick.

Fred and Charlie had got the roof on the house, held up by the studs, and a solid one-by-six wooden floor, but they never could afford the board and batten for the siding. In the summer they took off the canvas they had tacked up for walls. There was no electricity, of course, but there were lamps hung from nails, the gnats and moths flying around them like they were part of the light. Charlie was there and he'd brought over two women from Coalinga. There was a gallon of Okie whiskey, white lightning, and Charlie had brought a windup gramophone, and Fred was dancing.

I'd never seen him so lively without some kind of tool in his hands. While Charlie was cranking the handle for the record Fred did a Russian Cossack dance by himself, hunkered down kicking out his legs yelling hey, hey until he fell over. He didn't just pretend to take big swigs from the jug like some did, putting their tongue up the neck. You could see the bubbles popping inside the glass jug when Fred drank. When Fred decided to do something, he did it right.

The two women looked at least ten years older than us. They had come for a good time too. Both were tall and long-legged, built for hard work and he hoped we knew what kind, Charlie said. I danced and took several slugs of the whiskey, but it did what it always did, made me want to lay down and take a nap. I tried to stay lively.

Fred was the life of the party, stripping down to his shorts to stay cool, he said. One of the women, the blond one, Francine, reached in and was using his pecker for a gearshift. We were laughing so hard I forgot to breathe sometimes. Francine was making car noises, *rrrnnn, rrrnnn,* and yelling first gear, no, no, reverse, while Fred danced with her. Francine took off her clothes then and things got even livelier. I stayed on the stool next to the gramophone to keep it cranked up. Richard took Patsy, the other woman, out of the lamplight, and Charlie and Fred were humping the blonde at the same time while they tried to dance. It looked unusual, all those arms and legs moving in different directions at the same time they were trying to stay stuck together. When they all fell over for the second time Francine took them on one at a time. After each one shot, she'd jump up and douche with Seven-Up, shaking the green quart bottle back and forth with her thumb on the top until it was all fizz and then sticking it up herself, yelling, "I promised my mother no kids until I'm at least fourteen years old." She was hilarious.

When Richard came back he didn't have any clothes on either except for a white sock on his left foot. They tried to get me to take off my clothes but I didn't want to. When I did, people always had to comment. I had more hair on my back than four or five men had on their heads, not to mention the rest of me.

Francine promised me around the world, so I took off my shirt. Then she wanted to run her toes through the hair on my chest, and I lay down and let her. She stood on my chest and skipped her bare feet back and forth through my chest hair one at a time. She didn't have to try very hard to get my pants off. Patsy said, "I'm not going to fuck no gorilla," to be smart, but Francine took me out of the light and did what she promised.

We ended up taking a ride in Charlie's Studebaker. I was on the roof, humping Francine, Charlie was driving, and Fred and Patsy were draped on the hood. It was Richard's idea; he said the motion of the car and the vibration of the motor would make things exciting. Richard didn't come; he had passed out after we worked out how we were going to do it.

At first Charlie drove slow down the middle of the dirt road, but it was still hard just staying where we were, up on top. There wasn't much of a grip on the roof, and Francine had ways of moving that made it hard to concentrate. Fred had it easier because he could straddle the hood with his knees and there was the hood ornament that stopped him from sliding back, but he kept complaining that the engine must be heating up because his balls were cooking.

Charlie went up and down the road three or four times, but I didn't think it was any better than usual. Francine tried beating her heels on the roof and yodeling, and Charlie honked the horn and blinked the lights and dug gravel. I started noticing the bugs then, not just the moths and the regular night insects, but one as long as your thumb, iridescent green with little wings, and some yellow ones, and one that looked like a dragonfly. They'd stopped getting in my nose and mouth but they were nesting in my hair, hundreds of them. You couldn't see the dark anymore because they were everywhere, lighting up the sky and surrounding the car. It seemed like we were screwing inside a flower, and it was holy, lovely, endless; I could feel their wings and their mouths all over my body.

Then Fred yelled out, "Try going faster, Charlie," and Charlie slammed the car into third gear and we took off with the insects trying to catch up with me at the same time I was pounding Francine and she was yelping and pulling the hair out of my back. Then Charlie hit a chuckhole and I bounced off the roof and Francine and onto the road and then rolled into a ditch.

They must have kept going because it was dark when I woke up naked and my leg was hurting bad and making me feel dizzy. I couldn't limp but a few paces without stopping, and the trouble was I didn't know where I was. I saw an irrigation ditch and followed that; they always led somewhere. I came to a shack, half cardboard, half tin. The sun was rising by that time and an old woman was up and starting a fire in an open pit with a grill and a coffee can on top. She acted like it was an everyday occurrence that she'd see someone in my condition come down the road. "You want some coffee?" she asked. I sat down on the chopping block and she handed me a bowl of coffee. She looked at my leg then and went into the cardboard side of the shack. I could see my leg good for the first time. From my hip to my knee was raw meat oozing blood. I couldn't look. The woman came back out doing something with a pint jar and a kerosene can. She looked familiar in a way, but old Okie women that age all looked the same.

Washed-out cotton dress, men's boots, and a pair of glasses, thin hair cut short. She came over with the jar and I thought it was moonshine she wanted me to drink and I was going to be sick, but it was turpentine and she poured it over my bleeding leg. It hurt so bad I took a deep breath to bellow but I couldn't make a sound, just started panting, and I realized I'd passed out and fallen off the chopping block. She tied a clean flour sack around my leg with string and found me a pair of trousers with all the buttons missing from the fly and holes in the knees and seat, and rubber knee boots, one cut off at the ankle. Some spare things, she called them. I thanked her, of course. Told her our road number and what our house looked like and she would be welcome for a visit. She nodded. And I told her I'd be back, and started down the ditch. It wasn't until I wandered around a little that I realized where I was, and I headed back to our place.

After a couple of days, when I was feeling better and I could get around, Fred and I tried to find her camp. People were all over, half hiding, camped on someone else's land, trying to find work and stay alive. I didn't know how far I'd walked to get there or how far after I left. We never found the camp or the woman.

I told my folks and the Zia a good woman might come by to visit and they were to be kind to her. They always were; I didn't have to remind them. No tramps or people out of work ever passed our place and went away without something, fruit or bread or eggs. The Hamadas were always helping people down on their luck. The Brazils too, but Hortense's mother made them do chores first before she fed them.

A couple of weeks later I saw a old woman with a sack picking mustard greens along the road. When I stopped the car and walked back to where she was, I could see she wasn't the old woman who had helped me. I had been changing my mind on what I wanted to give her back, and now I knew I was never going to find her. I tried to give this old woman a dollar bill, a box of chocolate-covered cherries, and a sweater wrapped in white tissue my Zia made me that was too small. "I don't take charity," she said. I tried to explain this was just a gift. I was almost yelling at her, but she didn't look convinced. Finally she took the stuff and I got away. When I told Fred later he said, "You should have kept the dollar for your own self."

HORTENSE

chapter 12

When we graduated from high school I was so damned happy. It was like we'd played a trick on someone, sitting up on the stage in our graduation gowns, getting our diplomas. Julian was next to me, blowing his nose with a big white handkerchief. Reiko sat on my other side, watching Fred in the audience. Fred had missed too much school to have enough credits to graduate. Richard was there too, sitting with my family. It was an occasion: all three of my sisters had graduated, but not my two brothers. Mr. and Mrs. Hamada and Grayson sat next to the Palestini family. I couldn't get over the idea that we had finally passed all the requirements and they had to give us a diploma now, and with that piece of paper you could get a job like Richard's in the bank. I wasn't going to have to get up at four-thirty every morning to milk, day in and day out. It didn't matter that there weren't any jobs; I could still get a job.

I received the twenty-five-dollar scholarship from the Cabrillo Club for the class of 1940. Reiko was the salutatorian, but she also read the speech the valedictorian, Luther Tamatsu, had written. Luther was too shy to speak. His speech was called "Working Together to Change the

World." It was a wonderful ceremony. After it, we had a dance. There was punch and cookies and someone was supposed to have spiked the punch and all the boys were acting drunk. I danced every dance with Richard.

I found out you could go to summer school at the junior college and I signed up. When I mentioned it to Reiko she said she didn't want to be a teacher anymore, just like that. "But you always wanted to be a teacher," I said.

Not anymore. She got a job as a waitress at the hotel. I went to school at the junior college in town. I didn't care what she did. College was harder than high school, but it was easier too: you were there because you wanted to be, and you got things done faster. I was trying to get some of the heavy subjects out of the way, English and history, before going up to Fresno Normal School for the two-year certificate to teach.

I helped pick at the Hamadas', but I didn't see Reiko like before, when we went to high school together every day. I heard she was thinking of taking a trip to Japan with her mother to see her grandmother, who was sick. We phoned each other a couple of times. Richard was promoted to head teller. I was so proud of him. I didn't see Fred; he was working over in Lost Hills in the oil fields with Charlie. Julian was working in the vines at their place and happy to be doing it, after that battle they had with the Land Company.

I was glad Julian had won. I could never forget that morning Grayson came over and told us what had happened at the Palestinis' over the cotton. Julian's father never knew he was signing over his vineyard against the lease contract from the Land Company and that there was a time limit on the repayment. We went over right away. Fred and the Palestinis had been picking for a couple days before we got there. Julian had tried to hire pickers, but no one would come out. Even the Okies wouldn't; they were afraid, too. We knew why, and who they were afraid of.

Cotton has no mercy on you. It's the worst kind of plant in the valley to harvest. You're dragging a ten-foot-long canvas bag behind you, and your hands reaching for the cotton get cut up on the branches, and then your arms get cut up and you get tired and the bag keeps getting heavier and heavier. By noon I could hear the old Zia crying while she talked to herself. It wasn't so hot by then, and that made it a little better, but you still sweated your brains out. My folks had come, Reiko's, some others. The Palestini girls and their husbands couldn't come: they all worked at a packing plant over in Reedley that the Land Company owned. Charlie was even out there; you could hear him swearing, "Jesus, take me, Jesus."

We got one cotton trailer loaded. It took most of the morning. They always looked to me like a twenty-foot chicken run on wheels, high wire mesh sides on a wood floor attached to two axles with two sets of car tires. Julian hooked it up to the sedan and took it over to the gin. It was a occasion: we all sat under the oak and swigged water and made jokes. As far as we knew, we were the first ones to take cotton to the gin this year. Everyone in the county always remarked on who was the first. It was fitting to be ahead of everyone; we had Mr. McInteer and the Land Company pushing us.

I was doing the Zia's hair into a pigtail—her bun had fallen apart—when I looked up the road and saw Julian bringing back the cotton trailer, still full of the cotton we had picked. The gin foreman had said they weren't authorized to take the cotton. We just had to wait our turn, he told Julian. Wait. We knew what that meant. Our turn would never come.

Charlie knew someone, and he started phoning all over the county to find out what gin he worked at. We finished the second trailer and there was still no place to gin the cotton. It was dark, but there was a moon. We had stopped to eat, but no one talked. When he was finished Fred got up and went back out to the field. I didn't think I could move, but I got up on my feet and started down a row. You could see enough in the moonlight to pick the white cotton.

We all knew that if they could take Palestinis' place, they could take ours too if they wanted to. I picked and kept going, but I must have fallen asleep along a row on my bag, because when I woke up in the middle of the field the third cotton trailer was filled and Charlie was hooking it up to take to Corcoran. He'd found a gin over there that would take the Palestinis' cotton.

We picked that field clean in a week's time. Never one speck of white to be seen: it looked like a fire had passed through the row after row of stripped branches on those plants. And Julian settled with the Land Company. Mr. Hart told him to take care of the business through the home office in Sacramento, and that's what he did. The next thing he did was get a tractor and plow down that goddamn cotton into the dirt so there was no trace left.

* * *

When Reiko did phone, it was to say she was going to be a nurse now; she'd enrolled in a nursing program up at Fresno Normal. She had a ride up there each day on a feed truck. I had almost talked myself into staying at the junior college for another semester at least. It was cheaper, and I could get used to things. There was a Portuguese woman, Mrs. Duarte, who taught there in the English department, and it made me feel confident every time I saw her. Fresno seemed like a long way off. "Are you coming with me or not?" Reiko asked.

"Pick me up," I said. "I'll be out on the road."

I'd always thought I wanted to teach first or second grade when I had my daydreams of wearing high heels and a dress all day, because the young Holsteins were easier to handle than the older cows. The program for the two-year certificate was taught by former teachers who had all worked in elementary schools before. They knew the ropes. The first week we learned how to use construction paper to make bulletin boards for the seasons of the year. We practiced writing on the blackboard: your handwriting had to be good enough for the teacher to read without her glasses from the back of the room. We learned how to make a substitute school paste with flour and water in case we ran out. We learned little songs: Brush, brush, brush your teeth, every single day, Once or twice or even thrice to keep the germs away. We made green crepe paper hats to go with the Celery Song: I'll brush out your stomach and make your teeth white, If you eat of me freely your eyes will be bright. Sometimes I felt like I was back in the second grade myself. I had got as far as trigonometry in high school, and now was doing adding and subtracting in college. They recommended we take piano lessons.

One afternoon I went over to the biology room to wait for Reiko. She was in the lab doing something with a microscope. It looked interesting, and I helped her with the slides. It was better than high school biology because no one was goofing off and you were on your own. You could work as hard as you wanted. I mentioned to Reiko that I thought the teaching certificate program was a waste of time. "You can always go back to milking cows the rest of your life," she said. We both laughed like old times.

The next day I asked if I could get into the nursing program, and they let me, with Reiko saying she'd help me catch up. It was just too hard at first. Reiko did everything like she'd done it before a hundred times, but it wasn't like that for me. I'd read those books, but it was like they were in Portuguese. I understood it, but when it came to actually talking for ten minutes in the language, I couldn't do it very well. I studied. I made it through the fall and we started the spring semester.

I was still helping with the milking, of course, and seeing Richard too. He was getting fresh with me. Put his hand up my blouse, and then tried to unfasten my bra. I told him no, but he did it again the next time, and the next time after that. I sewed my bra closed at the snap and put it on over my head. He could never get that off.

Reiko didn't go out with anyone; she stayed home studying or working at her place. Every morning she'd be sitting on a sack in the back of that truck for our ride to Fresno. We were out of the wind, since there was a canvas top, and it was comfortable as long as they weren't hauling something that had been milled into powder and got all over our clothes. We wore bandanas to keep our hair clean.

We were walking toward the campus one morning when Reiko took her bandana off and shook out her hair. It was as orange as a persimmon. I didn't know what to say. It was hard to see the same person as before. "What do you think?" she asked again.

"It matches your sweater," I said.

"Peroxide," Reiko said. "It was supposed to be blond."

Fred was coming over from the oil fields that weekend to start picking the second crop of strawberries. I wasn't there when he showed up at the Hamada place, but later that morning I saw him staring at Reiko when he didn't think she was watching. She had let her peroxided hair hang loose so the sun could lighten it some more. Life was like a movie, but you had to know what to watch.

Julian showed up a little after eight. He was funny; he and Fred acted like they hadn't seen each other for a hundred years, slapping each other on the back and hooting. "You big dumb Okie, how you've been?" he yelled.

Fred yelled back, "You Wopaho! Mats, this Italian picker has been here for five minutes already—we better bring out the refreshments; it's lunchtime."

Mr. Hamada peered at them from under his new pith helmet and asked, "Is it time?"

"He's kidding you, Pop," Reiko said, and Mr. Hamada snickered, lifting his wrist up to show his watch.

It didn't matter where they were with the strawberry harvest, every Sunday at ten-thirty Mr. Hamada took his family into town to the Presbyterian church. The dairy came first in our family. We'd stay and pick, and in about an hour and half they'd be back, change their clothes, and we'd all be out in the field together, bent over, our backs all hurting the same.

A couple of times Richard came out to pick. Richard wasn't from the valley, so he didn't understand a lot of things. He was always trying to explain that he was Castilian Spanish and that Cortez was a common name in Castile. Hernando Cortés was Spanish. He explained that to my father one time. Later my father said, "He's okay by me, whatever he thinks he is." Richard even tried signing his name Cortes sometimes. He didn't understand that people didn't need a real good reason to look down on you, and that trying to change yourself to suit them was a mistake. As long as you minded your own business, you had a chance. The Japanese were like that; they were like shadows in the county. They just worked their place and kept their mouths closed. I never heard the Hamadas mention any of the articles in the *Bee* that spoke bad about Japanese Americans. Never. That's what was so puzzling about Reiko. She was Japanese American like I was Portuguese American; we were born here, so we were Americans, but you couldn't change what you happened to look like. How could you not want to be Japanese if that's what you were? Peroxiding your hair didn't change anything. Her mother and father were still Japanese. The other Japanese girls didn't act like she did. It was like she was always saying look at me; I'm different. She was doing this to herself.

My father thought Italians were all crazy. That's what he called them, crazy Italians; he thought they all had a screw loose. My sister, when she was in high school, went to a dance and danced with an Italian. When my father heard about it he was going to disown her, throw her out of the house. And all that time he liked the Palestinis; he'd be the first one there to help. I asked him one time how he could be the Palestinis' friend and not like Italians. "Don't get smart with me," he said. Richard thought the Italians were just funny. He told stories about when they came into the bank: here's a dollar for you and here's a dollar for me. And Richard was always talking about how he made Julian back down when he tried to pick a fight. I worried he might try that again with Julian. My father had seen the end of what happened when Julian and Elton McInteer got into it. He was walking through their vineyard to get home and he heard the noise: this was after the cotton had been ginned. Julian was trying to upend the car, rocking it higher each time, getting ready to turn it over on the roof; that's how Elton got his nose broke, hitting his head against the steering wheel like a battering ram, my father said. The bumper broke off and Julian had no grip left so he went and got his shovel and started whacking the car, tearing big holes in the metal. Julian would have killed him if Elton McInteer hadn't got the car started and got out of there.

We were still harvesting the second crop when I went over to pick strawberries early on Saturday morning. The Hamadas' flatbed went by our gate with a load of full crates they were delivering to a shipper. Grayson's folks were in the cab and he was sitting in the back. "I'm going over to pick," I yelled, and they waved. It was still dark; the moon was trying to decide if it was going to stay or disappear. I went into the shed to get some crates and I heard a sound. I thought it was their cat. I took a step closer. It was Fred and Reiko on the gunnysacks.

I had never seen humans couple. The animals, of course, one time or another. That always seemed violent, the rooster pulling feathers out of the hen's neck, the drake nearly drowning the duck, horses biting each other. A bull mounts a cow like a locomotive ramming a coal car. Fred was on top and Reiko's knees were bent and splayed. This wasn't violent: it looked like their bodies were joining and separating again in some slow, deliberate motion like a butterfly's wings when it's stopped on a flower. It was like they weren't really touching. Then Reiko made a sound, a sigh, their lazy shadows swaying against the wall, and I understood how strongly they were connected. I had never heard a sound like that before. I backed out and went into the field and started picking.

I thought Mr. and Mrs. Hamada or probably Grayson would notice something. It seemed like every time I looked at one of them that day all I saw was Reiko on her back or Fred on top. If Julian noticed, he didn't say anything to me. It was embarrassing. "You better be careful, Reiko," I whispered once when she brought a jug of water around the field to us. She acted like she didn't know what I was talking about.

She phoned me the next morning that she wasn't going to school anymore; she and Fred were going to Bakersfield to live. I caught my ride on the feed truck, and when I came home from school we passed the Hamadas' and Reiko was there in the field picking strawberries. The next day she was on the feed truck going back up to Fresno. She didn't say anything. The next weekend Fred didn't come up to pick. Reiko didn't seem to notice.

In July Richard was drafted, the first peacetime draft in the country's history, my father said. He got me into the backseat of his car but I wouldn't do it. He said he might die protecting the United States of America, but I still wouldn't do it. Richard left for Wisconsin without asking me to wait for him, but I planned to anyway.

Some people thought we were going to get into the war in Europe and some didn't. It depended on who you talked to. But something was happening in the valley: the government was building several airfields, and people were leaving for federal jobs in other parts of the state. It wasn't just the government; things were picking up for dairies, too. My father started milking ten more cows. Workers were making up to seventy-five cents an hour now in the factories. My father said that before the Depression started you could make five or six dollars a day, but the average after 1930 had dropped to about twenty cents an hour. He liked repeating all those figures he'd read in the paper. With all the countries at war, he said, they weren't going to have time to grow any crops over there, and the valley could make some money. It made sense to me. I didn't mind doing my chores. My folks had always given me room and board, and they were helping me pay for the nursing program at Fresno Normal.

One part of the nursing course required you to work in a hospital. It was all arranged in town. I liked the hospital; it was a lot like the dairy. During your shift you went around to the patients and cleaned them up and then fed them, made sure they were comfortable. It didn't bother me about the bedpans or the gore when someone had a baby. I'd reached up a cow the length of my arm to my shoulder to get a calf started in the right direction, and the hospital paid us fifty-five cents an hour.

Right after we went back to school in September the Army drafted Julian, sent him to Camp Roberts over at the coast. Richard they had sent from Wisconsin to Texas. We hadn't seen anything of Fred all summer. And we only heard about Julian. He was supposed to have made some big money, almost a thousand dollars, somehow, speculating on commodities, my father thought, and he shook his head. He didn't have to say crazy Italians out loud anymore.

Second-year students got to wear the white uniform but not the cap yet. I used to wash and iron that uniform every night, the cotton so stiff with starch it was like cowhide. I was so happy sometimes I'd start singing like a canary, no words, just chirping, glad to be alive. If I said so myself, I was getting prettier. I cut my red hair short, and my head looked smaller, Reiko said. I was wearing a size eight uniform, the smallest I'd ever been able to get on. My rear end was narrower, too.

Julian was able to come home from Camp Roberts for a couple of days at a time. You never saw him in a uniform if he could help it. He was the same old Julian, laughing it up with everyone, but he was different too; I couldn't say how. With that money he'd got he built a bathroom onto the back of the house, had some Army friends sneak over some equipment from the coast, and they used that to dig the leach system and trenches for the pipes. When my father saw that, he had to have one too, and Julian came over and did the work. It took four or five hours to do the trenching with the Army equipment. He did the Hamadas' and Fred's too. Indoor plumbing, you never realized what a wonderful invention it was until you didn't have to go outside in the rain anymore to where the black widows were waiting for you sit on them. The old Zia was supposed to have asked Julian if he was going to put two commodes in their bathroom like the two-hole outhouse that she and Mrs. Palestini used at the same time. He took Mabel Hastings' tank house apart board by board after the city ran water pipes out to her place, and hauled the boards out to Fred's shack. He got some more Army friends to come over and they put up those old redwood one-by-twelves for board-and-batten siding. The unweathered sides were purple and looked like new wood. My father was over there to watch; he couldn't keep away with all these changes happening on the road. One of the soldiers was an electrician and he wired Fred's house, though there was no electricity that far out yet. It looked like a different place now. Someone could actually live in that house; it wasn't just a pile of loose boards with a tin roof that looked like it might fall down of its own weight.

Grayson was there when Fred came back from Bakersfield and saw his place for the first time after Julian got finished. Fred started crying, Grayson said, and didn't even know there were tears coming out of his eyes. He couldn't even speak, just picked up an old broom and started sweeping the new porch.

On Sundays when Julian was home they'd have a feed over at the Palestinis' that was like a feast. It was still warm enough to eat outside, and they'd set up a table twenty feet long with benches running down the sides full of the soldiers and the Palestini family and some of the neighbors; Grayson was always there and so was I. The soldiers were homesick, probably, and happy to have a home-cooked meal, and after a couple of glasses of wine they'd all be laughing and shouting.

Julian was always up to something. If he heard of a farmer who'd got one of the jobs that were opening up and wanted to sell his place, Julian was right there with his cash and the bank's money too. He bought twenty acres once and fifteen another time, near his home place. There were a lot of people willing to sell: they could think of better things to do than spend twelve hours a day working and not make any money doing it. Then he got a thirty-acre place and everyone was holding their breath. There was cotton on the thirty-acre parcel; the others were planted in vines. It was like he'd forgotten what happened with the Land Company. And my father had heard Mr. McInteer didn't like it. When Julian came home now, if he wasn't at his place he was in town at Mabel Hastings', overnight sometimes, I heard.

One afternoon he stopped by our place just to talk. These days Julian seemed relaxed, like he was always happy with himself. "How's Richard doing, Hortense?" he asked me. "Is he a general yet?"

"They sent him to a school to learn watch repair," I told him. I laughed too, though I didn't know why it was funny, Richard fixing watches.

Julian gave me a ride into town then, to the hospital. He never asked about Reiko anymore; we just talked. I asked him, "If the Army sends you somewhere else like they sent Richard to Texas, who's going to take care of those new acres of vines?"

"We'll hire the picking, contract it out."

"Julian, haven't you noticed the Okies are disappearing now? You can't go out and get a dozen to pick anymore. The Army is taking them too now. What if there's a war? There won't be anyone left, and your folks and the Zia aren't going to be able to work that much land." I don't know why I was talking to him like this. The way we were talking now reminded me of when we were kids and we'd be in the vineyard pruning the old canes and just to be funny he'd put me up on his shoulders and we'd go down a row pruning like that, me getting the high ones and Julian the lower, telling each other things. He was never going to marry a woman with a mustache and a big rear end like all the women in his family, and I was going to be the princess at the Holy Ghost procession. We must have been eleven or twelve.

"I never thought of the harvesting part, but I did about my family," he said. "That's why I thought it was worth the risk. I wanted us to own enough land so we didn't have to worry that we'd spend more than we made, like you do with forty acres, always feeling you can never get ahead. I won the money in a payday crap game, never rolled a pair of dice before in my life. I couldn't lose. With that kind of money in my pocket, I thought I should spend it as fast I could. Farming is a crap game too, and I should have thought it out better. I still think it's not going to be as bad as you say. There'll always be someone left to work in the valley. I only paid twenty-seven dollars an acre, so I don't owe the bank too much. I couldn't stop buying; I had to have that land."

He rubbed his head. "You've got me worried, Hortense." Then he started laughing. "If there's just one man left to work around here, Hortense, I hope it's Fred Leeds."

We milked that Sunday like always and were eating our breakfast when Julian drove into the yard. We knew something was up because he was running. He jumped over the porch steps and called through the screen door, "Pearl Harbor has been bombed. We have to get back. Hortense," he yelled, "go over to the place when you can."

"I will, Julian," I yelled back. He had four other soldiers with him waiting in his car. My father turned on the radio and you could hear the word *war* all over the house. Then I thought of Richard; was I ever going to see him again? Or Julian, for that matter?

When the Hamadas went by on their way to church, Reiko dropped off the nursing manual we shared so I could study. "Stupid Nipponese," she said. "We'll show them."

We went to school Monday like always. The wind was blowing and the feed truck was hauling flour that was coating us with dust. "The first thing I'm going to do when I get a nursing job is buy a car," I told Reiko. "This is a goddamn pain in the ass." There were all kinds of rumors once we got to school. They were going to shorten the program. Registered nurses were being recruited into the Army as second lieutenants after they graduated.

We went on doing the same things we always did. The war didn't seem to interrupt anything in the valley. The cows still had to be milked. It was winter, so there wasn't much going on other than the citrus packing sheds, which were going full blast. Richard wrote and said they were sending him to another school again, in Florida. Julian came back two weekends after Pearl Harbor to finish pruning the vines. He told my father that the Army generals would be the last men in this country to know how to fight a war.

It was only just before Christmas that we started wondering what was going to happen next. Two Border Patrol agents came and picked up Mr. Hamada as an enemy alien. No one knew what to think. The rumors started up fierce: we weren't safe from getting our throats slit by the California Japanese.

Not everyone thought that way. I'd go into the college library and read the newspapers, one after another, to try and understand. They kept writing about the difference between the generations, the Issei non-citizens like Mr. and Mrs. Hamada and the Nisei citizens like Reiko and Grayson, about loyalty to this country and to Japan, and who was a potential saboteur, and what happened in Hawaii.

There were government people who couldn't leave it alone. Every time they opened their mouths they talked about the Japanese threat, spies and saboteurs and fifth columnists. It made you wonder where these people had been living the last twenty years: certainly not in California. The Japanese worked hard; how could they have time for all this other bullshit? Reiko didn't say much about it, called the politicians nitwits.

My father, who liked a good argument as well as anyone, said they did the same thing to the California Germans in the First World War. "They just need a scapegoat," he said. "They'll run out of steam. Mats will be back before long. If they try to round up the Japanese, they'll have to round up everyone from Germany and Italy and the rest of the Axis countries too." The Hamadas were receiving letters from Mr. Hamada from somewhere in Nebraska. He was okay, he wrote, and they might let him come back pretty soon.

Fred showed up. He'd broken both his forearms in an accident on a drilling rig. He couldn't do much with his hands in casts, but he tried. He painted the outside of his place by wedging the end of the paintbrush between the plaster cast and his hand. He was driving himself crazy, not being able to work. Reiko was with him a lot. She still went to school most days, but she was over at Fred's place too. I heard her ask Grayson what he thought of Fred for a brother-in-law.

Then a notice went up on the store bulletin board that all persons of Japanese ancestry were to be sent to assembly places. The Japanese from our district were to go up to the Fresno fairgrounds. "Can the government do that?" I asked my father. He had the top part of an old calendar printed with the Constitution and the Bill of Rights pinned up in the barn. He'd studied the Constitution to get his citizenship papers. He just looked at me without answering and went over to milk another cow. On the way up to school I asked Reiko, "Are you going?"

She seemed surprised. "It's for our own good. It's protective custody; we heard that at church. You know what people are saying." It wasn't only what they were saying. I'd read that a Chinese man in Los Angeles had been beaten to death by some Filipinos who thought he was Japanese. "How long can it last?" Reiko said. "As soon as things calm down, we'll be back. My father wrote last week that Grayson and I are American citizens and the law will protect us. He wants us to just do what they say for now."

They could only take as much with them as they could carry. They needed bedding too, besides kitchen things to cook with. Grayson was loaded down like a packhorse. It was like a game to him, trying to see how many suitcases and bags he could carry. Fred and Julian and I drove them up to Fresno. "You all look like a bunch of Okies," Fred said when we picked him up at his place. We had the suitcases tied on the roof. Everyone was trying to make light of the trip, like we might end up having some fun.

The Hamadas were assigned a stall in the old stable where they kept the horses for the fair races. We swept it out. It was full of dust and old hay. The walls only went up halfway to the roof, and you could hear all the noise from the families in the other stalls along the row. There were soldiers with fixed bayonets on their rifles on guard outside. People were milling around trying to find their places, dragging their luggage, their kids shouting and running. We weren't even supposed to be inside, but Julian had told the guard that he was a minister of the church of the vines and these were his parishioners he'd come to deposit. The soldier waved us through, probably because Julian was in uniform. I heard Julian say to a soldier posted near the Hamada stall, "Hey, buddy, you think this is necessary?" and he put his finger on the point of the bayonet. It's orders, the soldier told him. "I suppose all these little kids can turn dangerous," Julian said. The soldier's face turned red and he took the bayonet off.

We'd brought a picnic lunch. We sat in the stall on the cots with straw-filled mattresses the Army had provided and ate our sandwiches. Mrs. Hamada had worn her Sunday clothes, her tan suit and silk blouse, her green hat with a little netting to one side, and white gloves.

Reiko and Fred sat next to each other but they only touched by accident. The neighbors' little kids kept coming into the stall, and we fed them too from what was left of our picnic. I hated to leave the Hamadas there, but they were announcing over a loudspeaker that all non-internees must depart at 1400. A little girl had fallen asleep on my lap, and we could hear her older brother asking their mother, "Are we in Japan, Mom? Is that why all the Japanese are around here?"

"Do you realize we had to help a family leave their own house who've never done anything wrong to anyone?" Julian said, driving back. "Their home place, their fields? This country is going to the dogs. It makes me sick to think about it."

I couldn't keep up with everything. With myself, my feelings, school, the dairy, going up to visit the Hamadas. I was sitting in classes two miles away from Reiko, who was sitting in a horse stall and not allowed to leave the center. My father didn't like what was happening. He'd passed a place in Fowler where they were auctioning off farm equipment for Japanese who had been evacuated at about ten cents on the dollar. "They're using this business as a license to steal," he said. "What's going to happen to their land?"

My mother caught two men and a woman coming out of the Hamadas' front door carrying lamps and dishes and kitchen chairs. She asked them what they thought they were doing. They argued with her that the Japs weren't coming back and the goods were for the taking. Fred came by in the middle of the yelling. He didn't say a word; with his casts still on his arms he picked up a board and tried to hit one of the men in the head. They dropped the stuff and ran. They had been well-dressed people too, not poor Okies. They had kicked the front door in. My father took a walk over to the Hamadas' now and again at odd times. He'd tried phoning the sheriff's department, but they just laughed. "Serves them right," they said. The Palestinis, who were closer, went over nearly every day to water the flowerpots and sweep the porch to make the place look like there was someone there. I went once with my mother, and the old Zia was sitting on the back steps knitting and singing in Italian.

We stopped in to see Mr. Hart one afternoon, Julian and me. Mr. Hart had tried to find out what was going to happen to Mats. He knew a lot more than most people because of the Land Company. We sat in his office while he talked to us. I'd never been in there before. He was speaking to Julian and me like we were adults and already understood the things he was saying about the government. "The FBI has its camps; that's where Mats is. And the War Relocation Authority has its camps; that's where the Hamadas are going after they leave the assembly area. President Roosevelt has signed an order that all the Japanese, citizens or not, can be moved out of the West Coast. No one knows what to do. The sorry fact, Julian, is that seventy percent of those people are American citizens like Reiko and Grayson."

"What about the Italians; are we going to get rounded up too?" Julian asked.

"I don't know. You have a lot more power; there are Italian American congressmen. The Japanese immigrants in this country couldn't own land, couldn't vote, and had no power. They kept to themselves, and now they're going to pay for it. The newspapers are all against them. I keep thinking if Ray Hamada were alive, would this be happening? He had the guts and the money to do something. When we were up at the hunting camp once I heard him tell the attorney general of the state to be quiet when he was spouting some crap about the Chinese, and the man shut his trap. Now this new one we've got is yelling at the top of his lungs, 'A good Jap is a dead Jap,' and no one is contradicting him."

Julian was still coming home from Camp Roberts every weekend now, and we'd go up to Fresno together. Each time it was worse. Everyone was more dejected, cooped up behind all those fences. They were starting to move people to the permanent camps, all of them far away—Arizona, Utah, Wyoming, or Arkansas. All this was happening, but no one seemed in control or knew why.

We always brought a lunch and anything else the Hamadas let us know they needed. Julian kept Grayson supplied with baseball equipment he got from the Army base. They had started a camp league for the boys his age. Julian would dump a sackful of gloves and balls and bats on the stable floor and Grayson and his friends would whoop and grab the stuff. Reiko kept studying our nursing books. She didn't ask about Fred when he didn't come. His broken bones had healed, and he'd taken the casts off himself and gone back to work in Bakersfield with Charlie. Mrs. Hamada just sat there in her cotton dress and hat like she was going out to the fields to pick strawberries.

We never knew each visit if it was the last time we were going to see them or not. We told them some of the things Mr. Hart had said, but saying it was mass hysteria didn't help them, locked up like they were, or that the people who were doing this would be sorry. I didn't believe that myself when I said it.

Then they were gone. We weren't able to go up one weekend, and the next Thursday I got a postcard from Arizona. "I never thought I'd miss the Fresno fairgrounds, but I do. This is worse. It's hot, with dust storms, and there are rattlesnakes. This is nothing but a goddamn prison, Hortense. They have guard towers with machine guns and barbed wire fences. They have us in a jail. Love, Reiko." I showed it to Julian when he came home that weekend. He just shook his head.

You never saw much in the papers. Richard sent an article he cut out of a Florida newspaper with a quote from our attorney general, Earl Warren, in big black letters: "The Japanese will be prevented at all costs from forming a fifth column in California to destroy our defenses." We had never heard any stories about the Japanese doing anything wrong here. They never broke a law before the war either. The feed store where we traded put up a sign reading, WE DO NOT SERVE JAPS. My father asked the owner to take it down and he did. The owner knew the Hamadas too; they bought there. "The American Legion brought these signs around," he said. He was shamefaced when he talked, my father said.

When Julian came over from the coast he'd do what he could at the Hamadas' besides working at his own place. He got the strawberry sets out in time, and when it got warm I irrigated. We had two big pickings and were lucky to be able to hire help. And we got a price, too; you could sell anything now, with the war. Julian got his raisins in too; there was supposed to be an early storm, but it didn't rain and he got the best price the Palestinis had ever got. Food was like gold now, and so was milk. We were selling most of ours to contractors who turned it into dried milk for the government. We were milking seventy-eight cows now.

Then Julian got his orders and was shipped out somewhere at the end of September. He had left me the money from the Hamadas' harvest to pay the taxes. Fred and I were going to try to get someone to work the place on shares. Julian had told his parents that they weren't to sign anything with anyone unless I read it first and said it was okay. They understood what could happen with the Land Company. When I passed the Palestinis' the morning after Julian left, I could hear the old Zia wailing.

GRAYSON

chapter 13

Two men in raincoats knocked on the door on December 19th. They gave my father an hour to get his things together and go with them. They sat in the front room waiting for Father, who was shaving in the bathroom. Mother was getting his clothes packed. "It's for the good of the country," one of the men told my father. But my father hadn't asked any questions after they had identified themselves and told him their orders.

Then Reiko came in soaked, laughing. She'd been over to Hortense's, studying. We could hear her kicking off her boots against the wall and putting on her slippers. My mother told her in whispers who the men were and that they were taking Father. I heard her go into the bathroom and talk to my father first. "Why?" she kept asking him. Then she went into the front room and asked the two men.

"It's a national emergency," one said.

"But my father hasn't done anything to the government."

"It's not a pleasant situation for anyone," he said.

"Then why do it?"

"It's orders," he said. They were Border Patrol agents. I saw the decal on their car door. I was watching them through the keyhole of the kitchen door. My mother started crying when my father came out, ready in twenty minutes instead of the hour they'd given him. Just tears were coming down her cheeks; she didn't make a sound. My father was wearing his Sunday suit, white shirt, and tie, carrying his leather suitcase and topcoat and fedora. One of the men stood up and took the case and went over by the front door.

Reiko was going crazy in her room like she did when she was mad at someone, slamming the closet door, stomping her feet against the floor, making the whole house shake. I shook hands with my father and he nodded at me and they led him out and put him in the back of their Ford. It was raining hard still, and the two men were getting in the front of the car when Reiko came running around the side of the house screaming at them, soaked to the skin, "What about our strawberries? You can't take him. We need him here on the place. Everyone knows our berries. What will people say?"

After that the house was always quiet. We would sit there as if we were waiting for another knock on the door. We didn't play the radio because of what we might hear: the war news, what soldiers from Japan were doing to us. I told my mother if they could just take Father like that, they would bring him the same way when they found out he hadn't done anything.

I went back to high school after the Christmas holidays. I didn't know what to expect, but I was ready with a knuckle sandwich for anyone that called me names or gave me any trouble. No one said a word. We went to church on Sunday like before. My father was the only one taken so far from our congregation. People came up and wished my mother well. White people. It meant something to her to have the old ladies take her hands, asking if there was anything they could do to help. Most of the Japanese Americans in the church were frightened. They didn't come near us.

We got a note from my father in January that we weren't to worry; he was fine. He never mentioned where he was. We were to keep on studying hard, me at the high school and Reiko in her nursing program. He didn't give us an address to write back to.

I had never really thought much beyond getting up and going to school. I'd never thought if I was going to be a farmer or not. I'd always just done what my father said. Now I had to decide about the planting; without him I had no choice. We usually rotated the fields, plowed under the strawberries every three years and replanted new sets. So I started to plow after school, getting the fields ready to plant. My mother and Reiko helped, and Julian was usually home from the coast on weekends if I had any questions.

It was the rumors we kept hearing that kept us off balance, like we were going to be the next ones taken. They can't do that, Reiko said. We're American citizens. A Nisei kid in my geography class, Wilbur Tamatsu, disappeared one day, never came back to school. I heard his family made a run for it. The father got everyone in the car one night and took off. Drove all the way to Minnesota, where they had relatives. You could leave the coast still. But we had nowhere to go, and we couldn't leave here because my father might come back home. It was not knowing what was going to happen next that made it so hard. We just had the rumors to think about, and they were always bad.

My mother acted like everything was going to be all right. She would say, When your father comes back we'll do this, or go there. One time Reiko said, "What if he doesn't come back?" My mother ignored her. But Reiko got louder each time Mother said it, and she started shouting once, "He's never coming back, get that through your thick Jap head."

When we heard that we were going to have to leave our house, our fields, the road, and go up to Fresno to the assembly center, I never believed it would really happen. It didn't seem like they'd actually make us leave. I told myself it was all a mistake, that they'd change their minds. I'd started spring practice with the baseball team, driving my father's car in to school and getting back in time to do the chores before dark. As a junior I had a good chance to make the varsity team. I had been waiting for this since I was seven or eight, when my grandfather first took me to a game in town at Recreation Park. My mother and father had come to every game I'd ever played in.

They took us in March, before our first game with Bakersfield. I still didn't believe they'd make us stay in Fresno until that night, when I was trying to sleep on the floor of the horse stall. I could hear one of the little kids crying next door, just sobbing her heart out. The walls only went up three quarters of the way to the ceiling. You could hear eight or nine stalls down on either side. We were all awake, listening. Someone on the other side said as clear as day, "I wish I were dead." A woman's voice. It sounded close, like the person was in the stall with the three of us. "Maybe we're already dead," Reiko said. And she started crying too.

It was the way Hortense, Fred, and Julian kept coming up to see us that gave us hope. They'd arrive and it was like Christmastime, the things they'd bring. And they'd act like this was only temporary and we'd be back on our road soon enough. And while they were there we'd forget the rumors. The latest was that the authorities were going to send us back to Japan in exchange for the American soldiers taken captive in the Philippines.

I never saw Fred so talkative. He would try to get my mother to talk too, but it was hard for her. Hortense was always the same, like she was in the middle of milking and she had to hurry, doing four things at once, telling us in one long breath that Mr. Hart sent his regards and five pounds of sugar, her father had tried to phone our congressman but couldn't get through, the nursing school would not allow Reiko to take her test in the camp because she'd missed too much lab work, our place looked good and the strawberry plants were loaded this year, a bumper crop.

And Julian stood outside, leaning on the half door because there wasn't much room in the stall. His big head and shoulders made a shadow on the wall like a horse was watching us. All the kids in our row knew Julian by the second visit because he'd bring raisins by the ten-pound sack and they'd come around and he'd fill up their pockets.

But the cheerfulness didn't last the whole visit. Even Hortense would run out of things to say. All of us knew the three of them were going back to our road, and we were staying here in some horse stall. We'd heard they were getting ready to move us again, and this could be the last time we'd ever see each other. We'd even heard they were separating families, sending them all to different places. It was terrible. My mother would look crazy and close her eyes when people around us talked like that. I just felt sick to my stomach.

The assembly center was mass confusion. The people who were running the place had no more idea what they were supposed to do than we did. By the time we came back from breakfast at the mess hall each morning, Reiko would have worked herself into a rage. She'd head for the administration offices. "Go with her," Mother would tell me, and I'd follow. I wouldn't have to go inside to hear because they knew her by now and they'd all start shouting at the same time.

"Where is my father?"

"We've told you before; we can't release classified information."

"Do you know what *habeas corpus* means? I asked you a question, sir. Your job is to answer our questions."

Finally they told her he was in Nebraska. "Does that make you feel any better?" someone shouted at her. "You come back here tomorrow and I'll have you arrested and put in the stockade."

Reiko yelled back, "Go ahead. Is it any worse than living in a piss-smelling horse stable and eating this slop you're feeding us?"

I liked the food myself. There was plenty. They heaped your plate if you asked, though a lot of the Issei weren't used to the American kind of food and never ate much. And we played a lot of baseball. They had set up a school taught by the Japanese American teachers in the camp. But nothing was organized, and I didn't go until Reiko found out and made me.

We were shut off from everything. We weren't supposed to have radios or cameras. We lived on rumors alone, plus the war news people passed along from secret radios. The Japanese had overrun Bataan and were shelling Corregidor. Then Corregidor fell, and then the Philippines. It was the biggest surrender in American history. There were a few old Issei who thought that was fine and bet each other how long it would be before Japanese soldiers would be at the gate to release them, but I kept thinking, how could this happen? We always won our wars. We beat England twice.

My poor mother was too shy for camp life. When she had to go to the bathroom, which was twenty toilets lined up in a row without stalls, it was impossible for her. She tried to wait until late at night when there was no one else there, but she wasn't the only one who'd thought of that. During the daytime Reiko would make her go with her; she'd sit next to Mother on the second-to-last toilet and open up an old newspaper for privacy. She'd have to go over the whole plan two or three times with her before my mother would budge out of our stall.

The older people had nothing to do. They hadn't been assigned jobs yet. And like my mother, a lot were shy and didn't know anyone. We couldn't find anyone from our church, much less our town, because the camp was so big. My mother sat on the edge of the cot all day with her hands on her knees, waiting, listening to the talk from the other stalls. We were going to be put in San Quentin or on Alcatraz next. Both Hawaii and Alaska had fallen.

The night before they were going to move us, Reiko found out and phoned Fred. They let him into the visitor center and we went over there. He was as happy to see us as we were him. He said he hadn't had time to pick up the baseballs that Julian had sent over, but he'd get them to me. He sent me to go get my mother. I was glad to get away by then. I didn't want to hear Reiko and Fred talking. They were arguing in whispers like they were spitting nails at each other with words, trying get the other in the eye. You told me . . . Fred's voice was softer and I could barely hear. What else could I do? What would your folks say?

When I came back in the center with my mother, Reiko had her arm around Fred's waist and she was smiling. Fred was telling my mother she was not to worry; he might have found a tenant for the farm who would take care of the place and do the work on shares. The guard started yelling Time, Time, Curfew. Fred tried to hand my mother a tin box of throat lozenges but she wouldn't take it. She told me in Japanese to say her throat wasn't sore. He handed the tin to me. He hugged my mother good-bye. She wouldn't let him go. The guard was yelling at the crowd saying good-bye for the last time. "Are you people trying to take advantage of me?" he shouted. Reiko unloosened Mother's arms. Fred laughed it off and shook my hand but couldn't get to Reiko to say good-bye before the guards came between us.

I opened the tin on the way back to the stable. It had fourteen ten-dollar bills inside and three fives and a five-dollar gold piece. I showed it to Reiko when we got back. "Doesn't he know there's nothing to buy here?" I said.

"Give it to Mother," she said. I handed it to her and she started crying.

The next morning at four A.M. we left by train for Arizona.

I could have groaned out loud when they dumped us off at the relocation camp in Arizona. It was like they'd decided to pick the worst place they could think of to put the camp. They'd scraped the ground flat and put up row after row of wooden barracks on stilts with tar paper siding. One room, a little bigger than the horse stalls, that everyone called an apartment. We were all trying to make the best of it. Reiko said it could be worse. And when the wind started to blow and all the dust they'd made when they scraped away the top layer of dirt sifted in through the tar paper, it was funny at first. "What else can go wrong?" she said. We had to walk a city block to the lavatory, but I never heard anyone complain.

Make the best of it. Ignore the electrified fences, the towers with machine guns, and the guards at the gates. We evacuees were colonists now, like at Plymouth Rock. The director was supposed to have called us that. We were in protective custody until everything was straightened out and we could go back home. More rumors. Everyone wanted to believe the one about going home. My mother was always saying home, home, like if she said it enough times it would transport us back to our road. These people are too obedient, Reiko would say, watching the older Issei line up for the mess hall or to see a doctor, standing out in the wind. My mother got the first job, cleaning up the lavatories at nine dollars a month. I went to high school. And Reiko was helping in the hospital at eleven dollars a month. Top wage went to the doctor, who was getting sixteen dollars a month. That's what a private in the Army was getting, and we weren't allowed to earn any more. The important thing to remember, Reiko said, was we were getting free room and board. That would always get everyone laughing. Reiko could be funny it she wanted to be.

I used to dream of the valley, our place, even picking strawberries. I'd pick twenty hours a day if they'd just let us return so I could play baseball. The war wouldn't last forever. Wars stopped sometime. And then I'd think of the Hundred Years' War. Jesus. We'd beaten the Germans in the last war. This one would end and we'd go home. Until then we'd stay here.

It wasn't that bad. They were having dances. There were musicians, kids who'd played together before, and they formed bands. I went a couple of times. I didn't know how to dance. Some girl came and got me and I went out in the middle of the mess hall and tried to copy what everyone else was doing. The girl kept saying, "You're doing fine," and I got so I could almost move along pretty good without looking at my feet when someone tapped me on the shoulder. I thought it was another boy cutting in to ask her to dance, but it was her grandmother, who told her she was dancing too close. We both were embarrassed. The older people didn't always like the American ways: the dances, their wives working alongside other men, the kids going to the recreation room at night and having a good time. Reiko didn't dance; she wrote letters, and she and Mother would take long walks around the outline of the fence, picking up dried plants to make flower arrangements for our apartment.

There seemed to be so much more time now. We sat out on our stairs at night just talking. Mother knew how to play a Japanese lute called a samisen, and she'd play that and our neighbors would listen. She'd tell us stories about when she was a girl with her two sisters and her mother, who she worried about a lot. She hadn't heard from them since the war started. At night we'd all be on our cots in our little room that was divided by the blankets we'd hung up, and we'd wait for her to start.

It was a continuing story she told, about her coming to the United States. It was different from the way Granddad had told it. It started out as a humorous family story: a cousin of hers had come to California as a picture bride. The cousin had on her own sent her photo to a girlfriend in California. A Japanese man sent his photo back, and they started to correspond. Then he sent her a ticket for the boat to take her to San Francisco. "We heard that story for years, as little girls," Mother said. "It was like Cinderella to me and my sisters. Everyone knew that California was a golden place where there were plenty of opportunities and you could do anything, be anything.

"My oldest sister decided she was coming to America. My parents were against it; they didn't want any of us to leave. The arrangements were being made and the rest of us watched. It was both terrifying and wonderful. We would never see her again, but she was going to California. At the last minute she decided not to go. After writing all those letters, and she'd got the ticket, been interviewed, she refused. I don't know why she didn't want to go."

Just as soon as we'd developed a routine and the Arizona camp life was starting to smooth out—we'd got used to the place a little and we thought we were safe here—the administrators started calling in each family member seventeen or over, both Nisei and Issei. We got in line and stood outside the Ad building waiting our turn. We were getting used to just standing around waiting for someone to tell us what to do next. When it was our turn at a desk, Reiko read the questionnaire. I was kidding my mother, "They heard you were raking the sand around our barracks to make a garden. That's against the rules."

Reiko grabbed my arm and pointed at the questionnaire. I read the part she was pointing at.

No. 27. Are you willing to serve in the armed forces of the United States on combat duty wherever ordered? If Julian could go in the Army, I could too. Hortense's brothers were in now too; they were from our road.

No. 28. Will you swear unqualified allegiance to the United States of America and faithfully defend the United States from any or all attack by foreign or domestic forces and forswear any form of allegiance or obedience to the Japanese emperor, to any other foreign government, power, or organization?

"I don't get this," Reiko said to the clerk sitting behind the desk. "On 28. The United States wouldn't let my parents become citizens. And if they put yes to this question, they can't be Japanese either. They wouldn't have a country. My mother has family in Japan, and she has family here, my father and my brother and me, who are American citizens, of course."

My mother had read the questions by then and was getting excited. She asked Reiko in Japanese, "Would we be separated later if we said yes? Could they make us go back to Japan and leave you and your brother? Ask him that."

"Miss," the clerk said, "this is just to find out if you are loyal to the United States of America. It's like the pledge of allegiance to the flag. You put *yes* if you are. There are other people waiting, I might add. Are you loyal?" he said louder, as if we were all hard of hearing.

"Loyal?" Reiko shouted back. "Loyal? You never allowed them to become American citizens in the first place. And now you want them to be loyal to you? You lock us up and you want us to be loyal? We were born here, me and my brother, the same as you. My mother has relatives in Japan, sisters and her mother; she loves them." It had got quiet in the office. The clerk tried to interrupt again with "Are you loyal?" and Reiko shouted back, "Loyal! Loyal! You stupid jerk, the United States of America is disloyal to us; do you understand that? Disloyal. There was no excuse to put us in these camps."

Another clerk came up now and stood beside Reiko. "Please step outside, Miss. You've made your point." Reiko acted like she'd run out of breath. When we got outside I was holding her hand and my mother's hand, the three of us standing in the wind. We waited a few minutes before walking back to our apartment.

Three weeks later we were told to pack; they were moving us again. We were going to another camp. We knew the rumors. Tule Lake. A place up north in Siskiyou County. I looked it up in the atlas at school. It was a place for troublemakers, the kids in my class ribbed me. You're going to a special prison, they said, for the hard cases. A place for the people who said no to 27 and 28. The no nos, they called us. Reiko was still raging, going over the I-should-have-saids and they-can't-do-thats. My mother didn't care where she went as long as we were together. She gave notes in envelopes with "Mats Hamada" written on the outside in Japanese and English to our neighbors to give to my father, if he showed up.

"Look at it this way," I pointed out to Reiko and Mother as we climbed up into the back of an Army truck to be driven out the front gate, "at least we're going back to California."

HORTENSE

chapter 14

I wrote everyone, of course: Richard, Reiko, and Julian. Fred stopped by our place when he came back for some tools. He had a job in Los Angeles now in an aircraft plant. The Army wouldn't take him because he had a bad leg; when he was a boy rabbit-hunting back in Oklahoma his brother Charlie accidentally shot him in the knee while they were going through a barbed wire fence. It was hard to talk to Fred. We were sitting on the porch steps looking over at the Hamadas' place, and after a while he just stopped talking. I wanted to ask him why he and Reiko just didn't get married, why all this off-and-on business? He could have kept her out of the camps, taken her out to the Midwest, where they were letting some of the Japanese go to work at ordinary jobs. But I couldn't say anything, not to Fred, who'd just go silent on me.

Then we heard that the Hamadas had been sent back to California, up north somewhere and Mr. Hamada had rejoined the family. Time was going by so fast now that it was only the events that affected you personally that could stop the clock enough for you to understand. They were fighting all over the world, it seemed like. Richard had been sent to Cuba because he could speak Spanish. Julian had been in one of the big battles in the Aleutians. I read the letters he sent to the Palestinis. Julian couldn't write Italian, so I read them his English, trying to explain what I could. Julian didn't really say much. He was hungry for Italian food. He missed them all, and especially his Zia Maria. Her pasta was the best in the world. I had to start making up things; he only wrote a few lines. I pretended to read about seals, Eskimos eating whale blubber, polar bears, whatever I remembered from schoolbooks. The Zia got it into her head that a polar bear might get Julian, but I explained they were all tame up there, like pets.

There was a piece in the paper when Julian came back, welcoming him home. He'd been gone for a year. It said he had been in the battle for Attu and had been recommended for a medal. He was going to be stationed at Camp Roberts again.

We had a big feed over at our place for him too. Fred came up, and Charlie. It wasn't the same old Julian. He'd lost a lot of weight, and his clothes were baggy. Since we were kids we'd weighed ourselves on the scale in his shed when we weighed raisins, and Julian had weighed two hundred forty-seven pounds when he left. He didn't look anything like that now, and he wasn't eating much either, but he looked like he was enjoying himself. Trying to, anyhow. Everyone at the table felt the absence of the Hamadas. Fred didn't know where to look when Reiko's name was mentioned. I knew he wasn't writing to her. She never said, but I knew. I even missed Grayson.

I got my cap in a ceremony that lasted ten minutes. I drove back home and was at work at the hospital on the second shift that afternoon. They needed nurses everywhere now. I never was so surprised in my life when Julian came into the emergency room. I thought he'd stopped by to say hello, he was still on furlough, but he'd started hemorrhaging. I stayed with him while they gave him tests and the rest. He was cheerful enough, making jokes that the Army food had caught up with him. He had a bleeding ulcer. There were all kinds of medicine for that, and they put him on a special diet.

I drove him home after. He hadn't got his color back yet, but he was saying he was going to be careful. I don't know how it started but I drove up into the yard and stopped and turned off the lights. We sat there a minute, not speaking, and I reached over and pulled his head around by his ear and kissed him. Then I did it again until he started gasping for air. Then again, and he started to kiss me back. But it was Julian that stopped. I wanted him to go on and on. But he stopped.

I saw Kenny Rodriguez, who was working for the town paper, a couple of weeks after Julian went back to the Army. Kenny's mother had had an operation and he was visiting her at the hospital. I happened to mention Julian. "I wanted to interview him when he came back," Kenny told me. "At the newspaper we got this handout from the information officer of his division—they send these to hometown newspapers, how the U.S. Army is winning the war—about this medal they wanted him to get. He was happy to see me, but he didn't want anyone to know what happened. He said he'd break my back if I wrote anything. He made me promise. But he didn't know that the whole story was already out on the national news wire.

"Why he was recommended for that medal, Hortense, was, in the last part of the battle about a thousand Japanese soldiers charged, banzai charge, I think they call it, where they come running at you yelling, shooting and waving swords and bayonets. Julian's platoon had dug in and was overrun. They ran out of ammuntion, I think. Julian—and they have to have eyewitnesses to verify all this before you're even considered for this medal—Julian killed seventeen Japanese soldiers with a shovel."

A shovel, I kept thinking. Seventeen. That was the number of kids on our school bus when we went into town. A shovel. I had seen a shovel in Julian's hands my whole life. No wonder he didn't want anyone to know. Could someone like Julian kill another person without harming himself too? Especially Julian, who was so strong; it must have been harder for him.

"Don't tell him I mentioned it to you, Hortense. Julian's my friend. He never made fun of anyone when we were in high school. I got my induction notice last week. I'm not looking forward to the Army, that's for sure."

After that, I would be doing something at home or at work and I'd think of Julian. I wanted to . . . I wanted to . . . I couldn't think past that point. Sometimes we'd be in the front seat of the car again and other times he'd be standing with a shovel like a rifle, and I'd wonder how hard it was to kill another man with a farm tool.

Julian tried to act the same when he came home on weekend passes, I could see him trying, but he didn't know how. And he wasn't eating, and the Palestinis were howling. He lost more weight. Between us we were back to kidding each other like nothing had ever happened. He told me the ulcer was getting better, that I was a better nurse than a milkmaid, and that he'd got word they were going to ship him to the European theater this time. And that he and Fred were going to drive up to Tule Lake relocation camp to see the Hamadas.

I didn't see Julian after he came back from up north. Fred stopped by, though. I was working in the dairy before I went to the hospital. My father and mother had gone down to see my brother, who had got hurt in basic training in San Diego. We'd been able to hire two Portuguese nationals as milkers; they'd been allowed into the country because of all the labor shortages. There were a lot of Mexican farm laborers now, too; never enough, but it all helped during harvest. We had some of the most modern milking equipment around in the dairy now, but you still had to do a lot of lifting. Fred came into the milking parlor and started moving the heavy milk cans for me. He worked for half an hour before he even opened his mouth. I asked him how the Hamadas were. Fine, he said. He never did say much, but this was ridiculous. I didn't have time to pry the answers out of him. I had to shower and get to work in town. Reiko hadn't written to me for weeks.

As I drove to work, I was thinking how most everyone was gone, my friends, the ones I'd grown up with there on the road. I didn't think it was ever going to be like it was before. And I had to wonder what was going to happen next.

GRAYSON

chapter 15

It was winter at Tule Lake and it was wet. If it wasn't raining it was overcast and drizzling. I almost forgot the valley sun. It seemed real only when I read the magazines in the library, the *National Geographics* mostly, looking for the photos of the naked native women. There was a lot of sunshine on the pages, and I could remember sweat running down my back while we picked our crop of strawberries.

There were farms around here, growing mostly vegetables: cabbages, potatoes, and snap beans. Some of the colonists were recruited to harvest. It was one way to make some money besides the usual camp jobs at government pay. Getting out of the camps and earning money were the two big topics of conversation when we first arrived at Tule Lake. We were in the first group of evacuees labeled disloyal to be sent to the paradise of the north, so we were the first to learn that because we were considered disloyal we weren't going to be eligible to be transferred to the Midwest to work or go to college. Because most of the evacuees had lost all their money when they were forced to relocate, they were always worried what they'd do if they ever got to leave the camps. Some thought if they went back to where they had lived they'd be killed by their neighbors, and they couldn't think of any place else to go. I didn't like to listen to the old Issei; they had no hope.

The camp was going to be big when it filled up. There was supposed to be room for fifteen thousand internees. We disloyals joined some loyal evacuees who had been relocated here originally and were too tired to move again when Tule Lake was designated the segregation camp for disloyal people. And because some of us were troublemakers, there seemed to be more soldiers up here. The camp administrators worked for the War Relocation Authorities, and no one could figure out how the government could consistently hire so many duds. Were these people 4-Fs, rejectees from the draft? Or people who were specially hired because they were stupid? To most of them we were so many subhuman cattle who would try to pull a fast one on the government if they gave an inch. That's what a friend of Reiko's said. It was the Quakers who finally made them put up partitions between the toilets, but they balked at putting up doors.

The soldiers, our guards, were fed the same line of propaganda the rest of the nation was given about the Axis: the Japanese were fanatical crazed enemies that must be killed. So although the inmates of Tule Lake were obviously quiet, respectful, family-oriented people, to the guards we were still the enemy. That's how Dr. Sato explained it in senior history. But it must have been hard on the soldiers too, away from their families. It must have been confusing to see all the little kids as enemies when whole classes would hold hands and sing "America the Beautiful" to them up in the guard towers. They'd throw down sticks of gum to the enemy.

We were lucky that a professional ballplayer who'd got as far as double A ball was sent to Tule Lake. He became our coach, Isaac Gozen. He hadn't been rounded up with the rest of us because he'd been in the Midwest and the government thought he was Jewish: the name confused them. He was Nisei and had been caught when he appeared for his draft notice and they saw he was Japanese. He had been a second baseman in the Chicago White Sox farm system, and to watch him was like seeing someone born to play the infield. Ike got me to try third base and I got the hang of it pretty fast. The hot corner. I was seventeen and I was sleeping with my glove underneath my pillow. Reiko would razz me, "What is this smelly thing?" and she'd pick it up with two fingers by the webbing. "Are you trapping the muskrats now, bringing these disgusting things into our home?"

We had a game outside the camp in one of the small towns. They had a good team, but going into the fifth inning we tied them. Up until then the spectators had been perfect gentlemen, just calling us Japs and Nips. The third base coach, a kid my age, told me, "You Japs can play baseball." I pointed out we'd rather not be called Japs, but Japanese was all right. It was okay with him and we shook hands on it. "Wesley," he said, and "Grayson," I said. But when we tied, the fans came up with the usual racial epithets and started to throw things. The game was called. "Hysteria," Dr. Sato called it when it was brought up in class. "The local people reflect the national malaise, the national panic that's been generated by newspapers and the government. Not by everyone in the government, but most go along with this injustice because it's easier. It's too hard sometimes for individuals to think things out for themselves. You can't always expect the ordinary citizen to see through the information he's fed. But he might surprise you, sometimes, the ordinary citizen."

There was no one incident you could point to or minute when you could say, This is where everything started to turn sour. It wasn't when the administration called us malcontents or belligerents or communists. I guess some of the people just got irate over the way we were being treated. There were work strikes and hunger strikes. Everyone knew about the shooting at Manzanar Relocation Center, where the guards had fired into a crowd of protesters, killing one man. But that didn't stop anyone on either side.

Dr. Sato, our history teacher, would try to answer all of our questions about almost anything in class. It got so it wasn't just his regular students that sat in his classroom, but anyone who had a question or just wanted to argue with him. Everyone was welcome. He couldn't have weighed more than a hundred pounds, and he was old, at least in his seventies, I thought, but I found out he was only fifty-five. His complexion was a faded yellow, the color of Julian's mums when they'd died. He had graduated in 1912 from medical school at the University of Oregon. The collar of his shirt was larger than his small neck, and the same purple-and-blue silk necktie hung down his chest every day. He looked taller than he really was, barely five feet, standing in front of the class of forty-seven seniors. We had fifteen copies of a history textbook printed in 1927 to share between us.

The first couple of classes there was a lot of laughing, not just because Dr. Sato was often funny. "Did anyone notice the flights of geese overhead yesterday? You know, of course, that this is a major flyway for migrating fowl, and Tule Lake is one of the great breeding grounds on this flyway. Our relocation camp director has put in a request for anti-aircraft gun batteries. It seems he fears that the millions of geese flying over us in those large Vs and Ws may really be guided by offshore enemy subs who are signaling us and giving us orders here in this camp." When we finally got it and realized he was being humorous, we all thought it was hilarious. But some of the kids laughed because he had some kind of palsy and his head and hands would shake like he was constantly in his own personal earthquake. That was why he was with us in the classroom instead of in the hospital. But he knew history. He must have read a lot or something. Reiko's friend Shig found out, when he still could get into the personnel files before he got into trouble, that Dr. Sato was married to a Caucasian, who had been at the Santa Anita assembly center but wasn't at Tule Lake.

I went to school, my mother was working in the mess hall on the cleanup crew, and Reiko was in the hospital as a nurse now, in obstetrics. Sometimes ten babies were born in one day at the camp hospital. She came home exhausted. We all did. Besides school and practice, the baseball team cut up logs with a two-man saw. Coach said it would develop our arms and shoulders and warm us up twice, once while we cut the wood into rounds and later when we sat around the stove. I could barely keep my eyes open after dinner. But one of us would always say, "Go on, Mom, tell us the story," and she'd begin again.

"When my older sister Takeko had second thoughts and then refused to go, I started considering the possibility of taking her place. I was the middle daughter and I used to dream of far-off places. Read about them, we had a lot of books that were filled with photographs. They were quite popular then. We had a whole book on California. It was like a land in a fairy tale. I decided to take my sister's place."

"Mom, how could you come here to marry a man you'd never seen before, even if it was Dad?"

"In Japan at that time, families usually arranged marriages for their sons and daughters. You didn't go out and find your own husband. It was your parents who decided. If your father had a photograph of me, I had the advantage of going to meet his mother in Osaka with my mother. Your grandmother was a fine lady."

"That was Grandfather Ray's wife," Reiko said.

"I just knew her son would be like her. She was kind to the bone."

"I still think you were taking a chance; he could have been like Granddad, too." We all laughed when Reiko said that.

"Once I got to California, I didn't have to marry your father if I decided against it. My own father made sure I understood that. He gave me enough money for a return ticket. But when I sighted land, California, I knew I had come to the right place. I had found a list of women's names in the back of my English dictionary, and I decided to rename myself. I was Harriet when I stepped up to the customs oficial's desk on the dock. And once I met your father, I never had any doubts. He was such a kind and gentle man. I was staying at a hotel with some of the women who I'd come over with, and your father and I had to get a marriage license, wait a few days for tickets for the train down to the valley. We went sight-seeing and took ferry rides on the bay. It was so exciting. Your father was a gentleman. I was very fortunate. Some of the other women were less fortunate, I think."

"You married Dad when you'd only known him for four or five days? How old were you?"

"I was twenty years old, and we didn't really become man and wife until seven months later. He wanted us to get to know each other. I always felt I was a very lucky woman to have found your father for a husband."

Besides baseball, it was Dr. Sato's history class that caught my attention. I'd anticipate the time that we'd dash into the classroom and crowd near the stove to get warm. There were rows of mess hall tables to sit at, but so many people had been showing up that we'd had to add benches made in our camp wood shops along the walls. The more people, the warmer it got in that room, and we'd start to peel off our hats and jackets and sweaters, all the time listening to the winter wind slamming into the tar-papered building. We all knew that some of the people in the room were probably finks for the administration, reporting whatever was said.

Reiko came in once and sat in the back. I didn't see her. After we discussed the chapter in our textbook, Dr. Sato would start where the last class had left off, answering our questions. Anyone could ask a question. He seemed to like the banter back and forth. Sometimes people would bait him, but he never lost his temper, just kept trying to answer the question. "Democracy means having patience with an imperfect system," he started out.

"You mean it's all right to lock us up here, and when they come to their senses they can say it was all a mistake and they're sorry, and we should accept the apology?"

"We're in prison, Dr. Sato, accused of no crime other than our race." I looked over in the back to be sure, and it was Reiko who said that. Shig had asked the first question.

"We have to understand that it's not only an imperfect system, but more importantly, we are imperfect human beings." He never seemed to have the palsy when he talked; it was only when he stopped to listen that he'd start shaking.

"It's better to die on your feet than live on your knees," some old man by the stove said.

"My father, a seaman, used to have a tattoo on his forearm, Death before dishonor. A noble sentiment. I used to think that he was right when I was a young man, but now it's not so easy for me. I want to see the end of this travail. I want to see justice prevail. A second stupidity never erases the first; it just compounds it. What we have to do is wait this situation out. Follow the Golden Rule; treat others as you'd treat yourself."

"I'm not a Christian," someone yelled from the back.

"That statement has nothing to do with religion."

"Our future is in Japan," someone else yelled.

"How many of you have been to Japan?" About ten out of the sixty or seventy people raised their hands. "I myself have never been to that country. I have no past with Japan. How can I have a future?" No one left until he was finished. Usually he got tired after a couple of hours. It was the last class of the day. Sometimes he assigned us students essays to write. On what, someone would ask. "On anything you like," he'd say. "History covers everything. It's what we did yesterday, what we do today, and what we're going to do tomorrow, all the human and inhuman acts that define man."

I wrote about baseball. I tried to explain that I thought games were a better way to solve problems than wars, and there wouldn't be any wars if the people who started them had to first play some game like baseball with the people that they thought they wanted to invade. They might get so interested in perfecting the game that they'd forget about the invasion. He wrote on the bottom of the paper, "I don't think it would work, but I like the idea. Keep thinking." I showed Reiko.

"He's silly," she said. "He's not a good teacher. Shig says Dr. Sato thinks he's Socrates or something."

After thirteen months my father showed up, wearing the same suit and carrying the same leather bag he'd left with in the winter of 1941.

We were sitting on the front steps to our apartment. It had just stopped raining and the ground was steaming. The people in our block hadn't come out yet, but we could hear them inside, a kind of hum of activity. About a dozen men came around the corner, looking at the numbers on the buildings, moving down the path on the muddy ground. None of us recognized him when he stopped in front of us. I was just going to say in Japanese, Can I help you find someone? when Reiko said, "Dad?" We were all down the stairs and trying to hug him at the same time. None of us wanted to stop or let go or give up our place. We just held each other like that until we noticed people watching us from their open doorways and we went inside.

He had changed. Not just the way he looked, but the way he acted. It was like he wasn't sure exactly who he was anymore. I'd watch him early in the morning after he shaved, checking himself in the mirror again and again. He'd open the door as if expecting to see our strawberry patch at home instead of the gloom of the camp and the muddy space between the two barracks. It took him a couple of weeks before he'd even mention what had happened at the place in Nebraska. He acted like we had never been separated, as if that time was just another inconvenience, like a late frost on our strawberry plants. There was no use dwelling on misfortune.

They put him on the maintenance crew, which he seemed to like. They sent him out to repair broken windows, doors that wouldn't open and roofs that leaked. I'd see him with his wooden carpenter's bench and tools in one hand and the paper telling him where to go and what the job was crushed in the other. He was making twelve dollars a month, my mother nine, and Reiko fourteen. I made four for cutting the wood. I tried kidding him, "Hey, Dad, we're going to be millionaires: we're making thirty-nine dollars a month now." Without cracking a smile he answered, "That's right, we will." We all tried to eat together at the mess hall but it didn't always work out. Reiko had to work late a lot of the time. When we did, my father would stare at the food like he wasn't going to eat it and my mother would tell him in Japanese, Eat, you'll feel better. In the apartment he'd talk in a whisper. We could barely hear him ourselves, much less the people on either side of the thin walls.

He told us one night why he thought he had been held in the FBI camp in Nebraska. When he was fourteen he'd won a national title for jujitsu in Japan. He'd been invited to the Imperial Palace in Tokyo to receive the award. "There were a lot of young men," he said, "and we were all so proud to be there, and we gave demonstrations and were introduced as a group to the Emperor. There were photographs and banquets, a lot of military men; they were the sponsors of the contest. There was a newspaper photo of another boy and me in our judo clothes standing on either side of a general, his hands on our shoulders.

"The FBI had that photo and wanted me to explain what I was doing there, and how well I knew the general. The other boy had ended up in the Navy as a fleet oficer. They kept asking me that question for days. Then the interrogation would stop and I wouldn't see anyone for a couple of weeks. Most of us never knew why we were there. Some were executives of Japanese corporations, businessmen waiting for repatriation. Enemy aliens, they called them. They kept asking me that too: do you want to be repatriated to your country? 'My family is here. I'm just a small farmer in the Central Valley,' I'd tell them. 'I want to stay here. This is my home.' I never knew if some night they would take me to Seattle and put me on a ship and I'd never see you again."

I had written to Julian and asked if he could send me some books Dr. Sato kept mentioning in class. The camp librarian had said it wasn't likely that she could get them for me, but she'd try. Julian sent me *The Prince* by Machiavelli and *The Federalist Papers.* It looked like he had lifted them from the Army. In his note he wrote, "No one reads those books here anyway. You always mention how cruelly cold it is where you are, but I'm another thousand miles north at least, and the spit freezes in your mouth here. I'd give my right nut to be home sitting under that oak tree in August watching my mums, their buds just ready to pop open. I thought you were interested in baseball; what's with these books? I looked through both and they gave me a headache. The others the Army doesn't issue. You're going to learn the most from the Italian anyway."

I saw Dr. Sato walking one day when I was with my father and we stopped and I introduced them to each other. I don't know what I expected, but they were very formal. When we walked away I asked my father, "Did you like him?"

"Is he a mandarin? Someone who is very learned but doesn't know anything else?"

"No, Pop, he's like us. He knows how to work. He was a fisherman, worked his way through college catching salmon. His father was a drinker, left him on his own most of the time. He was a houseboy for a rich doctor in Portland before that. That's when he decided to become a doctor. Tuesday he told us his wife wanted to come here with him but he asked her not to. There was no reason for her to suffer this indignity, he said, and she could better use her time outside trying to help some of the cases that are going through the courts that will prove we are here illegally. She's a lawyer. A Caucasian." It was surprising to realize how much I knew about our teachers. It was like it was important for me to learn about their own personal history before they could teach me what they knew about their subject.

The camp was jammed with eighteen thousand internees now, when there were only supposed to be fifteen thousand. I knew the people on our block to say hello to, and the neighbors on either side of our apartment were friends, but that was all, except for the kids I played ball with and had classes with. There wasn't any time. They wanted my father to be our block captain representative with the administration, but he refused. He had always helped people on our road or at church, writing letters, even going into town with them to talk to someone at the county building. Now he wouldn't even leave the apartment on the night of a meeting, and when the trouble really started, he didn't go out and didn't want us to either.

Some of us in camp pretended that this was just like the outside, wherever we'd come from. But it wasn't; everyone knew that. "It's a nightmare," one woman said in Dr. Sato's class, "and I don't think most of us will ever wake up."

"Did I ever mention," Dr. Sato said, "that I was a surgeon in the First World War, and served in France?" Everyone listened when he spoke. It was sleeting outside and the ice was striking the building like it was broken glass. It made a racket, and we huddled together. The room was jammed.

"We were doing quite a few amputations. At this point the Armistice had been signed, but both sides were firing their artillery, using up all their shells, until the cease-fire at midnight. The loss of the arms and legs I was cutting off was a matter of bad luck for the victims, but this was also a senseless cruelty. An unnecessary cruelty; the war was over, but not officially, so the slaughter went on. The orderlies couldn't keep up with carrying the severed appendages out of surgery in garbage cans. On the one hand the war was over, and on the other the stupidity continued. It was beyond reason. The waste of killing is truly amazing. For me that was a nightmare I thought I would never forget. But I did put it aside. Now if there is another nightmare beginning here in this camp, I think we will have to learn how to put it aside also."

Kibei, Nisei—we'd never made these distinctions before we came to this camp. The Kibei, who had been born in the USA but had gone back to Japan for school or for one reason or another, were suspected as spies, and they were bitter. They weren't the only suspects; a lot of Nisei and Issei were too. There was a lot of talk from this group: if they got the chance, they were going to renounce their citizenship and go back to Japan to live. Agitators, my father called them. The problem was, you were either with them or against them.

They left me alone at first because I was on the camp baseball team and all the players stuck together. We didn't have time to argue with them. We practiced every chance we got after school, and sometimes before. There was talk we could maybe play the other camps. I loved baseball, third base, and my mitt and Louisville slugger in that order. Dr. Sato's wife, who was a baseball fan, somehow got us old uniforms, discards from some semipro team. Julian, before he left Prince Rupert in Canada to go further north, sent a complete catcher's outfit—mask, glove, shin guards, and chest protector, besides a dozen bats. You could see where he'd inked over "Property of the U.S. Army."

The trouble kept growing. It was like the drizzle that never stopped and then got worse and turned into sleet. There was one group that wanted to make the best of the situation and help the administration run the camp as well as possible. There was another group that wanted everyone in the camp to strike, refuse to work, stop everything. Another group was going to show the bastards, renounce their citizenship and go back to Japan. And there were groups in between that thought they had all the answers too. Most people just wanted to be left alone. I just wanted to play baseball. Coach said some of us, and he didn't mention any names, had the potential to play professionally. I thought it was me he was talking about.

Reiko started telling me, "You can have this country, Grayson. I'm going to Japan, one way or another." She was going around with a group of tough guys who shaved their heads like Japanese soldiers and wore headbands with the rising sun showing. They spent most of their time talking loud about camp policies, strikes, escape, and finks and white rats.

Reiko tried to talk to our mother and father about leaving the country and returning to Japan, but she just confused them. She'd end up yelling, "They're going to send you back anyway. Look what they have done to us. Our future is in the Orient: why stay where we're not wanted?" Both our parents knew which way home was. I didn't have to say anything to remind them.

We had built a good backstop, and the ground was drying out for spring practice. All I wanted to do was play baseball. The goon squad caught four of us in the lavatory. Some rabble-rousers grabbed our best pitcher, Leonard, and when they threatened to break his throwing arm if we didn't demonstrate with them in front of the administration building, it was too much for his brother, Robert, and he started throwing punches. I got out of there. There were too many of them.

It just kept getting worse, all summer and fall, one thing after another. Riots started in November, and the Army took over. They locked people up and there were shootings and stabbings. You couldn't trust anyone. I didn't trust Reiko anymore. "Leave Mom and Pop out of it, Reiko," I told her. She glared at me. She was going with Shig now, who'd been a first-year law student in San Francisco before he'd been relocated. He was a ringleader, who came into Dr. Sato's history class to be rude. "Explain to me again, Dr. Sato, while we sit here listening to the tanks patrolling the fence like we are maddened convicts, how democracy isn't a perfect vehicle." And Dr. Sato would. He couldn't resist, any more than Shig could.

"With our system there are weaknesses. It makes errors. Worse, it takes a lot of time to right itself, like a turtle on its back that keeps kicking its legs and squirming until it regains its feet and is on its way again. This period of waiting for the turtle to feel the ground under its feet can seem interminable, we all know that. I hope you are all aware too that the Supreme Court of the United States is getting ready to hear the first test case dealing with the legality of our incarceration. We here in this room would all agree that what the government has done wasn't right, but there are people on the outside who agree with us also and are working to stop this injustice."

"You have more faith in the American system than I have," Shig said. "We have watched as lawyers from the ACLU have come and gone, as well as the Spanish counsel who is supposed to be representing the Japanese government here during this war, a U.S. senator and his wife, and a complete committee from the House of Representatives, none of which has ever helped us or got us out of here. And you keep telling us, trust the Caucasians. But then again, in your personal life, I guess you have no choice."

Dr. Sato just smiled at him. After class I went up to him . "He's just a hothead," I told him. "He didn't mean anything."

"Words can't hurt you unless you allow them to. Have you got used to Jap yet, Grayson? Or slant eye?"

"I don't like that word," I said, "but I can't punch everyone in the nose that says it. That's all I'd do."

Shig called me a kiss ass and a brownnoser. A friend of his, a big guy who was at least thirty years old, came up to pick a fight with me, to punish me in public. It was after practice, and he had a big crowd behind him. When I walked away they jeered me. Coach had told us, you have to be an example for the other kids your age and the younger ones. I believed him. None of us smoked or swore or got into trouble. We had to spend time with the younger boys, umpiring their games and hitting batting practice, showing them the fundamentals, and we had to do well in school, get at least a B average, to play. When they were jeering at me, I remembered how I could hit the curve. I hit one two hundred seventy feet, over the fence, once, when we played the civilians and soldiers at the camp.

Reiko and I had another talk. She'd taken the books Julian had sent me and loaned them out, and they got lost. We had used them in class already, but they were mine. Her hair had grown out black again; all the orange was gone. She looked much better, and I told her so. We were alone in the apartment. I had started out yelling at her for taking my books, but later we started talking like we used to. She asked me, "Grayson, are we always going to be here?"

"We're going home someday," I said. "This is only temporary."

"I miss the valley, Grayson. I wake up some mornings thinking how nice it would be just to walk over to Hortense's. Just to go into town on a Saturday afternoon." I listened to her and it was like putting words to my own daydreams.

The Army team thought they could get to us. When we ran out on the field they gave a big yell, "Here come the monkey men." They thought they were being funny. Jungle bunnies was another one I'd never heard before. Coach said, "Get mad if you want to, but take it out on the ball. Don't even look in their direction." We beat them seven to four with everyone on our team playing. They didn't like that. And to make it better we gave them a cheer: Two four six eight, who do we appreciate? The camp guards, hooray, hooray.

Coach Gozen got a notice that he was being relieved as recreation department coordinator and manager of the baseball team. The team was to be disbanded. He went in to talk to the assistant camp director and was told the baseball team was a source of dissension in the camp and that was the reason it was being disbanded. We all decided we were still going to practice; they couldn't stop us from doing that. They came around and took some of our personal equipment. We played catch, but there were no bats, and we couldn't use the diamond. I'd had enough. I went in to see if I could graduate from high school early. And I thought of a way I could get out of the camp.

When Shig's enforcer gave me some more crap again I broke his collarbone for him and would have got Shig too if the others hadn't stopped it. But he looked scared enough to suit me as I tried to nail him too. "Come on, Shig, bigmouth, let's hear you talk me out of kicking your ass." He was backing up. He wasn't so tough. "Come on, you big bully, let's see what you're made of." Reiko was there; she saw. The yellow bastard.

I got a letter from Julian. He was back in the valley, stationed on the coast again. He wrote that he and Fred had a plan of getting in to see us, if they could get enough gas ration stamps to drive up. I didn't want him to come all the way up here for nothing. They weren't going to let them in here. This wasn't like the assembly center at the fairgrounds in Fresno; this was the maximum-security incorrigible criminal nuthouse camp. They ran the place like they were using a fortune-teller to decide things. They locked Dr. Sato up in the stockade with a group of block leaders that had been trying to help them run the camp. They let the troublemakers like Shig loose and locked up the others. It was all too much for me anymore.

I signed up for the Army. They didn't get many requests to enlist from Tule Lake Asylum, and they were more than happy to see me go. The rumor was we were going to be sent to a suicide unit and no one was coming back, but I'd take my chances.

We'd come back from the mess hall together one night. Reiko stopped on the way to our apartment to talk to a girlfriend. We were sitting in the chairs my father had made out of scrap lumber, and I was finishing homework, a paper I was writing. I looked around the room, the three blankets separating our sleeping places, the bare wood walls and the rag rugs. I had to tell them I had signed up for the Army before they found out from someone else. My mother had saved back some dessert, two sugar cookies, and she broke each in two to share. She said what she always said when we sat down for a minute: "I was thinking it won't be long before we go home." We'd got another envelope from Fred with the receipts for the rent for our place. She always talked like that after one of those envelopes came.

I told them I was going in the Army.

"We have to stay together," my mother said.

"I have to go. I can't stay here anymore. Try and understand. They don't respect us. They never will, unless we do some of the fighting. If we sit here we're always going to be guilty for what Japan did. You have to see that. We can't allow them to say we're cowards. We have to fight for our country."

Reiko came in, took off her coat. She'd been eating with us the last couple of weeks. "I'm tired," she said, and she went behind her blanket. We sat there a while longer, not speaking, listening to Reiko get into her nightclothes and get comfortable on her cot. She started breathing evenly, like it was the easiest thing in the world to go to sleep. I wanted to go on talking, trying to explain, but they weren't looking at me anymore. I wanted to say, this is important, what we do now: when we go back home we're going to have to know we did what we thought was right. Dr. Sato said that's all you can hope for.

Hortense had sent the clipping from the paper about Julian, and then another one when he was awarded the medal at the White House. I didn't show Reiko, but I did my mother and father. I was the only one who wrote Hortense now, and she wrote me back. I missed seeing her red hair that she could never get to stay combed out. It would curl up like electricity was running through each strand. I used to watch it when I sat behind Hortense and my sister on the school bus. For years and years I saw that red hair up close. It was like watching a tangled garden in front of me.

I went to the camp church services with my mother and father just to be together with them. I had stopped being interested in the Presbyterian Church a couple of years before we got to the camps. Not Reiko, she started going to the Buddhist church with Shig and some of the other troublemakers, who were on a food strike now. They fasted, broke curfew, hung big signs on the electrified fence around the camp: ELEANOR IS HALF JAPANESE; WHY ISN'T SHE IN HERE TOO? and JESUS WAS BUDDHA'S SON.

I didn't mention to anyone else what Julian had written about Fred and him coming up because I didn't think they would, once they found out they couldn't get in. And my parents didn't mention my plan about leaving the camp to go in the Army. My application was being processed. That's what they said when I'd go in to check. They'd let me graduate early. I had enough units. I didn't want to have to go back into Dr. Sato's empty classroom. He'd left a quote on the big sheet of plywood that was used as a blackboard:

"You may think that the Constitution is your security—it is nothing but a piece of paper. You may think that the statutes are your security—they are nothing but words in a book. You may think that the elaborate mechanism of government is your security—it is nothing at all, unless you have sound and uncorrupted public opinion to give life to your Constitution, to give vitality to your statutes, to make eficient your government machinery. Chief Justice Charles Evans Hughes."

I'd read it when he wrote it, before they locked him up, and now it was left there. No one touched it. It just stayed leaning against the wall. Dr. Sato had hanged himself in the stockade with his blue-and-purple necktie.

I was working full-time as a plumber's helper. An old Issei was the foreman; he'd been a plumbing contractor when he was on the outside. He was always making jokes. He reminded me of Mr. Brazil. "There's only three things you have to remember," he'd say. "First, the hot knob is on the left, the cold on the right. Second, shit doesn't run uphill. And third, we get paid on Friday." And every time I'd go into the lavatories with my plunger I'd think of the time Julian put in a toilet for everyone on the road. It was only three years ago, but it seemed like a hundred. He'd had an extra toilet at the end and decided to put a second one in his house in the Zia's bedroom closet. It was unheard of to have two in the same house. The old Zia would take people inside the closet to flush the toilet for them. I'd be on my hands and knees in a lavatory, working the snake, trying to get through the blockage and I'd be thinking of home and I'd start getting teary-eyed; I couldn't help it. It was worse when we got a package from home, when Hortense would send one and everyone would have put something inside the box. The old Zia always sent something for me, a salami or socks she knitted, something. I'd get to sniffing sometimes and the men I was working with would ask, Grayson, you catching cold? I'd nod, unable to even speak.

I didn't know what was up when I was told to report to our block mess hall where my mother worked. I went running, worried that something could have happened to my mother. There was a civilian car parked out in front by the steps, and as I came up, the back door of the sedan opened and Julian got out. He was half asleep still. My mother and father and Reiko and then Fred came out of the mess hall. I couldn't believe my eyes. Julian acted like he wasn't sure of his welcome, or like we might not have remembered him. He looked different; he'd lost weight and his face was chalk white, like he hadn't been outside for a long time.

My mother, who never did this kind of thing, went down the stairs first and kissed Julian on the lips. I was trying to shake his hand, then Fred's. My father was patting Julian on the back. Reiko kissed him and was crying. No one knew what to say. It was such a surprise to see the two of them. But all the thoughts we'd had about home came true, now that we had two people that were in all those daydreams.

"Well," Fred said, "you should have seen Master Sergeant Palestini get us into this place. What worries me is can we get out?"

"It was my battalion commander who knows someone on General Dewitt's staff who's in charge of these camps who wrote the letter that got us in," Julian said. "It wasn't because of me being a sergeant. That wouldn't get us past the tanks." Fred started talking again and didn't stop. After we'd hauled all the things they'd brought up inside the mess hall, I stayed outside with Julian, who had to tighten the fan belt, which was slipping.

I was holding the generator and pulley tight with a tire iron, stretching the belt taut while Julian tried to tighten the bolt on the bracket that went around the other pulley. He had to take his overcoat off to keep his sleeve from getting greasy. "Fred wouldn't stop driving once he got behind the wheel," he told me. "He'd have gone clear through the state of Oregon if I hadn't woke up and told him we were here. The goddamn car was overheating. He drove twenty hours straight." I had to laugh; it was the old Julian who was speaking.

I told him I was going to join the Army. "This place is bullshit, Julian; it's not fair what they're doing to us. I'll take my chances." I went on, Julian looking up once in a while as if to hear better. I went from the baseball team to Dr. Sato and the woman I found in the lavatory who had cut her throat after choking her child to death because she thought she was going to be separated from her husband. He let me go on until it was all out in the open and I started feeling like I could see better now, look back on all that happened as if it were a picture I had put into better focus.

Every time I'd read one of Julian's letters or hear something about him from Hortense, I'd want to be like him. And I was starting to feel better by the minute, just standing next to him. An oficer and two guards came over to where the car was and yelled out before they saw Julian, "Hey you, Jap, what are you doing to that car?" When the oficer saw Julian he asked him, "Do you have a pass, soldier?" Julian wiped his hands before handing him over the pass. The lieutenant didn't look at it very closely; he was looking over Julian's ribbons on his chest. The combat infantry badge I knew, but not the ribbons. "We have to check everyone, Sergeant; this place is nothing but a pest hole. It's a madhouse all the time. If the evacuees aren't raising hell, the civilian administrators are. We can't do anything right. Then there's the townspeople and the bigwigs that keep the pot boiling. I've put in for transfer four times already, and they won't let us go. If you don't like it here, neither do we," he said to me.

I had never talked to an officer before. "None of us like to be called a Jap," I said.

"I know that, but I forget. Some old man told me it was offensive to him too. I just forgot. I apologize to you." I couldn't think of what to say. "You were on the baseball team. I saw that triple you hit. They didn't disband you because you beat us. I was told you didn't want to play anymore because you thought the Americans might enjoy watching the games."

"I happen to be an American citizen, the same as you," I said. "It was the soldiers who came around and confiscated our baseball equipment. We wanted to play."

It wasn't getting us anywhere, and he must have realized it too, because he asked Julian, "Where are you stationed, Sergeant?"

"I'm on furlough now. I've got my orders for the European theater. North Africa is the word."

"Good luck. It was nice talking to you," he said, handing Julian back the pass. "Both of you," he said, and he saluted Julian and went off.

To be funny I asked Julian, "You think I'm going to like the Army?" He started laughing in his old way then. "You'll be the first," he said, giving me a whack on the back. "Just think about the mountains," he said. "That's what I thought about—the big trees up there. It makes you forget what's happening to you. I'm going to go fill this," and he untied the canvas water bag from the grill. "You go inside and get warm and I'll be in right away. This wind's got a bite to it."

I was feeling better by the minute, like I had taken some medicine. Old Fred, it didn't seem possible he'd be up here. He was chuckling in that Okie way, holding up a good wool overcoat for my father that had been Mr. Brazil's. All kinds of winter clothes for all of us. Reiko was trying on a pullover sweater with "Hubba Hubba" across the front. "How does it look?" she asked me. Fred got down on his knees, trying to put a pair of fur-lined boots on my mother's feet. She was giggling, embarrassed that anyone would wait on her like that, holding her skirt closed tight against her legs.

Fred had given my father a ledger to look at with all the farm accounts written inside and an inventory of all the equipment and household goods we'd left. I was trying on a pullover vest that Fred had handed me, I could tell it was homemade, that either the Zia or Mrs. Palestini had knit it for me, when Shig came through the double doors of the mess hall. He looked so ridiculous with his shaved head in that cold place where everyone wore a hat, I couldn't help thinking he was nuts or just plain silly. Before, everyone thought him so brave when he phoned the new governor of the state, Earl Warren, to call him a bigot—"You were a bigot when you were state attorney general and you're a double bigot as governor"—yelling at the top of his voice from the pay phone in front of the administration ofice. No one even knew if he was really talking to the new governor or not. What happened next unfolded like the melodramas we used to see at the Fox Theater in town. Reiko yelling, "Shig!" Me looking surprised, with a lightbulb lighting up over my head. Shig and Reiko. Shig was jealous; she must have told him about Fred. Fred standing up from helping my mother to shake hands. Shig socking him in the mouth, knocking him over the bench next to the table.

You don't have to hit an Okie twice. Fred was up, but not fast enough. My father yelled and took a judo stance. That surprised Shig, who stepped back, and Fred nailed him three or four times. Shig went down slow, but he didn't get up. It happened so fast no one had a chance to speak. My father was the first to recover. In Japanese he said to Reiko, "What have you done?" One of the cooks started screeching, and there was a lot of yelling in the back from the kitchen. Fred's lip was bleeding down his chin, and my mother got a wet towel from the sink and made him hold it to his mouth. Reiko didn't move. Shig was trying to get up when a guard came running in with fixed bayonet, and then another one. Then Julian came in after them. Fred tried to explain, "I butted heads with him is all. It was just an accident. No harm done." The soldiers didn't buy it and they marched Shig out.

The incident kind of put a damper on their coming up. Julian tried to make a joke: "I leave you a minute, Fred, and see what happens." My mother and I laughed. Fred's mouth wouldn't stop bleeding. Every time he took the towel away, blood would start dripping again. My mother wanted him to go to the clinic, but he said it was nothing.

Julian and Fred had been planning the trip for weeks and had driven twenty hours to get here, and we all ended up just sitting there looking at each other. Hortense had made about thirty pounds of cookies and the box was open on the table but no one was eating any. Fred mentioned people from home who wanted to be remembered to us. Mr. Hart, of course; he sent us all gloves. Hortense and the rest of the Brazils. Charlie was a superintendent now and had got exempted from the draft to work in the oil fields. Some people from our church. Bud, the fruit broker we sold our crops to. The owner of the grocery where we traded had sent up the new calendar for 1944. Fred would stop a minute to think, holding the towel to his split lip.

The mess hall crew started setting up lunch then. My mother got up to help. We started to say our good-byes. It wasn't like the hellos; it was depressing. These were our best friends, and we couldn't even visit with them without someone getting punched. They didn't want us to come outside; it had started to really rain now. You couldn't even see the guard towers across the way. We watched Julian and Fred make a run for it to their car through a blur of rain against the windowpane. Then two shafts of yellow from the headlights, and they started to move away across the sheets of rain.

After they had gone my father stood up, saying something to himself in Japanese that I didn't understand. My mother stopped wiping a tabletop and watched him. He took the two steps between him and Reiko where she waited and slapped her hard across the face. His hand left an imprint of fingers on her cheek. Then he walked out of the mess hall into the storm.

He had never touched us before, never laid a hand on us, no matter what we did. My mother would swat us, but not him. He wouldn't even kill a fly. He caught them in his cupped hands and walked outside of the house to let them go. My mother looked away. Reiko stood there, so surprised she couldn't move, trying not to raise her hand to touch her face.

JULIAN

chapter 16

It felt like I'd spent my whole life doing this: the troop train, the boredom of waiting around an Army base, this time in New Jersey, with four thousand other soldiers before embarkation on a transport, wondering how long the war was going to go on, how many more times I'd be getting on a troop ship headed for a war zone. The word was the Germans could last to 1950 and the Japanese forever if there wasn't a truce before that; that was the good news for 1943.

I was a master sergeant so they put me in the chief petty officers' compartment. All of them had stashes of booze, which we drank at night, sitting around in our shorts playing pinochle, chain-smoking, telling stories about women in civilian life that nobody else believed. No one knew how long we'd be in port, waiting for the rest of the ships to arrive to fill out the convoy. I'd been assigned to an infantry regiment, like before in the Aleutians. It was all the same to me. There was no avoiding the fighting, and I knew I had to do my part. But I wasn't sure I could anymore. When I thought about it, I felt like I'd rather die myself than look down at another person I'd killed. It was my own face I'd seen when I'd looked at the dead Japanese soldiers on the frozen ground at Attu, as if I'd killed myself. I had to stop thinking about that.

I was feeling better: the ulcers had stopped bleeding so much and at times I felt like eating. Once in a while I thought of trying to see someone about what was happening to me now. Sometimes for no reason I'd start bawling. Tears would stream down my face and I couldn't breathe right. I pretended it was hay fever, but it was hard to stop sometimes. But any Army doctor I'd ever met would call me a goldbrick, a malingerer, laugh at me and send me back to my unit, I knew that.

When things got bad for me, I tried to think about the place: the vines, my mother and father, the Zia. Everyone on the road: the Brazils, Fred and Charlie, the Hamadas, like it used to be before the war. The hunting camp: I could almost see it from our front porch, up there in the snow-covered Sierras. If I made it back this time, I'd never leave again. I'd stay in the valley forever.

One of the chiefs was talking about the ship's newspaper. I'd seen it around, a three-page mimeographed sheet so faded it was hard to read. A few jokes, ship's hours for the store and church services, an article about Mrs. Roosevelt, who was visiting the servicemen in Hawaii. For something to do, I went to the newspaper office the next morning and got on as a reporter. "Write what you want," the editor, a second class who'd been a Linotype setter in civilian life, told me. "But give me a full page by thirteen hundred."

The fifty-one-ship convoy sailed late one night, no lights on the shore to watch fade away because of the blackouts. The troops were kept below until we cleared the harbor and got out to sea. I went down ladders to the big compartments. With the ship's engines right underneath, the noise was deafening; everyone had to yell to talk. The bunks were stacked ten high, equipment was piled on the deck, men were everywhere there was a open space. They'd been waiting in the compartments a day and a half at the pier, and when we hit the open water there was a sudden pause of almost quiet: they knew we were in the Atlantic, finally, that we were on our way to the war. I started talking to some men from a National Guard unit in Arizona. The bow of the ship smacked against the waves. Sitting on someone's seabag, I started feeling a little queasy. Then I heard someone vomit, and then someone else. Once it started, the seasickness spread as if just the sound of vomiting was enough to get the next person sick. I went back up topside feeling sorry for the poor bastards who had to stay below. The fresh air made me feel better right away.

I wrote my first article as a scientific survey: Why is it the soldier on the top bunk gets sick first? How green should your buddy's face get before you should suggest he go to sick bay or the latrine? And why the sudden stop in complaints about the Navy chow? I went on for a full column, then filled the rest of the page with a profile of one of the merchant seamen on board, William Mauer from Lomita Park, California, who'd been torpedoed three times on the run to Murmansk, Russia, and lived to tell about it. "I never gave up thinking I was going to eat another hamburger and root beer float at the Avenue Fountain," I quoted him saying. I ended the page with Government Issue Gripes. I couldn't print a lot of the genuine gripes I heard every day, like Why are all corporals such assholes? or Why do I get a TS chit every time I try to see the CO about transferring out of the Infantry into the Navy? or How come we have to put up with the chaplain telling us Jesus Christ was an officer, not an enlisted man? But I did use one I'd heard that morning from a first class bosun mate: Is it true that after the war officers will have job preference?

My page was a hit. I wrote another one and signed myself Buck Private Smith. I liked doing the pieces; it filled in the time. I was typing away in the yeoman's office right after the third paper came out when an officer walked in. "You must be Buck Private Smith. I might have a slot for you with the division paper when we get ashore." We had a long talk. I listened, mostly. As an information officer, the major was on the lookout for reporters. We shot the bull for half an hour, which was the longest I'd ever talked to an officer.

There was a submarine sighting and the convoy went south, almost parallel to Brazil, and then cut east again toward the Mediterranean. Eleven days, and it seemed like we had been on the ship forever. When we finally landed in Tunisia, the Germans and the Italians had given up in North Africa, and I had been assigned to the division newspaper. The major wasn't just BS-ing me. I wasn't going to have to carry a rifle. I was so relieved I slept right though roll call and missed breakfast.

There was so much confusion in the port when we disembarked—troops and equipment were massing for a big invasion coming up—that it took me three days to find my unit. I didn't care how long it took. I was safe here in the rear. When I did connect, I found the division newspaper editor in a pyramid tent. Most of the men on the paper had no more experience than I did, but everyone knew what a good deal this was. There was an officer somewhere who was supposed to be involved, but the editor was a first sergeant, and it was supposed to be a soldiers' paper, written by and for GIs.

I was feeling better by the day. I was safe in the rear echelon and I was in the Mediterranean, close to Italy, which I'd been hearing about my whole life. My father had made me promise to write, and I did, every chance I got, thick letters this time. I knew my folks got Hortense to read them the letters: she'd go slow on the English, throwing in some Portuguese and Italian and lots of gestures until she got the meaning across. It always made me smile to think of her sitting at our kitchen table, elbows on the oilcloth covering, trying to explain my letters to my folks and the Zia. I tried to be funny; there was no sense writing about how screwed up the Army was and that the war might never end. Hortense wrote me back every week now. My father wanted to know if I'd met any Italians yet, especially Marchegiani, especially Urbinati; he hadn't talked to anyone from the town he'd left in 1901 since a couple of immigrant cousins had come through the valley twenty years ago. I wrote that I was close to Italy, but not there yet.

I had a photo, a three-by-four snapshot of all of us on the road, sitting at a table outside the Portuguese Hall in town. It was from when Hortense was queen of the Holy Ghost festival. My father in his black wool suit and the Borsolino he wore when he came to the U.S., the Zia in a dress made out of the same blue-and-white polka dot material as my mother's dress, my mother next to her. The long table with pans of sopas down the middle, bowls of fava beans and bottles of beer and and wine. The Hamadas in their Sunday-best clothes, Grayson, Reiko sitting next to Fred, her arm around his neck. Patrick wearing his gray derby. That couldn't be Ray next to him; he was dead by then. Hortense with her red hair like wire, fake diamond tiara already askew. Richard Cortez. Her mother and father, two of her sisters, one of her brothers. I was in the photo, standing in the back in my shirtsleeves, though it wasn't hot yet, next to two other people I couldn't remember. April was when the festivals started, the vines already leafed out by then, the grape clusters formed. I looked different in the photo, different each time I held it close to my face to see better. I had changed, but if I could get back to the valley I'd change back to my old self, forget everything that happened since the war started.

I was just feeling comfortable with the division newspaper routine, typing out the stories, making every deadline, when the editor called me in. I didn't know what it was about. "Palestini, you're to report to the First Parachute Battalion," the editor told me. "You've been to jump school so you should enjoy the assignment. It'll give you a different perspective than this rear echelon point of view. We need more news from the front-line troops."

Front line. Everyone knew there was something up, an invasion somewhere, maybe Greece, Sardinia, or Corsica. I'd volunteered for jump school when I was drafted because of the extra pay. It had never seemed hard then to leap out of an airplane. I pretended I was just letting my soul fall through the air while my body was safe in the plane and the two would join up on the ground again. I'd seen soldiers freeze at the door, or unsnap themselves from the static line and take their parachutes off, while the sergeants cursed and called them names. The First Battalion paratroopers weren't afraid of jumping; it was the invasion that had them worried.

Soldiers had a sixth sense for disaster, like dogs did just before a California earthquake, bristling and howling. Some of the paratroopers had already fought in the North African campaigns, but most were replacements, wide-eyed, not sure of themselves, like me scared but unwilling to back out, unwilling to say forget it, unwilling to let their friends down. When we were told Sicily, no one went AWOL.

It was a beautiful day for an invasion. We sat in a plane on the runway in the July sunshine for seven hours, pissing down a funnel attached to a three-inch pipe in the tail. When we took off, it was to fly in circles for another hour before heading out over the Mediterranean for Sicily. I could see other planes through our open doorway, flying in some kind of formation like birds. I was calm. Tears I couldn't control were streaming down my face along with the sweat. Everyone was perspiring in that hot plane. As I watched, one of the planes next to us exploded, split open, spilling the paratroopers inside across the sky. No chutes opened. I was positive that wouldn't happen to us. Our plane was hit, then, shuddered with the impact of metal passing through the wings. Everyone remained calm and the plane flew on.

The light went on to jump and everyone stood up. We were moving, leaving the plane, just like we practiced. I jumped and felt the rush of air and counted to ten, then pulled the rip cord. I opened my eyes and looked down. Water, only water, as far as I could see. I couldn't see any land, much less Sicily. I wasn't going to have anything to tell my father.

I started getting rid of my equipment, field pack, rifle. I got my boots off just before I hit the water, then slipped out of the harness before the parachute dragged me down. Floating on my back, I watched the others sail down from the sky. There was nothing I could do except yell myself hoarse, "Get rid of your gear, get rid of your shit." Some hit the water like stones, weighed down by their equipment. Others were taken under by their chutes.

I took off my trousers and tied a knot at the bottom of each leg, then filled them with air, holding the waist closed. The float lasted for eight or nine minutes. Then I did it again and again. There was no direction to swim toward. I couldn't guess which way land was.

After I was picked up by a destroyer, along with more men than I thought possibly could have survived, I found out that the planes that were shot down were fired at by our own anti-aircraft. Why we weren't put down over our drop zone on Sicily was never explained. I took it all calmly. For some reason, I was always calm after the disaster. We were transferred to an LST and landed on a Sicilian beach that had already been secured. It was amazing, I thought, that after all the Allied snafus we still had a toehold on Sicily. It meant the Italians and the Germans must be as fucked up as we were.

I knew the censors wouldn't even let me write to my folks about what had happened, much less put it in the division newspaper. Stupidity wasn't news in the Army, and a certain number of casualties was expected. Everyone was expendable, when it came right down to it. War was like farming in a lot of ways: you did everything you could, but it was mostly luck in the end. But no one ever died pruning vines.

The natives were friendly enough, waving as the trucks full of GIs passed, but I could barely understand their Italian. My father thought all Sicilians were thieves, but neither of us had ever met any before. I watched another Italian American, an Intelligence captain, talk a whole battalion of Italian engineers into surrendering—they had already thrown away their rifles—and then into unloading an LST. I didn't know where my unit was, but I didn't look very hard either.

The Signal Corps unit I was following moved toward Catania. I'd never seen such poverty. These Sicilians made the valley Okies seem rich in those old cars with mattresses tied on the roof. There was no food. People were dying of starvation. The Germans had stripped the country before they retreated. There were no farm animals or machinery. Bridges were blown up; everything useful to the Allies or the people themselves was destroyed.

The civilians had given up too, just like the Italian soldiers I'd seen. Girls were selling themselves, mothers with children were offering themselves, their younger sisters. I didn't know where to look sometimes. There'd be kids with old pots waiting at the garbage cans where we scraped off our mess gear, waiting for the scraps. I'd end up going back through the chow line for another helping just to give it to some little kids. If you finished a cigarette and went to snuff out the butt with your heel, four or five little hands would be trying to grab the butt. The older kids, eight or nine, maybe, would steal anything. I lost two fatigue caps in the same day.

I found out where my unit was located but didn't report for almost a week. "Well, look what the cat dragged in," the editor said when I showed up. "Palestini, we thought you'd bought the farm. Welcome home, Sergeant."

I moved around freely among the different units in the rear, shooting the bull, looking for something interesting to write about. My profiles were a weekly feature, and I tried to make each one different. I wanted to cover all kinds of units in the theater of operations. I got a ride from a Canadian corporal who was heading back to his unit and got an earful. The Canadians were pissed at the English generals, who were a little too free in spilling Canadian blood, they thought. Their complaints were a lot stronger than any I'd heard from U.S. troops: a Texas division complaining about a useless National Guard unit on their flank, for instance, or any of the rear-area echelon versus the front-line troop gripes. I ran into some Polish troops who crawled around at night behind enemy lines, looking for Nazi throats to cut to avenge their country. The Moroccans were just as bloodthirsty. I wrote a short piece on each unit. The editor liked them and wanted more.

By August the Sicilian campaign was almost over. I had kept away from the fighting. That first day had been plenty for me. I'd toured most of the British units: Australian, then New Zealand, Scots and Irish and South African. The only noncomplainers were the Gurkhas and the Sikhs. The English conscripts hated being in the Army and disliked their officers as much as any GI did. It seemed to be the same all over: brains had very little to do with making it into the officer corps. It was class that counted: sons from wealthy families were treated better than anyone else. "Born to be staff officers," a tech sergeant from Philadelphia told me.

I'd never thought much about class in California, but it wasn't so different at home in the valley, from what Hortense had written me. Rich men's healthy young sons were being exempted from the military draft because they were supposed to be needed to raise food on their fathers' big cattle ranches or farms. No one in the Land Company was going into the Army either, she wrote. "And they are not ashamed at staying home. They still look you in the eye and act like they own the whole world."

It was probably better that the people on the home front didn't know what was really happening here; it was good there was a censor. Would they work those sixteen-hour shifts like Fred did in an aircraft plant if they knew how many planes were lost with their crews because of bad planning or bad weather or just human error? What if the people who worked in the shipyards knew that ships were just abandoned when they broke down because no one knew how to repair them? The waste over here was horrific. A cartoon in the Army paper showed a GI looking through mountains of wrecked trucks and Jeeps and yelling to his buddy, "Hey, here's one with bullet holes." The kids who collected paper and scrap metal, the women who were working men's jobs because of the labor shortages, they were the ones who believed that winning the war was important and possible. I'd seen it when I came home from the Aleutians. Here everyone was interested in staying alive, in making sure they got back home.

It was only a request, but the editor treated it like a direct order: "Get going, Palestini," he yelled. A division PR captain had invited me to a news briefing for the big-time civilian correspondents. "I've read your profiles," the captain told me. "I've seen enlisted men read you first, before the cartoons. That should tell you something. You are a morale booster of the very first order."

I liked to hear the praise but I didn't trust the captain. Officers didn't talk to you like that unless they wanted something. "And if it's convenient, Sergeant Palestini, I'd like you to attend the reception after the briefing. It's for a select group only." All I could do was nod and say yes sir.

I put on a khaki uniform, wrinkled from two months in a seabag, and got a ride to the hotel in Messina. The Germans and Italians had been overrun in Sicily the week before. Most had got away across the straits to Italy proper, and now all the Allies were preparing for their first landing on the mainland. That's what the briefing was about. I put on my Infantry badge to show I'd seen combat once. What a hypocrite, I thought, fastening the clasp.

I didn't know what to expect, but the correspondents from the big national papers and magazines back home seemed old men compared to most of the soldiers—in their forties, at least, and proud of their rear-echelon pressed and immaculate uniforms, proud of their equivalency rank on their collars, as if they'd earned it by years of service instead of by writing from the safety of a city newsroom. They were trying to look military and dapper, like General MacArthur.

The briefing began. Officers traced lines on maps with pointers and gave long explanations of strategy. They said how well the Sicilian campaign had unfolded. How well the Allied armies had worked together. How surprised the enemy had been. How wonderful . . . I started thinking of Hortense. I should have married Hortense Brazil. Asked her, at least. It would be too late, once the war was over. I'd had my chance. That night when I took her home and we parked by their barn. We were like two magnets. I couldn't stop and she didn't want to either. She was tearing at my shirt trying to get to my skin as I was burying myself in her soft, warm breasts.

It was a combination of things that stopped me finally. The voice that said no, no, this isn't right, along with what happened up in Canada at Prince Rupert after the Aleutian campaign. A woman Red Cross worker picked me up in a bar. I couldn't do anything. I was more surprised than embarrassed. I couldn't believe my penis would ever let me down. "I think it's refusing to rise to the occasion," the woman said. The same thing happened in Seattle with a ten-dollar whore, the most I'd ever paid. She tried everything, but it was like my dick wasn't part of my body anymore. I gave up after that. And that's what I remembered while Hortense and I were grappling with each other, half undressed. I couldn't think of anything to say, once I got my breath back. We just sat there for the longest time, until finally I got out. She wrote after that, a letter a week, full of news about the road, my family, and she always signed it the same way: Your friend and neighbor, Hortense.

In her last letter she'd written that Grayson had finished basic training and was shipping out to the Mediterranean. They were sending all the Japanese American troops to the European theater because they didn't trust them in the South Pacific. I didn't like to think about the Hamadas. My head ached every time I went back over that visit Fred and I made up to the Tule Lake relocation camp. Hortense wrote that Grayson's unit was the 442nd, an all Japanese American combat team. Considering all the other nationalities with the Allied Forces in Italy, they might as well send over some Japanese Americans too to join in the fun. Hortense. Her breasts had smelled like soap and carnations.

"Sergeant Palestini, I presume." I came back with a start, stood up, and the officer surprised me by putting out his hand while I stood at attention. The PR captain was introducing us: "Colonel Green, Sergeant Palestini."

I sat next to the colonel during the reception, which was really a banquet. He kept asking me questions. I explained I was a farmer in civilian life; the newspaper business was a sideline. The colonel said he was a historian; he taught at a university and wrote history books. "This war is going to change the world in ways that we can't even imagine," he told me. I listened to the colonel and watched the war correspondents get tanked up. The Italian brandy was flowing along with the vino. Rigatoni, veal, fish, then big platters of game. It was like being home at Sunday dinner when my sisters came back to visit and my mother had time to cook. I ate until my ulcer started acting up, and tried to pay attention to the colonel to be polite, but he didn't need an audience. "Napoleon had historians in his entourage, you see. Of course, Xenophon was a general himself."

One of the correspondents with a young girl on his lap started hitting a fork against his wineglass, and the hum of noise started to abate. The correspondent slid the girl onto the next man's lap and stood up. He was short and homely. His hair stood straight up as if it were being sucked up by a big fan, and his ears stuck out.

"Officers, men, and correspondents, may I have your attention," he said. "It should be noted that this wonderful banquet given by the U.S. Army for members of the press corps covering the war in the European theater is only our just due and reward. There has never been a group of men and women who have risked so much in the service of their country to bring the news to the people." There was some clapping and calls of "You tell 'em, Elmer."

The colonel beside me was going on and on. I wanted to listen to Elmer. He reminded me of the old tramp reporters I'd met when I was a stringer for the valley papers. They never lasted more than five or six months on a paper, and a lot of them were alcoholics, but they could sit at a typewriter and pound out anything you asked them to, from obituaries to editorials. The only difference between them and most hoboes was that they could read and write.

"I'd like to make you a proposition," the colonel said. "I want you to do some profiles, say of some of the staff officers at the division or corps level. I think your profiles could bridge the gap between them and the enlisted men and junior-grade officers. There's a human and compassionate side to our leading generals, Palestini. It isn't often understood how egalitarian they really are." I was nodding; I'd had too much brandy. "And you deserve a bigger audience too. This assignment would be as a special correspondent to the official Army paper. You could leave a poignant record of what the GIs really thought of their generals." I would have to look up *egalitarian,* I was thinking. "This could lead to a professional career in journalism, Palestini. I might be able to help you later."

They wanted me to make the generals look good? I was nodding in agreement. Why the hell not? "Generals. I'd have to be in a position to observe them," I heard myself say.

"That's not a problem. I'll have you reassigned to my unit. You'll be a witness to one of the most brilliantly executed invasions in the history of modern warfare. It's top secret, but you'll see the Allied Military Command at its best."

Elmer, the short correspondent at the middle table, was still speaking, though most of his audience had stopped listening. "I'd like to make a toast," he shouted finally, and he raised his glass. The waiters rushed around filling glasses and the speaker waited. "To newspaper people," he called out, "this special group of brownnosers and various sorts of deviates who have fed off other people's misery for most of their professional lives." Someone threw a pear at the speaker; others were yelling, "Bullshit," and more fruit began to fly. I got down under the table with the colonel and we finished off the brandy.

I'd had it easy in the peacetime Army, drafted before the war started, but not as good as this. So plush, this new assignment, the sweet life. A maid woke me at seven-thirty with a café latte. After a long hot bath, I dressed in a uniform the hotel staff had pressed and shoes they'd spit-shined and went down for breakfast, which the hotel served family style. What a life. By ten o'clock I was ready for work, which meant wandering around the hotels and palazzos requisitioned by headquarters units. Colonel Green had told me I had carte blanche; no door was shut to me. I could attend any meeting, approach any officer and request time for an interview. Any officer; he emphasized that, *any.* I tested the order the first morning by walking between two MPs stationed at either side of a doorway with a wink and then sitting in on a planning session for the coming invasion. I listened for an hour to a brigadier general of engineers talk about beach terrain, tides, and approaches at Salerno. Then I closed my eyes and went to sleep because of the big breakfast I'd had.

The colonel had given me thick files with biographies of almost all the important Allied commanders, colonels and above. All the American generals had gone to West Point, I noticed. Some had served together in the First World War. All had families and dogs. I convinced myself I didn't need to talk personally to any of them. I decided I didn't have enough experience as a journalist to interview a general. It would be too complicated, trying to get past the man's reputation to the person behind the rank. And I wasn't sure I wanted to find out what lurked there. If he were a dummy or a candidate for a Section 8, I didn't want to know.

I sat around for days trying to write something based on the bios. I'd eat a big lunch and then spend some time at my typewriter cleaning out the letters *D, O, P,* and *Q* with a straightened paper clip. I couldn't get a handle on any one person. I'd observed a dozen generals at meetings, but they didn't seem human enough. I'd sat at a lunch table with a major general and two lieutenant generals plus Colonel Green. They were nice enough joes, passed the butter when I asked, but I couldn't break through the feeling that most of them were just acting out some part. There was one at a briefing who wore a polished helmet, spit-shined riding boots, jodhpurs, and two big silver six-shooters. He was probably Patrick Hart's age, forty-five or fifty, but he acted like he was twenty-five and a Hollywood star waiting for someone to bring on the movie cameras. He kept a white horse and strutted around jingling his spurs and whacking his leg with a riding crop. What could I write about a poser like this? He wanted to be called Blood and Guts? Did his wife call him that, his mother? Old Blood and Bull was what the GIs called him. What enlisted man would want to know more about this ham actor?

I was in a group of several hundred reporters who were listening to this general at a briefing when I noticed that Elmer Pope, the Reuters reporter who'd got the fruit thrown at him at the banquet, was standing next to me. He had a long gold toothpick sticking out the corner of his mouth. "Have you ever seen such a horse's ass in your whole life?" he said in a stage whisper loud enough for anyone within ten feet to hear. Some of the reporters laughed. "He knows we can't write the truth, but that doesn't stop him from bullshitting us." Another general came up to the podium. This one was even taller and had an immense nose. He kept turning his face to present his best profile for the photographers. "Now this one is not only arrogant, he's a genuine imbecile. Someone dubbed him the American eagle and he thinks it's a compliment. Here, have a drink." He passed me his silver flask.

"Where you from, soldier?" he asked me after the briefing. "The San Joaquin Valley; hell, I never thought anyone actually lived in that desert. I worked on the *San Francisco News* but never got further south than San Jose."

Things started happening too fast. On September 3rd the British Eighth Army landed on the toe of the Italian mainland across the straits from Sicily, and Italy surrendered. The Germans didn't, and they still held the boot. The U.S. Fifth Army was getting ready to follow the British to the mainland: embarkation was set for September 8th. "This is it, Julian," Elmer said, yanking my tie. "We'll be drinking tea with the pope next week." I made myself get lost in the shuffle when I learned the invasion date. I wasn't ready. I got myself sent to Palermo, on the other end of Sicily, for an interview with an Air Force general on the 8th. When the first U.S. assault troops hit the beachhead at Salerno on the 9th, I was sitting down to a meal in a hotel in Palermo. I would have got away with it, except for Elmer. He knew. He had to know what I knew: I was scared shitless. I could admit that to myself after my jump with the paratroopers.

The first reports on the landing were good. They stayed good until a few days later, when the Germans counterattacked. I stopped reading the reports and went out and got drunk. I went to bed each night pretending it was just another September day, that no one was getting blown up and dying, up the boot at Salerno.

I hid out until the fighting had moved away from the beachhead and there was no danger, and then I caught a ride to the mainland on a supply ship. I got a lift in a Jeep with an engineer battalion headed north. They let me off in the dark outside some little town just before their route veered east. Once I found the central piazza, I saw it was posted off-limits by the MPs. They were always doing that, saving a town for themselves. I ignored the signs and found a place to eat and ordered a big bottle of vino and a plate of pasta with clams. As I ate at one of the tables outside the door, women started walking by, speaking to me in a dialect I didn't understand. But one was picking up English fast: "GI, hey, look—blond pussy," and she showed me, but it was a tied-on wisp of blond curls like a miniature wig. "Sorry, Miss, I'm a priest," I told her in Italian, holding my hands up in prayer, and she laughed. I didn't want to catch a disease, I told myself.

I finished my bottle of wine and ordered a cognac and then another. There was no end to the Italian brandy; they must have hidden it from the Germans. I felt relaxed now, sitting back in the chair. The food had been good. Inside the door, hanging from a hook, was a fedora like my father wore. I tried it on. It fit okay. The restaurant owner tried to give it to me, but I paid him some invasion money. It was a Borsolino, the same kind my father wore with his Sunday suit, the hat he'd worn when he came to California. I started writing a letter to my father and mother, wearing the hat, writing away at the restaurant table, making Italy sound like the place they used to describe when they sat around the dinner table, eating, talking, reminiscing. If they could forget the poverty that forced them to leave this place for California, I didn't have to describe what the war had done here. I filled five pages in my notebook, wrote until the owner had turned off most of the lights.

When I left I didn't ask directions. I just started walking the opposite direction from the way I'd come. I didn't care where I ended up. This was the rear; the front had moved toward Naples. After a couple of hours I wished I'd asked, because I was lost and no vehicles were passing. I walked until I stumbled and almost fell. Then I sat down on the side of the road, said the hell with it, curled up, and went to sleep. When I woke up it was gray morning and I was sitting in a small square. It must have rained a little in the night, because my overcoat was damp and the stones were wet. The place was ruined, rubble, just a few columns still standing, and eerily quiet. What awful thing had happened here? I walked around; the place was ancient. An old man with a donkey loaded with sticks appeared. What is this place, I asked him. "Ercolano, Ercolano," he said, and it took me a while to put it together, Herculaneum, the Roman city near Pompeii, covered by volcano eruption and uncovered in this century by archaeologists. We'd had a calendar at home with a picture of Pompeii. Was all of Italy going to end up like this?

It wasn't hard to find where the correspondents were staying, once I got to Salerno. All I had to do was find one of the better hotels that had survived the bombardment and had a bar intact. I felt sheepish, was leery of what Elmer would say. I lied to myself that I'd had a legitimate reason not to be in on the invasion; that interview was important. When Elmer saw me come into the lobby he yelled out, "It's the California kid. Come on, you look like you need a drink." And I did, I really did.

I felt awkward with the correspondents now. How many had Elmer told? He knew I was yellow, a coward. "This is a major invasion, Julian; it's important. That interview can wait," he'd told me. He'd thought I didn't understand the significance of Salerno. When I'd said the general was being rotated stateside, this was my last chance at him, he had to know I was hiding out.

First Salerno, and then about a month later Elmer came rushing into my room. "Julian, want to go on a raid over Berlin? I've got us a ride in a B-17. Come on, it'll be interesting. We'll pee out the bomb bay on Hitler." I broke down in front of him. It was like I couldn't get my breath. I started to gasp for air. Then the shaking started. Tears. I stood up from where I was typing, trying to hide my face in my hands. Elmer didn't look disgusted. He punched me on the arm. "Don't worry about it," he said, and left. Elmer treated me like he always did, after that, and he never mentioned what happened. But he never asked me on any of his adventures, as he called them, again.

He'd been a foreign correspondent even before the U.S. got into the war, I found out. He was evacuated with the English troops at Dunkirk and covered the blitz in London. He was there when the Germans marched into Paris. He was in on the first American landing in North Africa. He was always taking off to cover some other part of the war: a submarine patrol, a practice landing in a glider. I wouldn't let him read my interviews with the brass. He kidded me about trying to make them seem human and normal. "You're looking in the wrong place for normal," Elmer said. "Regular Army staff officers are ruined men; the Army guarantees that with long separations from their families. They don't know their children or their spouses. Who they know best are their West Point classmates, because they're competing with them for rank. This war is a godsend to the officer corps. Promotions, recognition; they're in their glory; forget egalitarianism. And sex. The Allied commander of everyone in Europe is fucking his driver, for goodness' sake. In this case, she happens to be female. And that other general you were going to write about, that lowlife pervert broke some whore's jaw the other night; I saw it with my own eyes."

Elmer didn't accept the patriotic line that everyone wrote back home. "There's an old axiom that the first victim of war is the truth," he said. "Our newspapers are just more propaganda agents to keep the home front hopping, just like the service papers are for the troops. We're not going to win unless we can stop the German factories." He'd been on a raid in a Liberator over Ploesti in Romania to bomb the German oil refineries. It turned out to be a slaughterhouse for the Allies, but even so it must have scared the Germans, he said, because they knew that without oil they were finished.

Elmer knew so much I thought he must have gone to college, but he laughed his head off when I asked. The college of hard knocks, he told me. He had gone through ninth grade, and that was plenty at the time. He was raised in Idaho; his mother ran a boardinghouse. Sometimes, when I saw him in his black derby with his Army greatcoat flung over his shoulders, the long gold toothpick either in the corner of his mouth or sticking up like a feather in his hatband when he ate, Elmer reminded me of Patrick, who always looked dapper, too. Neither one of them was a phony.

Elmer was shy with women until he had a few drinks. After a few drinks, there was no telling what he'd do. He'd go after some officer's special claim, a pretty WAC or an exceptional civilian Red Cross worker, keep cutting in when they were dancing or patting the woman on the rear as he passed. There were fights, which Elmer never won. I'd look the other way. Some bruisers would pound Elmer until he couldn't get up. One time an officer, a major, was standing over him yelling, "Have you had enough?"

Elmer wiped his bloody lip and said, "No, but I've decided I'm a better lover than I'm a fighter, and I plan to spend more time doing that."

Almost everyone gambled, but Elmer didn't play cards or roll dice. He'd lose his money buying old gold coins that sometimes turned out to be made of brass and sometimes weren't very old. That never stopped him, though, or even slowed him down. "This is my nest egg," he'd say, holding up an old Army sock that jingled when he shook it. He was always on the lookout for more bargains, asking everyone in GI Italian, "Vecchio dinero? Dinero d'oro?" Nearly everyone had some hidden away or knew someone who did. And Elmer paid top dollar.

I knew Elmer referred to me as the country bumpkin; he'd call me that to my face when he was drinking. I wasn't offended; at any rate, I tried not to act like it when I was with the other correspondents. I was imitating Elmer myself, wearing the black Borsolino like he wore his derby. But I didn't have a gold toothpick in the corner of my mouth yet. When Elmer would slap me on the back and say, "Entertain us with a story from the Great Central Valley, Julian," sometimes I'd make something up and sometimes I'd embellish an old story. One night I told about the hunting camp up in the sequoias. I started out talking about the whores but got to describing the country, the giant trees so tall that you couldn't see their tops, and as big around as the moon. You could build a whole town out of one of those trees, I told them. Some are older than Pompeii, older than Jesus Christ himself. "Not that old," someone said. "A damn tree?" As I talked about the place I could see it all again, the way the sun filtered through the tall trees and finally reached the ground in patterns of shadow and light. The silence, as if the canopy of trees filtered out all sounds except the jays' squawks and the fern-lined stream's rush and burble.

I could have listened to the planning for the next invasion, which was supposed to take place after Christmas—in January '44, everyone guessed—but I kept thinking of how many men were going to die. I could have attended the meetings where the generals stood before maps with their pointers, but the maps didn't show some PFC with a stomach wound and a medic shooting him full of morphine and drawing a big M with his own blood on his forehead, or a sergeant with his arm blown off, his buddies trying stop the bleeding while he screamed and kicked and shit all over himself. None of the plans mentioned that. But that's all I could think of when I sat there in those briefings. I was safe, I kept reminding myself. I was safe. And the safer I was, the more I worried about not being safe.

I wrote a long letter to my parents describing the mainland, my photo of the Holy Ghost festival propped against an ink bottle as I wrote, my fingers near the faces of everyone on the road. I told them about the black market dinners for the correspondents, and that I'd seen a bunch of Italians make the sign of the horns to ward off the evil eye when a priest crossed their paths, as if he were a black cat. I knew they'd laugh at that. "This part of Italy is a little like the valley, but they get rain in the summer and it's always green. They can get three crops of wheat or two of corn. This is going to be my first winter, but here where I am now I don't expect too much weather, no snow. I remember, Papa, you always talked about the vegetables, how Italian soil made them tasty. I know what you mean now, especially the tomatoes." I went on for ten pages that way. I could imagine my folks' faces as Hortense read them the letter, tears coming down from their eyes, the Zia blowing her nose. When I touched my face with my hand, I realized my cheeks were wet too.

The division newspaper kept forwarding me mail from readers, even though I'd stopped writing the column four months before. They were always the same. "What ever happened to Buck Private Smith? Did they promote him to first sergeant or lieutenant because he could spell?" I missed writing for the division paper; I missed talking to GIs like me who came from some particular place they could describe down to the cracks in the sidewalk, some little fishing town in Maine or wide place in the road in Nebraska. Writing profiles of generals based on their biographies was like writing about statues in parks.

A couple of days before Christmas most of the correspondents and PR officers and a few VIPs left for an organized tour to the front lines. Elmer didn't invite me, but I went too. Elmer had been drinking all day in the Jeep, and when we stopped for the night at an artillery unit, he fell asleep with his head on the table at the officers' mess. After dinner four soldiers carried in an immense cake on a door to celebrate some officer's birthday. A woman in a Red Cross uniform popped out of the cardboard cake and started taking off her clothes. The noise produced from the striptease revived Elmer, and he started yelling, "Take it off, take it off." The woman was stripping as she danced on a tabletop, and men were trying to grab her, though their friends held them back. "Back, you peckernecks," she yelled at them. I guessed she was from Texas.

I wasn't drunk enough to really enjoy this, I decided when the woman finally got down to her bare skin and got the two propellers spinning in opposite directions on her tits. Her sequined G-string glowed red in the semi-dark. Elmer was beside himself, yelling, standing on his chair. He stuck a five-dollar bill in each ear—they stuck out like green calves' ears—and tried to bury his head between the woman's breasts, making *glub glub* noises with his lips like he was half under water. The stripper plucked the two fives and danced away. A captain tackled her around the knees and buried his face between her legs.

I didn't see who started it, but Elmer wanted to play horse too. He jumped from the tabletop onto my shoulders and started head-butting with the others, who were all yelling giddyup, giddyup. We used to do this in the irrigation canals at home, trying to pull each other's rider off into the water. Here, Elmer had his head forward like a battering ram, and we'd charge another team. Elmer's nose was running blood. I always protected my face by leading with my elbows first. We stopped to drink from a bottle of cognac and spotted two majors with their backs half turned as our next target. When we charged them, I lost my footing on some blood on the floor, and we rammed into a wall. That was all I remembered until the next morning.

I spent the next afternoon in the back of a Jeep, hanging over the side being sick, hearing the laughter from the other vehicles following behind us. It started to rain as we got closer to the front. I felt miserable, and when Elmer handed me his flask of brandy I told myself not to but I drained it.

We stopped for C rations with an engineering company that was clearing a minefield. The men with metal detectors looked like they were scything the muddy fields. I couldn't eat anything but the can of pineapple and a cracker. A couple of the correspondents were interviewing GIs, asking their hometowns, what they did in civilian life, trying to find some connection to their readers back home. When a PFC said he was from Reno, Nevada, and added, "the biggest little city in the world," it got a few laughs. Elmer took his name, and one of the VIPs told him, "I'm a Nevadan too, soldier; I represent Washoe County in Washington."

I'd hardly noticed this quiet, gray-haired man before, but it turned out he was a congressman from Nevada on some War Department fact-finding commission. He started taking down some of the men's gripes: they didn't have enough winter clothing, the food was bad, they hadn't got any mail in three weeks, the usual things, but the congressman kept writing it all down like it was the first time it had ever been said. When GIs complained to the correspondents, their notebooks snapped shut; they didn't want to hear anything they couldn't print. Give them a hero, a GI who wiped out a machine gun nest single-handed, or an oddball, a private with ten kids and only one good eye who still got drafted and was doing his part now to fight the Axis.

Getting closer to the front after three months of watching behind the scenes with the correspondents, I realized that none of the brass knew what they were doing here in Italy. Strategy? The country was one big kill floor; these mountains were going to be another slaughterhouse. The Germans were going to bleed the Allied armies dry of men. When the generals had talked about the next invasion that would finally break the Germans' line and defeat them once and for all, Elmer had whispered, "The Apennines go down the length of Italy like a spine. All the Germans have to do is move back to the next hill. If these blockhead generals from West Point are so smart, how come they can't beat these Germans led by a former corporal? The Germans are kicking half the world's ass, and our ass specifically, here in Italy."

We kept going. It kept on raining. Our group of about a hundred had dwindled to about thirty-five correspondents and VIPs when we got hit by German artillery fire. I'd never been under such accurate shelling before. I was scared but I couldn't stop watching as vehicles were destroyed. I was in a muddy ditch on my stomach, not moving a muscle, and when it got really bad I forced my mind back under cover of the vines, picking table grapes into a tub.

Four Jeeps were destroyed, but there were no casualties. No one made any jokes as the group broke up. "I'm going all the way to the front," Elmer said. I went too, I don't know why, along with a few others. We drove as far as the Jeeps could go. A major came out of the CP tent, the executive officer of the regiment. A whole string of mules was being loaded, the mud up to the animals' hocks.

Only about a half dozen of us were left from the original group. It was raining hard now, washing the ditch mud off our shoulders as we slogged along behind the animals. The major talked as if he'd explained it a million times before. "The men on the line are the big shots in this battalion, the infantry. And it boils down to three things: they need food, ammo, and water. That's what they've got to have to keep their eyes on the sights of their rifles and do their job."

It was quiet except occasional rifle shots in the distance. The major had stopped talking by the time we came to an aid station. There weren't any wounded. "It's slow now," someone explained. "We had a couple of trench foot cases this morning." In half a mile or so we came to a creek that was overflowing its banks and we had to leave the mules. The supplies had to be packed up the rest of the way on our backs.

Out of our group, only the congressman, Elmer, and I went any further. And when the congressman, Ted, who must have been older than Elmer, slipped a packboard with a five-gallon can of water onto his back, so did Elmer. I picked up a case of C rations on my shoulder and we waded across the creek. The major went back, and we were led by a lieutenant who was packing a box of ammo and a Thompson. I could hear Elmer breathing like each gasp was going to be the very last. He was taking two steps up and sliding back one in the mud. I wasn't scared out of my wits, yet.

When we crossed an open field we heard a machine gun close by open up, and we all hit the dirt. The rounds splattered into a bank near us. Until then, the closer we'd got to the front, the more peaceful it became. It was like you could leave your worries behind. We lay there while the lieutenant crawled away and then came back for us. It was almost dark when we came to the forward CP for the battalion. The CO, a lieutenant colonel, was sitting on a wooden ammo box in a dugout, eating bacon out of a frying pan with crackers and hot coffee for dinner. "Join us," he said.

It didn't take long to realize that the lieutenant colonel was an unusual officer. It wasn't just that his men treated him with respect—they liked the old man; he treated them the same way. He knew most of the men's names. The NCOs and junior officers weren't allowed to bully the ranks. The battalion worked together to get back in one piece. Some platoons had even made pacts that they were all going to go home together. There was none of the usual tension, old-timers versus green replacements. This wasn't regular Army; these guys were draftees, but they functioned like a military unit; there was discipline. I was amazed.

The first night it was awful. I was used to a warm, dry bed, and my clothes were still soaking wet. I was sharing a hole dug into the side of a gully with the congressman and Elmer. A tarp hanging down over the opening kept out most of the wind and the rain, but no one could sleep. Elmer was telling his old stories about life in the western fleshpots, going from San Francisco up to Reno to see the ladies, back in the thirties. "There was probably just as much vice available in the city, but we liked to take that ride over the Sierras."

"We had a summer sheep camp in the mountains when I was a kid," the congressman said, and he went on to talk about his father, who'd come over from a Spanish part of the Pyrenees, and how his mother boarded him in town in the winter so he could go to school. Lambing, sheep shearing, carrying a ewe on his shoulders in the snow.

When it was my turn I told about our forty acres of vines, and how I could really appreciate my life in the valley after seeing . . . I couldn't find the right words, and settled on *everything.*

Around four we gave up any attempt at sleeping. I pulled in my helmet, which had filled with water from the rain, and I got a fire going by pouring gas in a dry, dirt-filled can with some chunks of wood. When the water in my helmet heated up, I put in six C ration cans. "And they say you don't learn anything in the Army," Elmer said. I let the water boil for ten minutes before I fished out the cans, then opened them into a pot someone had left behind. I stirred all the cans together, pork and beans, hamburger patties, spaghetti, noodles, and meat, and started spooning it out to the others. Colonel Burnett lifted the tarp and came in then with a sergeant. "I thought I smelled home cooking," he said. We gave them a mess kit of hot food too. "Call me Bill," he said.

I had borrowed Elmer's typewriter after listening to the CO brief his men, and was working on a profile. Elmer and the congressman had crawled up with the colonel to the front line and the men in foxholes to get a look at the Germans. I titled it "Bill Burnett Is from Brooklyn." I had rough copy of two thousand words before Elmer came back. The congressman had walked down to the creek to help bring up another load of supplies. "That man is going to make me revaluate politicians, if he keeps this up," Elmer said. He started reading the first pages I'd finished. "Not bad for a bumpkin from the San Joaquin Valley," he said.

That night the three of us were invited to the CP for Christmas Eve with the battalion. There was a cask of brandy, but even Elmer didn't overdo it. A lot of the men had got mail that day and shared their Christmas packages with everyone: fruitcake and cookies, big hunks of fudge that had melted together on the trip to Italy from the States. There must have been a couple hundred of us jammed into an old German bunker in the side of a hill. Wind came through the shell holes and made the candle flames point in the dark like fingers. Someone started a Christmas song, and everyone joined in.

In the almost dark I heard a falsetto voice that had to be Elmer's in disguise announce, "Men, officers, and gentlemen of the Fifth Army . . ." which got a few laughs. "We are honored tonight to have a United States congressman in our midst, the perfect guest to answer the big question, When is this damn war going to end so we can go home?" There was some laughing and clapping.

"I wish I knew," Ted said. "I wish I could tell you tonight this would be the last day. But I don't know. No one does. A year and a half ago I was in Washington, D.C., listening to all the bullshit we have to listen to. Now, fourteen months later, there's a totally new focus there and across the country: not the New Deal to end the Depression, but an all-out effort to win and end this war. The United States of America is on a war economy and one hundred percent behind the fighting men. You'd be proud of the folks on the home front: everyone is trying to help, from the bond drives to kids saving tin foil. And they are making sacrifices too, and will until the war's over. But in the final analysis, the war has to be won here, in these muddy ravines in Italy and the jungles of the South Pacific. I'm making a speech," he added, "and I don't want to do that."

There was some clapping. The voice asked another question: again, I was sure it was Elmer. "Why would a decent man want to be a politician?"

"I've asked myself that many, many the time." There was more laughter. "I'm going to try and answer that seriously. I could say that because I'm a sheep rancher, I was used to dealing with dumb animals. But I thought I could do something, make a difference; I really did. I started out that way. When the Depression hit the West, I saw people lose everything they'd worked for their whole life. And I thought I could at least help them, and I ran for office. And you go on thinking that during your first term and your second term and so on. You vote for the general good, not just of your constituents but for everyone in the country. You know, if you're old enough, about the New Deal. I voted for those programs. And they did help; they put men to work. But that's not answering your question; I'm speechifying again. I found that one man doesn't make a difference. There are five hundred thirty others in Congress, all with their own opinion, with their own constituents. You have to wait in line a lot, to get on the right committee, to build up seniority before you can get anything done. While you wait, the job becomes a habit you can't quit, even when you realize all the hypocrisy, and I don't want to go into that. I've been there twelve years now, and the other day I looked around and I realized I'm just like the men that I thought I'd never become, that I came to replace, like the ones who were sitting around me that moment. That was probably the worst minute of my life." He stopped for a while. Then he said, "This is supposed to be a joyous occasion. Why don't we sing another carol? My favorite is 'While Shepherds Watched Their Flocks by Night.'"

We hung around until midnight to wish each other Merry Christmas. There was no shooting; the Germans were celebrating too. A lot of men left then to go back to their positions. There was more talk, speculation on who was having it rougher, the GIs fighting the Japanese or us here in the European theater. "Ask Julian," Elmer said. "He fought the Japs in the Aleutians."

There were a dozen questions all at once. "What was it like, Sergeant? Do they ever surrender or always fight to the death? The Germans will give up if you flank them. They know how to say Kamerad fast enough when they have to. Let the sergeant speak."

"To tell you the truth, I didn't see that much, the short time the campaign lasted. Most of the time I was too busy praying and saying my rosary." Laughter.

"Then how did you win the highest medal they give for bravery, Julian? Did you find that in a ration box?" That goddamn Elmer.

"I was lucky, just like we all are, to be alive after getting shot at. The Germans and the Japanese are the same. You just have to believe you're going to survive, that when it's over you're going home where you don't have to fight anyone. There's no difference between people who are trying to kill you, whatever the methods they use or what they look like."

Christmas morning they got hot chow to us up on the front. I got a warm turkey leg and cranberries and some biscuits. Bill had got a box of cigars from his wife and he was going around giving them out, shaking hands. After I ate I volunteered to be a stretcher bearer at the aid station so someone else could go back and get some hot food. Elmer and I were going to leave the battalion at noon. It was quiet. The rain was beating down hard. I heard the shooting and knew what was going to happen before I heard the words, "Medic, medic." I started running too, with the stretcher. Until then I'd been calm; my mind hadn't betrayed me.

Some corporal had left his foxhole and crawled out to hunt souvenirs and got shot by a sniper. I followed the medic out; the Germans usually didn't shoot at the medics. But I was shaking so bad my teeth were making a noise. The corporal had been hit through both his upper legs. We loaded him onto the stretcher and took him back.

There was no more firing. But I was scared so bad I almost ran down the side of the hill to get back to the creek, where we'd had to leave the Jeep. "What's the hurry?" Elmer said, puffing after me. "I was just starting to enjoy myself up there." I couldn't stop myself from shaking, but I didn't cry this time.

Elmer was punishing the brandy, as he said about everyone else who drank too much, and he insisted on driving the Jeep. When he hit a stone wall that pushed the radiator into the fan he kept saying, "I knew you should have driven, Julian." It had taken us four days to get back from the front. We were only eight or nine miles from the villa where the rest of the correspondents were staying.

We started walking and were overtaken by a column of Sherman tanks. The tank commander nodded okay when Elmer asked for a ride. We climbed on. I sat under the cannon with my back against the turret. The rain had stopped the day before, and the tank treads were turning the mud into dust. I could barely see Elmer on the back of the tank ahead, sprawled out over the engine to keep warm, the First World War helmet he'd found somewhere a couple of days ago strapped to his head. The noise was unbelievable. When I tried to talk to the tankers through the open hatches, they couldn't hear. No wonder they said all tankers were deaf.

A driver with "Sgt. Webster" stenciled on his tanker's helmet motioned from the hatch for a cigarette, and I lit a Camel and handed it over. Ahead of us, Elmer rolled over and stood up, unbuttoning his fly to take a leak off the moving tank. I closed my eyes for a nap. All at once, everything stopped, the movement, the engine of the tank I was riding on. I slid off to find out what happened. Some tankers were yelling directions to the driver of a tank behind us, who reversed and backed up, then turned off the engine. Just in front of its treads, a mashed body was pressed into the soft dirt of the road. I recognized Elmer by his clothes. The First World War helmet was squashed flat. "The war's over for your buddy," the driver said. It had happened too fast; I couldn't grasp that Elmer was dead.

Two medics put him on a stretcher and slid him into an ambulance. "Take this stuff," one of the medics said, handing me Elmer's pack. "You can send it to his family." I was going to explain that Elmer didn't have anyone that I knew of. I just stood there when the tanks started up again. I got a ride in a water truck into the outskirts of the city. The driver had liberated a demijohn of cognac, and I filled my canteen cup a couple of times.

I found where the correspondents were staying. One of the blowhards from a big magazine was holding forth at the bar on his advice to the general regarding the coming invasion. I found a friend of Elmer's from the *San Francisco Call Bulletin* and gave him Elmer's old Underwood. The word got around then that Elmer was dead. I'd ordered a drink at the bar. "How did he die?" someone asked me. I still couldn't believe Elmer was dead, that he wouldn't walk into the bar any minute yelling, "News-hounds!" I heard myself say that he'd jumped on a German potato masher to save two wounded GIs. Elmer would have liked that ending.

I asked the correspondent from the *Call* if he could think of anybody I could send Elmer's things too. He thought for a minute and shook his head. "I don't know of anyone. Just women, he liked them all, but I can't remember any names." We had more drinks. When I remembered the sock with Elmer's nest egg of gold coins, I had another drink, then put on my Borsolino and wandered outside the villa. I stuck Elmer's gold toothpick in the hatband. I'd keep that. I wandered until I saw the streetwalkers trying to keep warm around a fire in a rusty oil drum. I went over and started passing out the gold coins. *Grazie, grazie:* they were polite when they realized what the coins were. I didn't try to explain. More women came running when they heard, and when there were no more coins I threw the old sock into the fire.

I tried to keep busy, finished and turned in the profile on Bill Burnett. Colonel Green liked it and sent me a box of cigars with a note that said keep up the good work. I collected my mail from home, there was a good stack, but I didn't have time to read any of it. I stuffed the envelopes in the side pocket of my jacket. The ships were being loaded for another invasion: no one was exactly sure where, but the word was Nettuno, a town up the coast north of here. I got an issue of gear, the new high boots with two buckles instead of leggings. I didn't ask for a weapon but took the .45 I was issued. I got myself attached to a Ranger battalion, which would be going in first. I was tired of being scared all the time. The hell with it. I was going to kill the coward inside me—some old first sergeant in training somewhere had used that expression.

We embarked in the morning and then sat around waiting for the rest of the invasion fleet. I had time for my mail, finally. I'd stacked the envelopes in order of arrival, my sister Mary's first. "I have bad news for you, Julian," she wrote. "Papa died in his sleep Wednesday. We all miss him so much. Mama and the Zia are coming to live with us in Lindsay, we plan to sell the place. You can't get help anymore, everyone's gone. Hortense Brazil is arranging with the undertakers over there. Fred Leeds is up here now, and Fred and Mr. Brazil are going to dig the grave in the cemetery in town. Patrick at the Californian got us some ration stamps for gas so everyone can go to the funeral. I'm working twelve hours seven days at the cannery now. They made me a floor lady and I get an extra dime an hour. Papa was an old man, seventy-nine, Mama says, but we miss him." I tried to picture my father dead, but all I could come up with was Elmer lying in a stretcher.

All the way north with the convoy, I couldn't get it through my head that my father was dead. My sister might be just saying that. But why would she? And she was going to sell the place? I had put my piece of ground in my father's name in case something happened to me. My father was dead? I kept seeing him alive, sitting at the head of the table, his mouth full of food, a couple days' growth of beard, his white hair floating over his bald spot in wisps.

The general quarters sounded and the ship went black; we were turning toward the coast. I sat with my back to a bulkhead trying not to recognize the sounds: the landing craft being lowered into the water, the sailors on the boom overhead trying not drop anything on the soldiers who were packed on the deck. The landing nets thrown over the side. I carried two boxes of ammo as I went down the net.

We hit the beach at Anzio, just north of Nettuno. I followed a machine gun platoon up the wet sand. When we got to the first building, some Rangers barged inside. We heard a lot of laughter, and they came out with prisoners. They'd found a bunch of Germans eating dinner; this was a rest camp, one said. They captured three officers on their way out to fish, and then a private and his girlfriend. The Krauts were caught completely by surprise. There were a lot of German prisoners. Was this landing going to be a success? A sign of what was to come in Italy? I wished Elmer was around; he always had an opinion.

It was the end of January and the weather was mild and the villa the Rangers had liberated gave a perfect view of the Tyrrhenian Sea. I hadn't bothered to find the correspondents. Without Elmer it wouldn't be the same. The first few days were easy living; the ships kept coming in; more troops, more supplies. There were stories that the advance wasn't going anywhere, that the Krauts were putting up resistance on the way to Rome. There were so many rumors. Meanwhile, it was hurry up and wait.

A group of intelligence officers waited until we had the villa in good shape, the stove fixed and the water running, before they evicted us. There was nothing we could do. We were enlisted men, and officers got what they wanted. But they didn't get a chance to enjoy the place long: that night was the first air raid, and German planes sank some of the ships in the harbor. The next day the whole encampment was under fire from German long-range artillery. I moved into the cellar of a ruined house, full of barrels of wine and brandy, and some old wheels of hard cheese I thought was parmigiano.

The Germans' artillery found plenty of targets. A bunker next to my cellar took a direct hit, and everyone inside was killed. I didn't open the rest of my mail until we'd been at Anzio for a week. I didn't want to think about my father or the road. The place, the vines, were gone. I'd composed letters in my head telling my sister that some of that property was mine, but it didn't go any further. I opened the letter from Hortense. "I hope this letter finds you well. Your father had a nice funeral. We knew he didn't want a priest, so my father said a few words. The Hamadas couldn't come, of course, but they were able to send flowers; they phoned that florist on Main Street. The Land Company sent a big wreath. Patrick and Fred, most of the Brazils, and the Rodriguez family were there. All of your sisters and their families came. Your mother is fine and so is the Zia."

The next envelope was from Hortense too. "I don't know how to tell you this, Julian; it's more bad news. Your sisters brought your mother to the funeral and she held up fine. But four days after your father passed away, your mother died in her bed. The Zia told me she wouldn't eat. But I don't think that was it. She didn't get over your father leaving, I think. She wanted to join him. We had another funeral this week and put your mother next to your father. There's nowhere to buy a stone; the place where they used to do the work is closed for the duration. I helped my father dig the grave. Fred had gone back to work down south. Mary asked me to write; your whole family is broken up over your mother's dying too.

"I got a letter from Grayson; he's over there near you and he's been wounded. You might want to go see him. He asked for news about you, how he could get in touch.

"I wish there was some good news to write. Richard got the recommendation he needed and was accepted for OCS. I think he'll be a good officer. You wouldn't believe the price we're getting for milk, even with selling it all to the government for cheese and powdered milk. If we had another hundred cows we'd make a fortune. I haven't heard from the Hamadas for a while. There's supposed to be a lot of trouble up there in the camp at Tule Lake, riots, and some of the internees were machine-gunned by the soldiers when they tried to escape. No one knows the truth of the matter. I just hope the Hamadas are okay. I'm sorry about your folks, Julian. And I forgot, I think your sister Mary has got a buyer for the place. I know the Land Company is interested."

My folks were dead. I remembered when I was embarrassed by them. They were old when I was in high school, and couldn't speak English. They dressed funny, my father in his old black suit, my mother's slip hanging down below her dress, her teeth stained brown. I didn't want to be seen with them when I drove them into town on Saturday. I'd drop them off at the hardware store and pick them up an hour later and pretend we had to get back to the place. I didn't even invite them for something at the coffee shop at the Californian. They would have liked that, a milk shake or a Coke, but I didn't want my friends to see them with me if they happened to come in.

After that, sometimes I'd find myself writing a letter in my head to my folks, forgetting they were dead. "You'd like this place, Mamma, fresh fish. The other day some engineers threw explosives in the bay, and tons of fish came floating up." Then I'd remember they'd died; they were both dead. They couldn't be dead. And I'd remember that I had no place to go back to. The vines were sold; I couldn't go back to the road.

I drank too much one night and got a ride in a boat back down the coast to Naples. The beachhead was completely cut off from the mainland now; the sea was the only way out of Anzio. I was going to look Grayson up. It wasn't easy, Naples was so big, but I found the hospital. I bought a couple of bottles of brandy off the street, which meant it could be anything from piss to rainwater. It didn't help to try to speak Italian; I was just another GI with too much money.

The hospital was in an old palazzo. There were a lot of big rooms with twenty-five or thirty beds. An orderly at the front desk gave me directions and I tried to act sober. I had bought some things from the black market to entertain Grayson, to take his mind off the war—a funny hat, I couldn't remember what else.

And there was Grayson. Grayson. Grayson. Good buddy. My pal. Neighbor. Staff Sergeant Hamada. The only trouble was, when I looked at him, all I could see was a skeleton that talked. All the flesh was gone; just the white bones were left. Had Grayson died and by some mistake they'd forgotten to bury him? I tried touching his face a couple times, and it was still flesh. I wanted to be funny and I made a lot of jokes, ones that Elmer told me, traveling salesman and the farmer's daughter jokes: was anybody still telling jokes during this war? Were there any farmer's daughters left?

I had never been wounded, never a scratch, not a hangnail; I was proud of that. One of the reasons why was I'd decided that every time I got a chance I'd take a shot of morphine just in case I ever got hit, to keep away the pain in advance. It started when I found a wounded medic on Attu with a big hole in his stomach. I gave him one shot after another from his first aid kit, until the medic started to smile. "That's better," he kept saying, "much better." I had been so nervous that I stuck one in my own leg, I wasn't sure if it was by accident or not, and I wasn't so scared then, not half as scared. "Help yourself," the medic said, so I took another one and lay back beside the medic, who wanted me to hold his hand, and I did until he died. It was foggy and sleeting ice and I thought I was back in the vines, the sun shining, keeping me warm.

I didn't remember leaving Grayson, but I'd found some morphine in the hospital, I remembered that. I still had some left. I always knew when I'd had some because I was back in the vines, picking. I got a ride back to Anzio on a LST bringing in more supplies. I wandered around, once the ship landed on the beach. I bought enough brandy to fill my two canteens from a GI who had a whole barrel. Time was running out. It was the end of March, and we were stuck in the same place after two months. We couldn't move. The Germans were shelling the whole beachhead at will, turning the place into a shooting gallery. I was getting tired of the war. It was time to leave. The LST I'd come in on was about to leave the port to return to Naples. I got back on it.

After Elmer died, I'd started listening at the briefing sessions to the officers with their maps and pointers. I'd pay attention. I'd go up and examine the big wall maps of Italy. Central Italy was only about a hundred fifty miles wide. Le Marche, the region my folks were from, was on the other side of the boot, the calf side, over on the Adriatic. It wasn't that far. I could walk there, I kept thinking, if I could get through the lines, past our own troops and past the Germans. I wouldn't be questioned, not with my correspondent's patch and master sergeant's chevrons. And no one in their right mind would be heading north from Naples toward the lines.

I didn't have to go back to California. I could stay here in Italy, find a place where I could live out my life. Where there wasn't any war. Where everyone could be left alone. I knew my father's stories by heart. I'd try to find a place near there, near those stories. Round hillsides, just like California, and you could grow anything. Over the hill. I liked that. It was better than AWOL. I was going over the hill.

FRED

chapter 17

Hortense kidded me when I got Julian's address from her that my letter to him would be the first letter I ever wrote in my life. That wasn't true; I wrote to Reiko five times. I wanted to tell Julian how sorry I was about his father, Mr. Palestini. He was a good man and a good farmer. I looked over their place before I went back south and just about all the vines had been pruned and tied. Those Mexican hands were fast: I went over and helped out for a couple of hours before I had to leave. Those people knew how to work. There just weren't enough field workers to go around because of the draft. The crops were getting planted and picked, but that was it.

The road was different without the Hamadas. The Army had the Brazil boys, and Kenny Rodriguez went too. There weren't as many folks around, but they'd put in an airfield north of Visalia and one east of Tulare, so there were plenty of soldiers. They made me think about what Julian said once, that you never had so much time on your hands as in the Army. Hurry up and wait is what you do, he said. I wondered sometimes what that would be like.

I was working as a riveter down south for Lockheed Aircraft. I put in a little over a hundred hours the week that I went up for another interview with my draft board and to take a look at my place and say hello to Hortense. I rented a room down there with eight other men that worked in the same section: we were on different shifts and slept three at a time. All I needed was a pallet on the floor. The eats at the company cafeteria were hot, and you got all you wanted. I couldn't ask for more than that. I lived close enough to the plant, four or five miles, that I could walk. I saved my gas coupons to drive north that way. All the rationing didn't bother me, once Charlie sent me a pair of his Army boots. My old ones had got so they couldn't be repaired anymore. I was nailing on plywood heels, but they didn't last too long.

I thought a lot about my place up on the road while I was working at the plant. I didn't get tired or have to sleep when I did, it was so restful. I thanked my lucky stars me and Charlie got off that freight train in Goshen and walked up the track until we got to the road. I'd got my eye on some of the land, forty acres of it, next to our house by the creek. They wanted thirty-eight dollars an acre, which was too rich for my blood, but on the other hand, the way I was going, if everything stayed the same I reckoned I'd have ten thousand dollars saved by 1947. I never thought I'd have that much money my whole life. I know my father never did when he was sharecropping, and he made a good living but he died young.

They drafted my brother Charlie after they reclassified him I-A. That one-year exemption he'd got to work in the oil fields ran out in February. He was going to gunnery school in Texas with the Air Force. He wrote that the only good thing about the place was he felt he was closer to home down there in the Southwest, even if we didn't have anybody left in Enid, Oklahoma.

When I went back up for the second interview with my draft board, they had two doctors examine my game leg before they rejected me. I had tried to volunteer three times, but they wouldn't have me. I asked one doctor for the Air Force, "How much walking can a person do in an airplane, anyhow? You know I can get around as good as anyone else." He told me to watch myself; he didn't need any smart-ass questions from a civilian. I decided then that I'd go if they drafted me, but I wasn't going to try and enlist anymore. I was helping the war effort making those planes; that should be enough for Uncle Sam.

I had Julian's address but it took me a while to get started on my letter because there was something else I wanted to tell him besides that I was sorry that his father died, and I didn't know how to say it. Finally I just sat down with a pencil and my tablet and started out, "Dear Julian," and then went on like he was in the room with me.

You've known the Hamada family a lot longer than I have but I've never had such friends before. I can't think of anyone I respect more than Mats and Harriet. Mats wanted to loan me some money to buy a place and he didn't have that much to spare for his own self. He was going to put a mortgage on his strawberry field. I wouldn't risk our friendship for a piece of land. I wouldn't want to ever offend them in any way.

You probably didn't notice but me and Reiko are sweet on each other. More than that, I guess. When she graduated we planned for her to come down to Bakersfield while I was roughnecking. She wanted it that way and got Mr. Hart to phone someone and got on in a hotel down there as waitress. I had explained that I was saving my money to get a place and in good time we'd be together up home. She didn't want that; she would work in Bakersfield as well as anywhere. Let people think what they want, she said.

This is hard to say because it all went wrong. Well, I told Charlie the truth of the matter. He talked to me man to man. What would Mama and Daddy say? But Charlie always says that when he can't think of anything else. But he's my older brother and took care of me when our folks died when they put us in the school. I had to listen to him. So I phoned Reiko and said we'd have to put off her coming down to Bakersfield and she should keep on going to the school in Fresno with Hortense. She was mad.

I just want you to know how it was with me and Reiko. You're the only friend I have that can understand the situation because you know everybody so well. I tried to do what was best for everyone, but it didn't turn out that way. I know I always let things go until it's too late, I know that. And I knew that I wasn't going to find anyone like Reiko again, I knew that too. Love, Reiko used to say it all the time, but I never gave it much thought before. I suppose if you want to be with someone for your whole life in your own house that's the same thing. Then the war started.

I came up when I could, but Reiko wouldn't understand.

Didn't care what her folks thought. She was coming down to Bakersfield whether I wanted her to or not. I went down to the courthouse and tried to get a marriage license. They were still letting Japanese Americans leave the coast and go inland then. I didn't want to hurt Mr. and Mrs. Hamada but I wanted to be with her. But the county people didn't want to issue me a marriage license because she was Oriental. Not because she was Japanese and we were at war with Japan, but because it's illegal for a white to marry an Oriental. It's the law of California.

I didn't know what I was going to do next. I found out that we could get married up in Washington State but before we could go they made all the Japanese Americans move up to the Fresno county racetrack. I went and talked to Mr. Hart, he's always treated me good, and he made a few phone calls. By that time they'd moved the Hamadas to Poston relocation camp in Arizona. I had promised Reiko we would get married. Mr. Hart found out that if Reiko could leave the camp on a special pass, I could marry her in Arizona if she said she was an Indian. By that time I was working for Lockheed and I knew they had aircraft plants in the Midwest, so I could transfer, and Reiko would be allowed to leave the camp if she was married and leaving the coastal zone. But then they moved the Hamadas back to California, and there was no getting out of the Tule Lake camp.

The whole business has worn me out. I don't know what I should do next. I never expected in my whole life to have someone like Reiko want to marry me. But there isn't one single thing I can do so we can be together. The only way now is to wait until this war is over; what other choice do we have? Let the whole thing play itself out and we can go back to everyone minding their own business again. Then go to another state and get married. I'd have my land then and we'd come back here and it would be like it was before. I wrote and explained things to Reiko, but she never answered.

When you and I drove up there to Tule Lake I was going to try and straighten things out. My plan was to ask Mr. Hamada for permission to marry Reiko and give her my mother's gold ring to wear. I never got a chance to talk to

Reiko before that boy came in and copped his Sunday punch on me and split my lip. I still don't know what that was about. But I'm not mad at anyone. I've written two letters to Reiko since then but they came back return to sender. Mr. Hart phoned and found out they have Reiko in the stockade. She can't receive any mail.

I'm glad I got that business off my chest about Reiko. It makes me feel better for you to know what happened because you grew up with her family and know me well enough too. It makes it easier when I go over it in my mind.

I'm sorry I've spent all this letter telling you my problems. They say you're supposed to only send cheerful mail to servicemen overseas but I can't think of anything cheerful. One thing I learned from all this is you can't trust the future to take care of itself. You can't be sure what's going to happen next. I still think the valley is the promised land. But I'm not sure anymore how you go about collecting on the promises.

Your friend,
Fred Leeds

I was going to put it in an envelope, but I realized I hadn't said anything about Mr. Palestini. Before I got that part written, I drove back up to my place on a Sunday. When I saw Hortense, she told me that Mrs. Palestini had died too. Then she showed me a letter she'd written to Julian that had just come back to her. MISSING IN ACTION was stamped on the envelope over Julian's name. Tears were rolling down her cheeks when she handed it to me. I thought about my letter and I realized I had never even put in a word thanking Julian for fixing up my house, nailing the siding on and putting in the toilet. Julian couldn't be missing. He had to be somewhere. I couldn't afford to be losing friends like him. He had to come back here to his place, to the road.

JULIAN

chapter 18

I got a couple of rides going north out of Naples. The first was in the back of a truck crammed with raw recruits, jolting for hours on the hard wooden benches. I never had a real plan. I kept thinking of my father and my mother, the farm, and how the big oak tree threw its silhouette across the acres of vines. I had plenty of cognac left. It was almost an official currency for bartering with the troops. I could hear the guns despite the weather, sky jagged with lightning, thunderbolts, rain beating on the canvas top of the truck. It was supposed to be spring. The Allies had been stalled at Anzio from the end of January. It didn't feel right to be killing each other in April. Warm weather was coming, by all reports. The second was in a Jeep with a couple of signalmen looking for their unit. Then I started walking.

I wasn't sure when I walked across into the German lines. I only moved at night, lay up during the day. I guessed by the stars that I was going northeast, doing about twenty miles a night, avoiding the small towns. There were no more road markers showing kilometers to the next place; they must have all been removed. Only a few farm dogs. The weather was improving. The rain stopped after a week on the road, and it was getting warmer at night, at least in the lower elevations.

I passed a lot of small farms, five to ten acres, each with its tile-roofed two-story brick house built like a bunker, small shuttered windows high up on the walls on either side of a heavy wooden door, livestock stalled on the ground floor, family upstairs. Property lines separated by a ditch thick with trees or brush. Everything was green from all the rain, and there were plenty of woods left to hide in; they went for miles sometimes.

I wasn't sure where I was anymore, somewhere in the mountains of central Italy, but I knew I was away from the fighting; there were no sounds of war. The sun was going down. If I was home in the valley, they would have started irrigating by now. I felt such tranquillity. It wasn't hard to be patient and wait for the dark to cover everything before I moved on. I was out of food, but there was half a canteen of cognac I'd been saving back, and two ampules of morphine I'd borrowed from a sleeping medic in a truck weeks before. I took a couple of slugs of cognac before injecting the drug into each forearm. I'd never felt better in my life.

I picked up my pack and started off. It was getting warmer; I had to take off my jacket after a half hour. I took another slug of cognac and drained the canteen. Instead of putting it back in its case, I threw it into a ditch. I needed to get rid of all my gear. I was out of the Army; I didn't need this government issue. I'd already left my helmet and pistol under a tree somewhere four or five days ago. I tossed my jacket, then my pack. It was plenty warm. Plenty, I didn't need all these clothes, and I shucked off my shirt. I was passing an orchard all in bloom in the moonlight, almond trees, and I realized I was starting over in a new land. This was important to understand: that I was going to begin my life here, without anything from the past.

I sat down on the stone abutment of a little bridge and unlaced my boots, then took off my trousers too. I felt better than I had in years. I was getting rid of my past and all my troubles. I'd start a family in this new land. Twenty kids, forty hands to help in the vines. I tossed my dogtags over my shoulder and heard them splash in the water. I was naked except for my hat, my Borsolino. I was ready to start my new life now.

My feet really hurt the first couple of days from walking without boots, but the roads I was traveling on now were soft dirt. I was staying off the main roads, going up higher, walking in the daytime. I'd worked naked in the fields before, in the summer heat of the valley. No one noticed the difference, not with all the hair on my body. I felt like a man looking for a piece of land to buy, looking over the countryside. With each step I started feeling lighter, like my feet weren't touching the ground. I was going home. Somewhere around here was where I was going to live.

I was getting sunburned, I realized when I stopped at an abandoned farmhouse for water. The place was a wreck: the tile roof was caved in; all the windows were broken. The farms up here were small, five-acre fields at most. The ground was covered with weeds; I'd yet to see a plowed or planted field or another person. The houses were empty: this must be where all the refugees in the cities were coming from.

I heard the wheels of a cart and stepped behind the well. An old man was pulling between the shafts. He was taking a load of firewood up a grade, resting after every three or four steps. I'd follow him home, ask for work. But not naked, no one would hire me that way. I looked down between my legs and saw my penis at rest, lined up with the toes on one of my feet, making it an even six. At least I wasn't thinking with my prick anymore. That made me smile inside.

I found a good white shirt in a trunk in that house, and an old woolen suit hanging in the attic of the next one I came to. I looked like my father must have looked, coming to California, I thought, buttoning the trousers. I had to look like a respectable, reliable working man. I passed two more abandoned farms, following the slow-moving cart, and picked up a pair of wooden clogs that were in pretty good shape. For tools, I found a broken-handled pitchfork and a milking bucket. I was hurrying along the road when the sound of the cart stopped.

By the time I got to the house, the old man was shutting the door. I hurried up the path and knocked, and the door was opened by an old woman. I could smell food cooking and I opened my mouth to explain but she smiled and let me in. The dinner was watery gruel like polenta, but they'd used acorns instead of corn, so it was bitter. But there was plenty of vino and the three of us shared a big yellow apple from last fall. The old woman did all the talking. They had a couple of days of work. When the old man got up, I followed him out. I had understood their dialect.

We spent the day trying to cultivate a small plot of hard ground for a garden with a grub hoe and shovel. Some little kids came over yelling, "Nonno, Nonno," to the old man, Grandfather, and when they saw me they ran back. The big fields were thick with weeds. When it started getting dark, we went back to the house for supper. It was the same as lunch, but no apple. It wasn't true that farmers lived well in wartime. The nonna had told me at noon that they couldn't feed me for long. When the garden was planted, I'd have to leave.

I slept under an old haystack with a pole sticking up in the middle. The nonno hadn't invited me in to sleep in the house. I hadn't seen any livestock around, I remembered as I fell asleep. I didn't dream. The birds woke me up and I didn't realize where I was until I saw the haystack. I was home, that's where, I told myself.

I found a plow under the house. There was a stall where a cow had been once, but now they didn't even have a single chicken. Fruit trees, a couple of pears, an apple, an apricot and an old fig. We worked hard on the garden. The kids from the other farm came with bottles and buckets to get water from the old man's well, two girls and a little boy. I went over and helped them crank the water bucket up. They filled their bottles carefully. They were polite little kids, thanking me for helping. They were thin, legs like sticks, and their stomachs stuck out from malnutrition. As they ran across the fields, I thought of Hortense, Reiko, and Grayson coming to visit me as I pruned the vines when we were kids.

I saw the mother sometimes, all dressed in black like most of the country women I'd seen in Italy, with a scarf wrapped around her head. She worked steadily; she was trying to break up the hard ground to plant her garden too. At lunch I tried to ask the nonno about her, but either he didn't understand or didn't want to tell me. The nonna told me their neighbor was a widow; her husband had been killed in Russia. Her name was Annarosa.

I walked back three mornings later with the children—Monica was eleven, Carlotta ten, and Mario six—carrying some of the water bottles. The woman must have been young when she had her kids, because she wasn't much older than I was, but she made herself look ugly, I thought. Her face had sores she picked at nervously, and she looked like she didn't wash herself or her clothes. Her lips were cracked, with little clots of dried blood in the corners. One of her front teeth was gone, and she sucked now and then on the empty space. She never looked directly at me. Didn't speak to me at first. Just gripped the handle of her hoe like it was holding her up.

The rope on her well had broken, and I went down, bracing my back and legs against the stone walls and got the bucket, then spliced the rope together. "Bravo," the two little girls said, clapping, when I pulled the first bucket of water up out of the well. I picked up the woman's hoe and started breaking up the clods of dirt. I was done at the nonno's; his garden was finished. She and the girls followed behind me, raking the dirt smooth.

I never worked so hard in my life, striking down with the hoe as if the dirt clods were trying to run away. Sweating, I stopped thinking of the war, my folks, the valley. I kept working until I noticed some men watching me from the road. It scared me at first. If they were Germans, would I pass for Italian? The nonna had explained that the Germans had come around during harvest time, taken their olive oil and grain, and slaughtered the pigs and the oxen. "Left us with no way to farm," she said. The partisans were the next worst, in her opinion, and then there were bands of men in the countryside, ex-POWs, deserters, and refugees, whole families passing through, who were starving, trying to find food, and would eat the very grass.

One of the men came over and said, "Good morning, Signora," to Annarosa. He introduced himself as the new partisan chief, Comrade Oscar. Annarosa ignored him and went on working. He went on in bad Italian, asking her if she could spare any food; his men were starving. "Just some prosciutto and bread would be enough for now, Signora. We are fighting for Italy's freedom from the fascists," he repeated, and went into a long story about how he, a foreigner, had got to Italy. The rest of the group were as starved-looking as he was, unshaved, dirty, wearing parts of old uniforms. Three didn't even have wooden clogs. They had two old Italian rifles among the nine of them. One wearing a jacket from a Canadian uniform interrupted, "Come on, Oscar, get the food and let's get out of here." Hearing English made me jump. Oscar waved the Canadian silent, intent on his story. He was born in the United States of America, but his father had returned to Armenia when he was eight years old. He was conscripted into the Russian army and was captured by the Germans and made to do forced labor. He escaped from them and decided to leave the eastern front with the Italians when they retreated, and that's how he'd become the new leader of the partisan brigade for this district.

"Here," Annarosa said, holding out her bare arm. "Take this." The partisan leader didn't understand. Annarosa gestured to the big knife in his belt. "Cut off my arm and you can have enough meat for two days. Go on. You fool, we haven't had any bread in two years."

"What's she saying?" the Canadian wanted to know. She reached for the knife, and the partisan chief jumped back. She was screaming at them now. "You've taken everything else; here, take both arms." Her cracked lips began to bleed and blood was running down her chin as she followed the partisans down the hill, shouting.

When she came back she was out of breath. "I should have been an actress," she said, picking up her rake, talking to me for the first time, her face still flushed. "Once for the English soldiers I filled my mouth with dirt. 'This is what we eat. I'll share.' They were disgusted, horrified. The only trouble was, I broke a tooth." She laughed. It was the first time I'd heard anyone laugh for days, months, it seemed like.

She went with her little boy into the woods above the property and came back with a bucket and went inside. I kept working until she called me and the girls. She'd brought just enough corncobs to get the stove hot, and a pan of water was boiling on it. She put two big handfuls of ground corn in, and then a handful of some kind of peas. The polenta was as good as any I'd ever smelled in my life. The kids and I waited, sitting at the table. Just before she brought the plates over, she took a bird the size of a sparrow out of the oven and broke the bones and roasted meat over the kids' and my plates.

By late afternoon we had enough ground cultivated to plant. Under straw in the empty stall she'd hidden dozens of sets, tomato, squash, beans, eggplant, that she'd grown from seed. I carried a bucket of water behind her to water the seedlings she planted. Then she motioned for me to follow and we went up in the brush above the house. She put her fingers to her lips and bent some brush out of the way. In a hiding place built with stone into the hillside, there was a half a sack of corn, some barrels of wine on their sides, and baskets of corncobs. There was also a little plot of cultivated ground hidden nearby, and we planted the rest of the sets there, and a patch of corn. We went further back up to another clearing and cut more brush for the rest of the afternoon for another hidden garden.

At supper, another mound of polenta, she explained that we were eating the last of the seed corn. It didn't matter, because she couldn't get the ground ready in the big fields to plant a crop. The Germans might come back. "What if we got the partisans to help?" I asked her. She smiled and didn't bother to answer. She showed me where to sleep, under the house in the empty stall.

We started work early and stopped at dark. She never asked me about myself or made any comment when I tried to think of the Italian word for something. I knew my Italian wasn't very good, and I looked a lot more healthy then most Italian men, but she didn't seem curious.

Annarosa didn't talk much about herself, either. She wasn't from this province; her husband, Mario, had met her over on the Adriatic coast at San Benedetto del Tronto, where she was raised. Her husband's uncle had owned the farm, and when he died they'd moved here to be safer. The old couple at the next farm weren't related, the kids told me. One morning, hoeing in the garden, she started to pick at the sores on her cheek and I reached up and took her hand away. She stopped doing it after that, at least around me.

I didn't want to become dependent on Annarosa. It was one thing to sleep in the stall under the house, but I had to stop eating her food. The next time I saw the partisans pass on the road and go down into the woods, I followed. There was a big wild berry patch, and when they were desperate they went down to graze. I brought a bucket to pick into. It was Oscar who did all the talking.

Because I looked Italian and was the right age to have been a former soldier, they accepted me as one. They trusted me. Everyone was hungry. They were planning a raid over on the coast and were desperate for more men. They needed a successful mission to gain the support of the Allies so they'd air-drop supplies and arms. They had rescued a downed Canadian airman and delivered him to a destroyer in the Adriatic, but it wasn't enough. They needed to do something, and big, to get some recognition.

Oscar could talk, was good at making elaborate plans, had contacted another partisan group who needed help. But I wondered if the mission would actually come off next week. I was ready; I had no choice. Until the vegetable garden and the fruit trees started producing, there wasn't much to eat. The partisans referred to Annarosa as *la strega,* the witch: they didn't even insinuate that I might be sleeping with a woman like her. And she was crazy, besides. Once, the story went, another partisan group was looking around her place and happened to go near her outhouse. She went crazy and grabbed handfuls of shit and started throwing it at them, yelling, "You think I'm hiding food? Here, have some." She wanted them to think she was crazy; she was smart.

I had noticed rabbit droppings and put out snares, but I didn't catch anything the first week I was there. Anna and the two girls had traps all over the farm, but the birds were so small that when they did get one you could barely taste it. The second week I caught a rabbit that must have weighed two or three pounds. It was a feast. Anna invited the nonno and nonna next door. It was the first real meat the Italians had had in months. I stayed upstairs later than usual that night, lying on the floor in front of the open fire. We had roasted the rabbit on a spit. It was so peaceful, the kids piled up around me, sleeping. Anna was pretending not to notice me from her kitchen chair.

The house was small, with an open loft where the kids slept on a cornshuck mattress. The kitchen and dining room were one big space, and the only bedroom was off the kitchen, with no door. There was a big double bed that I didn't like to look at. It wasn't dread I felt. What was it? I kept telling myself I wasn't afraid of sleeping with her. But when I caught Anna watching me I untangled myself from the kids and got up and left. She knew I was going to leave with the partisans early the next morning, and I needed my rest.

No one knew how long it was going to take to get to the coast, but I estimated we'd walked fifty miles. It took two days. They'd got permission from some central partisan authority to join another group in wrecking a pier on the Adriatic. The pier was important because the Germans unloaded supply barges at it before dawn nearly every morning. Then the cargo went into waiting trucks. We'd had nothing to eat on the two-day march. The country here was as ruined as the place we'd come from. But the other partisan group on the coast had food. They led us into a house with a table with a big pot of fish stew, loaves of bread, bottles of vino. I ate so much I couldn't move. Even Oscar didn't talk, just ate bowl after bowl. The other group was better-armed and more disciplined, but no one had any explosives. They had got a stack of rusty saws they planned to use to cut through the wooden pilings.

We waited until low tide and started sawing through the half-rotten wooden supports. It took hours in the moonlight, but by three in the morning most of the pilings had been cut through. The incoming tide would either float or knock the sawed-through pilings apart. Fog had come in to replace the night sky, but we could still see the outline of the pier from our hiding place in the sand dunes. The supply boat came in slow, the water shallow, the sailors ready to throw a rope down onto the pier. They worked fast, using the ship's boom to unload the cargo onto the pier. We could hear the first trucks coming down the sand dunes toward the beach. "Wait a few more minutes; don't collapse yet," Oscar kept saying to the pier.

The partisans spread out, their rifles pointed at the road, but before the trucks came into view, without any warning the whole top of the pier, loaded with cargo, tilted and slid into the water. Our plan had worked. The Germans started yelling, and the barge moved away into deeper water. There was a burst of machine gun fire, and the trucks, warned off, turned around.

When the boat was gone, some of us ran down to the beach. We'd missed the chance to shoot up the trucks but had stopped the unloading and wrecked the pier. There were big wheels of wire and crates of generators and motors in the water. One chest had tools, and I took out a twelve-pound hammer. We had only a few minutes before the Germans would send a patrol down. There were a lot of small wooden boxes. I cracked one open, full of nails. Another had military decorations. Oscar ripped the broken top off another: a whole case of half-pound tins of French marmalade.

We grabbed the case and ran, not stopping until we got back to the coast partisans' hideout. Oscar was euphoric. "The Allies will reward us now for a successful mission. Send us food and arms." We ate again before leaving for the interior. I traded some tins of my marmalade for four kilos of baccalà, the dried cod that made such good fish stew.

When I knocked on the door early in the morning and handed the fish wrapped in newspaper to Anna, she didn't say anything, just took it inside. The kids came running outside when they saw me, calling "Julio, Julio," and I opened a tin of marmalade, bent the lid back enough for everyone to dip a finger inside. Carlotta started crying when she tasted the sweetness on her finger. When Anna came back we were all having another turn, and I held the tin out to her, but she took my hand and put my jam-smeared finger in her mouth to take off the marmalade. She didn't let go of my hand until I stepped back.

I saw over her shoulder that a group of men were watching us from down on the road. She saw where I was looking then and started yelling obscenities, going into her crazy-woman act for them until they moved off. They didn't look like partisans or refugees. "English POWs," she said. "They've been here before." I realized they were marching away in some kind of order in a group, as if they were on parade ground. It looked strange, such discipline on that narrow, dusty road.

When the nonno saw the pocketfuls of nails I'd brought back he got excited and talked so fast I couldn't understand him. Anna said to give him the nails so he could try to barter them for something. For supper we had the fish stew, and Anna let the kids eat as much as they could hold. She had washed her clothes and her hair was pulled back in a bun, with Elmer's gold toothpick, which I'd left up on the mantel, stuck through it for an ornament. In the light from the flickering clay lamp she looked beautiful.

The kids were up in the loft hanging over the edge of the bed, listening to her stories, half asleep. She had a harsh speaking voice, as if she didn't like words, and she kept turning over a soup spoon on the table as she talked. "When Il Duce asked all the married women to send their gold wedding rings to Rome, I didn't want to. My mother did; all the women I knew." She took off the ring she was wearing now and put it on the table. "Mussolini said he needed the gold to help our fighting men. Everyone was sending their rings, so finally I did too. He sent us back these ones made of steel." She held up the ring. "Mussolini was just another Italian thief. He stole our country and then our gold."

There was a knock on the door, and she stopped talking. Another knock, and she put out the lamp, then looked out of one of the small shuttered windows, then opened the front door wide. I saw the nonno's toothless grin and then a big white ox. I couldn't believe my eyes at first—it was the same color as the moon—until the animal made a noise.

We had the use of the ox until first light, and we ran to get ready to plow the fields. Anna held a lamp up and led the ox by a rope in the moonlight. The girls ran at the animal's side, feeding it grass. The old couple brought it a bucket of fresh water to drink when I turned him around at the end of a furrow. I'd never plowed with an animal before, and I liked the absence of tractor noise. It was pleasant to feel and see the blade of the plow slice open the layer of the ground at my feet. We plowed the three acres that couldn't be seen from the road.

We plowed the nonno's field after that, then disked them both. It was the nails that got us the ox. A farmer had hidden the animal from the Germans and bartered its use with the other farmers. I'd never seen Anna so excited. When we'd finished plowing, she couldn't wait and she started planting the last of the seed corn. She didn't want to rest. "This is a miracle," she kept saying as she dropped kernels of corn in the holes the girls were making with sticks. The sun was up, and I watched across the way as the old nonno broadcast the wheat, taking handfuls from a bag strapped over his shoulder, walking his field. We were working the land. I was a farmer again.

Farming here took more concentration, more attention to details, though it was still based on the usual farmer's luck. If you made a mistake in California, you lost your crop or your farm. Here you could lose your life, your family's life. The cherries were getting ripe, the first apricots. The girls spent their time chasing the birds away. The vegetables in the kitchen garden were growing; we'd already had some early beans and squash blossoms.

Oscar had come around the week before, wanting food. He'd walked right into the kitchen and was looking around the back shelves. If Anna had caught him, there would have been hell to pay. I hustled him outside while he complained, "They dropped us automatic weapons and radios we don't know how to use, but no gold sovereigns." That was a myth that every partisan group believed, that the Allies would give them gold coins by the sackful. "No food. No food." I couldn't help liking Oscar. He was only about five feet tall, with blue eyes that got bigger and bigger when he talked, as if they were going to expand and take over his whole face. Oscar took himself seriously as a partisan leader. After a vote, he'd put a member of his unit up against a wall and shot him for attempted rape.

Sometimes at night I could hear the sounds of the war. Bombs, I thought, and sometimes heavy artillery, miles and miles away. I could hear Anna turn over in her bed on the floor above. Her bedroom was right over the stall where I slept. I could imagine her lying there diagonally across the iron bed. I'd seen her bare back once in the morning. She always came out of the bedroom with all her clothes on, but she forgot one morning to button the back of her dress. I could see the bare skin of her shoulder blade when she reached for something, and the deeper crevice of her spine down at her waist. Monica noticed and did up her mother's dress. Her feet were small and white and bluish at the same time. She sat down in her chair and pulled on a man's wool socks and then her clogs. I couldn't sleep some nights, thinking of Anna. But I had to stop. How could I take a chance on failing again?

We were caught out in the open one morning, returning from an abandoned farm where we'd been getting manure out of the animal stalls for the garden. I was pulling on one shaft of the nonno's wagon with Oscar on the other, going up a steep hill with two partisans, brothers, and the nonno pushing from the rear. When we got to the top of the rise there was a German truck waiting. The officer must have been watching us for the last half hour, like a cat with mice. It was a good thing the partisans had left their old rifles at the farmhouse. These Germans were tough-looking, well armed. They looked altogether different from the ones I'd seen as prisoners. They looked like MPS.

They didn't take Nonno, but they loaded the rest of us into the back of a truck. Only Oscar argued; he said he had sworn allegiance to the Japanese and was an ally. The bored officer called him a Schweinhund and the truck drove off. The other two partisans, ex-soldiers who had fought in Greece, looked as scared as I felt. I wasn't worried that they'd find out I was an American and figure I was a spy: I was afraid I'd end up in Germany as slave labor in some mine or factory getting bombed by the Allies and never see Anna again. Only Oscar was calm. "We're heading south," he told us.

It was dark when the truck finally stopped. I could hear shelling. "Eighty-eights," Oscar said. "We're close to the front." We spent five and a half days digging holes in the hard-packed road so the Germans could plant anti-tank mines. We were fed twice a day and kept in a guarded barbed wire enclosure at night. When the job was done, we were told to go home.

There had been about a hundred fifty men working on the road. Oscar and four others were the only ones who wanted to take a chance and go further south and try to cross the lines to join the Allies. The partisans had made a map of the layout of the mines and knew the Allies would be interested. The brothers were already walking as fast as they could north, where they had families, as Oscar yelled after them, "Wait, it's a chance to fight for your country." When Oscar asked, "What about you, Julio?" I started walking too, following the brothers north. When I turned to look behind us, Oscar was hurrying to catch up. "You're all crazy," he said. "I gave my map to one of the other men who's going to try to cross the lines, with a message. We're all going to starve to death up there," he added.

We walked for a long time to get back. Oscar talked the whole way. He told us about living in California as a boy. His father had gone around the farms in a wagon, selling Watkins products, spices and flavorings like lemon extract and vanilla, he explained; that's how he'd learned English. He'd lived in a place called Yettem. I almost forgot and said in English, "I know that place." *Yettem* was Armenian for "promised land": it was a little town on the east side of the valley by Orosi; in high school I'd written a story about that town. I didn't give myself away; it was too much of a risk for anyone to know I was American. As far as Oscar knew, I was as Italian as the two brothers. We were lucky; fruit was getting ripe in the abandoned farms, and we found enough to eat.

When I started recognizing the countryside, I filled my jacket with early apples, and we all started hurrying, not sleeping at night, walking by moonlight. I got to Anna's just as dawn was breaking, dirty, tired, out of breath from almost running the last section of road. I could hear the clang of the cast-iron stove as she started the morning fire, and one of the girls saying something. Then I knocked.

"Julio, Julio." The kids hung on to my arms and legs as I tried to walk across the floor. "Two pigeons have come back and are laying eggs," Anna said, embarrassed, putting her hands behind her back. I could hear them cooing under the roof. "Listen. It's a good omen." Anna was pretending she wasn't surprised that I'd come back, that I wasn't gone for good, or dead. Did she feel as awkward as I did? She didn't greet me; it was as if I hadn't been away, had slept under the house last night. I drank a cup of acorn coffee and ate two big hard rolls she must have been saving for me. "I traded vegetables," she explained. I was so excited to be back I could hardly eat. I stroked the kids, made them sit down and I peeled them apples. I was able to peel one whole apple without breaking the coil of peel: they watched in amazement. I remembered my father doing the same thing for me.

I still thought of the San Joaquin Valley sometimes, but not as much as I used to. I still saw the winter vineyard sometimes, pruned vines reaching through the morning fog like fingers. I could wonder about them, even though I couldn't own them or see them anymore. I was going to stay here. When the front came this far, I'd be ready, and we'd hide in the cave up above the house. There was even a chance there wouldn't be any battle here, that the Germans wouldn't defend the area. That was wishful thinking.

It was Carlotta who saw the boar first, driven, probably, from the higher mountain. It had been shot; a wound was festering on one of its hams. I was able to kill it with a couple of blows from my hoe. The nonno showed me how to dig the pit and roast it in the coals behind the house. All of Oscar's partisans were there waiting for the meal to start. They brought a dozen loaves of bread, I don't know where they found it, and there were bowls of fruit from the trees and vegetables from the garden, a demijohn of wine from before the war that Nonno had been hiding. We ate until there was no more food left. Oscar started singing in Armenian when it got dark, and no one wanted to leave. The nonna sang, it started to rain, and then it was over.

A couple of days later a group of five men came into the yard, herding Nonno in front of them as if he were a big dog. It was the first time I'd seen the English officers up close. Some still had their entire uniforms. They were clean, their boots greased, their hair cut, shaved. There had been a POW camp for English officers on the main road, and after the Italian surrender in the summer of '43, they'd been released or abandoned. In good Italian, a colonel asked for food and then did a dumb show, pretended to put food in his mouth, then rubbed his stomach, going "Ahhh." "Where is the porker?" he asked. None of them were armed. Anna and the kids were up working in one of the hidden gardens. Nonno was mumbling in dialect, "It's gone, eaten, you're too late." The colonel shook his finger under Nonno's nose and said in English, "Where's the pig, you stupid Wog?"

I picked up a wood-tined pitchfork and put it near the colonel's face. He stepped back. I thought of answering them in English, but that would complicate matters, and then it would get out that I was American. They left, threatening me and the old man.

It rained every day for two weeks, turning the dusty roads into long ribbons of slick mud. There were no refugees, and all the brigands, as Anna called the partisans, stayed in their shelters. Anna mended clothes, the front door open for the light. The kids played on the floor with stacks of old buttons. The water came off the roof in long streams. I told Anna I wished it would rain forever.

With the maize and wheat almost knee-high, the animals were coming back. There were more rabbit droppings. Birds were everywhere. Before the rain, we were snaring a couple of wild doves a week. A flock of pigeons was roosting under the eaves. I held Monica out the attic window so she could reach the small eggs. We had spinach frittata one night.

I looked around at the kids playing on the floor. They had filled out, gained weight. And Anna was a different person. She seemed happy sometimes, smiling. Most of the sores were gone from her face. She took my arm when we walked around the fields. She'd never put her wedding ring back on, after that night she took it off. I tried to make her laugh while we waited for the rain to stop, told funny stories like my father did about my mother and her family.

I knew it was time, now was the time, but the longer I waited, the harder it was to try. It wasn't like killing the coward in myself when I saw the Japanese at Attu with long bayonets on the end of their rifles charging and everyone who wasn't wounded dropped their empty weapons and panicked. There was nowhere to run. I told myself then, no you don't, you sonofabitch, die here like a man. And I stayed, I was a man. This was different. I wanted to touch her hair, stroke her arm, make love to her, but first I'd have to get upstairs. Caress her, feel her moving under me. The last time I'd felt anything like this was with Hortense, and I'd stopped myself rather than find out. I'd had plenty of women in the past. I'd just have to try again. I didn't shake anymore. I hadn't cried in months. That was all over with, I was sure. I could hold my hand out and it was as steady as a rock.

Every day there were new rumors. Rome was occupied by the Allies sometime in June. The Germans would leave Italy now. If they did, it was going to be with a shovel, trenching all the way. They were building a new line of fortifications all across the boot, about thirty miles south of us. Oscar had made a raid and returned with sacks of real flour. We were eating pasta, for the first time in two and a half years, Anna said. There was supposed to have been a successful invasion on the French coast. That I doubted. Italian fascist units were in the region, looking for the partisans, setting up roadblocks, asking for papers.

In the evening I lay on my back by the field of corn, more than waist-high now, the ears big and juicy, almost ready to eat, the children next to me, watching the sky for tomorrow's weather. We saw big flights of Flying Fortresses, in patterns like geese, going over so high up they made no sound, on their way to give some German town a pasting. The Invasion in Normandy was a fact; Oscar had heard it on a radio. And the Russians were coming from the east through Poland. This war couldn't last forever.

The world was in turmoil, but I was at peace. I thought of Anna, up in the house. Tonight I'd take her by the hand and lead her into the bedroom. I was ready now. Thinking about her made me so hard I had to hide it with my hat. I'd used up a bucket of water, washing, taken off all my clothes and scrubbed with the rough homemade soap.

I'd used a green twig to brush my teeth like the valley Indians did; Mabel had told me that.

I was carrying the boy and the girls were following me up the ladder to the loft, half asleep, when I heard the wooden clogs on the stone steps, then Oscar's voice, "Julio, the fascists are here." I was out the door and running in the dark, away from the lights of the trucks coming up the hill. I couldn't allow myself to be caught now. Anna shouted something after me, and I heard the heavy front door slam closed.

This was an all-out drive to clear the area behind the German lines of partisans, we learned when we caught up with the other groups. It seemed like we were running for days. We'd get away and then get cornered again higher up in the mountains. I was carrying the base plate to a mortar, and I was always out of breath. There were hundreds of Italian fascists combing the woods. The whole countryside was in an uproar. There were German observation planes overhead, and half-tracks patrolling the roads.

Our group was ambushed by a German patrol, and only a few men got away. Oscar, the brothers, and I made it past and started working our way back toward the farms. There was nowhere else to hide. The fascists were everywhere. They were hanging men they only suspected of being partisan; you didn't even have to have a rifle.

I crept up on Anna's house late one night. There was a slight wind. I could hear the cornstalks brush against each other. I was just going to whisper, Anna, I'm back, and then head up to the cave behind the house. But something was wrong. On the top step the wooden doorstop was gone. When Anna left it on the right side of the door, it meant it was all clear. I crept over to Nonno's and hid in the orchard behind the house.

When I woke up the next morning, I saw the wheat had turned color and was almost ready to harvest. Bright-red flowers were scattered like butterflies over the surface of the grain. When the nonna came out with a tray to pick figs, I heard the news. Anna's husband had returned a week ago, minus the toes on both feet from frostbite. Mario was back. I smiled for the nonna, but I was stunned like I'd received a blow to the head. I had to close my eyes.

I watched Anna's place until I saw the husband. What was I going to do? I had to think this out. I watched all day, heard the old treadle grindstone turn as Mario put an edge on the scythes and then the other tools, getting ready for the harvest. I couldn't stay here now. I couldn't think about Anna anymore.

I left that night at soon as it got dark. I could have gone over and introduced myself. I wasn't guilty of anything. Neither of us had anything to be ashamed of. I could have said good-bye. I was going to miss Anna and the kids. I started back up into the hills, looking for Oscar. I didn't have any choice. It was either that or head south to Allied lines, and I wasn't going to do that. There had to be someplace for me here.

Partisan life was a lot like playing at cowboys and Indians. We slept during the day and at night attacked the German convoys on the main road going north, just like a wagon train. We'd pick out a slowed-down truck on a steep grade and open fire, shooting out the tires. The driver would flee, and then we'd hurry to unload the truck before the armored cars in the front would come racing back. One night, half drunk, I started whooping it up, giving Indian calls, *wha wha woo,* with the flat of my hand against my mouth. Oscar told me to stop it; I was scaring everyone.

We got a whole crate of schnapps that way, cheese and canned goods in another raid. Five-gallon tins of olive oil. Boots and blankets. We used wheelbarrows to haul the goods away and hide them in the woods. Sometimes we were chased by the Germans but mostly by Italian fascists, who would give up when they got higher up in the mountains, afraid of an ambush. One night we wounded one of the German drivers, who later died. The next day the Germans went into the nearest town and rounded up seventeen men and boys from the piazza and shot them. We heard about it the following morning.

There was a vote, and we decided to stop the raids for a while. We loaded ourselves down with goods to trade with the farmers and headed back down to the hill farms. I followed the others, carrying a big tin of olive oil. I could knock on Anna's door now; I'd worked it out. Say hello, introduce myself. I might buy the nonno's place; he was always talking about selling out. We would be neighbors then.

When we got to the farms it was quiet. The wheat and corn had been harvested; crows were still working over the fields, looking for grain. Too quiet. There was a dead odor, and that sound of flies. We found Nonno's body first, shot in the back of the head. He lay face-down. It looked like he'd been running away from Anna's. He'd been chased down. Oscar and I crawled on our bellies to the next body. It was the husband, Mario. His chest was riddled with bullet holes. He still had an axe in his hand. The little boy was a few yards further. His throat had been cut. The two girls were nailed by their hands to the wooden door of the stall. Monica was still alive. They'd both been raped. I couldn't get the nails loose from Monica's hands. Oscar found a hacksaw, cut the nail heads off, and pulled her hands free. She was unconscious. She'd been beaten up, and blood was running down from between her legs.

We wrapped her up in my coat and took her over to the nonno's house. The brothers had got the nonna to open her door. She was hysterical, couldn't talk. The brothers were asking, "Who did it: Tedeschi? Fascisti? Who? Who?" We went back to Anna's house, and I went up the stairs. Oscar wouldn't come. Anna was hanging naked from a ceiling lantern hook by a wire under her arms. She was dead. She had been mutilated. Blood was still oozing out of a big wound in her chest.

It took all afternoon to dig the graves for the bodies wrapped up in blankets. It was one of the brothers who found the bloody rag in the woods. The husband must have wounded one of the murderers, they decided. It was getting too dark to follow a trail, if there was one. We went back and talked to the old woman. As soon as she'd heard shots, she'd hidden; she hadn't seen any of it. Monica died that night.

I was leading, almost running, with the first light, Oscar behind me, the two brothers following. There was no more blood, but the tall grass had been bent over, leaving a trail up into the mountains. That ended in some boulders, but we kept moving up higher. When it got dark, I thought I smelled wood smoke, and we stopped for the night. The next morning the brothers didn't want to go any further. "We're following ghosts," the older one said. "Let's go back." Oscar and I went forward carefully. If we did find them up ahead, how would we ever know if they were the killers? We saw the group of men just after dawn, camped in front of an old abandoned farmhouse. We lay in some brush and watched for a while. "What now?" Oscar asked. I shook my head and started crawling closer.

I was probably two hundred feet away when I saw the face of the English colonel. He was the only one up, sitting on a stone near a fire. Oscar recognized him at the same time, and stood up. We walked in. When the colonel saw us he yelled, "Fuck off, we have just enough food for ourselves." Some of the other officers woke up in their blankets and looked around. There was no panic; no one grabbed his rifle. They must have come back from a raid on the convoys, because there were cases of German beer stacked near some boulders.

There was no one hurt that I could see. The colonel was standing behind Oscar now, telling him to quit poking around their goods. We'd followed a false lead; there was no one hurt here, and none of this stuff belonged to Anna's family. A pot of tea was heating on a grill and Oscar nonchalantly picked up a glass and said, "Tea time, gentlemen," in English and poured himself a glassful.

The English were well armed now, with German Mausers and even a machine gun. Several had pistols on their belts. Oscar finished his tea and started off, calling over his shoulder, "Good morning to you all." I followed. We walked a couple hundred yards and Oscar dropped into the grass. "They look innocent," he said. "Too innocent. I think they killed the Italian family. Let's wait." Oscar had been too quick to decide that, I thought.

We crept back. Some of the officers were shaving, washing up, others were cleaning their weapons. I counted fourteen. They had an informal field inspection, the colonel looking over each officer's uniform, then weapon, the men standing at ease. I could smell meat frying. A bell rang, and another officer came out of the house. He was limping. They had started their breakfast when Oscar stood up again and walked into the camp.

"We're getting tired of your infernal intrusions," the colonel said. He was young for a colonel, in his late thirties, wearing one of those full mustaches the English officers liked, tall, fit, disdainful. There were blank looks, surprise, when Oscar explained that an Italian family had been massacred and that we were on the trial of the killers. He'd like to see the captain's leg, he added.

"This is tiresome," the colonel said. "Jack, take down your trousers, show the man. He was bayoneted last night when we ambushed a convoy." Just above the captain's knee was a bandage soaked with blood. The colonel had finished eating and now took out a toothpick and started working on his back teeth. I watched the colonel's Adam's apple bob, as if he were swallowing something.

The next thing I knew my thumbs were in the man's throat and I was trying to kill him as we were rolling on the ground. I lost my grip and started bashing the colonel in the face with my fists. Three of the officers were trying to get me off. Oscar had fired a couple of rounds in the air with his machine pistol to stop the others from getting their weapons. The colonel's throat was bleeding and he was spitting out broken front teeth.

I shook myself loose from the officers and went over and picked up Elmer's gold toothpick. The colonel had dropped it. "She wore this to pin her hair," I said in English. "You scum killed her." I was shaking with hate.

"A bloody Yank," someone said.

"We're all on the same side; we should remember that," a lieutenant said. "That family isn't the first to die in this area. Your group was the one that killed the German driver and caused the reprisals."

"That evidence won't hold up at a court-martial; the colonel has had that gold toothpick for years; I'll swear to that," someone else said. And someone else added, "Jack's father is in the prime minister's cabinet."

The colonel got up. "You're going to pay for that," he rasped. "We'll see who's court-martialed."

Oscar looked at me. We both knew there was no way we could get these men moved to anyplace where they could be tried, not this many. "You left one of the girls alive," Oscar said. "She'll be able to identify you. You and all the men involved." He swept the muzzle of the machine pistol across the group. "Then we'll have our own court-martial. We'll see if Jack's father has any influence here in Italy."

One of the officers, a subaltern, yelled out, "We didn't all go down there with Jack."

"They bragged to us what they'd done," another shouted.

"You bloody idiot, don't get the wind up; they can't prove anything," Jack said.

"I was here with Albert the whole time," the subaltern said. "It was Jack," and he pointed at the injured captain. "Jack and his souvenirs. He brought back the woman's breast. Show the Yank, Jack. He was going to make it into a tobacco pouch."

"I'm the senior officer here," the colonel said, leisurely reaching for his pistol, unsnapping the catch on his holster, taking the luger out, cocking it, but never getting a chance to point the muzzle because Oscar blew the top of his head off with a burst from his machine pistol. Everything happened fast after that. Three officers made a run for it, zigzagging. Oscar kept the others covered and I cut them down with my rifle one by one, just before they reached the tall grass. The brothers came rushing into the clearing, out of breath, rifles ready, and everyone froze where they were.

We used the rope from the well and hanged Jack the cabinet member's son first. Then the others. I put the noose around each neck. I felt no pity for them. Oscar shot each one in the chest after they'd stopped kicking and jerking. When it came to the five who said they hadn't been down to the farm, Oscar wanted to hang them too. "They would have done the same thing," he said, pointing the muzzle of his weapon in their faces.

"But we didn't join them," the subaltern shouted. "We knew what was going to happen, and we wouldn't go along with it. The colonel knew they had food down there now. That crazy woman had never helped us, and the colonel said they didn't deserve to keep their harvest. We couldn't stop them. They said it was wartime and they could do whatever was necessary, just like the Germans did."

"Mi senti un momento," the sandy-haired lieutenant said, and I realized with a start he'd said it in Italian. "Listen to me. Some of us were rescued by Italian fisherman when our ship hit a mine on a commando raid. We could have taken their boat and escaped, but we couldn't do that after they'd saved us from drowning, so we went ashore with the catch and we spent two and a half years in a POW camp because of it. We weren't all like the colonel and Jack. They thought because they could die at any moment, it didn't matter what they did. It didn't count."

After a three-to-one vote, we left the rest alive and went back down into the hills. We took the long way to avoid the farms but still came within a mile of Anna's. When we came to the main road we sat down to rest. We could hear the bombardment, close now, four or five miles away. Oscar couldn't sit down; he was pacing in the ditch. It was warm, an August afternoon. "This is our chance," Oscar kept repeating. "We can sit tight, let the front roll right over us. Then we go, bring in a few prisoners, officers, and join the Allies. Julio is an American; he can tell them we're good soldiers." The older brother, the one who didn't talk much, said something fast in their dialect to the younger, who stood up, unslung his rifle, and laid it down on the grass. The older one went over to Oscar and handed him his pistol, then hugged him and kissed him on both cheeks. Said "Good-bye, Julio" as he passed and headed down the road with his brother. Oscar looked at me for a minute. Then he shook my hand. "I'll see you in California, Julio." He started walking toward the front, rifle slung across his back, talking to himself.

To the east, I could see the flashes of ships' guns shelling the coast. In the distance over the hill I could hear the high-pitched squeaking sound that tank treads make, coming closer. German tanks. Did it matter? Did I want to go on with it, after the things I'd seen, the things I'd done? Trying to cut Anna free from the wire. Burying the family, covering Monica's small fingers sticking out of the blanket with dirt. Memory was too permanent. Too absolute. Worse than death.

I sat there on the side of the road hugging my knees, looking at the sunset. The summer haze was as thick as valley fog in November, like a layer of dreams, I used to think, when I was pruning by myself out in the vines. You could be anything or think anything or be anywhere when it was like that, the fog as thick and hard as the ground you stood on. Some silly verse we'd recited in third grade came into my head: "I am a California child; I love my native state. Its mountains high, its valleys wide, its people good and great."

Did the place matter that much? The big oak, the vineyard, the forty acres of rows and ditches that my feet and hands knew by heart? The road? Or was it the people: the Brazils, the Hamadas, old Fred Leeds? I could stay here in Italy. With any luck, I could outlast this war. Or I could just go on listening to the German tanks creaking toward me and be done with it.

I rested my head on my knees, thinking, trying to recall the faces of everyone I'd ever known in my whole life in all the places I'd ever been, one after another. It was the people that made the difference, in all those places. Our oak tree covered with chrysanthemum flowers: it was Mr. Hamada who'd shown me how to grow them.

I'd like to go back to the valley, walk down our road just once more, I decided. I stood up, found myself headed for the ditch and down the ravine toward cover. The valley. I didn't have to own anything there. Just take a look at the vines, whoever they belonged to now, see if they were okay, and then walk down to the Brazils' dairy and say hello to Hortense.